NOVEMBER

THE ALPHA ELITE SERIES

USA TODAY BEST SELLING AUTHOR
SYBIL BARTEL

Copyright © 2022 by Sybil Bartel

Cover art by: CT Cover Creations, .ctcovercreations.com

Cover Photo by: Wander Aguiar, wanderaguiar.com

Cover Model: Zakk Davis

Edited by: Hot Tree Editing, www.hottreeediting.com
The Ryter's Proof, www.therytersproof.com

Formatting by: Champagne Book Design

All rights reserved. No part of this publication may be reproduced, distributed, or transmitted in any form or by any means, including photocopying, recording, or other electronic or mechanical methods, without the prior written permission of the author, except in the case of brief quotations embodied in critical reviews and certain other noncommercial uses permitted by copyright law.

All characters in this book have no existence outside the imagination of the author and have no relation whatsoever to anyone bearing the same name or names. They are not even distantly inspired by any individual known or unknown to the author, and all incidents are pure invention.

Warning: This book contains offensive language, alpha males and sexual situations. Mature audiences only. 18+

BOOKS BY SYBIL BARTEL

The Alpha Elite Series
SEAL
ALPHA
VICTOR
ROMEO
ZULU
NOVEMBER
ECHO
WHISKEY
DELTA
KILO

The Alpha Bodyguard Series
SCANDALOUS
MERCILESS
RECKLESS
RUTHLESS
FEARLESS
CALLOUS
RELENTLESS
SHAMELESS
HEARTLESS

The Uncompromising Alphas Series
TALON
NEIL
ANDRÉ
BENNETT
CALLAN

The Alpha Antihero Series
HARD LIMIT
HARD JUSTICE
HARD SIN
HARD TRUTH
THE ALPHA ANTIHERO SERIES: BOOKS 1-2

The Alpha Escort Series
THRUST
ROUGH
GRIND

The Unchecked Series
IMPOSSIBLE PROMISE
IMPOSSIBLE CHOICE
IMPOSSIBLE END

Join Sybil Bartel's Mailing List to get the news first on her upcoming releases, giveaways and exclusive excerpts! You'll also get a FREE book for joining!

NOVEMBER

Airman.

Hacker.

Mercenary.

Hacking one of the government's top agencies was my first mistake. My second was thinking they wouldn't find me. Nineteen hours later, five armed men kicked down my door.

They gave me a choice—prison or recruitment.

The Air Force took me in and trained me to be the best Cyberspace Operations Officer they'd ever had. Being the gatekeeper for the military's strategic operations was an honor, but it put a target on my back. I never traveled without security—until I made my third mistake.

Twenty-two hours later, covered in blood and barely able to stand after events I wasn't at liberty to discuss, I erased my past, changed my identity, and went off the grid. Then I joined Alpha Elite Security. I was invisible…until she saw me.

Code name: November.
Mission: Disengage.

NOVEMBER is a standalone book in the exciting Alpha Elite Series by *USA Today* Bestselling author, Sybil Bartel. Come meet Nathan "November" Rhys and the dominant, alpha heroes who work for AES!

DEDICATION

For my only child, my beloved son, Oliver.
You were my greatest gift. The world was a better place with you in it.
Everything in my life was better because of you.
Thank you for teaching me unconditional love, perseverance, and compassion.
You are and will *always* be my entire world.
I love you, Sweet Boy, and I miss you beyond measure.

Oliver Shane Bartel 2004-2020

For my readers, thank you for all of your love and support.
Gratefully yours, XOXO

PART ONE

Four Years Ago

ONE

The Hunter
Headquarters Air Force, the Pentagon.
Arlington, VA

Deputy Commander Bradley looked over my shoulder at my monitors. "You find them yet?"

Switching screens, I lied. "No, sir."

"Keep looking. They were heading somewhere when they left Havana Bay on that boat three months ago. At this point, get the Coast Guard involved if you have to. They've been off our radar too damn long, and Cuba is the closest they've come to U.S. soil. I don't like the optics on this one, and I sure as hell don't want it coming to a head under my command. The sooner we zero in on them, the better."

"Yes, sir."

He glanced at his watch. "I'm stepping out. Unless they land on our banks or the situation escalates, debrief tomorrow at oh seven hundred. When Perkins comes in, download everything you chased today and let him know we've got a change in mission status that came down at sixteen hundred hours."

"Copy, sir."

The Deputy Commander lowered his voice. "We've got a lot of brainpower in this room, but you're the best I've got. Find those Russian cyber terrorists. They need to be eliminated."

"And the female, sir?"

"I don't care if she's the brainchild of their operation or

collateral damage. Once we get a lock on their location, we have our orders."

My jaw ticked. "With all due respect, sir, she could be a source of intel."

"If POTUS wanted profilers, he would've called the FBI. This is U.S. Cyber Command. We're not fucking babysitters."

"Sir—"

"Mission stands. Lock-in and eliminate. We've already traced all known associates, and these four men are the nucleus of their cell. Our job isn't to detain. Once we find them, we send in a drone. If we can't narrow the field, or there's risk of U.S. civilian collateral, then we know who to call."

"Understood, sir."

"You better. We're disabling this threat. You have your orders." The Deputy Commander leveled me with a warning look. Then he strode out of the command center.

Toggling back to the screen I was on when the Deputy Commander had walked up, I stared at the lines of code I'd found with two hidden words embedded in them. Two words I hadn't seen together since I was eighteen years old, but ones that had come up three months ago. I read them again.

Check mate.

Thirteen years ago, those same two words, embedded deep within code, had spurred me to hit the final keystroke and breach the NSA's firewall. Nineteen hours later, five armed men kicked down my door and I was given a choice. Jail or the Air Force. I chose the latter, and the hacker with the two-word signature had dropped off the radar.

Until three months ago.

I'd discovered the signature the day I found the terrorist cell in Cuba. The same day the four armed terrorists boarded a forty-six-foot, 1975 Bertram sport fishing boat named the Nalleli Rose in Cuba.

The day I first saw her.

NOVEMBER

Pulling up her image, I stared.

Black hair, teal-blue eyes, she was beautiful.

She was also young.

Too young.

Thirteen years ago, she couldn't have been the hacker leaving me a two-word taunt. She wouldn't have been much older than a child, and the profile didn't fit. Same as the profiles of the four men who were the tip of the terrorist cell didn't fit. They wouldn't leave a signature flagging their location.

But Check Mate would.

It was the same MO as thirteen years ago.

Staring at the young woman, I allowed myself two more seconds to take in every inch of her. I knew she wasn't anything more than a pawn in this terrorist cell's operations. I knew it when I watched the four men board her boat, but I couldn't put together what the connection to Check Mate was. As of sixteen hundred hours today, it no longer mattered. She was caught up in the storm, and her situation had just become critical.

Taking in her unusual eyes one more time, I deleted her image and wiped all trace of my digital footprint today as well as the code with Check Mate's signature. Then I hacked the security cams for a private airfield I'd gotten a hit on earlier and double-checked the footage before rerunning the parameters through traffic cams one more time.

I found the same thing I'd found an hour ago.

The four known terrorists and one unidentified female with unusual eyes landed on U.S. soil fourteen hours ago when they moored the Nalleli Rose at a residential dock in Key Largo, Florida. Then an SUV left that same residence in Key Largo and drove to a private airstrip in Cedar Key, Florida. A Cessna took off from that airstrip and flew to a small airport outside Louisville, Kentucky. Ten minutes after the Cessna landed, a Pilatus PC-12 turboprop charter left the Kentucky airport. Seventy-two minutes ago, that same turboprop charter landed afterhours at Tipton Airport in

Fort Meade, Maryland, where the pilot signed the registration log without adding passengers, refueled, and took off again.

But a prearranged rental vehicle was waiting at Tipton.

Hacking the rental company's servers, I tracked the vehicle's GPS, then double-checked the intel against traffic cams.

The rented SUV came here.

Washington, D.C.

Driving straight to a dive bar in Dupont Circle.

Staring at my screen, I watched the four terrorists, then her, get out of the SUV. Capturing her image as the men surrounded her, running it through the facial recognition program I'd designed, I already knew what I'd find.

No hits.

The woman didn't have an official ID, driver's license, passport, or arrest record, and she hadn't traveled through any commercial airports in the past five years. She was a ghost.

Wiping my keystrokes from the system, I was replacing them with ones I'd done yesterday when Perkins strode into the command center.

"What's up, hacker genius?" He pulled out his chair in the setup next to mine. "You find our hottie and the four horsemen yet?"

Ignoring his nicknames and attempt at camaraderie, I said what I needed to not make him suspicious, but I left out the crucial detail of our new orders. "Day's activities are all recorded and downloaded. You can follow the trail." One I'd purposely thrown a detour in to.

"Copy that." He grinned as he sat. "Any more pics of our sexy femme fatale? I need something to distract me from the fact that I'm working tonight instead of getting laid at twenty-four hundred."

I fucking hated him. "Everything's in the log." I stood. "I'm signing out."

He chuckled. "Enjoy your workout, loner," he baited. "But fair warning, one of these nights, I'll break you like I do these codes, and you'll agree to a beer with us after work instead of your insane workouts."

I didn't drink or socialize. Ever. "Good night."

Bypassing everyone else in the command center, I scanned my access badge to exit, and two paces down the long corridor, the security detail fell in on my six. No other officers in Cyber Command had a security detail, not even the Deputy Commander. But I did. The cover story was my rank, security clearance, and the classified intel I was privy to necessitated it. The real reason was the Deputy Commander. He knew I was a flight risk. I had been since he'd brought me in the day after I hacked the NSA.

"Mathers," I stated, acknowledging his presence and following protocol.

"Evening, sir. The gym?"

"No, strained muscle," I lied for the second time tonight. "I won't need you until oh six hundred tomorrow."

"Understood, sir, but I have my orders. I'll escort you to your residence."

Then he'd sit outside in his unmarked vehicle all night.

I didn't comment.

Mathers drove me home.

Then he swept the perimeter of my converted warehouse space and did a cursory glance inside after I opened the front door for him. "Clear."

My entire place was wired. I had eyes on every corner, inside and out. With one look at my cell, I could've told him the entire block was clear, but I didn't. "Thank you. Good night, Mathers."

"Night, sir. You know how to reach me if you need me."

"Understood." I closed the door and slammed the bolt home for effect.

Opening the app on my cell, I watched him get back in his car. Using another app, I set the lights to go on and off at timed intervals in the kitchen, living area, bathroom and bedroom.

Then I got to work.

Changing out of my uniform and into civvies, I grabbed my leather jacket, keys, another jacket and two helmets. Shoving aside a bookcase in my living area, I unlocked the hidden door to the warehouse next to mine that I owned through a shell corporation buried so deep it'd take years for someone to find it if they went looking.

Crossing the expanse of the twenty thousand square feet that was filled with the remnants of a defunct packaging plant, I headed to the loading dock. Checking my app, I pulled up the security feeds for the cameras outside the small bay door and scanned the side alley.

Empty.

Switching feeds, I checked the front of my unit.

Mathers was in his car.

I opened the bay door.

TWO

The Hunter

STANDING IN THE DARK HALLWAY, I SCANNED THE BAR.

Thirty-seven minutes ago, from my desk at the Pentagon, I was staring at her from my screen.

Eight minutes ago, I'd walked into this bar through the back exit.

Now I was watching.

Waiting.

With one downcast, furtive glance around the room, she stood to excuse herself from the four men at her table. Before she could escape, one grabbed her by the upper arm. She winced, he handed her a cell, and she slid it into her pocket with a shaking hand. Then he released her, and she moved through the crowd in a flitting, haphazard pattern. No eye contact, not touching anyone, she took the last seat at the bar.

The one closest to me.

With a slide of a twenty-dollar bill across the wood, she caught the attention of the bartender before she discreetly grabbed and pocketed one of the matchbooks bearing the name of the place.

The bartender smiled, she spoke without looking at him, then she turned her back on me and the security camera covering her position.

Pulling out my cell, I hacked the bar's security feeds and recorded for forty-five seconds. Feeding it back into the system, I gave it a single loop, buying myself less than a minute.

As the bartender delivered her drink, I glanced one more time toward the table she'd come from. Then I stepped out of the hall and fell in on her six.

"Name," I demanded, low enough for only her to hear.

Startled, she flinched, almost spilling the drink.

Reaching around her, taking the glass by the rim, I set the vodka neat on the bar.

Tracking my movements, staring at my hand a beat, her gaze traveled up my arm. Then she turned her head and looked over her shoulder.

Unusual blue eyes, dark hair, fine features—I knew every inch of her face and body. But until tonight, I'd never seen her in person.

"Your name," I repeated.

Quickly averting her gaze, indecision crossed her face.

"I'm not going to ask again," I warned.

"Sub," she barely whispered.

For a split second, I fucking stilled. Then I put the pieces together. "Permission to speak freely, sub. Give me your real name."

Soft, submissive, mesmerizing, she spoke. "Atala."

Atala.

The blue Atala butterfly.

Native to Florida, the Caribbean—the almost iridescent teal-blue color of her eyes—it couldn't be a coincidence.

"Atala," I repeated, sinking my career. "You now have two choices."

Lifting her gaze but not her head, she gave me a wary, cautious glance with the same innocent eyes I'd seen on my screens, but she said nothing.

Maintaining eye contact, picking up her glass, careful not to touch where her prints were, I dumped the Stoli. Then I committed treason. "Leave your jacket and purse at the table, wait ten seconds, then follow me out." I tipped my chin toward the table she'd come from. "Or stay and take your chances with them." Holding her gaze, stepping back, I took in every mesmerizing inch of her in case it was the last time I saw her alive. "Ten seconds, sub."

NOVEMBER

I turned and left.

Striding down the hall, pushing out the back door, I scanned the alley and the security camera I'd already put on a twenty-minute loop, but I was cutting it close. Holding the glass up toward a streetlight, I took a photo and isolated the print before initiating a search on an app I'd created. Then I wiped the glass, tossed it into a dumpster and checked the time.

Seven more minutes.

Zipping my leather, I swung my leg over my Ducati Streetfighter V4 S. I was putting my helmet on when the back door opened with a rush of warm air and bar noise. Then the door shut, the sounds muted and a blue-eyed butterfly was staring at me.

Black sweater, tight jeans, high-heeled boots, she crossed her arms against the cold.

Unzipping my tank bag, I grabbed the new leather jacket in her size and held it out.

Glancing up and down the alley, she hesitated.

I didn't tell her we had seconds before her captors came out.

She looked back at me, but her decision was already made.

I knew it. She knew it.

She dropped her head and inhaled.

Then her heels were barely making a sound as she crossed the alley and took the jacket before sliding her arms in and zipping it up.

It was a perfect fit.

Handing her the second helmet, I issued two orders. "Give me the cell they gave you and secure your hair. Tuck it inside the helmet."

As if she'd been trained to do exactly as she was told and knew every detail mattered, she handed me the cell, then twisted her hair into a quick knot. "I don't know your name, sir." Holding her hair, she put her helmet on.

Sir.

I fucking inhaled and cataloged exactly how the single word

left her lips. "You don't need to." Removing the SIM card from the cell so I could check it later, I wiped both our prints off the phone and tossed it. Firing up the Ducati, I glanced at the back exit, then at her. "Get on."

She hesitated.

"Get on, sub," I added, pulling on my gloves.

Bracing a hand on my shoulder and stepping onto one of the foot pegs, she swung her leg over and wrapped her arms around my waist like she'd ridden before.

Dropping my face shield, shifting into first, I revved the engine and let out the clutch as the back door to the bar burst open.

Two of the four men spilled out, weapons drawn.

The Ducati's two-hundred-and-eight horsepower unleashed, we were already turning on to the street when the first shots rang out.

THREE

Atala

"Get on." His voice deep and reserved but commanding, he issued an order like the other men gave me orders, but this man was different.

Very different.

He'd given me a choice. He had a jacket for me. A helmet. He looked at me like he saw me.

I couldn't remember the last time I'd had a choice.

I didn't even want to because remembering that time also meant remembering….

Inhaling, I buried it all.

The new man, the only person who'd said my name in three months, he repeated himself, but this time he added one single word. "Get on, sub."

Sub.

My heart jumped, fear spread, but then my mind shut down and I did what I was told.

I got on the new man's fancy motorcycle and put my arms around him.

Lowering his face shield and revving the engine, he expertly shifted the bike into gear and released the clutch.

The door I'd walked out of in both a panic and with a sense of desperate hope burst open, and the leader of the bad men rushed out.

Shouting in both English and his native language that I didn't understand, he pulled his gun as his second-in-charge came out behind him. Then both men started shooting.

My heart beating so fast my chest hurt, my arms tightened around my rescuer as the bike leaned and we flew out of the alley, turning onto the main road.

Then we were weaving in and out of traffic so fast, fear gripped my panic and suffocated it.

My arms started to shake first, then my legs. My teeth began chattering, and my whole body followed with shaking tremors, but my rescuer only took on more speed as the bitterly cold wind slapped against us faster than the readout on his speedometer.

I was going to die.

After everything that had happened, everything I had lived through, this was going to be how it all ended.

I was going to die on a motorcycle with a stranger with not one living soul knowing my full name.

A sound of despair I had not let myself indulge in for three months escaped past my trembling lips.

Then a gloved hand covered mine, and his deep voice came through my helmet. "Atala."

I sucked in a sharp breath.

It was the second time he'd said it.

Atala.

The blue butterfly she loved. The color of the tropical waters she loved. The fluttering she told him she felt every time I moved in her stomach. At least, that was what I remembered Captain muttering one night, long ago, after he'd had too much to drink.

"Speak," my death-defying rescuer demanded.

With his hand still on mine, the bike racing down the freeway, with concrete and cold and the starless night sky all around us, I did as he commanded.

I spoke.

"Atala Rose."

"Atala Rose," he repeated, his reserved voice filling the small, windless space around my head.

My first name, my middle name, my only name.

No surname.

No birth certificate, no government ID, no driver's license, no passport, nothing traceable—I was no one, living nowhere, because that's how Captain had raised me.

That's all I had known.

But I had my name.

That was who I was.

A butterfly, free and fluttering across tropical waters.

Or I had been.

Now I was here, in a cold, harsh, unforgiving world, speeding away from very bad men as I raced toward my death.

Except now someone living knew.

My rescuer-killer knew my name.

Now I wouldn't be no one from nowhere.

I would die with a name.

FOUR

The Hunter

T HE SECOND I TOOK ON SPEED, SHE STARTED TO SHAKE. THEN A pained cry sounded through the speakers in my helmet.

I covered her bare hands with one of mine. "Atala."

Her inhale was sharp and fast.

Watching the speedometer, the traffic, the freeway behind us, I didn't have time to pull over and take her helmet off, demand that she look at me.

But I wanted to.

I wanted to see those eyes of hers and drown in them right before I broke her, taking every single part of her apart, because that's what I did.

I was a hacker.

Methodical, technical, without your consent, I accessed and dissected every part of your life, stealing your control without remorse. But with this woman, it was different.

From the first image of the innocent brunette that'd populated my screen, I didn't want to be the nameless, faceless hacker compromising her digital footprint. I'd wanted to put my hands on her. I wanted her to breathe my air, my scent, my dominance.

Except I always knew I couldn't touch her.

Not like that.

Instead, I was doing for her what no one had done for me.

I was giving her a way out before it was too late.

I knew the statistical probabilities of failure, the punishment for treason, and the danger I was putting us in. If I made even one wrong keystroke, the consequences for both of us would be fatal.

Except I wasn't going to make a mistake.

This wasn't thirteen years ago, I wasn't an impulsive teen, and this wasn't a game of chess.

Nothing about tonight was impetuous.

My plan in place for weeks, I had contingencies. I learned the hard way to never make a move without one. Nothing in life went as directed. My childhood a roadmap of shit circumstances and unforeseen events, the only thing I'd ever relied on was a global computer network and a keyboard at my fingertips. The internet never slept, drank or set your fucking subsidized housing on fire.

I lived behind screen time. Every dark corner of the web, I'd been to. Now I was here because of it, Check Mate or not, with a woman holding on to me who'd said her name was *sub* right before telling me she was a butterfly and crying in her helmet.

Someone should've told her butterflies didn't cry.

They emerged from a cocoon and lived bright and vibrant before their short life span snuffed them out.

Maybe that was her lot. I didn't know, but I had contingencies for it if it was.

Foregoing words of comfort because I wouldn't lie to this woman named after a winged species more fragile than her digital security, I issued her an order. "Speak."

She was quiet for two miles.

Then her shaking eased, her grip around my waist loosened, and her hauntingly quiet voice filled my helmet right before it sank into my resolve. "Atala Rose."

My grip on the Ducati precise, my movements controlled, my muscle memory at peak performance, I held the Streetfighter steady at ninety-six miles per hour.

But my fucking mind imploded and every plan, contingency, and regimented facet of my life hit the concrete divider at full throttle.

My life span suddenly shorter than a butterfly's, I dangerously tasted her name on my lips. "Atala Rose."

She said nothing.

Exiting the freeway, I drove in a preplanned, circuitous route through my industrial neighborhood. Making sure we weren't being followed, I pulled up to the warehouse.

Using my cell, I opened the bay door only long enough to get us inside before killing the Ducati's engine. Then I immediately reset my security cameras and the traffic cams along the route we'd taken. Throwing the kickstand down, I pocketed my phone.

She got off the bike without comment.

Swinging my leg over the Streetfighter, reaching for her before I could check my dominance, I took her helmet off for her.

Her hair slipped from her makeshift knot and fell down her back.

She glanced across the expanse of the warehouse as I took off my helmet and stowed it with hers on the bike.

Testing her, I aimed for my place. "This way."

The key purposely left in the Ducati, my back intentionally turned, I gave her an opportunity to run.

She didn't.

With her heels quietly clicking, she followed.

I led us into my place.

Tossing my leather on the couch, I turned on my three monitors and sat down at my desk. "Bathroom's down the hall. Kitchen's on your right. Last name?" Pulling up a program I'd designed, I double-checked to make sure there was no digital footprint of my movements tonight before I opened the app I'd used to scan her fingerprint. No hits. I accessed the security feeds for the bar.

The two men hadn't gone back inside, and shortly after we left, all of them had gotten back in their SUV. Hacking the rental company's servers, I entered the GPS's tracking number I'd memorized from earlier tonight, but it'd been disabled after I'd taken her.

My hands poised over the keys, realizing she hadn't answered my question, I asked again. "Last name?"

No movement behind me, she didn't speak.

I spun in my chair.

Standing in the jacket I'd given her, head dipped, her body language throwing off fear, she didn't so much as glance around my place.

For two seconds, I allowed myself to go there.

Her body against my back. Her arms holding on to me. Her thick, dark hair. Her complete and total vulnerability, being at my mercy... those haunted eyes.

I wanted to break her.

Then I wanted to put her back together in a way that made her only mine.

But I didn't keep anything.

Not even my birth name.

I'd learned a long time ago that nothing in this world was permanent, and sitting here staring at a woman I'd taken wasn't going to change that. I didn't take her to keep her. I didn't take her at all.

I'd given her a choice.

She'd chosen.

Now I had to get her out. But I couldn't wipe her from the grid unless I knew who the hell she was and where she'd come from. Except she wasn't talking, and in every damn contingency I'd planned for, I hadn't planned for this.

A submissive.

One almost tailor-made for me.

Except I didn't fuck women frightened by other men, and I sure as hell didn't touch unwilling subs—something she wouldn't know. Maybe something Check Mate would know, but I'd scanned every single line of code in relation to my life for the past thirteen years, and there weren't any breaches except for the one three months ago.

My personal life, what little there was of it, was still private.

Clasping my hands to let this frightened woman know I wasn't a threat, purposely staying seated, I lowered my voice and tone. "Have a seat, Atala."

She didn't move.

"Permission to sit or speak," I amended.

"You type very fast, sir."

"I'm a hacker," I admitted, tilting my head so I could watch her eyes, which were now more teal than blue, and look for markers of trauma or any sign that she might know another hacker.

She didn't nod, blink, or look directly at me, but she also didn't look away. No tells.

"Speak freely," I commanded.

"You drive very fast, sir."

Studying her, I wondered what she'd come from before the terrorists had gotten their hands on her. "I was in control of the Ducati at all times." There was more going on with this woman than the current situation I'd removed her from. "You've ridden before."

Her head dipped lower. "Yes, sir."

"Where're you from?" She wasn't Cuban. I'd checked.

"Nowhere, sir," she answered immediately.

Any other time, I would've respected that answer. "Where did they take you from?" I amended.

Her hands fidgeted, her throat moved with a swallow, her feet shifted. Tells.

I stood.

Flinching, she crossed her arms like she had outside the bar, but she didn't step back.

Two paces and I was directly in front of her. Height, weight, physical description, body language, gait, mannerisms—I'd studied all of it. But towering over her five-foot-six height, four inches of which were her high-heeled boots, I'd never taken into account what she would smell like when there wasn't a bar or a Ducati between us.

Soft, citrus, ocean, plumeria—*mine*.

Mentally shaking away that last thought, I grasped her chin and tilted her head, but she averted her eyes.

"Look at me," I ordered.

"I-I can't, sir," she barely whispered.

Testing a theory, I dropped the gentler tone I'd been speaking to her in and used my natural voice. "Eyes on me, sub."

Her gaze cut to mine without hesitation.

"Good," I praised, then I gave her parameters. "When I tell you to speak freely, you're allowed to say whatever you choose. That's a conversation. But if I have my hand on you, like I do right now, and if I give you a command, that's no longer a conversation. I tell you to do something, you do it. I ask a question, you answer as if your life depended on it, no hesitation." Because there was going to come a time when her life would depend on doing exactly what I told her. And that time was coming sooner rather than later if I didn't get back to work. "As far as you're concerned, Alekhin is dead to you. He is not your master. You are not his sub. He is no one to you. I'm your lifeline now. I became it the second you walked out of that bar. That means when you're in my presence, you do not see, hear or speak to anyone except me. Outside this warehouse, unless I tell you otherwise, you are no one. Inside these four walls, you're Atala. Do you understand?"

She stared at me, but she didn't answer.

I repeated the question in words she'd hear. "Do you understand, sub?"

"No, sir," she quietly replied.

"Which part?"

"I do not know who Alekhin is, sir."

She could've been lying. She could've been the best operative I've ever seen, and this whole thing was an act and she was a plant. But I'd been watching every scrap of footage I'd had of her for months. I saw her when the four terrorists boarded the boat. I'd watched her body language and theirs. Before that, I'd been behind my screens, watching cells and terrorists and bad fucking people for over a decade, and I knew the signs.

I also knew every one of those people had one thing in common.

No matter how good they were, no matter how deep they were, eventually, they all slipped. It could be something as subtle as a glance in the direction of a camera they shouldn't have known was there, or it could be as violent as murder from a single momentary loss of control. But sooner or later, that slip happened, and I caught it on screen.

Except this woman hadn't slipped.

She hadn't known those men when they'd gotten on the boat.

And now that I had her, now that I could see her eyes when she spoke, hear her voice, watch her body language, I knew without a doubt. She wasn't a part of the cell. But she was submissive as hell, and it'd been bred into her long before those fucks got a hold of her.

Making a calculated move, sinking us both deeper, I gave her classified intel. "Vladimir Alekhin is the name of the man who took you."

She blinked.

"Do you know what the men you were with are planning?"

"No, sir."

Truth. "Do you know why they came to D.C.?"

She averted her eyes. "I wasn't aware we were in D.C., sir."

"Look at me," I demanded.

She gave me her gaze, but not her focus.

I filed away her reaction. "How do you not know where you are?"

Still not focusing on me, she answered the question. "I have never been here before, sir."

They drove past the Washington Monument, National Mall and Lincoln Memorial. She was telling me the truth, her body language backed it up, but how could she not know where she was? "Are you American?" Her accent, or lack thereof, was.

"I am no one, sir."

Right answer, but fuck. "Before they took you, who were you?"

She hesitated for two seconds. Then she whispered, "Atala Rose."

I was missing something. "Where were you raised?"

She tried to hide it, but fear and grief flashed across her face. "On the water, sir."

On the water. Atala Rose, the *Nalleli Rose*, the boat was hers, or her parents. I missed that because it wasn't registered anywhere and she seemed too young. "Which body of water?"

"The Caribbean, sir."

"Be more specific," I ordered, suddenly realizing why this woman had no digital footprint.

She frowned. "I'm sorry, sir?"

"There are hundreds of islands in the Caribbean." She had to have been on land at some point. "Name the ones you've been to."

"The Bahamas, Turks and Caicos, Dominican Republic, Haiti, Jamaica, the Caymans, and Cuba, sir," she answered, rattling off an entire geographical loop of the Greater Antilles.

Five countries and two territories. I needed to get started on a more detailed facial recognition search immediately. "Going back how many years?"

Her voice dropped again. "My whole life, sir."

"Age?"

Her hands fidgeted, and she pulled her bottom lip in.

"How old are you, Atala?" Jesus, she looked young, but now I was wondering if she was underage.

"I do not know, sir."

I watched her closely. She wasn't lying. "Because?"

"Is this a conversation, sir?"

For two seconds, I let the urge to dominate her take hold and I imagined every way I wanted to top her. Then I reined it in and dropped my hand. Testing her to see if I was making any progress, I issued an order without touching her. "Speak."

She didn't hesitate. "You're asking more questions than the men who took me, and I just want to go home, but I don't think I can. I don't think I'm safe anymore."

She was right, she wasn't. "Where?"

She blinked. "I'm sorry?"

"Where's home?"

Her chest rose with an inhale, and her features softened. "A small atoll off the coast of one of the southern, uninhabited islands in the Bahamas."

An unprotected, remote location in the middle of hurricane alley. "You're right." I turned back to my computer to start the search. "It's not safe for you to go home."

FIVE

Atala

"You're right." Turning back toward his desk, the formfitting, long-sleeved, thermal T-shirt showing the enormous size of his muscular arms, he leaned his tall frame over his computer. With his fingers flying across the keys, he told me what I already knew but didn't want to think about. "It's not safe for you to go home."

Straightening to his full height, he spared me a glance, but this time he didn't stare unwaveringly into my eyes. He looked at the perfectly fitted leather jacket he'd given me. Then he tipped his chin. "Stand behind the desk, facing me, two steps back from the middle monitor." His focus went back to his keyboard.

I did as he asked.

Adjusting the tilt of the monitor, he glanced at me, hit a key, and issued another one of his orders. "Take the leather off, remain in position."

Unzipping the jacket, I placed the nicest article of clothing I'd ever had on the ground and looked back at him.

He repeated the slight adjustment of the monitor and hit another key. "Do you have a shirt on under your sweater?"

I nodded.

"Remove the sweater," he ordered.

I hesitated. The warehouse space he'd turned into living quarters was cool, but not nearly as cold as outside or the bone-chilling ride here. I'd been far colder over the past three months, not being allowed to use a blanket to sleep or dress in any clothes that could conceal a weapon—not that I had any. Or at least I thought it'd been three months. I'd stopped counting. But none of those reasons were why I hesitated.

Taking my sweater off in front of this quiet but commanding man felt… dangerous.

Almost more dangerous than being held hostage by the men who'd taken me.

Staring as if he could see right through me, the man with almost vacant blue eyes slowly removed his hand from his keyboard and let his arm fall to his side. The size of his muscular frame, the controlled intention of the movement, the way he looked both frighteningly lethal and expressionless, I naïvely thought for one heartbeat that his reserved manner was to put me at ease.

Then, in his deep voice, he quietly spoke with more dominant authority than the man who raised me and the men who took me combined.

"Remove the sweater, Atala."

I pulled the only sweater I owned, the one I'd thankfully grabbed from the boat before the men had dragged me off, over my head.

My rescuer's unrelenting stare went straight to my bare, bruised arms.

Perfectly still, nothing in his expression changing, his gaze swept the length of each of my arms before taking in my braless, bikini-topless state under my thin tank top.

From more than just the cold, my nipples hardened to sharp peaks, and an unfamiliar clenching pulsed low in my belly. Involuntarily, I shivered as both a rush of heat flushed through my body and a chill swept across my bare skin.

Then I made a horrible mistake.

Crossing my arms, I covered my breasts with my hands.

Faster than I could step back, he was around the desk and gripping my chin hard as he towered over me. Forcing me to look up at him, he bit out a lethal command. "Say no."

NOVEMBER

My core pulsed hard, and my mouth went dry.

"I gave you an order, sub. *Say no.*"

Whatever the reason was, I suddenly didn't want to say no to him, but something in my mind, in my body, it listened to this man. "No," I whispered.

"Again," he demanded.

"No."

"No, what?"

Heat flooded into every part of my suddenly aching body. "No, sir."

Instantly dropping his hand, he stepped back. Then he spoke again in his quiet, controlled tone. "That is your safe word with me." His gaze hardened. "Use it only if you mean it. Now drop your arms."

Releasing my breasts, letting my arms fall to my sides, my nipples pebbled to even harder points.

His gaze, now cold and hard, stayed locked on my face, but his chest rose with an inhale. "Why did you cover yourself in front of me?"

I said nothing. I couldn't. I wanted to both put my sweater back on and take off the worn tank top. I didn't understand what was going on with my own body or how this man could speak to me in such a way that made me want to do things my own mind didn't understand.

But he did.

From the moment I first heard his voice, my body had reacted. Then I saw his eyes, saw how he looked at me, how he studied me, it was as if he knew me even though we'd never met.

"*Speak,*" he demanded.

"I…" I swallowed past the sudden lump in my throat as tears threatened. "I don't know. Sir," I added.

"Conversation," he bit out. "Lose the 'sir.' Try again."

I said the first thing that came to my mind. "I'm afraid."

"Of me, the situation, or the men who bruised your arms?"

"All of it," I admitted, lowering my gaze because I didn't want to see his face when I told him I was afraid of him.

"Did they force you to have sex?"

I couldn't help it, my arms crossed protectively around myself again. "I don't want to talk about it."

"We're not talking about it. I'm asking you a yes or no question, and you're going to answer."

"No," I barely whispered, still not looking at him.

"Sexual acts?" he added.

Remembering that horrible second night of my captivity, I wanted to disappear. I wanted none of this to be real, and I wanted to be back on the boat in the tropical waters I knew, but now I was afraid the men would come after me.

I didn't know if I'd ever feel safe being alone on the boat again, but that was all I knew. That was the only life I'd ever lived. It was also my only source of income, and I couldn't bear to think about what might've happened to the Nalleli Rose by now. I prayed she was still at that private dock, but I wasn't even sure how to find her. I knew it was in the Florida Keys because I saw several of the famed mile-marker signs on the side of the road once we'd gotten in the car, but that's all I knew.

Growing up, Captain had always kept the Nalleli Rose away from the Keys. He'd said we should always avoid U.S. waters and their Coast Guard, so we had. Then the men who'd taken me and my boat said we were going north after months in the Caribbean, and I'd gotten scared. Foolishly telling them I didn't know US waters, the oldest of the men had taken over the helm once I'd gotten us to Key West. Then he'd navigated the rest of the way, and I wasn't even able to get GPS coordinates off the radar equipment when we'd docked. I'd tried, but the man who was the leader, the one who'd left the bruises, had grabbed my arm so hard and squeezed, I'd cried out when he'd dragged me off my forty-six-foot Bertram.

"Look at me and answer the question," my rescuer snapped.

Inhaling, holding my arms tighter, I forced myself to look up and focus back on the conversation when it was the last thing I wanted to do. "The youngest one tried."

"Vladimir, Ivan, Pavel, or Anton?" He rattled off four names, including the name he had given me before. "They're all relatively the same age. Which one was it?"

"I don't know their names. They only referred to each other by a first initial."

He amended his question. "V, I, P, or A?"

"It was none of those. It was the fifth man. The younger one. They called him Z."

For a fraction of a second, so fast I would have missed it had he not demanded I look at him, a murderous fury contorted his austere face. "There's a fifth one?"

"Yes."

"When?" he demanded. "How much younger? Full description."

"When they first got on my boat. He was closer to your age, maybe mine. I don't know ages, but he was younger than the other men, and I don't really know how to describe him other than arrogant and mean." The bad kind of mean that was delivered with a smile. "That's what stood out the most. Other than that, he had brown hair and brown eyes. He was shorter and much thinner than you. Like the others, he had an accent, but I don't know from where. I'd never heard an accent like it before, but I didn't ask them where they were from. I didn't ask them anything. I just tried to avoid them, especially the younger one."

"In Cuba?" Moving with both speed and grace, he was back in front of his monitors, and his hands were flying across the keyboard. "Tell me exactly where and when that was."

"In Habana Bay. They boarded at Guanabacoa. I do not know the date. It was about three months ago."

"Where is the fifth man now? He wasn't with you when you docked in Key Largo."

Key Largo. That's where my boat was? How did he know that? "We dropped him off in the Caymans about a week ago, near Grand Harbor, but at a private dock. How do you know where my boat is now?"

Looking up from his fancy keyboard, focusing his intense stare on me, he repeated what he had told me before. "I'm a hacker."

The word was familiar. I'd heard the men say a version of it as they'd set up their computers in my small galley and used devices I'd never seen.

"I don't know what that means." I'd never had a computer. The boat's outdated electronics were the closest I'd ever come to modern technology. But the younger man, Z, he'd had as many computers as my rescuer did.

The man who'd found me in a bar and quietly told me to come with him or take my chances stared at me for a heartbeat.

Then he said four words that chilled me to the bone. "I've been watching you."

SIX

The Hunter

A FIFTH MAN. *A FUCKING FIFTH MAN.*
It was Check Mate. It had to be. None of the other four men had fit the profile, and unlike Check Mate, I'd been able to trace all of their backgrounds. None of them had been careful enough. But this fifth man had kept away from all security cameras or anywhere I would've captured an image of him. *Goddamn it.*

"How do you know where my boat is now?" she asked nervously.

I reran a search with new parameters through all the footage I had a second time, but still hit a dead end. Looking up at her, I gave her the easiest answer. "I'm a hacker."

The confusion that etched across her face was steeped in anxiety. "I don't know what that means."

Staring at her, at her purity, knowing Check Mate had attempted to put his hands on her, that he'd brought her into this, it only enraged me more. He was a fucking dead man when I found him.

I gave her the one truth I could safely give. "I've been watching you."

Fear stiffened her body, and she sucked in a breath. "Why?"

Not taking my eyes off her, my hands already on the keyboard, I captured her image with a single keystroke. "It's my job." I wouldn't keep the picture or use it for one of the passports. But later, after I got her out of here and away from whatever the hell

Check Mate and Alekhin were planning, I'd look at it. Once. Then I'd wipe my whole system before I melted down the parts in the warehouse next door, leaving nothing to chance.

Terrified, she stared at me. "I-I don't understand."

"Good." The less she knew, the better. "Arms down, look at the middle monitor."

Anxiety rolling off her, her gaze shifted, but she fidgeted.

"Atala."

Her eyes jumped to mine.

"Take a breath," I ordered.

She inhaled, but it did nothing to still her. Like her namesake, practically fluttering in place, she stared at me with a need I was one hundred percent certain she didn't realize she was giving off. A need I couldn't ignore. Before I talked myself out of touching her again, I was in front of her, grasping her chin.

"Inhale. Slowly." I matched my breath to my command.

Her eyes on mine, she inhaled.

"Hold it." Releasing her, I toed her boots apart twelve inches. "Back straight, shoulders squared, unclasp your hands and exhale slowly."

She did as I instructed.

"Good. Again." As she inhaled, I grasped her wrists. "Fully extend your fingers, rest your right hand in the palm of your left, and interlock your thumbs." I showed her parade rest position but with her hands in front. "Every time you experience anxiety, center yourself and assume parade rest as you inhale deep and let it out slow. Understood?"

"Parade rest?"

"A military stance."

Not questioning me, keeping her eyes on mine, she inhaled and held position.

"Good." I strode back to my screens. "Eyes on the middle monitor." Taking another picture, I glanced at the search for

Russian hackers with first initial Z that I'd initiated moments ago, but there weren't any hits. "Stay there."

Quickly bringing up the harbor in Guanabacoa, Cuba, I entered parameters and started a new search before I strode into my bedroom and grabbed two shirts. Mentally going over every cyber terrorist's name on the running watch list we kept in the command room, I tried to remember any that fell within the parameters of the description she'd given me, but I hadn't memorized more than the top twenty, and none of them fit the profile.

When I came back, her arms were crossed again, but she wasn't dropping her gaze. She was watching me.

Bypassing my desk, I held out a white shirt. "Put this on."

She slipped her arms into the long sleeves, and I rolled the cuffs before hitting the top buttons. When my hands got near her neck, chill bumps broke out across her flesh.

Cataloging her reaction, I purposely brushed the back of my hand across her neck before sweeping her hair off her shoulder.

She shivered.

Playing with fire, I dropped my voice. "You like me touching you, sub?"

Her eyes closed, and her voice came as a whisper. "Why do you call me that?"

Tucking a strand of her hair behind her ear, my hand stilled. "What did you tell me your name was when I first asked?"

She dipped her head and spoke even quieter. "Sub."

I tipped her chin. "Look at me."

She gave me her teal-blue eyes.

"Why, exactly, did you tell me that?"

Fear, confusion and innocence all played across her features. "That's what the men called me."

She was bruised, traumatized and frightened, but they hadn't forced her into sex. For three months, they'd left this stunningly beautiful creature untouched. Alone, the pieces of intel painted one picture. Terrorists, boat, hostage, illegal entry on U.S. soil. But I was already putting together another scenario. One that made me both enraged and turned the fuck on. A scenario that I couldn't afford to entertain, let alone execute, but my head was already going there.

"Do you know what a sub is, Atala?" I traced a finger over the pulse in her neck.

"No," she whispered.

I fucking stilled.

My chest rose with an inhale, and her eyes stayed on mine. Nothing in the room moved, but my entire fucking existence pivoted on its axis.

She was innocent.

Truly fucking innocent.

Possession on a level I'd never experienced sank into my head, and my first thought wasn't that I was going to take her innocence and fuck her until she felt the pain so deep she'd never forget me. My first thought was how I was going to kill Check Mate. Slowly. Painfully. And without mercy.

Staring at the only woman who'd ever made me feel regret for the life of solitude I'd carved out, I selfishly gave her only a partial answer. "Sub is short for submissive." I purposely didn't ask if she understood the term. I wanted to sink inside her and taste her innocence without her knowing. But there was something I was missing. She didn't address me how she did because of manners. There was more to it. "Why do you call me sir?"

"That's how I was raised." She looked away. "That's what I called the man who was my father. Sir or Captain."

More intrigued with every piece of intel she dispensed, I increased the pressure of my grip on her and gently, but firmly, turned her face back toward me. "Your father raised you on the boat?"

"Yes."

"Fishing charter?" I guessed, running my thumb across her cheek.

Subconsciously, she leaned into my touch. "Yes."

"You worked the boat."

She didn't physically move, but the sexually tenuous grasp I'd had on her seconds ago dissipated. "I rigged and maintained the gear, cleaned the decks and cabin, and cooked. Captain chartered and did the engine maintenance."

Captain. That was twice now she hadn't referred to him as her father. "Where's your mother?"

She looked past me. "Captain told me she died in childbirth."

Then he raised her to call him sir and do his dirty work. Now I knew what it was about her eyes that drew me in. "Where's your father now?"

"A couple years back, he didn't wake up one morning. He told me when he passed, he wanted to be buried at sea where he'd buried my mother." Clasping her hands how I'd just taught her, she shook her head. "I don't know why I'm telling you this."

"Because I asked." Because she'd been deprived of attention. Deprived in a way I understood. Which made her dangerously more vulnerable than I'd anticipated. "Continue."

"Captain told me to never give any personal information, which I never understood, because I don't have anything to tell."

She had a lifetime of hard living to tell. "What did you do when he died?"

She nodded twice, a tell I'd seen on my screens before today. "I did what he asked. I took the Nalleli Rose north and east of Abaco Island in the Bahamas, and I let him go." Her gaze met mine, but her muscles tensed. "Were you watching me then?"

"No."

"When did you start?"

"Three months, two days ago." September twenty-eighth, eleven minutes past oh seven hundred, when four terrorists walked down a marina toward her forty-six-foot Bertram. She was hosing off the decks in a yellow bikini covered by a thin blue tank top and short white shorts. She looked as innocent then as she did now.

"You count days?"

Only the last ninety-four. "Yes."

She frowned. "What day is today?"

"Day or date?"

The lines between her eyes grew deeper. "The number of the day of the month."

"December thirty-first."

She blinked. "New Year's Eve?"

"Yes."

Her gaze drifted. "That makes twenty." She looked back at me. "I can answer one of your questions."

"Your age." She measured time in events.

"Yes. I've seen New Year's Eve fireworks nineteen times before tonight that I can remember. If I was on the boat, it would be twenty." For a brief moment, her wary expression lifted and was replaced with one of shy pride. "I am at least that."

Guileless, living off the grid, untouched, innocent and vulnerable.

I was dangerously wrong before.

There was no *almost*.

This woman was made for me.

But possession wasn't part of the plan. It wasn't even on the radar of any of my contingencies. I couldn't keep her.

No one could keep a butterfly.

Releasing her, I stepped back and issued an order. "Look at the middle monitor and hold position."

SEVEN

Atala

I THOUGHT I COULD PLEASE HIM BY ANSWERING ONE OF HIS QUESTIONS. I thought giving him my age would make him… I don't know what I thought it would do. But I didn't think he would immediately back away and give me a stern order.

"Look at the middle monitor and hold position."

Feeling like I did something wrong, wanting his hand back on my face, wishing I hadn't told him about the fireworks, I focused on the monitor he said to look at.

He hit a key, then strode back to me and silently unbuttoned the white shirt he'd put on me that smelled more like fresh laundry than him. Or what I would imagine freshly washed clothes would smell like coming from a washing machine. I didn't have anything like that on the boat, and more times than not, the fancy-smelling laundry soaps I knew you could buy were an expense I forwent.

I saved my money for my favorite shampoo that smelled like the wild plumeria growing throughout the Caribbean islands. I saved my money, period. Or I had been saving it. In a small tackle box I hid under the floor in the galley, I had been putting away as much cash as I could. The Nalleli Rose was old. She was seaworthy, but the engine was going and it needed repairs I didn't know how to do. I was getting close to affording them, but then I'd taken the foreigners that'd wanted a deep-sea fishing charter.

I should've known the double rate they were offering to pay me was too good to be true.

Pulling the white shirt off my arms, my rescuer tossed it over one shoulder before taking a blue shirt from the other and holding it up like he had the last one. "Speak your thoughts."

I slid my arms into the cool, soft material. "I don't know your name."

Rolling up the sleeves for me and swiftly buttoning the top buttons, he didn't answer at first. Then he swept my hair to one side, bringing it over my left shoulder, and his cool gaze took in my appearance. "They call me Hunter."

I listened to every word this man spoke.

I soaked up the sound of his voice, and I tucked it away because something told me he would become a memory. I was used to that. The customers on the boat all became memories, even if some of them returned. Other people cycled through the life I led, mainly workers at marinas where I bought gas or the few places onshore my father told me were safe enough to purchase supplies at. With the exception of my father, everyone in my life had been passing through.

Or I was passing through theirs.

I'd never dwelled on it. I didn't dwell on anything I couldn't or wasn't going to change.

Then the four men with guns came on my boat and led me to this place. A cold, cavernous building in a concrete city where my past life was destroyed and a mysterious hacker with ocean-colored eyes was dressing me like he wanted to undress me.

For the first time in my life, I didn't want someone to pass through my days.

I wasn't waiting to be alone so I could jump into warm waters with my speargun or lie on the bow and listen to the sound of soft swells or close my eyes and imagine distant breezes through palm trees.

I was staring at a hunter.

One who'd all but said I was his prey.

I wasn't educated, but I wasn't ignorant. I'd already figured out he'd been following the men who'd taken my boat and my life. I just couldn't figure out why he'd taken me.

Tasting his name on my lips, I whispered it into the cave-like place he lived. "Hunter." Harsh, foreboding, it sounded as it tasted—dangerous. Before I could think through what I was saying, I gave him more of my thoughts. "I wish I had finished *Moby Dick*." Then maybe I would know how it ended. Maybe I would know what happens to the prey of a hunter.

"You read." He strode back to the other side of his desk and glanced at me as he hit a key. Then his gaze dropped, and he was typing.

"I never went to any school, but Captain taught me to read. The controls on the helm at first. Then it was channel markers before he tossed a book in my lap one hot afternoon."

"*Moby Dick*," the hunter stated as he kept typing, his attention now fully focused on his screens.

"It was one of three books he had on the boat."

The hunter looked up, his hands pausing as his gaze immediately found mine, like he knew I was still standing where he'd told me to. "Put your sweater back on." His focus shifted back to his screens, and he was typing again. "What three books?"

"*Moby Dick*, *Kon Tiki* and *Call of the Wild*." Reluctantly taking his blue shirt off, even though it was much too big, I picked up my sweater and pulled it over my head. "I never finished any of them." The coarse material of the sweater was worn and stretched, and the hem fell almost to my jean-covered thighs. I hated how constrictive the material was around my legs. I hated all pants, but I was thankful for the warmth, even though the man named V had all but forced me into my warmest clothes before we left the Nalleli Rose.

"Why?" the hunter asked, never looking up from his screen.

"They were all…" I stopped myself from saying frightening. What I used to think was terrifying was nothing compared to having men with guns threaten your life every day for months, then shoot at you as a hunter on a motorcycle stole you away. "I didn't like them."

"Because?"

All at once, I noticed I was not calling him sir and he wasn't correcting me, and suddenly, I was more uncomfortable than I'd been for the past three months. Glancing away, crossing my arms, I answered his question, wondering at one word he'd spoken to me. *Conversation.* "I did not like stories, sir."

Was this a conversation? Was this what Captain had been doing with all those customers over the years? Speaking to them more than he'd ever spoken to me. Did he ever converse with me? Is that why I didn't cry when I pushed his body into the ocean, because we never had a simple conversation?

I didn't realize there was a new mechanical sound coming from the hunter's desk until heavy, black boots were in my line of sight a split second before a knuckle was under my chin and my head was being lifted.

The hunter stared down at me. "*Sir.*"

It wasn't a question, and it wasn't an order. It was more of a statement, but never in my life had a single word made me want to both shake in fear and drop to my knees. "Yes, sir," I barely whispered.

"What just changed?"

His voice was quiet, the deep quiet how he'd spoken to me before, almost as if he had been saying something comforting, but he wasn't. He wasn't even asking a question or requesting insight into my thoughts. He was demanding an answer. One I didn't know how to explain. "I don't know what you mean, sir."

"Why did you start calling me 'sir' again?" His thumb braced against my jawline. "Is this no longer a conversation to you, Atala?"

He had so many questions, but I had more. "I don't know. I'm not sure if I know what a conversation is supposed to be like, sir." Up close, when he touched me, he was right. There was no room for conversation. There was only him, and he was air. The air I needed to breathe.

"This isn't about a conversation." His fingers spread around my neck like the soft touch of an ocean breeze. Then his palm covered my throat, he closed his grip, and his tone became disarmingly quiet as the look in his eyes turned all predator. "This is about you being a sub."

Fear coated every inch of my body, but deep in my lower belly where a baby would grow, my muscles clenched with an empty ache.

I choked on my own ignorance. "Sub." I was wrong. This man wasn't my rescuer.

He was exactly as he said he was…

A hunter.

EIGHT

The Hunter

Closing my grip on her throat, I watched her fear sink in, and my cock hardened.

"Sub," she repeated, her voice breaking.

I held firm. "Are you beginning to understand exactly what that means?"

Innocence joined the fear in her eyes. "No."

I thought about the small, tight peaks of her nipples. How they would feel between my teeth, the texture of them against my tongue. I wondered how she'd taste as I sucked her into my mouth. "Are you a virgin?"

Watching my lips, she blinked.

I clarified. "Have you had sex?"

Color flushed her cheeks, and she immediately tried to turn her head, but I already had a hold of her. This was exactly what I was anticipating when I asked the question, which was why I'd dominantly put my hand on her. I wanted to see her eyes. I needed to know if she was capable of lying to me. "Answer the question."

"No," she whispered.

My cock pulsed, and I went there.

Fisting a handful of her hair, gripping her throat, pulling her head back sharp and fast, I both lost control and fucking embraced it. Letting go of the Cyber Warfare Operations Officer the Air Force had molded me into, I became the dominant I was.

Bringing my mouth to her ear, imagining taking her virginity hard and merciless, I allowed one touch of my lips to the soft flesh of her neck. "A sub is someone who is sexually submissive, Atala. Someone who submits to the commands of their partner."

Her entire body trembled. "Is that what you like?"

Inhaling her purity, wondering if she would be wet enough for my cock right now or if her virgin cunt would give me resistance, I answered the question she should have asked. "I'm dominant." I only fucked submissives. "What do you think?"

Her small hand landed on my arm. "I—"

"Did I give you permission to touch me?" Gripping her tighter but immediately pushing her back, I put half a foot between her body and mine.

Same as on the Ducati, she started to shake. "I-I'm sorry."

I raised an eyebrow. "Sorry, *what*?"

Unable to move her head, she squeezed her eyes shut. "I'm sorry, sir."

"Arms at your sides, eyes on me," I demanded.

Dropping her arms, she looked at me.

"Listen very carefully to what I'm about to say."

Still trembling, she nodded as much as she could with my grip on her.

"You do not touch me, you do not question me when I give you instruction, and you do not close your eyes when I'm speaking to you." I gave the one caveat. "Unless I give explicit permission. Understood?"

"Yes, sir."

I asked again. "Why did you switch from conversation to calling me 'sir'?"

"I'm not sure, sir."

"Not repeating myself. Answer the question, this time with honesty."

As if my instruction gave her room to breathe, she inhaled deep and the shaking eased. "I suddenly realized I was not calling you 'sir' and it felt… not right."

"Why?" I knew why. Increasing the pressure of my grip, I could taste it on her. This woman was as rare as her eye color.

A tremor hit her spine before quickly dissipating, and she subconsciously leaned into my hold. Then she began to speak.

"You and what I think you're capable of frightens me. But when you touch me, especially like you are now, it terrifies me more than the men who took me because I suddenly stop being afraid when I know I shouldn't." Her voice quieted. "But it's more than that. I stop being everything that's in my head, and I just… float. Except it's not like floating in the warm Caribbean Sea on a hot summer day. It's like plunging into icy waters, and that shouldn't feel good, but it does. It feels more than good. It feels safe. Like I don't have to think about being afraid or worried because I forget about everything except you." Color flushed her cheeks as she gave me more honesty than any female ever had.

"It also makes me feel things I don't know how to explain because I don't have fancy words or anything to compare it to. All I know is that it's like the kind of hunger that pains you when you haven't eaten and you don't have any food in sight." She drew in a breath. Then her voice turned as quiet as her submissiveness. "Something happened when you first spoke to me. Then I saw your eyes and how you look at me, and now I can't unsee or unhear you. I don't want to. I just… I don't know how to say what I want."

She didn't have to.

I already knew.

She needed someone alpha enough to strip her control so she could do precisely what she said—float. She wanted the freedom of total submission. Craving the headspace that only came from being truly dominated, she needed my exact brand of dominance.

Not reprimanding her for not using sir, I gave her the name for it. "Total power exchange."

"I'm sorry?"

"You're submissive, Atala."

"I… is that bad?" she barely asked.

NOVEMBER

It was perfect. She was perfect. "Yes."

Hurt crushed her features, and she shrank in on herself despite my hold on her. Then she dropped her gaze. "I'm sorry, sir."

I already knew her weakness, what she craved most, but she never should've handed it to me with her unfiltered honesty. "Take your eyes off me one more time and that will be the last time you have my attention."

She instantly focused on me.

"The level of submissiveness you exude makes you vulnerable and susceptible to the wrong kind of men." Already knowing I was going to kill the men who put those bruises on her arms didn't stop the dangerous thoughts of continuing to track her after tonight and eliminating any man who got close enough to touch her. The repercussions of which wouldn't only jeopardize the very thing I was trying to accomplish, but it would break the one self-preserving rule I had.

I didn't keep anything.

I couldn't afford to.

This innocent creature was no exception. She was never going to be mine. Not only was it not part of the plan or in any of my contingencies, she couldn't afford to have me thinking otherwise. Not if she wanted to live.

Unaware of how much danger she was in, she naïvely asked the last question she should have been worried about. "Who would be the right kind of man?"

"Someone worthy of that level of trust." Releasing her, I turned toward my desk.

"Someone like you?"

Pivoting, I grabbed her chin with a punishing grip. "Do *not* trust me, Atala."

"Then why did you take me away from those men? Why did you risk getting shot at for me?"

I should have noticed she didn't flinch or so much as blink

when I'd turned on her. I should've cataloged the fact that she was waiting for me with eye contact.

I didn't.

Instead, my punishing grip was expanding to encompass her entire jawline as I grasped her as hard as I would have had I been shoving my cock down her throat. "Do not mistake what I'm doing here, sub."

Slipping back into a submissive dynamic as easily as I'd lost the control of a trained military operative, her voice quieted. "What are you doing, sir?"

"Making sure you don't die."

Before her inhaled breath of shock hit her lungs, my hands were off her. "From here on out, you trust no one. You do not speak to anyone. You do not tell a single person your real name, and you never divulge where you're from. As of this moment, Atala Rose is dead."

Her hands going to her throat, she stared. But unlike every other time she'd looked at me, she tried to hide her expression.

Having repeatedly watched and studied every second of security camera footage and satellite imagery I'd captured of her, I knew this woman. I knew her expressions. I knew her body language, and I knew those eyes.

She was looking at me as if I'd betrayed her.

And I had.

I never should've touched her.

But what was done was done, and now I had a job to do.

Striding back to my desk, glancing at the time on one of my monitors, I issued her an order as I pulled the passport photos out of the specialized printer. "Get your leather and bring it here."

She didn't move.

The clock ticking, my dick hard, I did something I'd never done. I let the two halves of my life merge. Military trained, dominant alpha, I issued the order again, but this time I did it without filtering or holding back. "Pick up your leather, walk to me, then drop to your knees, sub."

Her eyes widened in shock.

"*Now*," I barked.

First flinching at my tone, she then scrambled into action. Grabbing the jacket, coming around my desk, she beautifully, submissively dropped to her knees at my feet and dipped her head.

Then she fucking signed my death certificate. "Please don't send me away. I can be whatever you need, sir."

Barely refraining from putting my hands on her and aggressively taking her virginity, I didn't give her a command. I gave her the best advice she'd ever get from me. "Don't ever tell me that again."

NINE

Atala

I STARED AT THE VEINS ON HIS LARGE HAND THAT SNAKED UP HIS FOREARM as he talked. They burst in exaggerated relief like flashes of lightning every time he moved.

I heard his words, but I didn't understand him, not now, not earlier.

I knew the content of what he was saying, but his eyes were saying something different.

I'd never conversed with the customers on the boat. I didn't engage with them at all if I could help it because Captain had made it very clear. I wasn't allowed to. Especially not any of the men, and for the most part, I hadn't minded. The ones who'd looked at me in the same way that fifth man had that night on the boat, I knew I'd been better off not engaging.

But that didn't mean I hadn't watched all those customers.

I had.

Same as I'd watched the bad men.

I watched their eyes and the way they spoke and the way they said things, because people spoke more with their expressions and movements than with their words. They were almost no different than the brightly colored fish that swam past me in the ocean when I had my speargun. Confident, daring, doing what they always did in their pursuit of life, never expecting someone was watching them, waiting to take away what they had.

Most people were like those fish.

They smiled, they joked, they bragged, they talked about a million different things, but none of it said what their eyes said.

Just like when the hunter told me to never tell him again I could be what he needed.

He hadn't meant it.

I knew he didn't.

But he still had his hand on one of the five passports laid open in front of us, and he was making me repeat the numbers of a house address followed by what he called a zip code. "Again."

I gave him the numbers that I didn't need to memorize because they were right in front of me. "Ten-oh-five-nine-four-three-oh-five."

The lights suddenly turned off in the living area of his warehouse space, momentarily throwing us into pitch darkness before a dim light turned on in a bedroom down the hall.

Sweeping up all the passports, he unzipped the tiny little zipper hidden under a seam on the inside lining of the leather jacket he'd given me and methodically placed the passports inside. Then he stood from his desk chair. "Come." Grabbing the leather jacket he'd given me and a laptop computer, he walked toward his bedroom. "Repeat the number."

Still on my knees, I quickly got up and followed him. "Ten-oh-five-nine-four-three-oh-five." The way he moved—the slight sway of his wide shoulders, the purposeful stride of his long legs—he was both controlled precision and stealth, like a predator. I couldn't help but imagine him on the Nalleli Rose, easily commanding the helm.

"Bahamas," he stated, short and fast, tossing the jacket on the bed before he sat next to his nightstand and opened the laptop.

I knew what he wanted, so I gave him the name on the Bahamas passport he'd put my picture into. "Naira Rios."

"Cuba," he quickly stated in the same abrupt manner.

"Novia Ramira." I'd noticed the pattern in all the passports, how they all matched the initials of the Nalleli Rose, but I didn't say anything. Just like I didn't say anything about the names. I didn't like any of them. None were my name.

"United Kingdom." He started typing.

"Natalie Rhoades," I answered, especially not liking that last name, as if I were to be condemned to roads and never travel on water again.

"Barbados."

"Naida Rhody." I didn't bother asking where he'd come up with the names, same as I didn't ask if any of these documents were real. I knew they weren't. Not that I had any experience because I'd never had a passport before, but I knew enough to know you couldn't legally make passports in a warehouse.

"United States," he clipped, asking about the passport that had the address numbers on it he'd made me memorize.

"Nicole Roberts." I didn't know why, but I disliked that name the most. "You went out of order, sir." He'd been making me memorize the names on the passports in alphabetical order by country.

"Drop the 'sir' for now. You need to know them in any order." Setting his laptop down on the bed, he pulled open a drawer on his nightstand and reached underneath as if to push something. A secret compartment dropped down, and he pressed his thumb onto a small screen. "Kneel. Repeat the number." A click sounded and a small door on the compartment opened.

I knelt in front of him, then I said the number without thought, realizing belatedly that I actually did know it by heart now. "Ten-oh-five-nine-four-three-oh-five. Is this a conversation?"

"Yes."

"Why do you tell me to kneel?"

He paused to look at me. "Because it's a physical act of subservience. It gets your attention, and it gives you something to focus on."

I heard his words, but I watched his eyes. "You like it?"

His voice lowered. "Yes."

Warmth flushed through me. Suddenly shy, I glanced back at

the nightstand. "Did you put that secret compartment under your nightstand drawer?" Captain had a small safe on the Nalleli Rose that was hidden in a storage compartment in his berth. It had a dial with numbers that you spun to unlock. It wasn't anything close to the elaborate compartment the hunter had, but I'd never opened the safe because I didn't know the combination.

"Yes, I installed this." He reached inside the compartment, then handed me a small switchblade. "Do you know how to use this?"

The cool metal, barely heated from the brief touch of his hand, fell into my palm, and I wrapped my fingers around it. For one heartbeat, I closed my eyes and inhaled the comfort of it. "Yes." After three months of nothing familiar, it almost brought tears to my eyes. I had never touched this knife, but I knew it. I knew its heft. I knew the spring action of the blade. I knew how fast it could be released, and I knew how to use it. A relic of my old life, the only life I'd ever known, I gave the hunter the truth. "I know how to use a knife."

"Fishing," he stated.

"Yes," I agreed, even though he did not ask it as a question.

"Do you know how to shoot?"

The momentary reprieve of familiarity, of safety, it disappeared in a blink. "No."

"Your father wasn't armed?"

He was, but I'd never been allowed to touch them. "Captain had two guns. One long, one short. I never fired them."

"Do you want a gun?"

I shrank back from the suggestion and from the memory of Captain cleaning his weapons once a week in the galley as the pungent smell of gun oil filled a space that I used for cooking. A space that I associated with the comfort of cooking smells but one that he violated with his gun cleaning. Until this moment, I did not realize how much I had hated that.

"I do not," I answered, trying to hold all emotion back from my tone despite the growing sense of dread that had been rapidly crushing my chest since he'd told me to never tell him again that I could be what he wanted.

"You hesitated," he accused.

Even though his voice never changed in nuance or held any emotion, there were fluctuations in his tone and volume and the force he used with certain words. This time I knew what he was saying. He thought I was lying.

I didn't bother to attempt to hide the truth from him. "The question made me remember a time on the boat."

"What time?"

"Every week when Captain cleaned his guns." I opened the switchblade and ran a finger over the sharp metal. "He did it in the galley. I didn't like the smell." This knife was nicer than the one I'd had to leave on the boat.

"Noted." Turning the laptop on the bed to face me, he pushed it toward the edge so it was closer to me. "Type in this website address." He recited a name by heart.

Panic struck, and I stared at the letters and numbers on the keyboard.

"Problem?"

"I..." Swallowing past the sudden dryness in my throat, I could no longer ignore the other growing anxiety, besides him sending me away, that was too overwhelming to think about.

"Speak," he demanded.

I looked up at him. "I'm not like you." It was an embarrassment to even say. His hands flew across his keyboard, he made official-looking documents, he had secret compartments and fancy things I couldn't begin to name, and he was more capable at everything than anyone I'd ever met. It was an insult to even say I wasn't like him, but I didn't know how else to express it. "I don't live in your world." I glanced nervously at the laptop. "I don't use computers. I didn't have a cell phone until the men gave me one, and even then I wasn't sure how to use it." I looked at his secret compartment. "I don't know anything about the electronic devices you or the men had." My fingers tightly gripping the handle of the knife, I held it up. "This is the kind of tool I know how to use."

The lines between his eyes drew together. "You don't have a satellite phone on the boat?"

"They're expensive," I admitted, suddenly embarrassed by the simple life I had been living, even though I preferred it over where this hunter lived with all of his expensive things.

"What did you do in an emergency?"

It was finally a question I could answer, but it wasn't one I had ever considered I should be ashamed of before now. "The Nalleli Rose has her marine radio, but Captain said there was no such thing as an emergency. He said I'd been born on the water, I could die on the water."

The hunter stared at me as his jaw ticked. Then he was back to his questions that I couldn't answer. "What kind of devices did the men have?"

My anxiety grew at yet another thing I knew nothing about. "I don't know. Lots of computers like you have and some other electronic devices."

"What did they do with them?"

"It wasn't all of them. It was mostly the younger one. He had the most electronics, and he typed on his keyboards like you type on yours."

The hunter's chest rose with an inhale, and he turned his laptop back toward him and started typing.

Like I had before, I watched his long, masculine fingers fly across the keys. He didn't even have to look at his hands. His focus on the screen, images and letters and numbers kept popping up and overlapping each other in a pattern of confusion that made my head spin but one that he didn't so much as blink at.

I wanted to both cry and stare at him in awe.

I could never fit into his world.

Even when I was swimming my fastest, my body didn't move

as quick or as sure as his hands. Nothing I could do would ever come close to what he was capable of.

No wonder he told me to never say I could be what he needed.

I wasn't anything close to what this hunter needed.

He needed a smart, sophisticated woman who could do what he did. A woman who lived in his world and who was his equal. That would never be me. All I could do for him was kneel. I would never measure up.

Before I sank further into the despair of my own thoughts, he turned the computer back to face me. With his eyes on me and a finger on the keyboard, he issued instructions. "Stop me if you see any electronics you recognize that the men had or anything that looks similar." He depressed the key, and an image filled the screen. He waited a second, then he depressed it again and another image filled the screen.

I stared at the pictures, and he repeated the process until finally I recognized something that looked almost similar. "There. Almost like that one."

Reaching over the keyboard, he typed. Then new images appeared. "Any of these?"

Leaning closer, I looked at the multiple images flooding the screen. Then I found one that did look exactly like something the arrogant man had had. I pointed. "That one."

"Copy," he said almost absently as he erased all the images from the screen, turned the computer toward him, and began typing again.

"What does that mean?" Did I displease him? "Did I say something wrong?" Why did I want to please this man so much?

His hands stilled, but they didn't leave the keyboard as he looked at me. Staring for a brief moment, he didn't answer right away. Then he said something that should've frightened me more than the fact that I would never fit into his world. "Those men are like me."

"Hunters?"

"Hackers," he corrected before turning the computer back toward me. "Use the touchpad, and open one of the internet icons. Then type in the website address I gave you."

I glanced at the keys. I had no idea what he was saying, and hacker and hunter sounded like the same thing to me, but I didn't ask because I didn't want to be embarrassed by yet another thing I didn't understand.

Suddenly fighting the urge to cry, I looked up at him and admitted my embarrassing truth. "I don't know what a touchpad or an icon is. I don't know how to use a computer." I didn't even know what half of the electronic things in his kitchen were. "I can't fit into your world." Tears welled. "Please don't make me. *Please*. I will fail."

TEN

The Hunter

"I can't fit into your world." Her eyes filled with tears, and she begged. "Please don't make me. *Please.* I will fail."

On her knees, about to cry, she looked more beautiful than any image I'd ever captured of her. The fact that she didn't know the first thing about modern technology only made me want to fuck her more. But I didn't walk into that bar tonight to dominate her.

"This isn't about fitting in." She wouldn't blend in with a room full of subs. "This is survival." This was how she was going to access the money I was giving her. "You're going to learn how to get into the secure bank account I set up for you."

Inexperienced at hiding her emotions, shock crossed her features. "You're giving me a bank account?"

Already having told her she was done with her old life, I reiterated it. "You're not going back to your life. You're not going to touch any bank accounts you or your father had. You're not going to contact anyone, and you're not going to retrieve your boat." I dropped the proverbial ticking time bomb in her lap. "You're going to walk away." For that, she'd need money.

Folding her arms protectively around herself, her eyes welled, but it wasn't my last statement she reacted to. "The Nalleli Rose is all I have."

"You can get a new boat." Literally, or one new to her. I didn't care. As long as she didn't go looking for hers or go anywhere near her old life where we'd already tracked her.

"I don't have the money for that."

Yes, she did. She just didn't know it yet. "Touchpad, internet icons, web browsers." I showed her where and what each one was. Then I typed in the web address I'd already given her before deleting my keystrokes. "Your turn. Hands on the keyboard. You need to know this." We were running out of time.

Pocketing her knife, putting her small hands on my keys, she mimicked what I'd just done with tentative slowness. "I don't even have a computer." She brought up the browser but stumbled on entering the address.

Standing so I could step behind her, I bent and put my hands under hers. "You're not supposed to. Any computer connected to the internet can be tracked. Watch closely." I showed her where to place her hands, then where to type in the browser. "You're going to use internet cafés or public libraries or go into the actual bank itself in the Caymans."

She glanced over her shoulder at me. "You opened a bank account in the Cayman Islands?"

Her hair smelled like flowers. Her hands trembled over mine, and she looked at me like I was her savior.

I wasn't.

I was the hacker committing her to a life on the run because I was too selfish to let her die.

"You don't recognize the name of the website." It wasn't a question. If she didn't know the largest bank in the Caymans in a region she was familiar with, she was more sheltered than I'd realized.

"I know it's a bank's name because you said as much."

"Type it in," I commanded, removing my hands from under hers, wondering how she could hold a switchblade with dexterity but be so uncomfortable with a keyboard.

Slow, deliberate, she typed.

The bank website came up.

"Top right corner. See the log-in prompt?" I didn't point. I didn't move from my position behind her. "Use the touchpad, swipe the arrow to it." Caging her in, issuing commands, teaching her the keystrokes, I was both controlling her and protecting her. "Login name is the Bahamian passport, no spaces. Password is the British passport, surname first, all lowercase. Type it in."

Using only her index fingers, she entered the letters and another prompt came up.

She leaned closer to the laptop. "It's asking for the account number."

Committing to memory the way her scent moved with her each time she shifted, I cataloged every detail about her that I could. "You know the number."

She looked over her shoulder at me.

Staring into her eyes, I gave her more than I'd ever given anyone. "Type it in."

Still innocent, still unassuming, she entered the digits.

Watching her as the screen populated with the account and its balance, I saw the exact moment she realized what I'd done.

Half my wealth to a woman I'd never met.

I could make more money, mine more crypto, but getting her out, this was a one-shot deal.

Rearing back, she lifted her hands off the keyboard as if it were on fire. "What is that?"

"Your bank account."

"No." She pushed back even more, which only cocooned her within the fold of my protection. "That is not mine. I don't have that much money. Take it back."

Dropping to one knee, wrapping an arm around her waist, holding her firm, I reached around her to access the keyboard. "Pay attention, Atala." I brought up the transfer prompt. "This is how you transfer funds, either to another account you set up later or to manually make payments on the credit cards, or to—"

"Credit cards?" Crossing her arms, she shook her head. "No. I can't have credit cards. Captain said to never use them. It's money you don't have."

"You have one credit card in each of the names on the passports. They're set up to automatically pay the balance once a month from this account." I toggled back to the home screen on the account. "You have money."

"No, I don't," she whispered, shrinking into me.

"Read the balance, Atala."

"I can't." Her head was shaking before I finished the sentence. "That's thousands and thousands of dollars, and that's not mine."

It was more than thousands. "It's five million," I corrected. "It's yours now."

"*Five—*" Her posture stiffening, her voice broke and she froze. Then she turned her head and looked up at me. "Why are you doing this?"

I gave her the easiest answer. "You were going to be killed."

She didn't move. She didn't blink. She didn't react. Then she asked the wrong question. "Why are you saving me?"

I wasn't the hero. Nothing about this was saving her. I was sentencing her. "I'm not."

ELEVEN

Atala

I HAD SO MANY QUESTIONS, MY MIND WAS REELING, BUT I ASKED THE ONE that stood out even more than all those zeroes in the bank account that didn't even seem real because it was so much money. "Why are you saving me?"

Hunters hunted.

They didn't save their prey, let alone give them access to five million dollars.

But he was focusing all his attention on me as if he were deadly serious as he stared at me with eyes that were more haunted than predator. "I'm not." He watched me as if looking for a reaction. "In forty-eight minutes, your survival's going to depend on you." One arm around me, the other on the keyboard, cradling my body between his legs and chest as if protecting me, he focused back on the computer and typed. "You'll have passports, credit cards, the offshore account, and ten grand in cash." The screen went dark, and he closed the laptop. "You're going to disappear."

Before the shock could register, before all the air left my lungs, he was standing and taking me with him.

Then words were spilling from his full lips, the lights in the bedroom were turning off and his body heat, his protection, it was gone as he moved toward the door, leaving me with nothing except my fate.

Disappear.

My knees gave out, and I sank to the bed.

I knew this was going to happen.

NOVEMBER

I knew it when the men first took me, and then again when the hunter showed me the passports, but I hadn't wanted to acknowledge it. I didn't even want to think about it.

I'd wanted to hold on to the last thread of hope I had that I could go back.

But this wasn't the bar. I wasn't getting a drink for the leader of the bad men as I stared at the front entrance, wondering if I could make a run for it before they caught me.

This wasn't the past three months I'd spent thinking about escape.

"Atala."

This wasn't even the desolate truth that the bad men had control of my boat, that they'd taken my cash, that they never all slept at the same time, and they were armed. It wasn't even the fact that jumping overboard into waters teaming with sharks and stingrays wasn't my biggest obstacle. I'd had nowhere to swim to, no one to help me, and no resources with which to survive on once I got there. I had nothing.

But I knew how to swim, fish, make a fire and build a lean-to.

I could survive in the world I'd grown up in.

"Stand up, Atala."

I'd had a fraction of hope, and I'd been waiting.

Foolishly, ignorantly waiting for months for one slip of the watchful eyes of the bad men so I could make a quiet escape and swim back to my old life. Except that moment never came, and I was never going to get my old life back.

Now a hunter was giving me the next best thing, but I wanted no part of it.

I didn't want to disappear. I hadn't wanted to before either, not completely. I just wanted to be invisible. But now that I'd seen haunted blue eyes and saw the way a hunter looked at me and heard his voice when he spoke low and commanding, I didn't want to be invisible. I'd been invisible my whole life. Now, I wanted to be seen.

I wanted to breathe in the scent of amber, musk, and wintery cedar as strong arms reached around me and typed on a fancy computer.

I wanted—

"Get up, sub."

Flinching as if slapped awake, I was on my feet before my mind registered my body was moving. Then a huge, firm hand was gripping my jaw and everything fell away.

"Speak your thoughts." Deep, commanding, his voice sank into my body, but my mind was suddenly floating.

"I'm not thinking, sir."

"Before I touched you."

Inhaling, I tried to focus, but his crisp winter scent filled my head, and I was wondering if he would smell the same on the Nalleli Rose as she chartered through tropical waters. "I was thinking about what I wanted, sir," I admitted.

"Which is?" he demanded.

Heat rushed from his grip and spread across my face as an ache pulsed between my legs. All of a sudden, I was thankful for the dark. "I prefer not to say, sir."

"Conversation," he clipped, still holding on to me. "Speak freely."

"I want to know your real name."

"I already told you."

"You said they call you Hunter." I didn't know who *they* were. I didn't want to know. "What do you call yourself?"

As if he could see me in the dark, he stared down at my eyes. "Hacker. Why did Alekhin give you a cell phone?"

I didn't know if I believed him about Hacker. It sounded like a bad name, and this complicated man was many things, but he didn't seem bad. "V gave me the phone to talk to the younger one after we dropped him off in the Caymans. Then when Z called, I was to put it on speaker and have a conversation with him while the other men listened. How did you know it was V who gave me the phone?"

"He's the leader of the cell. What kind of conversation?"

"He would ask questions about the weather or where I was or how I was doing. The other men would quietly tell me how to answer and what to ask back. Usually I was told to ask what Z had eaten for dinner the night before."

"What were some of the repeated words or phrases used?"

The question, the way he asked it, maybe he truly was called Hunter. "The Nalleli Rose's directional headings, he always said he had eaten seafood, and then he would sign off by saying he would see me soon."

"Did you notice any other specific patterns?"

"No, but the last time he called, he said he had eaten steak and that he would see me tomorrow. That was the day before we docked in Key Largo."

Dropping his hand, he turned toward the door. "We need to move."

Desperate, I asked. "Do you look at other women the way you look at me?"

His tall frame and broad shoulders, his muscular arms and thighs, every part of him froze mid-step, but he didn't turn around.

I had to know. "Do you give other women money and passports?" My throat went dry, and pressure squeezed around my heart, but I pushed the next question out. "Did you call them sub and save them too?"

He spun on me, and even before he had his punishing grip back on my jaw, I could taste his anger.

His fingers dug into my flesh, and he loomed over me with all the might of a merciless hunter. "Do *not* mistake me for a hero."

"Why me?" I dared to ask.

TWELVE

The Hunter

S HE ASKED THE ONE QUESTION I COULDN'T ANSWER.
Staring down at her, I gave her exactly what I had to offer—nothing.

She tried to work me from another angle. "I'm not asking who you work for or why you think I was going to be killed. I knew when the bad men first pulled a gun on me that I was in trouble, with little to no way out. I understood that much." I felt her throat move with a swallow. "But I don't understand you. The money, the passports, the credit cards, why are you doing all of this? You don't know me."

Every vulnerable word out of her mouth made me want her more. "White shorts, blue tank top, yellow string bikini," I stated, increasing the pressure of my grip.

Inhaling sharply, she reached for my wrist but stopped herself halfway. "I'm sorry?"

"Your outfit. Cuba." When she'd picked up Alekhin and his crew.

Lines formed between her eyebrows. "Are you saying you know me because of what I wore?"

"No." I knew her body language in the footage I had. Repeated glances over her shoulder as she'd pulled out of the harbor, furtive glances at Alekhin as he'd stood with her at the helm, her stiff posture on a boat she'd grown up on—all were signs of distress, but one crucial fact was missing. I dropped my hand. "There was

NOVEMBER

no fifth man with Alekhin and his crew when they boarded your boat that morning."

"I am not lying."

"When did he get on?"

"Habana Harbor."

It was the second time she'd used the local pronunciation instead of the American one. I switched to Spanish and asked another question. "Did he get on the boat with the other men?"

Her frown deepened. "I don't understand what you just said."

I repeated myself in English. "Did the fifth man get on the boat with the others in Guanabacoa?"

"Guanabacoa, yes, but not at the same time, and not from the marina. The younger man was on a sailboat moored just past the main marina. V directed me to charter past it and circle once. Then we pulled up alongside the twenty-seven-foot Albin trawler, and Z boarded."

I couldn't verify her story. I had footage of her boat leaving the marina with the men aboard, but once they got out of the marina's security camera range, I didn't have eyes on her again until they got to the Keys. If I was in the command center, I'd use military satellite imagery to try to verify her story, but accessing those satellites from here wasn't a risk I was going to take with her in the warehouse.

Not that any of it mattered anymore.

I'd taken her, and now I had to let her go. "Time to move."

"I don't know how to disappear."

She'd been invisible her whole life. "Yes, you do. You're going to drive south to Miami. Hire a charter to Cuba. Pay extra for anonymity. Only use the U.S. passport if you need it to get out of the States, but do not come back here. Then use the Cuban passport to get to Barbados. You won't need a visa. From there, pick one of the hundred-and-sixty-three countries you can legally travel to visa-free from Barbados. UK is one of them. Then keep moving. Rotate which passports you use, don't establish roots, stay off the grid, and relocate at least every couple months, but stay away from the Greater Antilles. The Cuban and Bahamian passports are for travel outside those countries only." I reiterated the most important factor. "Remember, do not come back to the United States." She'd forever be on the terrorist watch list here, and the U.S. was the easiest place to track someone with our infrastructure of security surveillance.

Shrinking in on herself with every word I said, she crossed her arms. Then she dropped her gaze and begged. "Please don't make me do this."

I wasn't making her do anything. That was the problem. I should've been dominating the hell out of her, not sending her away. But taking this little sub's innocence and virginity wasn't a panacea. If I was truly a dom, I wouldn't still be standing here. I'd be pulling the trigger on the escape plan I'd spent years putting in place. Faking my own death, disappearing off the grid, taking her with me, protecting her—that's what a true dominant would do.

Protect her with my life.

But I wasn't.

I was still fucking straddling both of my worlds.

Keeping one foot in the military, throwing her into an existence she wasn't prepared or equipped for, I was selfishly fucking her over as sure as if my dick was sinking inside her unprepped virgin cunt.

Weak, telling myself I was doing the right thing by giving her a life free from my obsession with her, I gave her dangerous hope. "If it becomes safe for you to return, I'll find you."

She looked up. "That's a possibility?"

No. "Yes."

"When?"

Never. "Years." If Perkins was worth a damn, he would've already gotten past my detour and figured out the terrorist cell hadn't only landed on U.S. soil, but the woman wasn't with them

NOVEMBER

when they left the bar. Then he'd sound the alarm, alert Deputy Commander Bradley, and I'd be called back in.

Her shoulders dropped along with her voice. "Years," she repeated dejectedly.

"Put your jacket on." The only light in the room ambient, I still had to turn away from her eyes. "Let's go." One pace and I heard it.

The same beautiful but reckless drop as before.

All her weight, no regard for bruising herself, she dropped to her knees on my finished concrete floors.

My cock grew hard, my hands fisted, and I had to force myself to center my thoughts. Focusing on my military training, I turned.

Head down, hands on her thighs, unspoiled by another dom's commands, the little sub sat kneeling. Waiting.

I knew what she was doing. "You're panicking."

"Please don't make me leave you."

Leave you. As if she was doing this to me. My cock pulsed, and my jaw ticked. She was so goddamn submissive, I wanted to drown in her.

"Don't test me, sub." It wasn't a warning. "Get up." Stand, kneel, move, don't move, it didn't matter. She'd already lost. Her fate was fucked the second I'd laid eyes on her.

"I-I can't, sir." Her voice trembled, her hands fidgeted, and she shook her head.

I wanted to break her of every one of those habits. Then I wanted to punish her small body with my cock until she begged me to stop right before I made her completely submit and fall the fuck apart under my command.

On the edge of control, I gave her one warning. "If you don't want me to hurt you, you'll get up right now, sub."

Her head lifted, and the moonlight hit her teal eyes.

Then she sealed her fate. "I want to be what you need."

The snap of my control was instant.

I moved.

THIRTEEN

Atala

WITH THE FORCE OF A HURRICANE, BUT UTTERLY SILENT, HE descended on me.

Faster than a shark cutting through the ocean, he sliced through the distance between us, picked me up and threw me on the bed. But the predator in him didn't stop there.

Coming down on top of me, gripping my hair so hard it hurt, grasping my jaw, he shoved my thighs apart with his knee as a heavy, silver necklace escaped the neck of his shirt and fell to my throat. Then the cuff of his long-sleeved shirt slid back, and a thick silver bracelet on his wrist dug into the thin flesh over my sternum.

His striking features transformed with lethal warning as he bit out a question. "You think I need anything from anyone, sub?" His grip punishing, he didn't wait for an answer. "You think you know the first thing about me, about what I *need*, little girl?"

Fear and shame shot through my body at his anger, but so did something else. Something so carnal, I didn't have a name for it, but I wanted to reach for it. I needed to reach for it. Air straining to get into my lungs, my skin both on fire and tingling from goose flesh, I suddenly ached with a bone-deep desire to have this man's hands on me. Tasting his anger as if it were my own, the familiarity of it intoxicating, I did something I had never done. I steadied my voice and spoke for myself. "No, sir. But I want to."

With the cast of shadows covering half his face, the other half bathed in winter moonlight, his nostrils flared. "You want me to hurt you? Take that virgin cunt?" The pressure of his grip increased. "Make you bleed."

My heart beat so hard, my chest hurt.

Then suddenly, moments of my life began to flash through my mind in a blur of clouded memories. My first hurricane when I was a small child, and Captain refused to bring the Nalleli Rose into safe harbor. Captain throwing me overboard into a school of sharks and telling me to swim faster. Captain sending me alone for the first time to get supplies, telling me he'd whip me if I got robbed or didn't come back with the alcohol I was too young to purchase. Heaving Captain's stinking body over the stern, then going below and grabbing every piece of his clothing and throwing it overboard after him. The man named Vladimir Alekhin smiling at me right before he pulled a gun and held it to my head. When I looked up in a bar and saw the hunter's haunted eyes.

Every memory played like they were flashing to tell me the same thing from my earliest recollection to my last.

I had nothing left to lose.

I'd never had anything to lose.

My life, the moments in between, the silence when I swam under the water, the quiet when Captain passed out from drinking—none of that was living.

But the hand gripping me tight, the hard, muscular body on top of me, the veiled desire I could smell in his wintery coolness that'd just turned to summer heat, it all felt like living.

He felt like living—a hunter threatening to make me bleed.

But he didn't know I'd already shed blood.

My whole life had been a slow drip of my soul bleeding out into the places in between life and belonging where I was supposed to fit in but never did.

With the hunter's firm grip on me and his pressing weight on my body that could crush me in one breath, I finally felt like I wasn't being fit into someone else's world.

In that moment, in that breath, in that fragile beat of my heart, I felt like I was his world.

I spoke the truth. "I want you to make me bleed."

I wanted to bleed for him.

I wanted to feel what it felt like to have him hurt me. I wanted to have all his anger, all his attention and all of his deep-voiced control. I wanted those strong, veined hands that moved lightning fast with exacting precision across his fancy keyboard to move across my body, lighting me up like a summer storm lit the night sky.

I wanted him to take whatever he needed from my body.

Because something deep in my heart, where I didn't ever allow myself to go, it'd awoken, and instinct was telling me that if I gave this hunter that control, he could erase my past. He could make me feel.

He could free me.

Hovering, barely a breath above my lips, he gave me more of his warnings. "You don't know what you're asking for, little girl."

Maybe I didn't. But all I had was this moment and the punishing ache of emptiness my body felt every time he was near, and I knew I couldn't disappear like this, like he'd so carefully planned. I couldn't live in his world by myself. I didn't want to. I'd only be trading all of the horrible parts of my life for a different set of bad, only it'd be worse because I'd meant what I'd said to him.

I couldn't unsee or unhear him now.

I didn't care how or why he'd found me. He just had, and that was all that mattered.

My life was present.

That's how I'd always lived. I dealt in what was or what was immediately coming next. Every time I'd strayed from that, the weak moments I'd dipped my thoughts into the ocean of what could be, it made me sad inside. And angry. Angry in a way that scared me because I didn't know if I let it out if I'd ever be able to get it back in.

So I lived for what was. I touched the sky with my face up

and eyes closed. I listened to the future only on the marine radio weather forecasts. I kept my hope focused on the next meal, next swim, next catch, and I never, ever looked past the fuel gauge of the Nalleli Rose or counted beyond the dollars I needed to fix her engine.

Those were dangerous waters I didn't know how to swim in. So I'd drifted.

Until four men with fake smiles boarded my forty-six-foot world and ruined everything.

Now I was here, knowing exactly why I'd never stared at the endless blue ocean where it met the horizon line at midday as the sun glinted off it just right. Because that picture-perfect sliver of hope didn't exist. I knew it didn't. Except I was staring at it. The exact same shade of picture-perfect ocean blue was swirling in the eyes of a hunter who focused all his attention on me as he spoke like the deep, quiet rumble of an incoming storm.

A storm that smelled like winter and that perfect sliver of hope I'd never allowed myself to reach for.

I couldn't disappear from that.

Not when it was this close and not without trying, at least once, to feel what living felt like.

Foolish, desperate, so far out past waters I could navigate, I ignorantly reached for the horizon.

"Please, sir." My whisper almost as quiet as an ocean breeze, I begged. "Kiss me."

FOURTEEN

The Hunter

I KNEW WHAT SHE WANTED.

I smelled her desire. I watched her beg. I could practically taste her frantic need to feel more than whatever shit life she'd come from.

Every ounce of her desperation, I recognized.

She coped with submission, I fed off dominant control, but we were the same.

I saw it in her eyes the very first time her face filled my screen.

I could give her exactly what she needed.

But I didn't.

"You think you want to be kissed, sub?" She didn't. She wanted to be dominated.

"Yes," she whispered, hesitant.

"What part of my grip on your hair and jaw makes you think I'll give you my mouth?" Pounding need straining my cock against the confines of my pants, I ground my hips into hers, intending to scare her off.

Her back arched, her head fell back, and a guttural sound I wasn't expecting erupted from her throat.

Driving forward again, I thrust against her cunt hard and punishing. "Answer the question, sub."

Hitching her knees in natural submission, groaning, her small hands gripped at my biceps. "I-I don't know."

No fucking hesitation, I reared back and flipped her, yanking her hips up. Before the shocked gasp had left her mouth, my hand was coming down hard on her ass.

She jerked in surprise as her mouth opened on a silent scream. I spanked her again. "Did I tell you to touch me, sub?"

Her whole body jerked again, but she closed her mouth without answering.

I gave her an out. "If you don't want this, now's your chance. Get off my bed, sub."

She didn't move.

I fucking drank in the moment like a man deprived. Then I issued an order. "Unfasten your jeans and shove them down to your knees."

Pushing up with her arms, she started to rise to all fours.

My hand came down again, hard. "Did I tell you to get up?" I didn't wait for a reply. "Face down, ass up, remove your jeans. *Now.*"

She didn't get up. Turning her head to the side, her hair splaying out across my bed, she reached under her raised hips with shaking hands.

Controlling my breathing but not my heart rate, I watched her slowly, almost hypnotically push her jeans over her perfect ass before she pulled her arms in close underneath her.

Cursing the lights I needed to keep off and who I was, I dragged a finger down the crease of her ass, deliberately not touching yet where I'd spanked her. Controlling my tone, I skirted her exposed cunt with my touch. "Did I give you permission to tuck your arms beneath you?"

"No," she whispered.

"No, what?"

"No, sir."

"What's your safe word, sub?"

"I-I'm sorry, sir?"

"What do you need to say if you want me to stop touching you?"

"No, sir."

"Say it again, without the 'sir.'" Gripping the flesh of her ass in each hand, giving her an excuse, testing myself more than her, I dug my fingers in.

"*No*," she gasped.

Zero hesitation, letting go of her, I leaned my hips back. No part of my body touching hers, I fisted my hands as my cock pulsed. "That's your safe word. Say it again."

This time she whispered it. "No."

"You say it, make sure you mean it." Leaning over her back, bracing my fists on either side of her, I didn't touch her as I brought my mouth to her ear. "Because all activity will stop. Understand?"

"All, sir?" she asked.

"Yes, Atala. All."

At the sound of her name, she shivered. "Forever?" she barely breathed.

Strangled by her innocence and both of our realities, I bit out the facts. "We don't have forever." I pushed myself up. "We have right now."

Turning her head, looking at me with her exposed ass in the air, her arms still tucked under her, her gaze cut from my cock to my eyes. Then she made the worst mistake she could've made. She green-lit me. "I want right now."

Staring at a wild butterfly, wanting to break her wings so she couldn't fly away, I did what I'd never done. I fucking asked. "Permission to touch you."

She blinked.

I amended. "Permission to hurt you."

Her voice came as soft as the fluttering insect she was named after. "Intentionally?"

I didn't answer. I stared at her teal eyes.

Understanding hit, and her lips parted as if to speak. Then she shut her mouth, locked down her expression and lied. "Permission given."

Fuck.

NOVEMBER

Three months studying her, I knew this woman's expressions. I knew the way her body moved, and I knew when she was under duress. That wasn't permission, and it sure as hell wasn't about me putting my hands on her.

Shoving back, hypocritically and irrationally pissed that something else besides me was fucking with her head, I stood.

"Wait." She started to get up but quickly leaned back down. "I mean, sir. Please, don't. Where are you going? I'm not ready to leave."

There it was. The slip.

She wasn't ready to leave, and fucking me was a tactic, not the end game. This was why I didn't do this. "Not how it works." I wasn't a goddamn diversion, and I'd never touched innocents. I also didn't fuck virgins. I vetted women online, hacked their backgrounds, then met them anonymously at a hotel I'd prearranged and secured. Then I fucked the demons out, leaving before they caught their breaths or my name. No repeats, no trace evidence. And I never fucking asked permission. "Get up." I glanced at the time.

"No."

My gaze cut back to her.

"Sir," she added, still holding position.

No control, staring at her exposed, virgin cunt, I didn't walk away. "What did you just say?"

"N—"

My hand came down on her bare ass with a hard crack.

Her defiance morphing into a shocked cry, she jerked, and her arms unfolded as she braced her hands on the bed.

I was already spanking her other cheek before she drew in her next breath. "Who's in this room?" I demanded, coming down hard on her again.

Her hands gripped handfuls of the bedding as she held back a grunt. "We're—"

"There is no we." My palm connected with the back of her thighs.

Her back arching, she reared up.

"There's me, my hands, my touch, and your body." Spanking her ass hard, I gripped the reddened flesh, hating myself for what I was about to say next. *"That* is not a we." My palm came down on her innocent ass again. "Understand?"

"Y-yes, sir."

My cock fucking hard, wanting to shove into her without prep, I dragged my palm over her heated ass and quieted my tone. "Do you want me to fuck you, Atala?" If she was smart, she'd say no.

"Yes."

Grasping her waist with one hand, I dug my fingers in hard enough for her to feel me. "Yes, what?"

"Yes, please, sir."

"Be sure." My hand already at my zipper, I purposely didn't use her name. "Last chance, sub. Say no." Leaning down, my mouth an inch from her reddened ass, I played dirty. "Or tell me to fuck away your virginity." Exhaling over her heated skin, I released my cock and stroked myself.

A tremor shook her small body. "Please, sir, take away my virginity."

Rearing back to my full height, I didn't hesitate.

Gripping her hip, lining my cock up, I shoved into her and encountered resistance an inch in before I broke her barrier and sank to the hilt in a heated rush of blood.

Her scream pierced my bedroom and struck my chest as my cock pulsed hard enough to come.

My head fucking twisted.

FIFTEEN

Atala

For one second, overwhelming fullness stretched me past reason, then pain exploded.

Flesh ripping, my body being split in two from the inside out, I didn't cry.

I screamed.

Losing myself to the agonizing hurt, clawing at the bed linens, trying to crawl away from this horrible invasion, I begged. "Stop!"

A hard slap hit first one side of my backside, then the other, shocking away all that was left of my breath right before two huge, warm hands gripped my hips with intent and brought me back, as the too-big, too-hard, hot invasion thrust deeper.

Then, holding me prisoner in this torturous pain, he went perfectly still and began to speak.

But it wasn't any voice I had ever heard from him.

Deeper, richer, but much, much quieter. He spread sinful words of dark seduction all across my exposed skin. "Feel me inside you, Atala. Feel the rush of blood." He leaned over my back. "Know that my cock took your virginity. Your blood is on me now." His fingers dug into my hips. "Breath in deep and feel the pain. Embrace it, sub." His touch softened. "But open that cunt for me." He stroked a gentle hand down my back. "Breathe in again."

Already inhaling, not realizing I'd done it the first time he'd told me to, I held perfectly still, afraid to move for fear of more pain, fear he would stop, fear he wouldn't.

"That's it, sub." His palm pressed against my rear. "Breathe again for me, this time deep."

My body his, I filled my lungs.

"Again," he demanded as his hard length pulsed inside me, stretching me even more.

Sucking in a shocked breath, involuntarily raising my back, I clawed forward.

A hard slap hit my sore backside a second before both hands were back on my hips, but he didn't just hold me against him. Rearing back, his impossibly thick length pulled out halfway, then he slammed back into me.

This time, my scream was silent, because the second the end of him hit the end of me, something other than horrible pain happened.

A spasm ran up my back, and goose bumps followed.

Harder, darker, he issued an order. "I said take a breath."

The need to apologize warring with the overwhelming urge to comply, my body chose for me, and I breathed in deep.

"Again," he barked.

Wanting more of whatever he had done to counter the pain, I didn't delay.

"Again, deeper. Open your mouth." Two fingers stroked down the crease between my cheeks and rubbed against a place I never imagined him to touch.

My body my traitor, I jerked in surprise as I gasped.

The fingers left my backside, he pulsed hard and deep inside me, then he shoved those same fingers in my mouth and barked out an order. "*Suck.*"

My lips closed, my throat moved, saliva came, and I was sucking.

Then it happened.

My mind blanked, and I was underwater.

But not under the surface of the warm Caribbean Sea on a hot summer day.

NOVEMBER

My core began to pulse, and I was drowning in the most starkly beautiful man I had ever seen. Sucking his skillful fingers with my worshiping tongue as every dominant, capable, intimidating thing I had seen him do magnified until all I felt was idolization at his touch, his invasion, his attention.

His fingers dug into my hips as his impossible length rocked in short, hard bursts, pulling back and thrusting forward, hitting both my entrance and something deep inside me until I started to shake.

Then his dark voice gifted me with praise. "That's it, sub. Just like that."

My womb heated to the point of pain more intense than his invasion. Greedily sucking him as he pressed down hard on my tongue, I began to pulse.

"Stop," he barked, gripping my jaw hard with his thumb and fingers that weren't in my mouth. "Release."

My womb ached worse, and I opened my mouth.

He slid his fingers out, and a second later, one pressed into my forbidden entrance as he thrust into me hard and ground his hips.

Shock tensed every muscle in my body.

"Relax, sub. Let me in." He pushed deeper with his finger. "You're taking my cock and my fingers."

That was all the warning I got before he was everywhere.

His hard length drove in and out of me in merciless thrusts. His finger invaded me. His palm came down hard on my backside before gripping my nape and holding me down. He dominated every inch of me as he overwhelmed all of my senses.

His musky, winter scent everywhere, his hands commanding my body, the taste of his fingers in my mouth, his deep, commanding voice, the sight of him behind me, taking what he wanted.

I was powerless.

"Now." He pressed down harder on my nape. "Come for me."

At his command, as if I had no will of my own, my vision tunneled, my breath left my body, and I began to shake as I splintered into a thousand fractured pieces. Sinking into the depths of the ocean as sure as if I were drowning, everything started to go dark.

Then my name viciously growled past his chest and shook the bed. *"Atala!"*

The hand left my neck, a slap echoed like a crack, and fire licked across my backside.

I sucked in air.

Before I could fill my lungs, his thrusts changed in speed and angle. Pain and pleasure hit a new plateau, and I cried out as if it were my last act of living.

His hips slammed into me, he sank too deep, his body stilled, then his roar erupted. *"Butterfly."*

Hot wet filled my womb, and I shot to the surface.

Every bright color I had never seen burst as from a kaleidoscope.

My back arched, my life suspended, and I pulsed and pulsed around his hard length until I had nothing left.

Then my body sank to the bed, and I was floating.

SIXTEEN

The Hunter

H ER BACK ARCHED LIKE THE BUTTERFLY SHE WAS, AND SHE SPREAD her wings, coming a second time on my cock.

Then she dropped back down to the bed, spent, winded and so fucking beautiful, my thoughts spun out of control.

Gripping a handful of her hair, I leaned over her and tasted the back of her neck where she still wore my handprint. Then I allowed myself to say it one more time. "Butterfly." *My* Butterfly.

Her eyes closed, her tight cunt constricting around me at the sound of my voice was her only response.

Weak, knowing full damn well I hadn't used a condom, I didn't pull out. I didn't glance at the clock, and I didn't start calculating time and logistics of stopping to get her a morning-after pill.

I fucking hovered, balls deep, and selfishly considered it.

My exit plan. The contingency I had set up and that was ready to go at a moment's notice. A single keystroke that would set off a series of events, erasing every last detail of my life.

A complete sweep.

I'd had it in place for years.

The military was never my long-term plan. I'd been caged into service just like my Butterfly had been groomed to crew.

My cock still hard inside her, fisting my fingers in her hair, I thought about pulling the plug.

Fuck, I thought about it.

But leaving now wouldn't only put the spotlight on her, it'd leave her in danger. I had to go back in. I needed to find Check Mate, end this cell, and make sure nothing came back on her.

Not wanting to pull out, let alone send her away, I did the only damn thing I could do. I hit the switch.

Flipping to my military training, I shut down every damn thing except the mission and gave her fair warning. "Pulling out now, Butterfly." Slipping on the name, I cursed myself and eased back.

A sharp cry of fear followed her shocked gasp, and her muscles tensed, pulling me back in.

Still fisting a handful of her thick hair, I twisted her head and did the last goddamn thing I ever did with a woman.

I covered her mouth with mine.

Sinking my tongue in, momentarily forgetting every reason why we needed to be on the move, I kissed my Butterfly.

Fuck, I kissed her.

Her desire smelled like heaven, but her fear tasted like salvation.

Stroking deep with my tongue like I had with my cock, I distracted her as I eased out of her tight cunt. Swallowing her half cry, half moan, I hovered for one more second. Then I let her go.

Pushing up and off the bed, I took in every inch of her.

Her ass still in the air, her cunt ruined, my seed dripping out, I stared as it mixed with her blood that was smeared across her inner thighs. "We need to move."

With a shaking hand and her hair splayed everywhere, she didn't respond. She reached between her legs.

Unleashed possessive dominance filled my head, and I barked out a command. "Don't you fucking dare touch my cunt." Using two fingers when I knew she would be sore, I swiped across her inner thigh and shoved my release back inside her.

Jerking away from me, she cried out at the invasion.

Grasping her hip and holding firm, I rotated my fingers that barely fit in her tight, swollen cunt, and I stroked deep against her G-spot. "Am I hurting you, little one?"

Her back stiffened, and she tried to press her thighs together as a small gasp escaped. "Yes."

"Good." Deep satisfaction filled my sick head before I forced myself to focus on the real reason I was doing this. Issuing another command, I stroked her roughly again. "Lower your back and hold your ass up." Leaning over her, I bit her shoulder before I dragged my teeth across her ear. Then I dropped my voice. "Exhale and take my fingers." I stroked again. "Bleeding, sore, and swollen, you're going to come again, Butterfly."

Her back lowered, she held her ass up, and her cunt pulsed at my words, but she sobbed once. Then she threw me. "Please, no."

For half a second, I froze.

Then I unceremoniously jerked my hand out, pushed off the bed, and forced my tone to impenetrable military calm. "Get dressed." Pulling my boxers up over my bloodied, hard cock, I zipped my pants.

Her jeans at her knees, her sweater bunched up past her perfect breasts that I hadn't gotten a chance to put my mouth on, she rolled to her back. Then her teal-eyed gaze met mine before dropping to the movement of my hands, and panic hit her expression. "I'm sorry, sir. I didn't mean…." She sucked in a shaking breath, and her eyes welled. "I did something wrong?"

"No." I had. Seriously fucking wrong. "Get dressed, Atala. We're leaving."

Anguish contorted her delicate features a split second before silent tears fell and dripped on her shattered innocence. Covering her face, her small body shook with soundless sobs.

Wordless, controlled, I reached for her ankles and dragged her to me. Pulling her jeans up and fastening them, purposely not cleaning her up or wiping away my release, I righted her sweater. Then I slid my arms under her legs and shoulders, picked her up, and sat back down with her in my lap.

Wrapping one arm around her, I gave her a command. "Let it out, sub."

Turning her face into my chest, she wept harder.

Stroking her back, her hair, I compartmentalized my anger over the fact that she'd said no to me, that she'd denied me giving her another orgasm, one I knew would've avoided this breakdown, and I let her cry.

She'd taken every rough thing I'd thrown at her, but I wasn't finished.

I'd needed to push her past one more boundary.

I'd needed to show her how strong she was, how much she could actually take. I wanted her to feel deep pain as she came one more time so she knew she could survive. Then I would've broken another rule for her, and I would've given her aftercare. Care she'd earned and deserved. Even though it would've been cutting my timeline dangerously close, I would've given her what I could.

I would've shown her me.

The real me.

The dominant man that'd make her bleed, then lick her wounds.

The hacker who made her feel safe.

But she'd denied me, so now I was denying her, telling myself it was how it had to go down. In less than an hour, she was going to be completely on her own. I wasn't going to be on her six. I wasn't going to be issuing her commands. I wasn't going to bring her up on my screens. I wouldn't look even once for her. I couldn't. Until Check Mate and the terrorist cell were terminated, until I'd dealt with her boat and destroyed all evidence of her ever being on my bike or in my bed, she wouldn't be safe.

Even then she'd never be safe from the watchlist her image, but not her name, had been put on.

Knowing the second I'd made the decision to go after her it would come down to this, I'd still done it. I'd selfishly traded her freedom for her life.

She'd always be on the run.

And I'd have to live with that.

NOVEMBER

No comfort in my touch, telling myself I'd done the right damn thing, I stroked her back, but I didn't give her more. I didn't hold her, I didn't embrace her, and I didn't give her any words.

I let her cry.

It felt like fucking shit.

SEVENTEEN

Atala

His muscles tense, his body hard, smelling like musk and amber and now sex, he let me cry, but he didn't say anything.

Clinging to his soft shirt, hating that I was showing so much weakness, hating myself even more for saying no to him, I couldn't control the tears until they decided, like shifting winds, to stop on their own.

I knew we were out of time.

I knew he was going to send me away.

I couldn't bear to even think about it, and yet, I didn't want to take back a single second of his body inside me, despite how much I hurt, both between my legs and in my chest.

Not wanting this to be his last memory of me, I swiped at my face and attempted to smooth a hand over my hair. My throat raw, my voice came out rough. "I'm sorry, sir."

"Don't apologize to me." His tone, his mannerisms back to the way they were when he'd taken me from that bar, he stood and set me on my feet.

A rush of wet heat spilled out from between my legs, soaking my already ruined underwear, and I couldn't stop it. I sucked in a sharp breath, both at the unfamiliar feeling that felt too much like loss and the soreness I knew I would carry for days.

His hand snaked under my hair and went to the back of my neck where I also felt the remnants of his touch. Then he spoke, not with question, but with authority. "You're sore."

All at once, a deep jealousy blindsided me and every single reason why he would know such a thing struck me with such force, I took a step back.

Short and terse, his arm extending as he kept his hold on me, he barked out an order. "Stop." His grip tightening, he issued another order. "Speak. *Now*."

My throat moved, and my mouth wanted to open and spill words. This was what this man did to me. He used his authority and his dominance against me. It made me feel safe. He made me feel safe, even when he was hurting me. And when I'd said no, as much as it hurt deep inside my chest, all the way to my bones, it also made me trust him like I'd never trusted anyone.

I didn't understand what was happening.

Not with my feelings, not with my body, not with whatever was going to happen next.

But I knew, in that moment, I couldn't tell him why I'd stepped back. If I did, it would somehow make everything that'd just happened real, and I couldn't handle real right now. Not when he was about to usher me out his secret door.

"Atala," he warned, low and threatening. "Speak freely. Tell me why you pulled away."

Tears I had never known I'd had before this hunter appeared at my back in a bar and used his voice, welled again. "I can't."

"Can't or won't?" he demanded.

I said the only thing I could to protect myself. "Why does it matter?" We both knew he would not keep me here.

Moonlight streamed in through the high windows and cut across his face, showing me his ocean-blue eyes but also making every sharp angle of his hard jawline and stern features stand out more. He looked as fierce as the predator he was named after, but for the first time since I'd laid eyes on him, there was something else in his expression.

He looked conflicted.

Stepping into me instead of pulling me to him, he stared down at me for two beats of my racing heart.

Then his voice came as deep and lulling as the calm evening swells lapping against the old hull of the Nalleli Rose that were now a memory.

"I took your virginity. My seed is inside you, and now it's occurred to you to wonder exactly how I knew you would be—and are—sore." His thumb stroked my cheek. "You're not going to go there. Understand?"

I closed my eyes.

His fingers gently squeezed. "Look at me, Butterfly."

Butterfly.

One single word, the fourth time he'd said it, but this time was the one that made what was left of my world crush in on itself and bury any piece of hope I may have foolishly still been holding on to. I had heard everything he'd just said, and I understood it, but his last word, that one single tease of affection, it only made it all worse.

"How do you know?" I asked, belatedly realizing how vague my question was, but I shouldn't have been so foolish as to underestimate him.

As if he knew me and my thoughts, he easily followed where my mind had taken this. "About the Atala butterfly?"

This hurt. This really, really hurt. "Yes."

Holding me tight like I mattered, like maybe he wanted to keep me, he didn't answer right away. His chest rose and fell, his eyes studied mine, then it was as if he had to make a conscious decision to speak to me in the manner in which he demanded I speak to him. "Your eyes, your hair color, is that why you were named after the Atala?"

I knew I had an unusual eye color. I'd never seen anyone else have the same color. But I couldn't answer his question. "I don't know for sure." More hurt came. I'd never asked Captain outright.

NOVEMBER

I'd assumed. But what if I wasn't? What if all this time, I was just making it up?

"Your father didn't tell you?"

I admitted a truth I'd never acknowledged to myself. "Captain never spoke to me about anything directly related to my mother or myself. I can't even remember a time when he actually used my name." Captain had never spoken to me about anything except the boat or our charters. He gave orders. If I ever questioned him, he'd say *his boat, his rules*. If I ever displeased him, he'd tell me to *get on board before you find yourself overboard*. With the exception of telling me once, when he was very drunk, to *never let a man put his devil between your legs*, he'd never taught me anything except how to read and how to crew.

This man named after a hunter had given me more attention in the past few hours than an entire lifetime of memories of the man who was supposed to be my father, but who I only thought of as Captain.

Looking down at me with his stern expression back in place, the hunter asked a question with anger in his tone. "What did your father call you?"

"Crew."

His nostrils flared. "How do you know your name then?"

"I don't know. I just... I remembered it." Didn't I? Did I remember Captain yelling it or saying it or speaking it in his sleep? Had he said it when I was a young girl? Or was I always *Crew* to him and I was just thinking I remembered it because it was easier than the truth? And where did I get the Rose part? Was that actually mine, or had I stolen it from the stern of the Bertram simply because I had read it so many times?

The hunter's warm, firm hand moved to my jaw, and he tipped my head up. "Listen very carefully to what I'm about to say. This won't change the circumstances of what each of us has to do, but I want you to hear the words. Understand?"

No. "Yes."

His hand slid up, and he cupped the side of my face as if I were his. "You are a butterfly, Atala. *My* butterfly. As rare and as beautiful as your namesake. You're not going to be jealous of my past or experience. There are no other women in this room. There were none when I was inside you. If this is the last time we speak, know that. Know that you took a piece of me the same as I took from you. No woman has ever been in the bed where I sleep, and no woman has ever had my seed inside of her." His lips touched my forehead. "Remember that, Butterfly."

The last word left his mouth, and suddenly an alarm was going off on both his cell phone in his pocket and the computers in the living area.

Not hesitating, he grabbed my wrist. "We're leaving, *now*."

EIGHTEEN

The Hunter

THE ALERT FOR THE PERIMETER ALARMS WENT OFF.

"We're leaving, *now*." Grabbing her wrist instead of her bruised arm, I rushed to my setup. "Put your leather on." Quickly typing, bringing up my external security feeds, then retrieving both of my Glocks from my desk drawer, I shoved the larger G17, already holstered, onto my waistband. Flipping through the screens, sighting the rented SUV less than a block out, I silently cursed.

Fuck, *fuck*.

How the hell had they found us?

Mentally retracing every step I'd taken tonight, hating myself for not getting her out of here sooner, I weighed the option of contacting Perkins, but I already knew my answer. Same as I knew the answer to how the hell we'd been found. Check Mate. But I wasn't involving Perkins or anyone else at Cyber Command until I got her out of here.

Sparing a glance at the woman I'd fucked in more ways than one, I cursed myself for not taking defensive measures the second she'd told me there was a fifth asshole.

"Come here. You ever shoot a speargun?" I grabbed the wallet I had for her from the lockbox in my bottom desk drawer.

Walking over, glancing between me and the screens with fear in her eyes, she nodded. "Yes, I use a speargun."

"Are you right or left-handed?" Stowing the wallet with the

credit cards and ten grand cash into a secured inside pocket of her leather, I zipped her jacket up.

"I'm sorry?" She nervously glanced from the screens to what I was doing, then looked back again as the SUV came into view on another camera angle.

"Ignore the computer monitors and focus on me," I demanded. "Which is your more dominant hand? When you write your name, when you pull the trigger on the speargun, which hand do you use." I didn't have time to think about how critically sheltered and inexperienced she was.

"I-I have never written my name, and I use my left hand. That's the car the bad men were driving."

"I know. You're left-handed." *Goddamn it.* What the hell was I doing sending this butterfly into the world? "The kickback's the same on a handgun, concept is identical." Lifting the side of her jacket, I secured my smaller Glock G19 and holster onto the waistband of her jeans on her left side. "Holster is Velcro secured. Release it and grab the gun by the grip. Use both hands, right under left. Glocks don't have a traditional safety you need to worry about. Just aim and pull through the trigger. It'll shoot. You're loaded with fifteen rounds." I glanced one more time at my screens. The SUV was on my street. Driving slow, passing Mathers, they headed toward the alley. There was no chance this was coincidental. They knew we were here. Worse, they didn't give a fuck about Mathers. This wasn't recon. They were coming for one thing and one thing only.

If Mathers sounded the alarm, we were fucked.

If I brought in Perkins, we were fucked.

If we didn't get out of here before they made it down the alley, we were fucked.

If they caught us, she was dead.

No choice, I typed the command, wiping my entire setup, security feeds and all.

Grabbing her hand, I barked orders as I strode into the

bedroom, calculating the speed of the SUV, the length of the street, and the time it'd take them to get to the end of my alley. "Follow my steps. Don't touch anything. If I give a command, don't hesitate. And no matter what happens, do not, under any circumstances, give anyone your name. You give the same damn answer you gave me when I first asked, and that's it. You speak to no one, you say nothing. In the presence of others, you don't know me, you don't know how you got here, and you know nothing about the men. Unless it's just me and you and I give you the phrase *speak freely*, you do not talk. *Understand?*" Grabbing the comforter from the bed, I used a corner to wipe the edge of the nightstand.

"Yes, sir. I know nothing," she repeated, watching me bunch up the comforter and following me as I rushed to my laundry room and shoved it into the machine.

Pouring a gallon of bleach over the comforter and starting the washer, I grabbed her hand and ushered us back to the main living area where I paused. "Wait." Releasing her, I stepped out my front door and closed it. Then I kicked it in, purposely splintering the wood of the frame.

Staring at me wide-eyed when I walked back in and closed the now ruined door partway, she didn't comment.

"Do you know how to drive a motorcycle?" Taking her hand again, kicking over two chairs in the kitchen area, shoving the table askew, I quickly led her to my hidden entrance into the warehouse next door as my cell sounded with another alarm.

She glanced behind us at my trail of destruction. "I know how gears shift, but I've only ever ridden on one. Why did you kick your door in and do that to the furniture?"

"Distraction," I answered vaguely, taking in her first comment. Ridden, not driven, fuck. Letting us through the door, then securing it behind us, I pulled my cell out and glanced at my security feeds as the SUV turned into the alley. "Do you know how to drive a car?" Down to seconds, leading us toward the Ducati, I switched security feeds on my cell to show the bay door.

"Is it much different than a boat?"

Fuck. She didn't even know how to drive a goddamn car. "Gas and brake foot pedals. Left is brake, right is gas. The gear shift is on the column of the steering wheel. D for drive, R for reverse." Taking three seconds we didn't fucking have, I turned and grabbed her face. "Gun, driving, passports, bank account, drive south to Florida, charter to Cuba, fly out from there, remember every goddamn thing I've told you, and get the hell out. No matter what, get yourself out. You hear me?"

Her eyes welled. "What about you?"

"I'm the hunter. You're the butterfly. We do what we do."

Tears slid down her face. "I fly away."

"I hunt."

"Hunter," she whispered.

"Butterfly," I whispered back.

Then I kissed her once, grabbed our helmets, and got on the bike.

She got on behind me.

Firing up the Ducati, using my cell, I checked the security feed one last time.

Then I programmed the bay door to open only long enough for us to race out, deleted the app, and revved the engine. "Hold on, Butterfly."

The bay door opened, her arms tightened around my waist, and I hit the throttle.

Scanning the alley, bypassing the ramp and the sharp left needed to use it, I drove us straight off the loading dock.

The Streetfighter landed hard, but the wheels gripped and I fucking hit it.

The SUV nowhere in sight, we shot down the alley.

Hugging the shadows, keeping the corner tight, glancing behind us, wondering where the fuck they'd gone, I turned onto the main road.

The SUV came out of nowhere.

NOVEMBER

I gunned it, but so did the other driver.

Only a split second to react, I didn't hesitate.

Letting go of the Ducati, palming my Glock with my right hand, I grabbed her around the waist with my left arm. "Legs up, legs up!"

Standing on the foot pegs, taking her with me, I unloaded into the windshield of the SUV as it slammed into the Streetfighter, broadsiding us,

We hit their hood, she screamed, the Glock knocked from my hand, then the driver slammed on the brakes.

Thrown from the SUV, one arm still around her, I grabbed her with the other and twisted midair.

My back hit the ground first, she landed on top of me, and both of our helmets cracked against the pavement.

Her scream stopped and everything went black.

NINETEEN

The Hunter

Noise. Road noise? No. Engine noise.
    I tried to open my eyes. Heavy.
    My ears popped.
Sleep.
Jolted out of unconsciousness, my ribs took a fucking hit, my arms stretched.
Fuck. Butterfly. *Fuck.*
"Sub?"
Voices, sharp sting, slipping…
Sleep…

Inhale.
Ribs.
Noise.
Out.

Noise again. Different. Canned, popping, clinking… shots. *Shots?*
Goddamn it, focus.
Voices. Yelling. Distant. Foreign language…
Russian?
Russian.
Fuck. *Fuck.* Butterfly. Ducati. Crash. Terrorists. *Butterfly. Come on, come on, surface… focus. Get to her.* Noise. Distant.
I listened.

There it was.

Not just noise. Shots, bursts of gunfire. Distinctive, familiar, closer. Where was she?

Inhale.

Inhale and assess. *Come on, fucking focus.*

Okay. Ribs sore. Arms stretched. Arguing. Russian. Gunfire. No quiet voice. No scent of flowered shampoo. *Where the fuck is Butterfly?*

Holding perfectly still, I didn't open my eyes.

I forced myself to listen.

Three, four, five different voices.

No, six.

All speaking in Russian while the gunfire sounded in the distance… not distance, outside. No wind, I was inside. My head still scrambled, I latched on to the Russian but only every few words filtered in. *Military. Hacker. Closing in. Time. Kill them. SEALs.*

Fuck, *fuck*.

Fighting to focus past the last of the brain fog, not letting on I was conscious, I assessed.

I flexed my toes. Still in boots.

Knees bent. Dressed. I was seated.

Breathing labored. Ribs broken or bruised.

Active bleeding, none.

Heavy footsteps sounded, then a seventh voice spoke. Argued. Too fast for me to pick up any words.

Arms stretched above my head, wrists touching, thin binding under thicker, courser binding—zip-tied and rope bound.

Injured, but not mortally. I hadn't been in and out of consciousness from the crash or hitting the ground. I'd been drugged.

Maybe Butterfly was too.

Shallow inhale, I kept assessing.

Head cool, no helmet. Mouth dry but copper tasting. I smelled blood, leather, mold, and air that wasn't dense enough to be city air. Air that didn't smell like anything I knew.

We weren't in D.C. We probably weren't in the States. That would've been the smart move on their part—to get out.

The only question was where was Butterfly?

And why'd they keep me alive?

Bursts of gunfire erupted outside, and one of the men switched to English. "Last chance. You're both out of time. Who is he, sub?"

A slap sounded.

Rage hit and adrenaline surged. My eyes opened, and I was scanning the room.

Eight armed men, four of which I'd seen from my screens, none of them young enough or thin enough to fit her description of Check Mate. I kept scanning. Industrial building, vacant, late afternoon light coming through second clerestory windows, and her. My Butterfly, on her knees, unrestrained, tears dripping down her reddened, bruised face.

Vladimir Alekhin stood over her.

My rage hit a whole new level, but I spoke with a lethal calm. "Are you injured, sub?"

Without hesitation, her head turned, and her gaze met mine as the four men I'd never seen instantly drew on me.

Terrified, panicked, my Butterfly sucked in a sharp breath as her bloodshot teal eyes said it all.

A chorus of Russian exploded between all the men except Alekhin. His attention cut to me.

Ignoring him and his fucking cell, taking note of the gunfire outside that'd ramped up, I locked my gaze on hers and issued an order. "Answer the question, sub."

She shook her head once.

Vladimir Alekhin chuckled as he crossed his arms, seemingly ignoring the firestorm outside that was closing in on us as he addressed me. "Ah, so she does respond. Interesting. And you are?"

I looked him in the eye. "The man who's going to kill you."

He smiled as he grabbed a fistful of her hair and yanked her head back. "Would that be before or after I show you what I was doing to your little sub girlfriend for the past three months?" He tipped his chin at his men. "What we all were doing," he added, thinking he was upping his psychological game. "It was a small boat. No privacy." He winked.

A couple of men laughed.

Butterfly silently wept.

I didn't take the bait.

Alekhin fished. "Your little sub didn't tell us she had a boyfriend in the military." Glancing down at her, still holding her hair, he kicked her in the stomach.

Trying to stifle a cry and unsuccessfully attempting to bend in at the waist, her arms went to her stomach.

My fury erupted with another burst of gunfire outside.

Whether Mathers heard the accident or Perkins had put it all together, they'd come for me. Top security clearance, over a decade's worth of intel on every strategic, classified, covert, defensive and offensive U.S. military operation—I was too valuable an asset to be left in enemy hands.

There was a reason they'd put me through extensive hostage-survival training.

Any form of torture these assholes could dish out, I'd already withstood. I'd been fucking immune to it. I'd called it survival. The Air Force shrinks had other names. I didn't fucking care what labels they assigned to me. Every man in this room was dead.

But Alekhin was going to suffer.

Glaring at him, I spoke to my Butterfly. "You with me, sub?"

Eyes closed, holding her stomach, weeping, she didn't respond.

"Reply, sub," I barked.

Her voice shook. "Right here, yes, sir."

"Good girl." Seething, keeping my tone level, I addressed Alekhin. "The sub doesn't have a boyfriend, I have nothing to do with the military, and real men don't kick women. Why don't you come over here and try that with me?"

"I am fine right here, and you lie." Alekhin pulled her hair harder. "You knew to call her sub."

Inconspicuously testing the strength of the restraints around my wrist and the rafter above my head they were tied to, I cautiously pulled so the asshole wouldn't notice. "I walked into a bar, asked a beautiful woman sitting by herself what her name was. She said 'sub.' I decided to take her for a ride. You decided to shoot at me. Now you're not man enough to come over here and see what happens when you kick me?"

Another chorus of gunfire erupted outside, but this time closer. Much closer.

Pavel, one of the original men with Alekhin, pulled out his cell and glanced at the screen before urgently striding toward Alekhin.

"I'll show you how much of a man I am." The fuck Alekhin was about to shove his groin into her face when Pavel came up on his six.

Whispering agitatedly in his ear, Pavel showed Alekhin his cell.

Alekhin threw Atala back, drew a 9mm, and started barking orders, rapid-fire, in Russian.

I only picked up a few words, but it was enough. They were out of time.

Weapon aimed, Alekhin moved in on me. His inner circle followed, and the four armed men pivoted from offense to defense and fanned out, directing their weapons to cover all four sides of the building.

Alekhin shoved his gun to my temple. "Last chance or you will both die. What do you know, soldier?"

"I'm not a soldier." I was an airman.

"Then why are they coming for you?" the fuck demanded.

The bursts now a constant firefight, I stalled. "They who?"

Alekhin swung out, the barrel of his 9mm connecting with the side of Atala's face.

Her cry echoed, the force of the hit knocked her over, and I was on my feet.

NOVEMBER

Kicking back the chair the assholes were too stupid to tie me to, I stood to my full height, giving me just enough rope length. Wrapping it around Alekhin's neck, I made him a promise. "Hit her again and I will gut you with my bare hands."

Not missing a beat, the fuck aimed at Atala. "Try it and I shoot her."

Panicked, Pavel spoke in Russian to Alekhin.

This time I understood it.

The SEALs breached the compound. We need to leave now.

"This is your final chance, *hacker*," Alekhin warned, spitting out the last word. "What do they know about us?"

Bullet spray hit the wall of the building, and the seven men closed in our position, protecting their leader.

I looked Vladimir Alekhin in the eye for the last time. "Fuck you."

The barrel of his gun left my temple, and he fired two shots with unerring aim.

Her head snapped back as the first shot hit her skull and the second her arm as a crimson spray of her blood coated everything.

Then her lifeless body hit the ground.

No.

NO.

The hot steel of a freshly fired 9mm landed back on my temple. *"What do they know?"*

A roar of rage echoed, and I snapped out of my zip ties. My knee hit his groin, my elbow struck his face, and my hand was on his gun, twisting with force before I fired once, twice, three times. Alekhin's body fell on me, I hit the ground, two more bodies dropped then bullets were spraying, hitting the already dead bodies and ground around us.

Grabbing an automatic from the lifeless hand of the fuck lying next to me, I opened fire.

And kept firing.

Then I grabbed the next gun, firing every fucking round until

I ran out of ammo. Kicking Alekhin's body off me, shoving to my feet, ignoring the aimed guns of the two men left standing, I charged the closest.

Dropping his gun, he pulled a knife and sank the blade into my side right before I tackled him. We crashed to the ground, smashing the wooden chair, and I grabbed for a splintered leg as he yanked his knife out and came at me again.

I was faster.

I jammed the makeshift wooden stake into his chest.

Blood sprayed, and a barrel hit the back of my head as the last fuck yelled in Russian.

My foot was kicking out behind me before I'd yanked the stake from the dead fuck's chest.

The last asshole hit the ground as I brought my arms up, plunging the chair leg into his chest with all my strength before he could get off a shot. His body arced, his chest gurgled, I wrenched the stake out and pivoted. Then I was stabbing the fuck out of Alekhin's corpse, over and over until I couldn't see past the blood spray covering my face.

Yanking the stake out, staggering to my feet, blood dripping off every inch of me, I clutched the splintered leg of the chair and spun in a circle. All eight men were dead at my feet, but she was gone.

My Butterfly's body was gone.

Blood, too much blood, pooled on the floor where she'd been shot, and I fucking stared as a burst of fire hit the outside of the building, then the door was kicked in.

Three SEALs breached, fanning out in formation, scanning every corner of the building through their scopes.

The one in front lowered his aim first and clipped out orders. "Echo, ID. Zulu, perimeter. Taking approach."

Chest heaving, stab wounds bleeding, I fucking stood there as the first and second SEALs approached me while the third jogged the perimeter.

NOVEMBER

The second SEAL, ink covering his hands and neck, glanced at the carnage at my feet and smirked. "Nice work, motherfucker." Holding his cell up next to my head, glancing between the screen and my face, he tipped his chin at the first SEAL. "ID affirmative. HVT acquired."

"Good copy," the first SEAL answered. "Document."

"Roger that." Using his cell, the inked SEAL started taking pictures of all eight dead terrorists.

The first SEAL glanced at my hand where I still held the stake before meeting my gaze. "I'm Alpha, U.S. Navy. We're here to take you home. Can you walk?"

Four words echoed in my head.

The very last thing she'd said to me.

Right here, yes, sir.

TWENTY

The Hunter

SEALs, exfil, helos, medics, cargo plane, landing at a base in Germany, debrief. Words, places, phrases—Bosnia, heavily armed cell, compound, ambushed, casualties, drone strike—it was all a blur.

I was too busy replaying the moment she got shot in the head.
Replaying the moment I fucked up.
Reliving the very second I got her killed.
Over and over, it played on repeat through every second of the past few hours, tuning out everyone and everything around me.
Except now I was in a small, cold, windowless room I'd been escorted to and told to wait.
Alone.
Still in my bloodied clothes I'd refused to take off.
I wanted to feel the rage.
See it.
Live it.
Breathe it.
The one called Alpha had sent the one called Zulu on an exterior perimeter search for her body before we'd evaced, but he'd returned empty-handed.
I knew who took her body.
There was only one answer.
The fifth man. *Check Mate.*
He did it because he could.
He did it to send a message.

NOVEMBER

He was better.

I'd failed.

Hours later, the door opened and Deputy Commander Bradley walked in with his usual stern expression until he saw me.

"Jesus fucking Christ," he muttered, shutting the door behind him before his hands went to his hips and he stared. "How the hell did you survive?"

I ignored the question. "I did my job." It wasn't a statement. It was a warning.

His tone quieted. "I know, son."

I wasn't his son, and he didn't fucking hear me. "The cell is eliminated."

He nodded once. "I heard. You took out the players. Perkins's drone strike wiped out the rest. I read the debrief. Medics said you were drugged. Hell of a rebound, son."

Compartmentalizing what else could've been collateral in the drone strike, refusing to go there, I waited.

He didn't ask about Butterfly. He didn't mention a body found in satellite imagery before the drone strike. He didn't ask about the motorcycle. He didn't even ask logistics on how I'd been taken.

I tested him. "They came for me."

His quieter tone and single nod came back. "I know, son. We found your door kicked in. Mathers has been properly dealt with. Perkins is looking into how this could've happened, but at this point, all security footage in your surrounding area was wiped before the incident. Perkins believes the cell was behind that."

Not reacting to his term *incident*, testing him one more time, I reiterated myself. "The cell is eliminated." Except for Check Mate. I didn't believe for a second that he'd been taken out.

"Yes, they are," the Deputy Commander confirmed. "The female was MIA when Perkins tracked them to Tipton. We know there was a private jet waiting, but we lost security cams at the airfield before and after they boarded. We're still piecing some of it together, but Perkins was able to track the plane en route to

Bosnia, and we called it in before you landed. A team was mobilized, and you know the rest. If the woman's still out there, we'll find her and she'll be dealt with, but the rest of the cell is dead and accounted for. They won't be coming after you again."

He didn't know I'd taken Butterfly or that there was a fifth man. Or they were covering it up.

I didn't care.

I knew what I had to do.

Staring at the Deputy Commander, I reminded him of his promise to me thirteen years ago. "We had a deal." When he'd recruited me, I'd told him I wouldn't stay. He'd threatened and followed through with a security detail to make sure I did. That's when I'd offered him a deal. I told him I'd work harder, better and faster than any hacker he'd ever had, and I'd stay through the mandatory military commitment. After that, I told him I'd tell him when I wanted to leave if he promised to let me go and wipe my record. He'd agreed.

The Deputy Commander's chest rose, then he let out a heavy sigh. "You sure about this, son? You're going to get the Air Force Commendation Medal and Combat Action Medal. It doesn't have to end here. You can—"

"We had a deal, *sir*." I didn't want medals.

Dropping the fatherly role with me that only he subscribed to, he slid back into the Deputy Commander he was. "Message received. I'll arrange transport back to the States, then—"

"I don't need it."

Staring at me a beat, he shook his head. "Less than thirty-six hours ago, this conversation wasn't on my radar. It wasn't even in my purview. My best hacker taken, a SEAL team ambushed, and you racking up headcount with a damn chair leg in hand-to-hand combat like you eat terrorists for breakfast. After thirteen years of your uncanny skill set, I shouldn't be surprised by what I'm staring at, not when it's right in front of me, but I admit, I'm fucking surprised."

NOVEMBER

I didn't comment.

He stared for a beat longer, then exhaled. "You're right. I made you a promise, and I honor my word." He held his hand out. "A deal's a deal."

I shook his hand.

"For the record, you stayed longer than I expected. You've done good work, son. You set the bar for both this branch and defensive and offensive cyberspace operations. It's been an honor and a privilege to have you under my command." He narrowed his eyes in warning. "But don't make me have to kick down your door again for hacking the NSA. You don't get a second pass, understood?"

I wouldn't need one. "Understood."

"Good. What do you need from me right now?"

"Change of clothes, shower, and an undetected way off base."

"Wait here." He left the room.

Ten minutes later, he was back with a standard combat OPC uniform and a clean pair of boots. Closing the door behind him, he handed me everything. "Shower's down the hall. Leave the building by the north exit, turn west and exit the base past the airfield. You'll have a twenty-minute window during which I'll be getting onto a transport back to Virginia that you'll supposedly be on. If you're spotted on base after that, you're on your own. Once I'm back at the Pentagon, assuming you're not caught, I'll handle the paperwork. You'll be honorably discharged and relieved of your duty."

That was only half of it. "My record of service?"

"Per our deal, all pertinent intel will be expunged," he promised.

"Thank you, sir."

"Don't thank me. We both know you would've found your way to a computer here on base and done it yourself within seconds. Hell, you'll probably wipe everything anyway the second I turn my back. But we're both going to deny this conversation ever took place. Give me a one-minute lead." Stepping back, straightening his shoulders, he gave me a proper salute. Then he used a name that was never mine. An alias I'd created long before the military had kicked my door down. One so deep that no one had ever questioned it. "Cyberspace Operations Officer James Hunter, the United States Air Force thanks you for your service." Pivoting, he walked out of the room.

I waited a minute.

Then I cleared the hall, stepped into the empty communal shower undetected, and checked for cameras. When I didn't see any, I reached in my front jeans pocket for the one fucking concrete lead I had, the SIM card from the cell I'd taken from her.

But it was gone.

Slamming my fist against the wall before leaning against it for support, I let the rage and grief eat me for one goddamn minute as I choked on her name. Then I stripped down to my underwear, shoving the blood-soaked clothes into a trash can. But when I dropped my boxers, I fucking froze.

Staring down, I looked at the blood of her innocence still on my dick, and her voice echoed in my head.

Right here, yes, sir.

TWENTY-ONE

November
Manhattan. New York City.
Ten months later.

Scanning the street, the front of the building and the side alley, I moved down the latter. Using the rear entrance, I took the service elevator up to the forty-seventh floor. Three swipes on my cell, and I temporarily disabled the tenant's security system before I entered the suite.

Glassed-in offices visible past the reception area, large conference rooms overlooking Manhattan's evening skyline, three initials in gold on the wall behind the empty receptionist's desk—I bypassed it all.

Striding toward the corner office, I silently opened the door and stepped one foot inside.

With the honed senses of a lethally trained killer, the office's occupant, a man standing at the windows who was on a call, glanced over his shoulder.

Expression locked, Adam "Alpha" Trefor's only tell of surprise was a split-second pause in his conversation as he turned to face me. "Understood, sir. My colleague Zulu will be in touch tomorrow to make the arrangements.... Yes. Of course. You as well." Ending the call, his gaze locked on mine, he pocketed his cell. "This is unexpected." He nodded at the chair next to me. "Have a seat."

"You need better security."

"Clearly." Unbuttoning the jacket of his custom suit, he sat behind his desk. "You bypassed both the building's and my company's security systems and walked into my office after-hours undetected. No small accomplishment."

A handful of people could have done it, him included. "You would've been able to do the same."

"It's my system. There's a difference."

Not commenting, taking the chair opposite him, I purposely glanced at his left shoulder where he'd taken a career-ending hit. "How's the arm?"

"Healed." Leaning his elbows on the arms of his chair, he steepled his hands. "I'd ask how you knew I was injured at all, but I think I'm beginning to understand exactly why the Air Force wanted you back. Speaking of, I heard you fell off the grid after Bosnia."

"You made inquiries." I hadn't caught that. I made a mental note to back-trace his steps and erase them.

"Singular. Only one inquiry after Bosnia, about six months ago," he admitted. "It was discreet. I learned nothing more than what I already told you. How's civilian life?"

I took note of his time frame. "Not as busy as yours." Six months ago was after his injury and right after he'd gone civilian and started AES.

He nodded once as if he knew the first fucking thing about me. "You want a job."

Want and need were relative. I didn't want a job. "You need cybersecurity." I'd searched every inch of Bosnia and the surrounding countries. No body. No Butterfly. No two hidden words in any line of hacked code in ten months. I needed better resources. Or I needed to get out of my own head and accept that the drone strike eliminated both her body and Check Mate, which wasn't going to happen.

"I do," Alpha agreed. "Are you offering?"

Cutting to the chase, I laid out my terms. "My system, my network, my software and hardware. All internal and external cybersecurity and monitoring, including but not limited to custodial cyber monitoring of all company, employee, and client assets as well as digital usage, access, footprint, and all device monitoring. Client background checks, mission and assignment overwatch, piloting on demand, boots-on-the-ground backup in critical situations only, and client interaction at my discretion, i.e. minimal to none. I stay behind my screens."

Alpha stared at me for three seconds. "Are you as good at flying as you are at hacking?"

Not yet. "I'm sufficient."

"Licensed?"

"For your Gulfstreams." As of last week. I knew the drill. Alpha hired pilots or put all his new hires through training and licensing. It was a smart business tactic. No other global security contracting firm had done it. There also weren't any that had a fleet of private jets as large as his.

"I have a Falcon," Alpha stated, testing me.

"The 10X is your personal jet. I can fly that too if needed."

"Salary?"

I gave him a number and pushed a small piece of paper across his desk. "In crypto currency. There's the wallet ID."

Alpha glanced at it. Then he stood and held out his hand. "Welcome to Alpha Elite Security. I'm assuming you already know, but Adam Trefor."

I didn't offer my name. "I know who you are." Standing, I shook his hand. "I'll start tomorrow. I'm bringing some of my own equipment, but you'll need more. I'll submit requisitions and set myself up in the command room. Your system will be upgraded by week's end. I'll train you and the rest of the team as they filter in between assignments." I turned to leave.

"Hey, Air Force."

I glanced back.

He gave me one last test. "Did you ever find her?"

"Find who?"

The trained SEAL with an impeccable service record and

untouchable reputation scrutinized me. Then he smartly dropped it. "I don't know your name."

I tested him. "You said you inquired about me."

"I didn't say I asked about you by name."

"You knew I was Air Force." That meant he'd done more than make one inquiry. It also meant he knew people and had connections, ones higher up than I anticipated.

He didn't deny it. "I also know you were Cyber Warfare."

Not knowing what else he did or didn't know, I said nothing.

Staring for another beat, he shook his head and almost smiled. "You would've made a hell of a SEAL." Then his expression locked back down, but he showed his hand. "I honestly don't know your name. We weren't given that intel on the Bosnian mission."

"Rhys, Nathan Rhys. R-H-Y-S."

Hands in his pockets to appear unassuming, the SEAL nodded once. "We use call signs at AES. You'll be November. Welcome to the team, Rhys."

The ghost of her voice played in my head.

Right here, yes, sir.

"See you tomorrow." I walked out.

PART TWO

Present

TWENTY-TWO

Nicole

Fanning out the five passports on the bed, I stared at them.
Bahamas.
Barbados.
United Kingdom of Great Britain and Northern Ireland.
Cuba.
United States.

All with pictures of me, all with different names, not one of which I recognized or even remotely remembered. No matter how long I stared at the young woman in each photo, the same woman I saw every time I looked in the mirror, I didn't recognize her or any of the names. I didn't remember going to any of the places where some of the passports had been stamped.

I glanced at the expensive-looking black leather wallet with gold accents and a zippered compartment that used to have ten thousand dollars in cash in U.S. bills but was now down to less than twenty dollars. I'd been careful with my spending, but it'd been three New Year's Eves since I'd found the cash, and I'd been to too many countries to count.

I didn't even know why I counted time relative to New Year's Eve when I never paid attention to the days or months, but I did.

Opening another compartment, I pulled out the five credit cards I had that I'd never used that were set to expire next year, and I laid them out next to the passports. Staring at the five different names that matched the five different passports, I wondered for the countless time if any of them were real. I wondered if the cards had ever been used at all or who would pay the bill for them if they were. Would someone be alerted if a charge was made or if I used any of the passports? Would someone come after me? Was I in danger? Were any of the passports actually real?

I didn't know, but I'd used one earlier today for the first time in an official capacity and it'd worked.

I'd flown on an airplane as a woman named Nicole.

It was frightening, and my ears did the same thing as when I swam too deep, and I had no idea if it was my first flight or not, but I had to come here. I had to come to this city.

I was out of options, and this was the last clue I had.

Desperate, my job on the yacht done for the season, nowhere to sleep for the night, no new crew job on another yacht available, I'd gone to the closest airport.

I didn't ever remember being at an airport.

I couldn't remember one single thing since waking up, covered in my own blood, almost four years ago with an older woman staring down at me, speaking a language I couldn't understand. Then she'd dragged me into an old barn that'd smelled like rot and earth, and for the next three weeks, I'd prayed for death.

But the old woman didn't let me die.

Forcing water and some kind of pills down my throat, changing blood-soaked bandages, pouring straight alcohol over my infected wounds once the bleeding had stopped, she'd left me in the ruthlessly cold barn. Fading in and out of consciousness, wishing I was dead every time my eyes opened, I watched her to take my mind off the pain.

She'd fed her chickens, tended to her one small goat that'd looked older than her, and she ran her small, decrepit farm as she kept a suspicious but watchful eye on me.

The weeks turned into months, and through hand gestures and stern facial expressions, I began to feed the chickens. Take the goat out. Rake the hay with my one good arm. The forced water she'd poured down my throat turned into scarce meals of dense

NOVEMBER

bread, eggs and goat cheese. The bread I ate. The eggs and cheese made my stomach hurt.

But I got stronger.

I picked up a hammer.

I tried to fix the rotting, gaping holes in the barn. I mended the broken fence she had around her small pasture for the goat. I fixed the single, sagging step that led to her one-room farmhouse, if you could call it a house.

I yielded the hammer and any nails I could find, and I'd tried to patch the old woman's barn back together while trying to remember even a single piece of my life before I woke up.

The more the barn took shape, the more frustrated I got.

Nothing jogged any memories, and the physical labor and cold weather stopped wearing me out enough to sleep at night in my corner of the decrepit, old, wooden structure.

I knew I had to leave, but I had nowhere to go and nothing I could remember to go to.

Then the first snowfall hit, and the old woman waited until after our evening meal, until after I'd gone back to the barn before she trudged through the already shin-deep winter prison.

Barely shoving the barn door open past the drifting snow, she quickly shut the door against the increasing flurries and came toward me. Holding out a leather jacket and extra blanket I knew she couldn't afford to part with, she'd insisted with a thrust of her hand and nod of her head for me to take them.

So I did.

Cold, despondent, I'd put the jacket on and started to wrap the blanket around my shoulders, but she stopped me.

Placing her hand on the inside of the jacket on the left, she'd silently stared at me for a second. Then she'd nodded toward the open land past her pasture where there was a single dirt lane before she left the way she'd come.

That's when I'd found the passports, a wallet full of cash, five credit cards, a switchblade, and a bloodied matchbook with two words printed on the front. None of it had been familiar.

I was as mystified then as I was now.

I thought in English. I read in English. I recognized the money as being U.S. currency, but otherwise, I didn't know anything. Not even the scent of the jacket was familiar, but the hole in the upper left sleeve that had been crudely stitched matched the location of the scar on my arm. The scar on the left side of my head, I tried not to think about.

Except sometimes I got very bad headaches and *it* happened. The bad thing.

But I didn't like to think about that either.

Instead, I thought about all the questions. The ones I couldn't stop no matter how hard I tried. Who was I? Where was I from? What had happened to me? How did I get here?

After the snow stopped, those questions were what compelled me to leave.

Early on a bright, cold day, I'd gotten up, fed the chickens, took the goat out to the pasture, and carefully folded the blankets of my makeshift bed. Then I'd placed ten one-hundred-dollar bills on top of the small pillow that had my bloodstains on it and left.

Walking out to the road that was no more than two dirt tracks with wild grass in the middle, I'd started walking.

I'd walked for almost sixty sunsets.

At first, foraging off the land, fishing in streams, making small fires at night—all things I somehow instinctively knew how to do—I'd walked until I'd gotten to more populated areas. Then I'd skirted paved roads as much as I could and stuck to areas where I could easily hide. But as my boots wore down to nothing and hunger for a real meal and somewhere soft to sleep became overwhelming, I ventured into a city that looked populated enough that I would not stand out.

Somehow knowing I needed to find a bank, I'd walked in and exchanged three hundred-dollar bills for local currency. It wasn't until I'd found a small hotel at the edge of the city that let me pay in cash, and I'd entered the room and saw a brochure on the nightstand did I realize where I was.

Prague.

The name was somewhat familiar in that I could pronounce it in my head. The brochure had some English, and it said Prague was in Europe. I knew Europe was an ocean away from the United States, but that was it.

Weary, I'd lain down on the small, sunken-in mattress that was the most comfortable bed I could ever remember, and I'd slept for almost two days. When my stomach was pained from hunger, I'd gone out for takeaway food before coming back and indulging in two long, hot showers because I could. After that, I'd ventured back out and found a place to purchase new boots, socks, a few articles of clothing, a small backpack and some toiletries. Then I'd left the city.

That was four yacht jobs and three New Year's Eves ago.

I didn't know how I knew to work on a boat. All I knew was after I left Prague, I'd wound up on the coast, staring at some marina. After so much time spent smelling the woods and forests and city smell that I didn't care for at all, the scent of the salty ocean air and the marina was comforting. So I'd watched the boats.

A couple hours in, it'd occurred to me that I knew names—bow, stern, galley, head, berth, mooring. I'd spent all day watching the boats in the marina come and go. Then a large, private yacht docked, and I'd waited till I saw some of the crew come ashore. Before I could change my mind, I'd walked over and asked for a job. That was my first stewardess position.

The first one I remembered.

Three more stewardess crew jobs and one airplane ride later, here I was.

At a hotel in a city I didn't remember.

I picked up the bloodstained matchbook, the reason I was here, and stared at it.

The very matchbook one of the deckhands had caught me looking at. When he saw the two words printed on the front that I had been looking at for years, he said he'd been there.

I'd asked where.

He'd told me, and I'd gone to the airport after the captain of the yacht had paid us our final wages. Using almost all my cash, I'd bought the plane ticket, but when I'd landed and taken a taxi to the location, the place wasn't open yet.

I'd asked the taxi driver to take me to an inexpensive hotel. I used the last of my cash to get a room for one night, and now here I was, sitting on the bed, staring at the matchbook, and it was time.

Inhaling, I shoved the stained, folded cardboard into my pocket. Then I slid all the credit cards, except for one, into the wallet and put it in my backpack. I zipped the passports into the hidden pocket of the leather jacket, fed my arms through the sleeves, and tucked the last credit card into an inside pocket.

With a single glance around the room to make sure I hadn't left anything behind, I shouldered my small backpack and placed the room key on the nightstand.

Then I walked out.

TWENTY-THREE

November

FLYING FIRST CHAIR WITH ALPHA AS SECOND, I LINED THE G650 UP for approach into Teterboro as air traffic control came through the radio.

"Gulfstream November four zero niner two whiskey, New York approach Newark altimeter two niner seven five. Fly heading zero two zero vector I-L-S six circle one. Contact Teterboro Tower, one one niner point five."

I confirmed with air traffic control, then contacted Teterboro. "Teterboro tower, Gulfstream November four zero niner two whiskey is with you on the I-L-S six."

"Gulfstream November four zero niner two whiskey, Teterboro tower, runway six, cleared to land. Where are you parking?"

Wearing his headset, Alpha looked up from his tablet and glanced out his side window as he muted his mic. "Parking at first."

I knew what Alpha was doing. Why he'd had me fly him to New York for a client meeting when he could've taken his Falcon or used anyone else as second chair.

Tipping my chin at Alpha, I answered Teterboro. "Teterboro tower, Gulfstream November four zero niner two whiskey, roger, cleared to land and parking over at first."

Alpha waited till we were on the ground and taxiing before he spoke again. "Zane says you've got new software tracking private airports."

Years of practice, I didn't react. Zane "Zulu" Silas, Alpha Elite Security's second-in-command after Alpha and everyone's first choice for piloting, had fucking told Alpha about one of my software programs.

Normally, I read Alpha in on everything I did on his servers. AES was his company. But on some things, all he needed to know was that I handled cybersecurity. The exact details of the software and programs I created, ones that benefitted AES and made the company more efficient, giving us an advantage over everyone else out there, including the military, he didn't need to know were the very programs I was using personally every day to search.

Because I was always fucking searching.

Except recently, after two false-positive hits on the new facial recognition software I'd designed using everything I'd learned in Cyber Command but improving upon it, swearing I saw her only to come up empty, I was questioning everything.

She was dead.

I saw her get shot. I saw her body fall. You didn't survive a close-range shot like that. I fucking knew this.

But coming up on the four-year anniversary, I still hadn't let it go. Bodies didn't just disappear. Not from me. Not from someone with my skills. Except now I wasn't only questioning what I was capable of, I was questioning every move I'd ever made—keystrokes, lines of code, hacks, programs, every goddamn decision because Check Mate and Butterfly were gone. I'd failed.

Before Bosnia, I'd only ever failed once. But getting caught hacking into the NSA when I was eighteen didn't come close to how badly I'd fucked up with Butterfly. I'd let myself get taunted into breaching the NSA's firewall. Butterfly was on a whole other level of fuckup. But I wasn't an eighteen-year-old kid anymore, this wasn't the NSA, and I wasn't playing a fucking game of chess. What excuse did I have for continuing to chase ghosts when there hadn't been one single lead in four years?

Parking the Gulfstream and contacting ground control for refuel, I took off my headset and glanced at Alpha. "Say what you need to say."

"You've been distracted."

Adam "Alpha" Trefor had two sides. At AES, with all the employees, with every client, he was Alpha—the unreadable, impenetrable Navy SEAL. Then there was Adam "Alpha" Trefor, the man.

I rarely saw that side of him.

But three words and I knew I wasn't looking at Alpha. I was dealing with Trefor. "I always do my job."

"Yes, you do," he agreed, glancing out his side window at the busy apron of Teterboro before looking back at me. "After I started AES, and you showed up on my doorstep, frankly, I was surprised. I'd heard rumors of what you were capable of. Then I saw firsthand how you handled a combat situation, and I wasn't going to pass up an opportunity to have someone with your skill set on board. We both know there are less than half a dozen people in the world that can do what you do. So I didn't ask questions. I just told you to name your price. In truth, I never thought you'd stick around. I was shortsighted enough to think it was about money." Fishing, he paused.

Neither confirming nor denying the money comment, I didn't say a damn thing.

Alpha nodded once. "Right. It was never about the money." He looked back out at the apron. "Did you ever read the full incident report of the Bosnian mission?"

I didn't answer.

He glanced back at me. "I did. Your name and identity were redacted, your position at the Pentagon wasn't listed anywhere, and the woman's body you insisted we look for when we were boots on the ground in Bosnia, a body that we both know was never recovered, wasn't mentioned anywhere in your debrief."

I showed my hand. "She wasn't in yours either."

"No, she wasn't. In all my years on the Teams and everything I've seen, every mission I've lived through, I've never seen anything like Bosnia. That terrorist cell knew we were coming. It was a total ambush. That doesn't happen, Rhys. Not to SEALs, and not on my team. Then we lost all communication, and I'm not talking about an EMP. Our gear was live, we were wired-in one second, blind the next. No overwatch, no comms, but everything digital still had a pulse. I didn't have time to wonder how the hell we'd been hacked because the fog of war was already FUBAR, and the firefight was raining down on us from all sides. Then, when we finally breached that building to retrieve our HVT, I wasn't looking through my scope at tangos and a hostage. I was staring at an unidentified Air Force officer who was standing in the middle of a bloodbath with eight dead terrorists at his feet and a broken-off chair leg in his hand." Trefor shook his head. "Do you remember the first thing you said to me?"

I knew exactly what I'd said.

Trefor didn't wait for me to answer because he knew I didn't talk about this. Ever.

"You said *search the perimeter*." Raising an eyebrow, Trefor repeated my words verbatim. "Search the perimeter. Female, brunette, early twenties, GSWs. They took her body." Trefor stared at me. "You specifically said body. You knew she was dead, so you must have seen her die."

I didn't say a damn thing.

"I'm not going to bother asking who she was. Hell, after all these years, I don't even know who you really are. And trust me, I've looked. The second we made it to our extraction point and were on that transport to Germany, I made inquiries. Quiet ones, using every back channel I had, but all I came up with was a what, not a who." Trefor dropped a piece of intel he'd never spoken of out loud. "They called you The Hunter."

The refuel truck approached. "You have a client meeting."

Trefor turned back into the Navy SEAL and cut to the chase. "I didn't mention the woman on my incident report for the same reason you created a software program to look for single female passengers traveling through any private airport or booking a charter service." Alpha leveled me with a look. "You think she's still alive."

NOVEMBER

Losing control, mentally replaying the two-second video I'd seen from the streets in Belize weeks ago where I'd stupidly thought it was her, fighting the same damn reality I couldn't fucking shake for almost four years, I shut Alpha down. "She was shot in the head." Unable to bring myself to say the words out loud that she was dead, I got out of the pilot's seat. "I'll handle refuel. Go to your meeting." I opened the main cabin door.

Alpha followed me out of the cockpit, but he didn't descend the airstairs. "I may not know your given name, but I know who I've been working with these past couple years." He leveled me with a look. "You don't chase ghosts. So I'm only going to ask this once, are you positive she's dead?"

No. "Yes." I didn't want her to be dead.

"Was she involved with the cell?"

Anger flared. "No."

"Then who was she?"

I gave him the only thing I was willing to give. "No one until someone made her a pawn."

Alpha nodded once. Then he showed once again why he was Alpha. His instincts unmatched, he asked the right questions. "Do I need to be concerned about who made her a pawn and how that relates to you?"

Holding on to the rage that drove me, that had been driving me for the past four years, the anger before that, the bullshit in my head over what I'd come from, who it had made me, I didn't speak.

Because that was who I was.

That was what I did.

I flew solo. I spoke to no one. I kept everything locked up tight.

Then Alpha shut the cabin door and waited. No judgment, no bullshit, he simply waited.

I broke. "I don't know. The landscape's been quiet for four years."

"Since Bosnia?"

"Since three months before."

Once again, as if he had a sixth sense, Alpha asked the right question. "Is four years unusual?"

"It was thirteen years before that."

In a rare show of emotion, Alpha frowned. "Seventeen years ago? How old were you?"

"Eighteen."

"In service?"

I didn't explain the events that led to my military career. "Not yet."

"You've had a stalker for seventeen years?"

"Rival hacker," I corrected.

"I'm going to assume you don't know who it is, or we wouldn't be having this conversation. That said, do you have any concrete intel?"

"No."

"Speculative?"

"Russian, male, first initial Z, brown hair, brown eyes, and he has a signature." None of which mattered because everyone who could identify him was dead.

"What signature?" Alpha demanded.

"Every time he hacks me, he leaves two words embedded in his code."

"Which are?"

For half a second, I hesitated. Then I told him. "Check mate."

"*Jesus Christ*, Rhys. That's more than a rival hacker. This has been going on for seventeen years?"

He already knew the answer. I didn't bother repeating myself.

Alpha swore again, then he put it all together. "This is why you came to work for me. You don't think the drone strike took out the hacker, and you needed more resources." He shook his head. "After the client meeting, we'll go over everything you know and come up with a plan of attack." He opened the main cabin door.

"There's nothing to attack." I'd fucking scoured every line of code, used every resource, and trekked across southeast Europe. There was nothing.

"Then we'll find the bodies, and one way or another, get answers." Glancing over his shoulder, Alpha leveled me with a look. "And don't ever keep shit like this from me again." Descending the airstairs, he got behind the wheel of one of the Range Rovers we kept in New York for the Manhattan office.

Maybe I wasn't chasing a ghost, but I sure as hell was chasing a delusion.

Resigned, I coordinated the refuel and was doing prechecks before Alpha returned when my cell vibrated with an incoming text.

Glancing at the screen, I fucking froze.

Then I read it again.

Credit card activity alert. Washington D.C. Taxi service.

No.

Not possible.

Stunned, still staring at my screen, another text came in.

Credit card activity alert. Washington D.C. Dupont Tavern.

I fucking moved.

Grabbing my laptop, hacking a security system I hadn't accessed in almost four years, I watched as the images populated.

Then I stared for three fucking seconds before I was moving into action.

Filing a flight plan, I shot off a text to Zulu.

>Me: *Alpha needs pickup at Teterboro ASAP.*

>Zulu: *Good copy. I'll head to executive now. Hour thirty.*

I sent a text to Alpha.

>Me: *Time sensitive matter, had to depart. Zulu en route to Teterboro. ETA ninety minutes.*

Alpha immediately texted back.

>Alpha: *Negative. You're not flying the Gulfstream solo. Leaving client meeting now. ETA back to Teterboro thirty minutes.*

I didn't have thirty minutes.

I may not even have the forty-two minutes it'd take me to fly to Tipton, let alone the drive time once I landed.

Another text came in.

Alpha: *November, copy?*

Turning my cell off for the flight, grabbing the headset, I powered up the G650. "Teterboro tower, Gulfstream November four zero niner two whiskey requesting emergency takeoff."

"Gulfstream November four zero niner two whiskey, Teterboro tower, what's your emergency?"

I lied. "Teterboro tower, Gulfstream November four zero niner two whiskey, medical emergency."

TWENTY-FOUR

Nicole

For a second time in one day, I pulled up to a tavern in a taxi, but this time I held my breath as I handed the small rectangle of plastic over and paid the driver.

When nothing happened, I got out of the cab and stood in front of the building, hoping against hope, that I would remember even one thing.

A scent.

A detail.

Anything.

But as I stood there, the only thing I felt was dread.

All this time, I had assumed the dried bloodstain on the matchbook was mine, from my injuries. That I'd somehow touched the matches in my pocket after I'd been hurt, but what if I hadn't? What if it was someone else's blood?

Or what if it was mine and I was hurt here?

Except that didn't make sense.

This place was a very, very long way from the old lady's barn in the woods.

How did I get from here to there?

Oh God. Had I even been here before?

What if I had come all this way and the matches were never mine? What if I'd never been here?

My head started to hurt.

The kind of hurt that I knew meant the bad thing was coming.

Instinctually, automatically, I did what I always did when this happened.

Inhaling deep, squaring my shoulders, I clasped my hands in front of me, and I held my breath against the dizzying headache.

Sometimes it worked, other times it didn't, and... I couldn't even think about it.

Praying that today of all days, for as far as I'd come, that it wasn't the latter, I willed my headache to dissipate. When I couldn't hold my breath anymore, I exhaled slowly, then sucked in another. By the third one, my body was stiff from holding the position, but my head was less fuzzy.

I could do this.

I *had* to do this.

I had to walk inside, look around, really look, and see if anything at all, even one small detail was recognizable. Then I'd know.

I *had* to know.

If nothing was familiar, then maybe this would be it. Maybe this would be the point where I let it all go and lived.

Maybe I could get a job somewhere warm. Maybe something more permanent than one season on a yacht. I liked warm. I liked the ocean. Maybe one day I could have my own boat.

All of that sounded better than this—this sea of concrete and tall buildings and the unshakable feeling of coldness closing in around me. Inhaling to clear my head but only getting a breath full of exhaust fumes and polluted air, I focused instead on the brick building in front of me with the seven steps going down. I stared at the place that had a sign that was the exact same as the matchbook. Two words. White script on black background.

Dupont Tavern

All I had to do was go in and look around. Then I could leave.

NOVEMBER

Leave and move on.

That's all I had to do.

I took a step forward, and a couple in business-type clothing who'd come up beside me suddenly shifted and gave me a wide berth before walking into the bar.

I looked down at my clothes.

No longer having a crew uniform, wearing a summer dress I'd bought in Palermo years ago on impulse when I'd had a day off, I knew I didn't fit in here. Not for this weather and not for a place like this, but I was already here, and I couldn't worry if a black leather jacket over a short, pastel blue sundress made me stand out even more.

Except I didn't like to stand out.

Which was why the dress had been an impulse purchase. That and I always saved my earnings because crew jobs were hard to find in the winter months. Staying in hotels when I wasn't on a boat, even cheap ones, and moving around a lot because I never felt safe being anywhere public for too long, it added up. So I'd saved.

Until today.

Or rather yesterday, when I'd purchased the last-minute, very expensive airline ticket from Marseille where my previous crew job had ended for the season, but none of that mattered now.

I was stalling.

I didn't want to go into the tavern. I didn't want to be disappointed. But I didn't want to have wasted all my money for nothing either.

Okay, I could do this.

Now or never.

Forcing my feet to move, quickly descending the steps, I opened the door and barely scanned the tables and the row of stools. Then I kept my head down and aimed for the last seat at the bar.

Before I'd sat down, a bartender tossed a napkin across the polished wood. Sliding in a perfect toss, it stopped right in front of me. "What'll it be, beautiful?"

Fear hit.

I didn't like men noticing me. I especially didn't like what he'd called me. Attention was bad, but what was under my hair was worse. I wasn't beautiful. Beautiful women didn't have ugly scars. Beautiful women remembered their names.

Thick arms leaned on the bar in front of me. "You okay, sweetheart? You look upset."

My hands started to shake. "Yes, sorry. I'm fine." I didn't look at him as I fumbled for the small piece of plastic in my jacket pocket and placed it on the bar. "May I please have a coffee?"

"Sure thing, sweetheart. You want cream and sugar, or even better, how about an Irish coffee? You look like you could use it."

I didn't know what an Irish coffee was. "All right, thank you."

A few moments later, while I was still keeping my head down, strong-smelling coffee in a glass mug with whipped cream on top was placed in front of me. "Here you go, sweetheart. You want to start a tab?"

"No, thank you." Still not making eye contact, I pushed the credit card toward him.

He ran the card, and I wrapped my hands around the hot mug.

Then he placed the receipt and a pen in front of me. "Enjoy, sweetheart. Let me know if I can get you anything else."

"Thank you." Barely finding my voice, staring at the paper, I nodded as he walked away.

I knew what the pen was for. I'd seen plenty of people use credit cards. But the taxi driver had a keypad thing, and I'd only had to enter the tip. I didn't have to sign my name.

NOVEMBER

I'd never signed any name that I remembered.

Picking the pen up, not remembering if I had ever written, visualizing the name on the credit card, the same name that was on the passport I'd used, I carefully wrote it out.

Nicole Roberts.

Adding a tip, I quickly dropped the pen as if it were on fire, pushed the paper away and picked the mug back up with unsteady hands.

Tasting the sweet cream on top a moment before liquid fire burned my throat with more than just coffee, I forced myself to swallow.

Then I turned on the stool and did what I came here to do.

I looked around the bar.

TWENTY-FIVE

November

THREE YEARS, TEN MONTHS AND SIX GODDAMN DAYS.

Double-checking the app on my cell, making sure all the security cameras were disabled, I walked into a bar I hadn't walked into since that night.

Nothing had changed, but everything was different.

She was different.

Sitting in the same seat, hair longer, face thinner, expression wary, those unusual blue eyes, *those eyes*—I'd know her anywhere. I'd know that jacket anywhere.

Except it wasn't fucking possible.

She was dead.

I'd fucking watched her die.

Allowing myself one quick inhale of stunned disbelief, I timed it with my stride. Then I fed off the anger, backfilling the shock in a rush of adrenaline and purpose.

Not hiding in the shadows, not standing back in the hall, I didn't even look at any other goddamn person in the room because none of it mattered.

Only one thing did.

How?

How the fuck did she survive that shot? How had I not found her? How did she get back in the country undetected, and why *the hell* was she reckless enough to come here of all places?

I'd given her money.

I'd told her what to do.

NOVEMBER

I'd made her memorize every alias I'd created, and I'd told her exactly how to disappear. She wasn't supposed to fucking come back here.

Yet here she was.

Exposed.

In the last goddamn place in the last fucking city she ever should've been in.

Unless…

Fuck. *Fuck*.

Halting mid-step, I did what I should've done before I'd walked in.

Scanning for the trap, I read the room. Faces changed, but the look never did. FBI, CIA, NSA, the Air Force's own Security Forces Specialists, MPs, I could recognize all of them. Staring at screens for the last seventeen years, I knew what to look for, but nothing popped.

I made a second pass. This time looking for Check Mate.

No one by themselves except for her. No men that fit within the parameters of the physical description she'd given me, and none that had a look I'd recognize.

No red flags at all.

I focused on the sole reason why I was here.

Facing the rows of bottled liquor, her hair windblown, her hands wrapped around a coffee mug, she was inappropriately outfitted in a thin blue dress and bare legs. Looking like she was coming off a beach instead of sitting seven feet below street level in a dive bar in D.C. in fall, she stared without seeing.

I waited.

I'd let the back door slam shut behind me. I hadn't masked my footsteps. She should've heard me. She should've at least had enough awareness to look up.

But she didn't.

Staring at nothing, she didn't even blink.

The bartender glanced over and tossed a napkin across the bar. "What can I get you?"

Finally breaking her stare, she watched the napkin slide past her and stop in front of me. Then she lifted her head, and I was met with teal-blue, haunted eyes.

Staring right at her, I gave an order. "Come."

Not waiting to see if she followed, I walked out the back door and into the alley, except this time I didn't have a Ducati Streetfighter waiting or a specially made leather jacket.

Fourteen seconds later, she emerged wearing said jacket and a small backpack.

Arms crossed, stance timid, gaze darting, she fidgeted.

The rush washed over me, and I issued a command. "Speak."

She blinked and went still for a second. Then she looked up and down the alley. "I-I'm sorry?"

I took a step toward her. "I didn't ask for an apology."

Her gaze cutting to mine, she took a step back.

I gave the command again. This time lower and with more dominance. *"Explain."*

"Wh-what?"

Automatic, even after all these years, my arm lifted and my hand was reaching for the side of her neck where I could practically feel the heat of her skin.

Flinching, her back hit the concrete building as panic contorted her features, and she spoke in a rush. "Do I know you?"

Midreach, I froze.

Emanating fear and desperation, she looked at me like she'd never seen me. "Do you know me?"

Dropping my arm, forcing myself to move, I pivoted. Two paces down the alley, and her rushed steps sounded on the pavement, torturing me with the sound of the past.

"Wait. Please."

Please.

One word and my cock pulsed as I tasted it—her, the

memories, the behaviors I suppressed every minute of every day. My stride lengthened.

Hers quickened. "No, please, don't leave. *Wait.*" Then she said the one thing that'd make me halt. "Sir!"

Weak, unfocused, same as the first time I'd heard her call me that, I stopped short. Then I fucking turned, but I didn't reward her with my attention. My expression locked, I stared above her head. "What?"

"I-I think you know me."

Using every ounce of strength and training I'd ever fucking learned, fighting not to pick her up and take her with me, I focused on the facts. I didn't know who the hell she was now or who'd gotten to her. She could be a decoy. "You're mistaken." Whatever had happened to her, physically, mentally, wherever she'd been for the last almost four years, the version of the woman standing in front of me wasn't the woman who'd gotten on my Ducati. Whoever she'd become, I couldn't trust it.

This woman was a direct threat to me now. What she once knew could have me tried for treason.

"You don't understand." Her voice broke. "*Please*, will you look at me?"

Knowing what I'd do before I lowered my gaze, I silently cursed myself. I had no control around her. I never had. Not since the first time she'd appeared on my screen.

My gaze cutting to hers, I gave her my attention.

Her shoulders dropped, and she exhaled. "Thank you."

I didn't speak.

Tension immediately bled back into her posture, but unlike the woman I used to know, she held her gaze and stared directly at me.

I let her, but I gave her the same damn thing she'd given me since Bosnia—nothing.

Something close to resignation crossed her features, and she nodded slowly, but then she clasped her hands. Except she didn't simply join them. Uncupped, fingers fully extended, right hand resting in the palm of the left, thumbs interlocked, her hands assumed a parade rest position.

A position I'd taught her.

Making a quick, purposeful glance at her hands, I met her gaze again.

Her cheeks flushed, and she immediately broke eye contact. Dipping her head, dropping her arms to her sides, demure, obedient, deferring, she became the submissive she once was. "I'm sorry. I just thought...." Briefly looking over her shoulder to where she'd backed up against the building, she brought her gaze back, but she focused on the ground. "I thought that maybe you...." She trailed off again. Then she lifted her head and looked directly at me. "Do you know me?"

"Who taught you to hold your hands like that?" It wasn't a question. It was a test.

Her eyebrows drew together with the same innocence of the woman I used to know. "I'm sorry?"

"Parade rest," I stated. "Where did you learn that?"

She glanced down at her hands. "I was in the military."

Neither a question, nor a statement. I ignored it because suddenly I knew where she'd been the last four years. "What's your name?"

"Nicole," she quietly answered.

Nicole.

Nicole Roberts. The U.S. passport. "How did you get here?"

The frown returned. "A taxi?"

My cell pinged with a new text. Enraged, thrown, needing a second to assess, I pulled my phone out and glanced at the screen.

Unidentified Number: *Check mate*

My nostrils flared, my head spun, and the rage I was barely holding back hit a new fucking level.

Fuck. *Fuck.*

"We need to move." I scanned the alley. *"Now."*

TWENTY-SIX

Nicole

"We need to move." Looking up and down the alley, his right hand disappeared inside his jacket. *"Now."* His left hand reached for the back of my neck and landed with a precise grip as if he had done it a hundred times.

All at once, the horrible anxiety I thought I knew the extent of took on a whole new depth. I wasn't only panicking, but the dizzying headache I was fighting laced with an awareness I'd never felt before, and it shot through my nerves like fire.

A fire that was suddenly terrifyingly familiar.

Shock struck me so hard, chills shook my entire body. My head started to pound harder, my breaths came shorter, and my vision narrowed. *"Wait,"* I cried.

"No." His grip tightened.

My body and mind splintered.

His huge hand, his strength, it was as if my body knew to respond, and the air I couldn't get into my lungs a moment ago suddenly came. But at the same time, my mind fractured with fear. Desperate to understand what was happening, not knowing if I was in danger because of this man or myself, I sucked in another breath. "Y-you don't understand." He hadn't answered my questions, and the bad thing, it was still coming, pushing at the edges of my vision.

"Keep moving." Propelling me down the alley with his unyielding grasp, practically pushing me to keep up with his long strides, he towered over me as he scanned every dark shadow.

His urgency feeding into my fears, of him, of the bad thing, of what was happening, I followed his glances. "Where are we going?"

Same as before, instead of answering my question, he asked one of his own. "What airport did you enter the States through?"

All at once, the prickling awareness his touch was sending to my nerves, the breaths his tightened grip made me take, it all turned to unfiltered panic. "I-I don't know what you mean." His question, the way he'd said it, he knew something.

"Airport," he demanded, leading me out of the alley and onto the street.

Instead of making me feel safe, the openness of the street, the people, the cars, the congestion, it felt too exposed, and the lie didn't come quick enough. "I live here."

"No, you don't." Using a key fob to unlock a black SUV with dark, tinted windows, his hold on the back of my neck still firm, he ushered me to the passenger door and opened it. "Last time I'm going to ask." Without warning, he jerked my backpack off, tossed it in the foot well, then grabbed me around the waist. Effortlessly, almost gently, he lifted me into the vehicle. Then any hint of his fleeting gentleness was gone as his cold, blue eyes met mine while he buckled me in and spoke in a lethally quiet tone. "Which. *Airport?*"

My lips parted, the answer formed in my mind, on my tongue, and I had to force myself to stop it. Swallowing down the overwhelming urge to do whatever this man told me to do, I had to force myself to demand from him what he was expecting of me. "Answer my question first."

Faster than a blink, he slammed my door.

Rounding the front of the SUV, getting behind the wheel, he turned the engine over and glanced behind us before pulling into traffic. "Which question?" Short and brusque, his tone was strangely void of any emotion.

Pushing at the dizziness, at him, at the way he wove in and

out of traffic as if we were being chased, I asked again. "Do you know me?"

So slight, had I not been staring at him from such close proximity that I could smell every breath of his cool, cedar musk, I would have missed it. His nostrils flared with the briefest, controlled show of anger.

Then he answered my question. "You knew me."

For one single breath, time suspended on a fantasy. Then it ruthlessly resumed with reality, and tears welled.

For years, *years*, I'd been searching for this. Praying, hoping, *wishing* that I could find just one person, one soul, who knew who I was. I'd imagined it, fantasized about it, and made up a thousand different scenarios about both a perfect life waiting for me and a horrific existence I'd escaped from. Each extreme came with its own minefield of emotions and anxiety, but I still wanted to know.

I needed to know.

But never, in all the scenarios I'd imagined, did I ever think I would be staring at a cold-eyed man who wasn't only unhappy to see me but was angrily demanding responses to questions I didn't understand. Even worse was how he had acknowledged me. Three words strung cruelly together.

You knew me.

That was purposeful. I didn't remember this man who'd practically kidnapped me, but I could tell that he was someone who said exactly what he meant.

That hurt on a level I was not prepared for.

Turning away from him, suddenly too tired to care where we were going or what was happening, I answered the one question of his I could. "Dulles."

"When?" he demanded, taking a sharp turn.

"What time is it?" The dizziness started to feel like fuzziness.

He rattled off the time. "Eighteen-forty-seven."

Military time. I struggled with the conversion as numbers

floated by. Six-forty-seven p.m. He was military? Former military? Was I? How did I know to convert the time?

My head hurt too much for the questions.

Shoving them down the same way I'd been doing for years, I recited the time the plane ticket had told me we would land. "Two-seventeen p.m." Not that I knew what time we'd actually landed because I didn't have a watch or a cell phone.

He fired off another question. "How did you get from the airport to the bar?"

My head throbbed with a new wave of pain, nausea came, and I couldn't do it anymore. The pounding on the left side of my head so much worse, I couldn't keep pushing everything back. "You already asked that."

"I'm asking again."

"Taxi."

"Which brand?"

The lights from the traffic started to spin. "I don't know." The word kaleidoscope filled my mind.

"Color? Make? Model?"

Did I have a kaleidoscope before? "I don't know cars." I didn't know anything. I could feel the bad thing. It was going there. To the point where I couldn't stop it or control it or make it go away no matter how hard I tried.

"Your plane landed over four hours ago. The bar didn't open until seventeen hundred. Where were you? Did you check into a hotel first?"

Where was I? "Hotel?" Inn? "Winslow?"

"Winslow Inn. Room number?"

Everything blurred. "Two… two-fourteen." My mind twisted, and suddenly it was like the first time the bad thing happened. My wounds were fresh. My flesh was fire hot, but I was freezing cold. My head pounding, fighting not to vomit, that was the last thing I remembered.

The last thing I remembered was always something bad.

NOVEMBER

"Where did your flight originate? Do you have any luggage?"

Originate? Luggage? Kaleidoscope? I fought from closing my eyes.

So many words. Too many. I lost the fight. The pounding incessant, my eyes closed. "I don't... I don't..." The bad thing, it was here.

Ringing.

Pain.

Panic.

Cold.

Shaking.

Can't breathe.

Can't surface.

Twisting, spinning, spiraling.

Heat covered the back of my neck, a dark voice barked into the void, and I was drowning...

Again.

TWENTY-SEVEN

November

FOUR FUCKING YEARS.

I had so many goddamn questions, like where the hell she'd been, but now wasn't the time. One text and everything had changed.

Checking my rearview mirrors, switching lanes, I cataloged every vehicle behind us.

No hits on any of her passports or credit cards, no withdrawals from the offshore bank account, not that I was expecting any because I thought she was dead, but I still had my programs running, scanning. Always scanning. Except, unlike Check Mate, I'd missed the passport swipe at Dulles.

Stupidly, I hadn't been tracking U.S. commercial air traffic for her. Everything I'd warned her about, the instructions, the money I'd given her, if she'd somehow survived, not that I'd ever told myself it was a possibility, but if she had, I was expecting her to fly private. Hell, I'd created a specific software program that scanned all private airports and charter services for single female passengers flying alone using passports that were within an age range of the ones I'd made for her.

Then she'd fucking flown commercial through Dulles. *Dulles.*

Silently cursing myself, I glanced at the rearview mirrors again, but close-range tailing wasn't Check Mate's MO. He'd tracked her, and now he was going to fuck with me, which meant he was fucking with her, and that was a deadly mistake.

This wasn't four years ago.

NOVEMBER

I'd been waiting for this moment, and I was ready.

Check Mate was a dead man—after I got us in the air and got her off the radar.

Once she was secured, I'd get behind my screens and unleash the software I'd been building for this exact moment. But before that, I needed to know where the hell she'd come from so I could wipe her digital footprint. "Where did your flight originate? Do you have any luggage?"

No response.

I glanced at her as I pulled into Tipton.

"I don't... I don't..." Shoulders slumped, facing the window, her head bent at an odd angle, and she jerked, hitting the side of her face hard against the seatbelt housing.

Then she was fucking convulsing.

"Atala!" Gripping the back of her neck, I slammed on the brakes.

Her entire body arced.

"FUCK." Holding her tight, I yelled at her like she could fucking hear me. "Atala!" *Goddamn it.* With both of my hands on her, I barked out the command for my cell phone's built-in personal assistant, then gave it an order. "Call Talerco."

"Calling Talon Talerco," the voice recognition software's AI responded before ringing came through the SUV's speakers.

Her arms at her sides, her entire body wracked with the jerking tremors, I scanned the left side of her head as the line rang a second time, but I couldn't see anything through her hair. "Come on, Talerco, fucking pick up."

After the third ring, the former Navy SARC who'd been deployed with a Marine Force Recon unit as their advanced trauma combat medic finally answered and his southern accent came through the speakers. "What up, Hacker Boy? Your fingers get tired of typin'? You usually text me when the shit hits the fan."

"Female, early to mid-twenties, four-year-old GSW to the

head. She's having a seizure." I glanced at the clock on the dash. "Over one minute. I'm holding her upright. Walk me through this."

Talerco dropped his usual Southern accent and turned all business. "Copy. First, you can hold her, but don't try to stop her movements. Ease her to the floor."

"We're in the fucking car."

"Recline her seat."

"I'm not letting go of her." No goddamn way.

"Recline her seat, Rhys. She's already having the seizure. You can't stop it."

"*Fuck.*" I let go of her for two seconds and reached over her to drop the seat back down. "Reclined. She's still convulsing."

"It's under two minutes. We're not going to get concerned unless it hits five minutes, but I'll worry about the clock. You put her on her side."

I turned her toward me. "Now what?"

"Anything tight around her neck? Is she wearing glasses?"

I undid her seat belt. "Negative on both counts."

"Good. Now we wait."

"There's nothing fucking good about this." How much longer could her body take this? "How long has it been?"

"We're still under five. What's her name?" he casually asked.

I didn't think. "Atala."

"Pretty name. Does she have a history of seizures?"

Come on, Butterfly. Stop fucking convulsing. "I don't know."

"Tell me about the gunshot wound."

"I can't." Jesus, I didn't even know if the bullet was in her skull.

"Patient confidentiality. Whatever you say stays between us."

"I can't because I don't know. I turned her on her left side. Time?"

"Not time to worry yet. She still shaking?"

"Yes, but its less." Maybe. *Fuck.*

"Good. Was it a graze wound or did the bullet penetrate her skull?"

"I don't know."

He chuckled without humor. "For someone who trades in hacked intel, you're coming up short tonight."

I fucking told him everything. "Bosnia. Four years ago. We were both hostages. I saw her get shot. Close range, 9mm. One in the head, one in the arm. I thought she was dead. I was extracted by Alpha's team, and I didn't see her again until tonight. She didn't recognize me. She asked me if I knew who she was, then she had a seizure."

"Time, two minutes. Is she breathing?"

I glanced at her chest, then reluctantly let go of her to hold my hand under her nose for a second. "Yes."

"Good. I heard rumors of the Bosnian mission. Didn't know there was a female hostage."

"No one did."

"What happened between the time she asked you who she was and the seizure?"

Her convulsions slowed. "I asked her questions," I admitted.

"Was she distressed?"

Still holding the back of her neck, I briefly closed my eyes. "Very."

Talerco didn't comment. "How is she now?"

"Not shaking, not awake."

"Takes a minute. She'll come around. Where are you?"

"D.C."

"You coming back down to Miami?"

"As soon as I can get us in the air." *Fuck*. Wait. "Can she fly? I need to get us out of here."

"Assuming you can't tell me what type of seizures she has, and not knowing if they're medically controlled, I can't recommend it. Hang on, I'm getting Roark on the line." The call went silent a moment, then ringing came through the speakers. "I'm back. I'm gonna see where he's at."

Roark "Romeo" MacElheran, former Marine pilot and part-time AES pilot, answered on the first ring. "Talerco."

"I've got November on the line. There's a medical situation. Can you give me a lift to D.C. right now?"

"Which airport?"

"Tipton," I replied. "But Zulu's flying out of Miami on the last Gulfstream that's flight ready to pick up Alpha at Teterboro."

"Where's Trefor's Falcon?" Roark asked.

"Executive," I answered, staring at her, willing her to be fucking okay.

"I'll take the 10X then. Talerco, meet me at Executive."

"On my way," Talon replied.

"Alpha'll be pissed if you fly the Falcon solo," I warned Roark.

"Falcon's faster than the Gulfstreams. We'll be back before he is. What he doesn't know won't hurt him. Hour forty." Roark hung up.

"Talerco?"

"Still here. Grabbing my gear. She awake yet?"

"No. What do I do when she comes to?" I checked again to make sure she was breathing.

"I'm going to tell you what you're not gonna do." He paused to make sure I was listening. "You're not going to stress her out, Rhys. No questions except to offer her water, but only if she's alert enough to drink. Be calm, be reassuring, help her sit up, tell her what happened, but that's it. Anything else, wait until I get there."

"What if she has another one?"

"Immediately take her to the nearest ER."

"That's not reassuring." I felt her pulse just to make sure.

"You're not a reassuring person, Rhys. You should be used to it."

"Copy." She looked so goddamn young.

Talerco chuckled again. "An amenable November. That's a new one. Can't wait to meet your woman."

"She's not mine."

"Sure." His southern accent came back in full force. "Keep tellin' yourself that. In the meantime, keep that agreeable attitude as well. No stressin' Miss Atala out."

More fucking wary than before she'd had the seizure, I wasn't going to stress her out ever again. And neither was anyone else. "She doesn't know her real name. Don't use it." I didn't want anyone to call her by her given name until I did.

"Copy that. On my way. Phone's on. Call if you need me before we land."

"Thanks."

"*And* a thank you." Talerco chuckled again. "Really can't wait to meet the missus." He hung up.

She wasn't my missus. She wasn't my anything. And she damn sure wasn't going to have another seizure because of me and my dominance. I was going to tell her who she was. Then I was going to eliminate Check Mate, make sure she was safe, and do the right fucking thing by her and walk away.

I gently brushed her hair from her face, and her eyelids fluttered.

Then a teal-eyed Butterfly was looking at me with an expression that was more lost than when she'd asked me who she was.

TWENTY-EIGHT

Nicole

M Y EYES OPENED, AND FOR A MOMENT, I DIDN'T KNOW WHERE I was.
I didn't care.

My body hurt, and I was so tired I couldn't lift my head, but I was staring at the most handsome, blue-eyed man I'd ever seen, and nothing else mattered. Except he looked… upset or worried, and I didn't know who he was.

Then the pieces started to fall together, and shame struck.

"The bad thing," I whispered.

A frown drew his eyebrows together. Then he spoke in a deep but very soft tone. "You had a seizure. You're all right now."

"Seizure?" It was my turn to be worried.

"You're all right," he repeated.

"No." I started to shake my head, then immediately stopped from dizziness. "It's the bad thing." I didn't have seizures. I just… the bad thing happened. Sometimes. And I couldn't control it. "You don't understand."

"It's all right." So gently it hurt my heart, he brushed a strand of my hair from my face.

I started to panic. "No. Stop it." This wasn't how he was before the bad thing. "Why are you being this way now?" I tried to sit up. "Where are we? Why aren't you being…" trailing off, I looked around, but I couldn't see out the windows. I was too low, and that was when I really panicked. "I have to get up." Weak, I reached for the door.

He reached across me. Grasping my hand and putting it in my lap, he then brought my seat up. "You're okay, Nicole."

"Who's Nicole?" I realized my mistake as soon as I said it, but it was too late.

Inhaling, looking like he was trying to keep his expression calm, his voice came out more firm this time, more authoritative. "What's your name then?"

Without thought, a word that wasn't on any of my passports came out of my mouth. "Sub."

Every muscle in his body froze.

Then he sucked in a deep breath, his eyes closed, and I couldn't tell if I had said something very wrong or something very right.

"I'm sorry, sir," I whispered, forcing myself not to even think about the question that I really wanted to ask.

His eyes opened, and he looked at me with a pained expression, but his voice, it was deep and soft again. "Do you know why you said that?"

I wanted to weep in relief at his tone, but I didn't trust it. "No, sir," I whispered even quieter, not understanding why I added sir, but only knowing it felt right to do so with him. As right as saying sub felt, which only brought more questions I couldn't answer.

"Do you know what sub means?"

The way I said it, the way he repeated it, I knew sub wasn't my real name or a name at all. It felt like a term. But the way he reacted, it suddenly made me wonder if I really did want to know my name. If three letters could get a man like him to pause and inhale and close his eyes, what would a name matter? Did he even know my real name? Did I have enough nerve to ask? What would happen if he knew it and said it?

Would I remember?

Would I be just as lost as I was now?

Did a name even matter anymore? I'd used all the different names on the passports at one point or another over the years, and I'd never used the same one twice on any crew job. Maybe I was focusing on the wrong thing. Wasn't it enough that I'd found someone who knew me?

Forcing down all the thoughts, focusing for a single moment on that one little word, I silently spoke it.

Sub.

Goose flesh raced across my neck and arms.

I didn't know what it meant, but I wanted to. I gave him the barest shake of my head. "No, sir."

His eyes closed briefly again. But this time, when he opened them, it wasn't with an expression of pain. It was determination, and he grasped the side of my face. "I'm sorry," his deep voice rasped.

Before I could ask what he was apologizing for, his mouth covered mine, and his hot tongue swept across my lips.

Gasping, my lips parted.

Then the man from the bar was kissing me.

Except he wasn't just kissing me.

He was invading every single part of me.

Hard, soft, deep, possessive, he swept his tongue through my mouth, curling around mine as if he were entwining our bodies in a heated embrace. Then he groaned, and the vibration shook my very soul like nothing I had ever experienced.

Reaching for him, reaching for more, my hands wrapped around his thick wrist, and he deepened the kiss.

Then all of a sudden, I was floating.

No thoughts, no worries, no questions, just him.

Everything was him.

Then, just as quickly as it'd happened, it was ripped away as he abruptly pulled back and stared at me with haunted eyes and the pained expression I'd seen earlier.

Roughly sweeping his thumb over my lips, he repeated himself. "I'm sorry." His voice deeper, heavier, it was more hoarse.

Before I could form a thought, let alone speak, he released me.

Turning the SUV's engine off, glancing around us, he opened his door. "Wait here, thirty seconds. You'll be all right." Without looking back at me, he got out of the vehicle and strode with purpose toward a private jet.

Caught up in him, his kiss, my brain still fuzzy, I was staring at his wide shoulders and the way his jacket stretched across his muscled arms as he opened the main cabin door to the aircraft and stairs unfolded. Then he was taking the steps two at a time, and it struck me.

Private jet.

Airport.

I glanced around. Private airport.

I should've been panicked, or at least afraid, of him, of what he'd said about what had happened to me, but my lips were tingling, I was still floating, and I realized he was right.

I did know him.

Maybe my mind couldn't remember, but my body did. I'd floated away in him, his touch, his kiss. *That kiss.*

You didn't kiss someone like that if you didn't know them… did you?

I didn't have time to think about it.

He'd already returned, and he was opening my door. Silently shouldering my backpack, he reached as if to pick me up.

The protest was past my lips before he got an arm under my legs. "I can walk."

His cool blue-eyed gaze met mine. "I understand." He picked me up anyway.

I started to argue, but the sudden movement of being lifted made my head spin, and it was instinctual. I tucked myself against his chest and closed my eyes.

Then his subtle, masculine scent surrounded me, and I was floating again.

Except I wasn't only floating, I was inhaling deep, breathing in with what felt like the first full breath of my entire life, and that breath was all him. Just like before, everything was all him.

By the time he carried me up the stairs and onto the plane, I was truly in trouble.

I didn't want this man, whoever he was, whatever he'd done to my equilibrium, to put me down.

Not ever.

I wanted to burrow into the strength of his arms and never have to think about my past again.

But life as I knew it had never been that giving.

Moments later, he was putting me down on a couch on an airplane, and dropping my backpack beside me before giving another one of his short commands. "Wait."

Merely nodding, I glanced around at the cabin. It was so far removed from my previous flying experience today that I just sat there with my hand running absently over soft leather as he went back toward the front of the plane. The couch was as luxurious as the ones on the yachts I'd crewed for, but I'd never sat on any of those. The crew always had separate quarters. I'd always thought they were nice, but I didn't have any memories to compare those places to.

After shutting the main cabin door to the plane, the man stopped in a small galley to grab a bottle of water and something else from what looked like a small freezer drawer. Then he picked up a laptop from a built-in table and strode back to me with his gaze locked on mine.

Suddenly feeling his kiss all over again, my face flushed and I shivered.

His already stern features grew more intense. "You're cold." He pressed a small ice pack to the right side of my face. "Hold this here."

His first statement wasn't a question, and I didn't have an answer anyway for how my body reacted to him, so I said nothing. I merely reached to hold the ice pack against a part of my face that was suddenly sore for reasons I couldn't explain.

NOVEMBER

Instead of thinking about that, or obsessively dwelling on questions I couldn't answer, I simply watched him.

The veins in his hands flexed and moved as he set the water and computer on the couch. His biceps bulged and pushed at the constraints of his jacket as he reached above me. He withdrew a perfectly folded blanket from an overhead bin and in precise, controlled movements, he shook it out, placing it over my lap and bare legs. Then he shrugged out of his jacket and draped it over my shoulders.

All at once I was immersed in the heavenly richness of warm cedar and musk.

But I also smelled something else.

Something familiar.

The scent of winter air.

The kind of winter that was all around the old woman's barn and the woods I'd walked through. Not pine, not trees, but cold, wintery air. I couldn't describe it any other way, but it was there, and he smelled like it. So much so that I spoke before I thought. "You've been there."

Taking a seat next to me, he opened the water. "Where?"

"The forest."

His hands stilled. "Which forest?"

The fear I should've felt earlier, the doubt, the questions, it came in a rush, and all of a sudden, I was wondering why I was here.

Anxiety licked up my spine, and every inch of me felt the chill before it sank bone-deep. "You know me."

Saying nothing, he stared. But he didn't stare like he had in the car. This time his expression was shut down.

I couldn't let it go. "You said I knew you, but you must've known me." My throat went dry. "You kissed me."

His chest rose and fell.

"Say something," I practically demanded.

"I'm sorry."

"No." The blanket warm, his jacket warmer, the thoughts

started to bleed past the point where I could hold them in, and it was as if a dam broke. Pushing away from him, everything came out like a rushing tide. "That's not enough. You knew me like I knew you. You must have. You don't kiss someone like that if you don't know them." I didn't have any experience, but I knew that. "You were angry at the bar." Oh my God. *Oh my God.* The bar. "You found me at the tavern. You came after I had gotten there. You walked in and came right to me. You didn't even speak to anyone else. You knew I was there. You came for me. How did you know I was there?" Forgetting about the ice pack, the blanket, his jacket, I pushed to my feet.

Instantly standing, blocking my escape, his impossibly tall frame towered over me as his hands fisted. "You're panicking."

Of course I was panicking. I was naïve and stupid and so desperate to be known that I'd just let this man take me. All because he'd said four little words in that back alley. "Why did you bring me here? Why did we have to go? You said that, you said, 'We need to move.' What does that mean? Why are we on a plane? Are you a pilot?" I glanced at his hands. "Why are you doing that with your hands?"

Releasing his tight fists, his nostrils flared, and he sucked in a deep breath. Then his voice came in that deep, soft tone, but it didn't match his stance or the look in his eyes. "You're safe with me. I won't hurt you." His jaw ticked.

He was lying. "You're lying."

"I won't hurt you again," he amended.

Shocked, everything stopped.

Then, just as his proclamation had struck me, the meaning hit. *Oh God.*

My knees going out, I sank to the couch and crossed my arms. Rocking forward, I tried to put it all together, but I couldn't. His last words just kept replaying in my mind. *I won't hurt you again.*

"You did this?" I looked up at a man who didn't have haunted eyes. He had guilty eyes. "You hurt me?"

He nodded once.

I wanted to cry.

I wanted to cry and scream and rage. I wanted to pound my fists against his chest and demand that he tell me everything, but all the fight in me had left, and after four long years, I was too exhausted to do any of it. Broken, dropping my gaze because it hurt to look at him, at the man who carried me here like I'd mattered, the man who was my last hope, the man who'd admitted to hurting me.

None of it made sense.

I didn't even know if I wanted to hear the truth, or his version of it, anymore.

What would it matter? What would it change? How would I even know what was or wasn't true?

My head starting to spin again, I did the only thing I could. I asked to leave. "Please take me back to where you found me."

"I can't do that."

Closing my eyes, not wanting to know the answer, I asked anyway. "Why?"

"It's not safe."

More tired by the second, I looked up at him. "If you're the reason I lost my memory and you're standing right here, then how is it not safe out there?" Out there in that desolate world where I was no one and nothing.

Just when I didn't think anything he could say would make things worse, he proved how wrong and how utterly foolish I was.

"I'm not the one who pulled the trigger."

Gripping fear choked my throat and my voice. "I-I was shot?"

The winter-cold man with guilty, haunted eyes and more muscles than any deckhand I had ever worked with stared at me for five impossible seconds.

Then he gave the answer to one of my questions that had been plaguing me for years.

"Twice."

TWENTY-NINE

November

"Twice," I answered, doing everything Talerco told me not to do.

Dropping her head, she rocked. "I would like to leave now, please."

Hating myself, hating the fact that given half a chance to touch her again, I wouldn't hesitate, I choked down her name and aimed for damage control in the form of stalling. "Drink." Sitting back down next to her but keeping a foot between us, I held the water out.

Not looking up, not taking the water, she spoke with both defeat and exhaustion. "Are you forcing me to stay here?"

I wanted my hands on her. She *needed* my hands on her. The second I'd picked her up, she'd curled into my dominance, and I fucking knew. She was still in there somewhere. If I could just touch her, get her to look at me, I could erase all this bullshit and her fear, but I had no goddamn business touching her. I never should've kissed her, but I was selfish enough not to regret it.

That kiss told me everything I needed and wanted to know. Not that it'd change a damn thing, but I was wrong in the alley. Dead wrong.

This woman wasn't a liability to me. I was one to her.

Fighting my dominance, not putting the water to her lips or cupping her neck, I held the bottle closer, but I left the blanket at her feet and the ice pack and my jacket on the couch where she'd dropped them. "You need to drink."

NOVEMBER

Still rocking, she didn't comply. "You're not answering the question."

Everything about her was different, and yet she was still the same. Her statement was defiant, but her tone, her uncertainty, her innocence, it was there. Except now it was coated in four years of what could've only been a shit existence.

Guilt eating at me, I gave her facts because I owed her at least that. "I'm not going to lie to you with half-truths."

"Which part is the half-truth?"

I'd taken note of how she wasn't calling me sir anymore. I'd cataloged her comment about a forest. I'd taken in every nuance of her body language since she'd come out of that fucking seizure, and I drank in the details. Then I weighed it against the woman I met four years ago who was a survivor, and the woman sitting in front of me now who was a fucking miracle.

Talerco's advice was sound. But he'd never met her.

I didn't lie. "I won't physically restrain you from leaving." If she left, I'd follow.

She looked up.

I gave her the rest. "The cabin door is locked." Electronically secured and I held the digital key—a security feature I'd added to AES's entire fleet of aircraft. "I won't tell you how to open it."

She looked back at her lap. "Are you going to fly us somewhere?"

"Not yet."

"What are you waiting for?"

"A colleague."

More wariness bled into her tone. "Why?"

"He's a former combat medic." Talerco had seen it all. "I asked him to come make sure you're okay."

"I'm fine."

She was anything but. I stretched the truth. "I asked him to clear you to fly."

"Why can't I? I spent all day flying already."

I took the opening. "Where did you come from?"

"Marseille."

France. "What were you doing there?"

"Crewing."

Crewing. Christ. Even with no memory, the ocean ran through her veins. "On a ship?" I was buying her a new fucking boat when this was all done. One she didn't have to be the damn crew on unless she wanted to.

"Private yacht."

"For four years?"

"Not just that one, there were others, but mostly, yes."

Mostly. "In France?"

She looked up. "Why do you get to ask all the questions and answer none?"

Because I hadn't been shot in the head, had my body disappear, then come back to life four years later without any memory of my past. "What do you want to know?"

She asked the last question I was expecting. "Why do I have a matchbook from that tavern?"

Relieved she hadn't asked her name or what exactly had happened to her, I gave her a straight answer. "You pocketed it the night we met."

"When was that?"

My cell vibrated, but I ignored it. Not giving a damn who was calling right now, I stared at her without replying because I selfishly wanted to see her eyes when I answered.

Like I knew she would, she looked up. But she didn't just look at me. Her gaze met mine, and whether she realized it or not, she stopped rocking.

I gave her the answer. "Three years, ten months, six days."

Shock widened her eyes, and her lips parted. Then she broke me with the same simple but telling question she'd asked me almost four years ago. "You count days?"

NOVEMBER

I gave her the part of me she'd already stolen. "Only since I met you."

Not waiting to see her response, I set the water down next to her, then stood and took the call. "November."

"We're here," Roark replied. "You're locked up tight. Expecting trouble?"

Talerco cut in. "The fact that one-man-army Hacker Boy called in the cavalry in the first place means there's trouble. Tell him I'm doin' a perimeter check, then he can let me in."

"You catch that?" Roark asked.

"Copy." I glanced out one side of the plane before moving to the other. "I need to get behind my screen. You mind doing exterior prechecks for me?"

"Done. Anything else?"

I wavered. "You bring Missy?" Roark had a golden retriever. She wasn't a service animal or a military K9, but he'd essentially trained her as both.

"She's here. You want me to send her up with Talerco or put her on perimeter? Apron's not busy tonight."

I glanced back at Butterfly. "Send her in."

"Copy, but fair warning, she has no experience with seizure disorders."

"Understood."

"I'm shutting down the Falcon and moving to your prechecks. Send Missy out when you're ready. I'll be on apron. Talerco flying back with you or me?"

"You." I already had a plan I was going to execute, and Talerco couldn't be on the plane for it, but I would need Roark's help with one more thing. "I have another favor."

"Go."

"Secure line?"

"You gave me this cell."

"It's never been out of your possession?"

"No, and Talerco and Missy are already off the Falcon. What's going on?"

"I need to bring a ghost plane down at your place and stow it in your hangar."

Silence.

"Temporarily," I added. At least until I could get the plane scrubbed and reregistered.

He still didn't reply.

"Romeo?"

"Start talking," he demanded.

I didn't have time for this. "The less you know, the better."

"That's not what I'm concerned about. You don't need my help to make a plane, or anything else, disappear. Alpha's blowing up my phone. You called in Talerco. No one at AES seems to be read in on this, and now you want to take a sixty-million-dollar aircraft off the grid. This is bigger than a medical situation."

I glanced back at Butterfly, but she'd closed her eyes. "Tell Alpha he can call me." I hadn't heard from him since I left Tipton, which normally would've caught my attention for the red flag it was, but I'd been exactly as he accused me of—preoccupied.

"Not a fucking secretary," Roark clipped. "How deep is this?"

Deeper than he wanted to know. "I can't answer that."

He fired off another question. "What am I risking bringing this to my private property?"

More than he should. "The sooner I get to my screens, the sooner I can get ahead of it."

"You're never behind it. You're AES's fixer."

"One week," I bargained.

"Seventy-two hours," he countered.

"Done. Thanks."

"Don't thank me. Three days. Talerco and Missy are waiting." Roark hung up.

Disengaging the electronic security lock, I opened the main cabin door.

NOVEMBER

Grinning, Talerco came up the airstairs with his full med kit followed by a canine. "What up, Hacker Boy?" He slapped me on the shoulder. "Never thought I'd see the day." He glanced down at Missy. "Go see the missus, girl."

Missy trotted down the aisle.

"This is gonna be fun." Talerco winked before following the dog.

THIRTY

Atala

THE MAN OPENED THE DOOR TO THE PLANE, AND ANOTHER MAN came aboard followed by a beautiful golden dog wearing a vest.

The new blond-haired man stopped to talk to the blue-eyed man for a moment, but the dog came right to me and nudged my knee before sitting.

"Hi." Tentative, not remembering if I'd ever had a dog, let alone if I liked them, I held my hand out for the dog to sniff.

The dog licked me instead.

Cold nose, wet tongue, hot breath, big brown eyes—if I remembered how to smile, I would have. "Can I pet you?"

The dog licked my bare knee in response.

"I'll take that as a yes." Cautiously, I patted the top of the dog's head.

The tail wagged, and I got licked again.

The new man came down the aisle with a large, black bag with a red cross stitched on it that he set on the couch across from me. "Seems you made a new friend, darlin'. Missy likes you. And trust me, that's high praise comin' from her."

I glanced up.

Smiling, green eyes, tan, muscular like the other man but not quite as tall, the new man looked down at me with both a hardness in his eyes and an air of mischief as he introduced himself. "Name's Talon, darlin'. Mind if I sit?" Taking me in with a single glance, he didn't wait for a reply. He sat next to me, and his tone became less casual. "Hacker Boy says you've had a rough night."

Sun and surf and coconuts. He smelled like the beach, but not the ones on the Mediterranean. I frowned. "Hacker Boy?" How did I know what coconuts smelled like?

"Talerco," the blue-eyed man warned in a low, threatening tone.

Talon glanced at the right side of my face. "Sorry, darlin'. Nicknamin's a habit. I meant November. But if you ask me, if the shoe fits...." He trailed off with a quick smile that didn't reach his eyes.

November? Hacker? Coconuts? A dull ache started on the left side of my head, then the right side of my face joined in. "November?" Winter, cold, his eyes, his scent—it fit.

Raising an eyebrow, Talon glanced at the man he'd called November.

His gaze locked on me, he replied to Talon. "She doesn't know my name."

Something in his eyes made me ask a question I had never considered. "Did I know it... before?" Missy stood and licked my knee twice before nudging Talon.

Still staring intently at me, he spoke to his colleague. "Talerco, give us a minute."

Talon glanced down as Missy nudged him again, but this time with a whine. "No can do." His attention cut to me. "You feelin' all right, darlin'? Missy's gettin' a little concerned, and she doesn't usually do that."

I didn't answer the coconut-smelling man. I didn't pet the dog and tell her it was okay. I didn't even get up and leave.

I stared at a man named after a month. "You said I knew you." A sharp pain shot through my head in a blinding flash. "How could I know you and not know your name?" *Oh God*, I had to ask. "Do you even know my name?" The sharp pain came again, and a small, involuntary cry escaped.

Whining louder, Missy pushed against my legs.

"Stand down, November," Talon ordered.

My blue-eyed kidnapper ignored him. "I know your name, but there were aggravating circumstances when we met."

"I don't know what that means." Everything around me started to crush in. "How could you say what you did? How could I have known you without even knowing your name?" Everyone had a name. Everyone except me. That was my painful, brutal reality. How could this be happening? "Was anything you said true?"

Missy pushed into me hard.

"All of it is true." Anger mixed with the guilt in his eyes. "You knew a name, just not my real name." His voice fell like an avalanche of boulders into the ocean, sinking to the dark depths. "I couldn't tell you."

This time, I didn't have any warning.

The man named Talon abruptly stood.

The dog barked.

A cold month reached for me.

Coconuts, hacker, November. Sub.

"Atala!"

I was drowning.

THIRTY-ONE

November

SHE FUCKING SEIZED AGAIN, AND I LUNGED FOR HER. "Atala!"
Missy barked, Roark came aboard, and Talon pushed me out of the way with a bullshit calm command. "Back up, Rhys. I got this."

I fucking snapped. *"Do something."*

Talerco didn't miss a beat. "MacElheran."

"On it."

Grabbing me from behind, Roark fucking wrenched my arms back.

Her body arced. I kicked out at Roark, and Missy attacked.

Canine teeth latched on to my boot-covered ankle, Butterfly twisted off the divan, and Talerco caught only her head. She hit the floor hard, I roared, and MacElheran dropped me.

A canine growling in my face. Me, her, and Talerco all on the floor in the small aisle. My arms pinned behind me, I couldn't fucking get to her. "I will break your goddamn arms, MacElheran. *Let me fucking go!*"

"Talerco?" the asshole asked calmly.

Leaning over her, holding her head, Talerco didn't stop her goddamn seizure. "Few more seconds."

"Copy," MacElheran replied, still fucking pinning me.

"Talerco, if you don't fucking—"

Letting go of her, Talerco pivoted and looked me in the eye. "It's not epilepsy."

I completely lost my fucking shit. "DON'T LET GO OF HER! GRAB HER HEAD!"

"I don't need to." Gripping my shoulder, he calmly repeated himself. "It's not epilepsy." He paused. "It's PTSD."

I fucking stilled.

He nodded at MacElheran.

My arms were released.

Grabbing her, cradling her head, I pulled her into my lap.

Talerco sat back. Then he started spewing shit. "Psychogenic non-epileptic seizures. PNES for short. It's a form of PTSD. An attack can look like an epileptic seizure, mimic the symptoms—shaking, jerking, blacking out. Everything you're seeing, but there are some signs to tell the difference. Out-of-phase shaking, pelvic thrusting, side-to-side head shaking. She's exhibiting all of those, and PNES occurs from wakefulness. Both events have happened while she was awake. I saw this downrange, brother. I've also seen epileptic seizures. This isn't ES. This isn't being caused by unusual electrical patterns in the brain. PNES have psychological triggers. Witnessing what just happened, I'm betting that's what we're dealing with, but she needs a specialist and testing so we know for sure. I will say though, that GSW on her head didn't penetrate her skull. It's a graze wound, a deep one that would've knocked her on her ass and bled like hell, but it wouldn't have done enough damage to give her epilepsy." His tone turned grave. "This is psychological, Rhys, and brother to brother, you're triggering her."

This was my fault.

All my goddamn fault.

I'd fucking broken my butterfly.

Not taking my eyes off her, knowing what I had to do, compartmentalizing, I asked for the intel I needed in that moment. "Can she fly?"

"If she's strapped in and you don't upset her."

"Give her something," I ordered. "I need to get her out of

here." She'd been in D.C. too goddamn long. I needed to get in the air and get her trail wiped.

"Rhys."

I looked at Talerco. "I heard you. PTSD. I'm fucking triggering her. I get it." Goddamn it, I got it. "But I can't protect her here. I'm flying this plane out, and you're not coming with us. If she can't safely get in the air for a couple hours, then fucking help her and give her a sedative. Otherwise, leave." Fighting not to glare at him, I glanced at MacElheran. "Prechecks?"

His hands on his hips, the fucker stared me down. Then he threw me. "Hold the woman. I'll fly you out."

"No." He knew why. "Get the 10X back to Miami."

He nodded once. "Prechecks done." He glanced at Talerco. "I'll be in the Falcon." Turing, he aimed toward the forward cabin. "Missy, come."

Talerco waited until MacElheran and Missy were off the plane. "Sedating her isn't helping her. Neither is antagonizing her. She clearly has memory issues from what I heard, and you need to recognize that there's a reason she's not remembering."

I was the fucking reason. Not Check Mate, not Alekhin, not the past four years. This was all my doing. I didn't get her out soon enough. If I hadn't been so selfish, if I hadn't killed time that we never had to rob her of her virginity, none of this would've happened. She wouldn't have been taken. She wouldn't have been shot. She wouldn't have PTSD. She'd be living free with her memory intact.

Ignoring the last part of what Talerco said, I forced myself to focus and address the pertinent part. "Sedation is a temporary solution. I'm not leaving her side till I get some things handled and make sure she's safe. Until that happens, she's stuck with me. After that, she'll be free of me." I had to let her go.

Talerco flipped back to his usual southern accent and attitude, the one he hid when he was dealing with medical emergencies, which told me more than the shit he spewed next. "Christ, for a hacker, you're dumber 'an shit." He stood and reached for his bag. "How long you gonna be up in the air?"

"Under two hours." Her body wasn't shaking anymore, but she hadn't come around, and Talerco was wrong. I was worse than ignorant.

Grabbing a bottle of pills, Talerco shook some out and handed me half a dozen. "Sublingual. One every four hours, *if* needed. That buys you a day to get her to a doctor. For the record, I should be on this flight."

"You can't." I pocketed the pills.

Tossing the small bottle back in his bag and zipping it shut before he shouldered it, Talerco threw me a look. "Not my first rodeo, Hacker Boy, so save it. I know what you're doin'. You could get in the air with me on board, and it wouldn't make a damn difference when you wiped this plane from existence."

I only confirmed half the reason why I didn't want him on board. "Then I'd have to erase your digital footprint today as well."

"A few extra keystrokes is nothin' to you." He glanced at Butterfly. "Do what you gotta do. Protect her, get her safe, do your hackin', but for fuck's sake, don't trigger her again or you'll be answerin' to me."

Her head in my lap, sitting on the fucking floor, my life came full circle. "She's not the only one I'm protecting."

Talerco looked at me like I'd lost my goddamn mind. Then he shook his head. "Me and Romeo, Alpha, every SEAL you got at AES—when are you gonna fuckin' figure it out, Rhys? This ain't a solo sport, and we all signed up for the risk long before you came along." Walking off the plane, he closed the airstairs behind him.

Taking advantage of the situation, I brushed her hair back on her left side. Then I steeled myself and looked.

Rage hit.

Over a third of an inch wide, running almost the entire length of the left side of her head just above her ear, the deep welt of the scar made me see fucking red. I wanted to kill Alekhin all over again, this time without the bullets first. Tracing a finger over the scarred flesh before I let her hair fall back down to cover it, I was only thankful for one thing besides the fact that she was alive. Talerco was right. The shot hadn't penetrated her skull.

But Check Mate was still out there, and I had work to do.

Pulling out my cell, I electronically secured the cabin door.

Then I shot off a text to a burner.

Me: *911. Protocol. Thirty minutes.*

Her eyes fluttered open.

Then a teal-eyed butterfly looked up at me with innocence and whispered. "Sir."

Fucking destroyed, I locked down my expression and gentled my tone. "Sub."

Her chest rose with a deep inhale, and her face softened, but then her gaze drifted past me, and the fear and panic were back in her eyes. "What happened, sir?"

Testing her memory, I lied. "You fell asleep in the car. I carried you aboard."

"I'm sorry, sir." She frowned. "Where are we?"

"Airplane. I'd like to take you somewhere."

"May I ask where, sir?" The lines between her eyebrows deepening, she pushed to sitting as she looked around. "Is this your plane?"

Helping her up, I treaded lightly. "I work for a security firm. This plane is part of our fleet."

Her trusting gaze came back to me. "Did I know you worked in security, sir?"

How the hell was I going to walk away from this woman? "No."

She blinked. "Are you going to fly this plane, sir?"

"Yes." Risking touching her while she was conscious, I carefully brushed her hair from the bruise on the right side of her face. "You don't need to call me sir right now."

She shivered, then she asked a question only a submissive would ask. "How will I know when it's time to call you sir again?"

"I'll let you know." I ran the back of my fingers down her cheek.

Her eyes closed, and her voice quieted. "I like when you touch me."

"I know." Sinking into my dominance the same time I sank my hand into her hair, I walked a dangerous line. "It's time to go, sub." I didn't tell her I could finally fucking breathe when I had my hands on her or that I hadn't touched another woman since her. I didn't warn her I was going to walk away from her because it was the only way I knew how to save her.

Eyes still closed, she tilted her head toward me. "Where are you taking me?"

"Somewhere safe." Her state, the situation, the less she knew the better. She didn't need to know Check Mate was fucking with us or that he'd already had a window to take her before I'd even known she was in country.

"Will it be warm? I like warm weather." She stilled, but her eyes opened. "Don't I?"

Her trust in me killing me, I told her what she needed to hear. "You do."

Her voice went whisper quiet. "What's my name?"

Looking for fear, panic, desperation, I studied every inch of her face. Hating myself, hating what I was about to do, I manipulated the opening and took advantage of her again. "I'll tell you on one condition."

THIRTY-TWO

Atala

My head fuzzy, I had a hundred questions. It felt like one minute we were in the car, then the next I was waking up in his arms.

I knew I got tired after the bad thing, and I could swear I remembered him picking me up just like he said. I remembered the smooth fabric of his shirt against my cheek. I remembered his strong arms, how close and how tight he'd held me. And I remembered his scent. It was all over me. I trusted what he'd said. How would I remember snippets of those things if they were untrue?

I didn't think I would.

But I wanted to ask him about it. I wanted to ask him about everything, except more than anything else, I wanted to know one thing.

The one thing I'd been avoiding.

I was afraid of it.

But waking up in his lap, seeing his face, his eyes, the hint of something in his expression that felt like he was searching for me as much as I was searching for myself, I couldn't not know anymore.

I wanted to know the name of the woman he'd known.

I wanted to know my name.

Frightened, resigned, full of anticipation, I asked. "What's my name?"

His hand in my hair, his fingers rubbing against the back of my neck, his heart steadily beating, it felt like everything went still.

Staring down at me as if he were searching for something,

he was quiet for such a long moment, I wasn't sure he was going to answer.

Then his throat moved and his full lips parted, but he didn't give me what I asked for. He bargained. "I'll tell you on one condition."

I agreed immediately. "All right."

"The condition is that you trust me. For the next seventy-two hours you do exactly as I say. You do not question me. You do not speak to anyone besides me unless I give you express permission. You agree to see a doctor, and no matter what you may see, hear or think, you trust that I will keep you safe. Seventy-two hours. Unquestioning, complete trust." He paused. "Then, I'll tell you everything you want to know."

A rush of yearning so deep it made my stomach riot collided with a spike of fear, and the two exploded. Scattering the debris of hope across my consciousness like the fall of spent fireworks, his promise rained down on me and gripped a hold of my deepest desire.

I'll tell you everything you want to know.

Playing on repeat, his promise tasted like sin, but I told myself it was salvation.

It had to be.

I'd waited four years for this. The truth would free me, one way or another. It was everything I'd been searching and hoping for. This was it. This man knew things about me. He had answers. That was salvation, and this was my chance. I could trust that.

I could trust him.

But I wanted a piece of trust in return.

I asked. "Why not tell me my name now?"

Saying nothing, his gaze didn't waver.

Not giving up, I brought up the other part of what he'd said, besides the time frame, that had bothered me the most. "Why a doctor?"

"Because of the bad thing."

Ever so slightly, he'd hesitated before he'd said *the bad thing*, and I suddenly remembered what he'd said in the car. The heat of shame washed across my face. He didn't believe me. He thought I had that other thing, the thing I had to force myself to say. "I don't have seizures."

"I want you to be seen by a specialist."

Specialist. I didn't know what that was, but it sounded like some kind of doctor. I'd never been to any doctor, at least none that I could remember. Every time the bad thing had happened, whenever I'd felt the dizziness, the headache coming, I'd hid. Fortunately, it'd never happened while I was crewing, but in the off months, when I was by myself, when I had been in hotels or traveling and I'd felt it coming, I had always managed to retreat or stow away somewhere until it'd passed.

Until today, to my knowledge, no one had ever seen it happen.

But what he was calling it, that frightening word, I knew it wasn't that.

I saw a young woman on one of my crew jobs have what he was saying. There'd been a party, and the other crew had told me later that the woman had taken drugs, but I saw her body twist and shake, and foam had come out of her mouth. Everyone said she was having a seizure, and a helicopter had come to take her away, but she'd never woken up.

That wasn't me.

I always woke up, and I never had foam in my mouth. Yes, I would be tired, and sometimes I had trouble remembering what had happening right before or right after, or my head felt fuzzy for a bit, but I wasn't that lady on the yacht. I didn't want to see a doctor or wait three days.

I tried one more time to bargain. "How about you tell me my name now, and I'll agree to all of it except the doctor."

His expression turned lethally fierce. "You will see a doctor."

I let my fear show. "Will you be with me the whole time if I do?"

"Yes."

I thought about that. I foolishly thought about what it would be like to have him beside me. Not just at some doctor, and not just for his seventy-two hours, but for the little things. A meal. An early morning cup of coffee as the sun came up. The sound of his breathing in the middle of the night, letting me know I wasn't alone.

I thought about all of it.

Mostly, I thought about him. The blue-eyed man who rationed every word and measured them for control so as not to let any emotion slip past his command. A man who smelled like winter and musk, who I called sir, and who had walked into the tavern.

Wait.

He'd walked into the bar after I was there....

"Then it's settled," he stated, interrupting my thoughts as he stood with both grace and power, bringing me to my feet with him.

I glanced down. "Why were we on the floor?" The plane was full of expensive leather seats. It even had two couches. Couches... something pricked at my memory.

"Would you believe me if I said I tripped while carrying you aboard?"

Taken aback, I didn't know if he was joking or not. I couldn't even imagine him being the type of man to joke. He was the most serious person, next to the old lady, that I ever remembered meeting.

Thankfully, I didn't have to answer.

He was already giving me a command and walking toward the front of the plane. "Come. You're going to have a drink before we take off."

"I don't drink alcohol," I blurted. I hated it. The terrible tasting coffee at the bar was a mistake.

"Water, coffee, tea, soda, juice, electrolytes," he rattled off. "We have other choices." Stopping at the first row of seats behind the galley, he turned and met my eyes. "Why don't you drink?"

Every time he looked at me, it was startling how handsome

he was. "I don't like the taste or how even a few sips makes me feel." I'd tried it once on one of the crew jobs when a deckhand had offered me some. It'd burned my throat, and I'd never tried it again. I was wary of most everything I ate or drank. If I couldn't identify it, I didn't want to eat it, especially since my stomach was sensitive to most everything.

Intently staring as if he were searching for something I wasn't saying, he nodded once. "Juice?"

I had always felt uncomfortable whenever any man looked at me, let alone gave me any sort of attention. So uncomfortable, that I avoided it. But with this man, each time he looked at me, it was as if it were a gateway. The door had been opened, and I only wanted more.

Realizing I was staring back, that I hadn't answered, I felt heat flush my cheeks. "I'm sorry. No, thank you." I didn't know if I liked juice. I couldn't remember ever having it. I always just drank water. It was safe, free and easily accessible. I also knew I liked coffee. I liked the smell, and if I had access to it, I liked a cup in the morning. But this wasn't morning, and I wasn't about to ask him to make coffee on this fancy airplane. Instead, I asked for one of the sodas they always had on the yachts that women would ask for. "Do you have Diet Coke?" Same as juice, I had never tried it, at least not that I remembered, but it seemed like an appropriate drink to ask for.

His fierce expression returned. "You don't need diet. You can have regular. Have a seat." He tipped his chin toward one of the seats, then moved to the galley.

I sat and glanced out the window, but everything outside was dark.

A moment later, he was handing me a small glass. "Drink."

I took a hesitant sip. Bubbles tickled my nose before they left an almost burning sensation as I swallowed. It tasted like it smelled, but much sweeter. Not caring for it, I set the glass down on the small built-in table next to my seat. "Thank you."

"All of it," he ordered, standing over me.

Regretting not asking for water, I picked the glass back up, but the second sip wasn't any better than the first. I started to set the glass back down, but he stopped me.

His hand under mine, he raised the glass back toward my lips. "Finish it, and I'll tell you your name."

A rush surged through my veins, and I didn't hesitate. I drank the entire glass, swallowing down the punishing bubbles.

"Good," he murmured, taking the glass and setting it in the galley before returning to me. His expression not giving anything away, he took the seat next to mine and reached over to buckle my seat belt. "Your name isn't Nicole. Or Naira, or Naida, or Natalie or Novia." He tightened the seat belt.

Shock momentarily distracted me. "You know about—"

"Yes. I made them for you."

Oh my God. "Why?"

"Seventy-two hours," he stated quietly but firmly.

Unease spiked, but a fluttering feeling had started to scatter across my nerves, masking it. "Why three days?"

"I need some time."

I wanted to ask what for, but I knew he wouldn't answer. He'd said no questions, and I didn't want to jeopardize my chance to find out everything he knew, so I didn't push it. "Okay."

So gentle, it was almost as if I imagined it, he brushed my hair from my shoulder. "Before I tell you your name, I want you to listen to me." He grasped my chin, his thumb and forefinger spreading out along my jaw. "I want you to hear my voice. Understand?"

My heart thudded wildly, but my body melted into his touch. "Okay."

"If you don't remember your name, if you don't recognize it, if nothing about it sounds familiar, you're not going to get upset. A name doesn't change who you are or who you're meant to be. All that matters is that you're safe, understand?"

NOVEMBER

My heart beat even faster, but his touch, his voice, it felt like a blanket of calm. "Okay."

With his cool, blue-eyed gaze holding me captive, he slid his huge, warm hand under my hair, and he cupped the back of my neck. "Your name is Atala Rose."

A shudder went through my entire body.

Then I was whispering a name I had no recollection of. *"Atala Rose."*

His voice deep and quiet and reverent, he gave me more. "You were named after the teal-blue Atala butterfly."

Teal blue. Oh my God. *My eyes.*

His hold on me tightened, and his thumb stroked across my throat. "I call you Butterfly."

THIRTY-THREE

November

I GAVE HER MORE THAN I SHOULD BUT I COULDN'T STOP MYSELF. Putting my hand on her, stroking her throat, I wanted her to know. "I call you Butterfly." I wanted to be able to say her name when it was just the two of us. I selfishly wanted everything I could take from her for the next seventy-two hours. Because once I wiped this plane, I was taking myself out of her life.

I had to.

"Butterfly," she whispered, her eyes welling. "Thank you."

My Butterfly, I silently corrected, and she wouldn't be thanking me if she knew I'd drugged her. "I'm going to do prechecks and get us in the air. I want you to sleep." Reaching over, not knowing how long it would take for the sedative to kick in, I reclined her seat.

"I am a little tired." Pulling her legs up, she turned on her side.

"Close your eyes, Butterfly." I stood. "I'll get you a blanket." I turned toward the aft cabin.

"Sir?"

I glanced back.

Her seat reclined, the cabin lights shining on her face, her eyes were bright teal.

She whispered, "I like Butterfly."

Not holding back, bracing my hands on the armrests of her seat, I leaned over her and hovered, my mouth an inch from hers. "What the caterpillar calls the end of the world, the master calls the butterfly."

"Master," she barely whispered.

"Sleep, little one." I kissed her once, but she was already out.

Grabbing the blanket, I tucked it around her. Then I pulled out my cell as I headed to the cockpit and made a call.

Vance "Victor" Conlon, AES's loose cannon, answered immediately. "Got your text. Secure line. You're a go."

I didn't give a shit that Conlon took whatever assignment he wanted, when he wanted or that he wasn't a team player. He was never a Teams man. He wasn't even Navy. He'd been Marines. Both of us were in the minority at AES on the Navy front, but that wasn't why I was calling him. I'd been training Conlon as my backup. It'd pissed off Alpha and Zulu because Victor was his own entity and answered to no one, but that was exactly why it made him the right choice. He fit the profile.

"You in front of a new machine?" Firing up the Gulfstream, I started prechecks.

"Hundred percent virgin, anonymous operating system and anonymizing browser ready to go. No one will even see her flirt online," he answered. "What's going on?"

"Six-seven-A-C-C-L-two-Z-three-M-V-L-W-J-A-E dot onion," I rattled off the dark web website.

"Typing… and I'm in. What am I looking at?"

"Lower left corner, click the icon and a login prompt will appear."

"Right, got it."

I gave him the login and password.

"I'm in."

"Top right, search bar, type my cell number and hit enter."

"Copy. What am I looking—*Jesus*. When the hell were you going to tell me about this? This tracking program is a hundred times more sophisticated than the software at all the alphabet agencies combined. Is this what you've been working on? Wait. Don't answer that. I want plausible deniability. In the wrong hands, this program would be catastrophic—"

"I know. Highlight my last text, then in the command prompt type *trace*, then *location*, then *reverse search*, then *four years*."

"Right. Executing, but I have to ask, where the hell do you have this program housed? This is not on the AES servers. This has to be massive. I would've seen it. Also, who the fuck is Check Mate? You need to turn your cell off and destroy that SIM card immediately."

"I'm about to, but I needed you to run the reverse search first, and I wanted it on in case another text came in. Results of the trace?" I finished the last of the prechecks.

"Right. Okay, it's a burner, purchased four years ago, cash transaction. Except it was never used until it was turned on today, and the only activity was the one text sent to your cell. Then it was immediately taken offline again. No other texts, no calls, but your software was able to grab its location when it sent that text, and it's… New York. West Bronx in Fordham, and the address is coming up as… that's odd."

"What?" I glanced back at Butterfly, but she was out.

"It pinged from the Fordham University campus. Looks like it was outside a dorm."

Fuck. It wasn't Check Mate. "Is Blade still at the New York office?"

"He was earlier."

"All right, run it down. Grab the exact GPS coordinates from when the text was sent. Hack the university's security cams, traffic cams, whatever you need to. See what you can find, then send in Blade if there's something or someone to follow."

"Copy. You going to tell me who the hell Check Mate is and why you raised the 9-1-1 flag for this?"

"If I answer that question, you'll have knowledge of treason."

Conlon chuckled. "Is that supposed to scare me?"

"Yes."

His tone sobered. "Right. Let me put it another way. I'm not Alpha. I'm not constrained by the responsibility of running the company and paying salaries, or maintaining decades' worth of connections in each branch of the military and every government agency you can think of. I don't play by the rules. Never have, never will. We both know it's why you picked me out of every prick at AES to be your protégé. You handle everyone's problems, but at some point the handler's going to need a fixer. Lucky bastard, you got me. So stop wasting time and lay it out. You need to get that SIM card taken offline. Not that you can't be tracked countless other ways, but let's not make it easy for this asshole Check Mate, whoever he is."

For two seconds, I looked back at Butterfly and stared.

I'd spent every day for four years looking at everything I had on Check Mate and Bosnia and that disbanded terrorist cell, and I'd come up empty. If I really wanted to protect her this time, I needed backup. Talerco and Conlon, even Alpha, they'd all made valid points, but Conlon was who I needed.

"All right." Fuck, this felt like I was betraying Butterfly, but if he was behind the screens for me, I could get in the air sooner. "Remember this." I recited another dark web site address. "After we hang up, go there. Use the same login and passcode I gave for the previous website, and you'll have access to everything I have on Check Mate. Before you do that though, I need something else."

"Shoot."

"I'm flying one of the G650s solo."

Conlon chuckled. "Alpha's overwatch breaking all the rules. For the record, I approve, but he'll rip you a new one for this."

I didn't care. Every reason Conlon had outlined regarding Alpha's constraints was why I was keeping him out of this. "I need you to wipe my flight data from today, then alter my tail number and put me on a ghost flight with a bogus flight plan."

Conlon's tone turned all business. "Right. On it. Which Gulfstream are you in?"

"November four zero niner two whiskey." I backed out of position on the apron. "Taxiing at Tipton."

"Roger, hold... All right, got eyes on you. Hacking into the flight tracker system now and deleting your history. Getting you a new tail number. Are we using one of the phantom tail numbers and false aircraft histories you created for AES?"

"Yes, and use one of my alt identities." I told him which one.

"Copy. Grabbed one of the false aircraft histories and entered your alias as the pilot on record. New tail number assigned." He gave me the number. "Initiating the bogus flight plan now. Location preference?"

"Athens, Greece. Get this tail number on the radar and out over the Atlantic." I glanced at my watch. "In five hours, have it go off flight plan, send a mayday, cite cabin pressurization issues, then cut to dark. After you kill the feed, wipe the trail from radar. Remember this phone number." I recited a burner cell by heart. "Call it from a secure line after you take the flight down and give the fake tail number. Tell him to intercept the mayday, initiate a ghost search and rescue, then declare no possible survivors."

"Christ, do I want to know who I'm calling?"

"A connection," I answered vaguely.

"Right. You just gave me an Athens area code. Let me guess, Hellenic Coast Guard?"

I didn't deny it. "Give him my alias. Tell him I was the only occupant on board and to have HCG issue an official statement."

"For the record, I'm undecided if this is brilliant planning or alarmingly unsettling. Ready on your go to file your ghost flight plan."

"Hold." Grabbing the headset, I contacted Tipton Tower and got us in the takeoff queue before muting my mic and putting my cell on speaker. "Victor, copy?"

"Here."

"Second in line at Tipton. Cutting the transponders on board now. Initiate the switch to ghost flight."

"Copy. Switched."

I glanced back one more time to make sure she was still

secure. "Once I'm out over the Atlantic, wipe the security feeds from Tipton and send a cleanup crew to the Winslow Inn in D.C., room two-fourteen. I need the room swept. After they're done, have them take care of the rental I left at Tipton." I gave him the plate number.

"Good copy. Any real flight plan for where you're heading?"

"No. Just keep me off the radar."

Victor chuckled. "Your confidence in my hacking skills are as alarming as this call is intriguing. I'll bite. Where am I bringing you down?"

"MacElheran's private airstrip. Have a company Range Rover waiting. Then take this tail number out of service and wipe your digital footprint from the flight tracking system. After you access the website I gave you, destroy your laptop and keep this conversation to yourself."

"Trust me, this isn't one I'm going to brag about." Conlon gave his signature chuckle again. "Although… swapping tail numbers with an aircraft that's already in service. Fake crashing a company jet into the Mediterranean. Killing you off. Reading in a foreign coast guard and relying on him to keep quiet. Sending in a sweep team to cover your tracks, and getting you back down, off the radar, at a private airstrip with no one the wiser… this is level ten bragging rights."

"Conlon," I warned.

"Right. Of course, no bragging. And I'm not intrigued *at all*," he added sarcastically.

"Just stick to the plan."

"Roger that, *boss*. Any other miracles you need while I'm waiting five hours to fake kill you?"

Tipton Tower came through the radio.

"Conlon, hold." Answering ATC, lining up the Gulfstream, I confirmed I was ready for takeoff. Then I muted my mic. "Conlon, you copy?"

"Yes."

"Taking off now and removing the SIM card to this cell. Follow the Bronx lead. Look over everything on the dark web address I gave you. See if you can find any connections to the burner in the Bronx. I'll check in once I'm back in the command room at AES."

"Copy. Anything in particular I'm looking for besides the originator of the text?"

"No." I'd handle tracking everywhere she'd been for the past four years and wipe her footprint myself. "I just need Check Mate."

"Do I want to know why?"

No, but he would once he read all my notes. "Access the website." I hung up.

Then I took the SIM card out of the cell and thrust the G650's engines.

The Gulfstream lifted into the air.

THIRTY-FOUR

Atala

Like the whisper of a breeze, a soft touch caressed my face. Then a deep voice stroked the peacefulness of my dream. "Butterfly."

Warm water, sun on my face, the sway of the ocean, I was floating.

"Wake up for me, sub."

My breath hitched, and my eyes opened.

For a single second, I thought I was still dreaming.

Cool blue eyes, sharp angles, fierce expression, he was impossibly handsome. But I wasn't dreaming or floating.

The sun on my face was his hand cupping my cheek. The warm water was a blanket tucked around me, and the sway of the ocean was him lightly shifting my body as he undid my seat belt.

His gaze unwavering, *always unwavering*, when he looked at me, he spoke again in his quietly measured tone. "We've landed. How are you feeling?"

Butterfly. He'd said it. I hadn't imagined it. "Is my name really Atala?"

Still cupping my cheek, he gently pulled the blanket off me. "Yes."

He didn't ask if I remembered my name. Maybe he already knew I didn't. Right now, in this moment, I didn't care that the pretty-sounding name didn't register even a hint of recollection. My body was heated, my nerves were singing in a way that I'd only ever felt when he was touching me, and there was nothing else right now except him.

And the way he'd said Butterfly—before, just now—the way his tone dropped and wrapped around the syllables, it felt like I meant something to him.

The way he'd kissed me felt like I meant something to him.

How he looked at me, how he handled me, how he'd said I was safe with him, all of it felt like it meant more. But maybe I was… wait.

Wait.

I frowned. "What am I not safe from?"

His warm hand, his gentle touch, it shifted from the side of my face to the back of my neck, and he grasped me with firm purpose. "Do you remember our conversation before we flew?"

Oh God. He'd flown the plane, and I hadn't even seen him do it. "Are you a pilot?"

"What did I say about questions?" His voice went deeper, quieter, and his eyes darkened. The dominant shift was barely noticeable physically, but it had the effect of a tidal wave.

The shiver raced up my spine and crawled across my entire body. His warm caress suddenly a distant memory, tingling awareness rushed in, leaving a wake of pulsing emptiness that erupted low in my belly before surging between my legs.

My breathy reply was fluttering past my lips with only one purpose. I wanted to please him. "No questions, Sir."

"For how long, sub?"

Sub.

There it was again. Except this time, knowing what else he called me, having heard him say it, and now hearing the switch in his tone, hearing this other name he called me—I shattered. A million pieces of broken nothingness flew apart the same time my body awakened. As if I had to break to feel alive.

As if three little letters crossing his lips were all it took for me to be real.

I wanted to drink him in. I wanted to own that one small word. I wanted to be what made his voice dip and his attention focus. I wanted his gentle caress on my cheek, and I wanted to be his Butterfly.

But I also wanted more.

Butterflies flew away.

Sub wasn't Butterfly.

Sub was the storm in his eyes, the command in his grip, the dominance in his voice. Butterfly was in my heart, but sub was the single word I felt in every fiber of my being. Except it wasn't just a word. Not when he said it. It was detonating and unbearable. It was explosive heat that swirled with raw, untamed hunger.

Sub was fire.

And I needed to unleash it.

I needed to set it free.

I needed it so bad I was trembling when I finally answered him. "For seventy-two hours, sir."

But then I was done.

The decision was made before I'd even formed the thought.

I would suffer, I would ache, and I would bare this relentless need that he'd ignited. For three days, I would do exactly as he commanded because I couldn't imagine ever telling this man no, but then I was going to ask.

I was going to ignore the hundreds of questions that swirled in my head every time he wasn't touching me, and I was going to ask for more.

"Good," he quietly replied as his thumb slowly stroked the length of my throat.

My eyes closed, a small sound escaped, and suddenly there was wetness between my legs as I drowned in his single word of praise.

My lips were moving, and I was begging before I even registered the thought that I wanted to drop to my knees in front of him. "Please touch me."

Sharp and commanding, he bit out an order as his hold on me tightened. "Open your eyes, sub."

I looked at him.

Every angle of his features sharper, he warned me. "You call me Sir when I have my hands on you."

I didn't hesitate. "Please touch me, Sir."

"I am touching you, sub."

Oh God. What if he stopped? "Please don't stop, Sir."

"Sub," he warned, low and threatening. "You're playing with fire."

Traitorous relief spread. "I want fire, Sir."

"This is not a game, Atala."

Heat rushed to my face and tears welled as my name struck like a kick to my chest. "Please, Sir." My heart pounding, my core pulsing, shame and fear and need dripped down my cheeks. "Everything is hurting." Why did he call me that? How did I do this? I couldn't ask questions. I couldn't ask for more. I couldn't take another second of this emptiness. "Please make the pulsing stop." I barely whispered the next humiliating, desperate, sinful words. "Please touch me, Sir."

His nostrils flared. "Touch you where? Be more specific, sub."

"Everywhere, Sir."

His eyes darkening to a storm, his fingers twisting in my hair, his deep voice came like a weapon. "I don't believe you want me to touch you everywhere." His free hand snaked under my dress and between my legs before roughly shoving my thighs apart. "I think you want me to touch you here, sub." He cupped me. Hard.

My back arched, my mouth fell open, and the sound of an animal crawled out of me. *"Please, Sir."*

"Please what, sub?"

"Please." My voice broke. "Make it stop, Sir."

"Make what stop?" he demanded, pressing his fingers hard against my soaked underwear and my most private place.

My legs started to shake. "The emptiness, Sir."

NOVEMBER

"Emptiness where?" His fingers, all pressed together, moved in a circle, spreading wetness everywhere.

My hips thrust and need eclipsed shame. "Between my legs, Sir." Crying, I begged. "Inside me, please, Sir."

"Say it louder, sub," he ordered.

"Inside me, please, Sir," I sobbed.

"Louder," he barked.

Throbbing with painful need, I lost all sense. "Touch inside me, Sir!"

Shoving aside my underwear, he did exactly as I asked.

He plunged two fingers inside me.

THIRTY-FIVE

November

I SANK TWO FINGERS INSIDE HER SWEET CUNT.

Her mouth opened with a sharp gasp, and she cried out in pain, pressing her legs together as she grabbed my wrist. "No, no, no, wait! Please, *Sir*."

Stepping between her legs to force them open, I gripped the back of her neck harder. "Did you ask for this, sub?" Widening my stance, spreading her thighs open, I pushed my fingers deeper. "Are you saying no, sub? Because that's your safe word with me. Say it one more time and I stop. My fingers leave this tight cunt. My hand leaves your neck, and I don't make you come. I don't touch you at all." I said the right fucking words, but I was two fingers deep into the past, and I didn't know what I would do if she said no to me again.

I didn't know if I would have the strength to stop before I forced her to come.

Hating who I was, I rubbed her clit harder. "Are you saying no to me, sub?"

She jerked back, and her nails dug into my wrist, but her cunt pulsed around my fingers. "I-I... *oh God*." She choked on a sob. "Please." Her voice broke. "*Sir*."

Sir.

Not a no.

I covered her mouth with mine and sank my tongue in, kissing her once.

Then I did exactly what she'd denied me from doing four years ago. I stroked her G-spot, thumbed her clit, and I took her past the pain until she fucking fell apart with pleasure I'd given her.

Her hips thrust, her legs shook, and she sobbed.

She was beautiful.

So goddamn beautiful.

But I hated myself.

Not giving her a single word of praise, I rode out her orgasm until her sweet cunt stopped pulsing around my fingers. Then I covered her mouth once more and slowly withdrew my fingers.

She flinched, but then she shivered and released my wrist.

My cock so fucking hard I could come just from looking at her, I stood to my full height and issued her an order. "Stand up, sub."

Her gaze unfocused, she pushed herself up using the arms of the seat.

Not sinking my fingers inside her mouth, then chasing her taste with my tongue like I wanted to, not bending her over and fucking her raw, I instead grasped her chin with my soaked hand. Then I gave her another order. "Take your jacket off and lift your dress up above your hips, sub."

Shrugging out of the leather, she let it fall to the seat. Then she gathered the blue material of the sleeveless dress by the hem and did as I instructed.

Innocent, sated, hair messed, cheeks tearstained, the scars of a through and through GSW on her left arm—she held her dress and looked at me with reverence. Then she threw me. "Thank you, sir."

I fucking hated myself more.

Releasing her chin, hooking my thumbs into the waist of her simple cotton underwear, I slid the soaked material down her bare legs. "Step out."

Her small feet in utilitarian hiking boots, she gracefully lifted one foot then the other.

Pocketing her underwear, my cock getting harder as I watched her face flush, I issued her another order. "Stay exactly as you are, sub."

Striding to the aft cabin, I grabbed her worn backpack and unzipped it.

Then I had to tamp down rage.

Barely two outfits and the wallet I'd given her comprising the entirety of her paltry belongings, I pulled out a replica of the pair of cheap underwear I'd taken from her, and I made a vow. Not only was I buying this woman a goddamn boat, I was buying her a house and filling it with clothes and shoes and whatever the hell shampoo she'd used four years ago that made her hair smell like flowers.

Her voice small and hesitant, she called after me. "Sir?"

Ignoring the insecure tone in her voice, I zipped the damn backpack before grabbing my laptop and stowing it in my TUMI briefcase made from ballistic nylon. Knowing she had next to fucking nothing, didn't remember the damn bank account I'd set up for her, and cognizant of every expensive bullshit item I had, my guilt compounded. I knew what it was like to have nothing. I knew what living out of a damn backpack was like. I knew the insecurity of not knowing where your next meal would come from. Knowing I'd thrown Butterfly into that hell was fucking unforgivable.

Shoving all the shit down so I could focus on what needed to be done, I shouldered both bags and strode back to her before I knelt on one knee. "Step in."

"Yes, sir." Her hand touched my shoulder.

My eyes briefly closed, and I fucking inhaled her. The scent of her desire, the natural smell of her that I'd know anywhere, I didn't want to walk off this plane. I wanted to get back in the air with her and go off the grid. But I couldn't.

I wouldn't sentence her to another second of life on the run or to the dominance I couldn't control that would trigger her over and over again.

I was going to end this bullshit with Check Mate.

Then I'd set my clipped-wing butterfly free.

Using Roark's seventy-two-hour timeline to wipe the G650

as my own damn personal timeline to find and end Check Mate, I'd already started the countdown twenty minutes ago when we'd landed because I knew myself. If I hadn't put a limit on my time with Butterfly, if I didn't force myself to set an expiration date, I wouldn't leave her.

I'd keep putting her at risk.

Resigned, pissed off and rock hard, I pulled up her underwear that I hated because of every shit circumstance they represented.

Goose bumps raced across her thighs as I touched her.

I hated what I was doing even more. "Let go of your dress, sub." She complied, and I grasped her chin again, searching her face for any signs of distress. Then I gave her an out. "You can walk away from me right now." I fucking choked on the thought. "No strings. No seventy-two hours. You'll have money and new passports, and you can go wherever you want." I'd put someone from AES on her. I'd bring in Neil Christensen, former Danish Special Forces turned billionaire developer. I'd make sure she was guarded, set up somewhere safe, and I'd do what I had to do without torturing us both with seventy-two hours of a life we couldn't have.

If she were smart, she'd take the deal.

But my butterfly didn't.

Hurt ruined her sated expression, and she crossed her arms in self-protection like she had all those years ago. "Is this a conversation, sir?"

Out of time, exposed on open land on Roark's waterfront property, I cruelly denied her. "No."

Her throat moved with a swallow, and she dropped her head. "Then no thank you, sir."

"Eyes on me when you speak to me, sub," I demanded.

She looked up with tears welling.

I forced myself not to touch her. "Walk away now or stay with me for seventy-two hours," I bit out, reiterating the timeline so I fucking followed it. "Make a decision, sub."

"I would like to stay, please, sir," she whispered, a single tear falling.

"Acknowledged. Here are the rules. You do not speak to anyone except me. You do not tell anyone who you are. You do not take note of where we are or where we go. The moment we walk off this plane, I'm 'Sir,' you're 'sub' and you stay on my left, one step behind. Understood?"

"Yes, Sir," she answered even quieter.

"Good." I grabbed her leather jacket. "Let's go." I turned toward the main cabin door.

"I'm sorry I angered you, Sir."

Fucking crushed, I turned.

Then I did the last thing I should've.

I gave her me.

Cupping her face, bringing my mouth to hers, I kissed her once. Worshipful, gentle, I stroked through her innocent perfection. Pulling back before I couldn't, I stared into the teal-blue eyes of a broken butterfly. "Every second I get to touch you is a privilege. Making you come was the second-best moment of my life. Never forget that, Butterfly." I swiped at the tears freely falling down her face. "No matter what happens, never forget it." Touching my lips to her forehead, I let her go.

THIRTY-SIX

Atala

M¹ HEART BREAKING, JEALOUSY ROBBING ME OF ALL BREATH, I followed him toward the plane's exit with tears streaming. Every word he'd said both broke me and gave foolish hope. Except I'd heard him say seventy-two hours enough times now that I could no longer ignore it. Allowing myself to believe there would be time with him after that was worse than foolish, but that was exactly what I was doing because I wanted nothing more.

I also wanted to know what was the first best moment of his life.

I couldn't bear to think it was with another woman, but maybe that was exactly what I needed to hear. Maybe that would stop the crushing sensation in my chest that felt worse than when I'd woken up in that decaying barn with blood stuck to me and wounds so painful I'd wanted to die.

I'd wanted my body to take its last breath because I didn't have anything to live for.

I'd remembered nothing.

No memories of even a single simple pleasure in life, I'd had no reason to be suffering through such horrible pain.

But now it was different.

I knew what it felt like to dive into the deep, blue waters of the Mediterranean Sea on a summer day. I knew what it felt like to float. I knew what fresh fish grilled outdoors tasted like, and I knew the colors of a sunrise cresting an endless horizon line.

And now I also knew the color of an intense, cool, blue-eyed gaze. I knew what a muscular man who spoke with the quietness of dominant control but looked at me with the force of a lethal warrior smelled like.

I knew how he tasted.

I knew every way he could make my body bend to his will.

And I knew how every nerve, every sensation, and every breath of my body came alive when I was simply near him, and I didn't want to die.

I didn't want to walk away from a dominant man who called me Butterfly with a whispered caress right before he touched my body in my most private place and made me see the true colors of stars as he called me sub.

I now had more to lose than when I'd woken up in the barn, and this felt worse than that physical pain.

Following him as he ducked to exit the airplane, he only broke my heart more when he paused on the first step.

Holding his hand out to me, shouldering my too-worn backpack, he gave me a warning that sounded like affection. "Watch your step."

Taking his hand because I would do anything to touch him, I felt the same heat flush my cheeks as when he'd first cupped me, and my core pulsed. "Thank you, Sir."

His fingers gripped mine, but he didn't reply.

I stepped off the airplane and was immediately engulfed in warm, humid air that caressed my bare shoulders, and for a single second, I closed my eyes. Blocking out the large airplane hangar we were in that had a huge open door to the darkened landscape beyond, I inhaled.

Fuel, concrete, new paint, briny ocean, and a hint of something sweet and floral that was so intoxicating it smelled almost as good as Sir, all swirled together as one, and suddenly, I didn't care where we were. The perfect temperature, the smell of the night, the gentle breeze stirring the late evening—I never wanted to leave this place.

Before I could remember the rules, I was glancing across the cavernous space that had a seaplane at the other end and I was asking a question as Sir led me down the airplane's stairs. "What is that sweet floral scent?"

Walking me toward a black SUV that looked expensive and brand-new that was parked just outside the smooth concrete floor of the hangar, Sir nodded at a tree with almost gangly looking limbs, long, thin leaves and exotic, yellow flowers. "Plumeria."

"It smells beautiful."

Pausing, he looked down at me. But he didn't just look. He held my hand tighter, his expression turned almost lethal, and he stared.

I immediately dropped my gaze and amended. "I'm sorry, Sir. It smells beautiful, Sir."

For two heartbeats, he said nothing and the sound of tropical night with its crickets or cicadas or frogs or other insects grew to a deafening chorus.

It grew so loud, I wanted to shift my feet or clasp my hands or look up at him to see his eyes, but I did none of it.

Remaining still, focusing on his hand holding mine, I inhaled again.

Sweet-smelling flowers and cool musk filled my head. Then his voice filled my soul right before it broke my heart.

"Don't ever apologize to me, Atala." Opening the passenger door of the SUV, he scanned the long driveway and property around us as he ushered me inside.

Sub, *Atala*, *Butterfly*, they all meant something different when he used them, and he was as mercurial as his abrupt switching of names when he spoke them.

It felt as if I would need a lifetime to figure out the difference in his nuances when he used them, but at the same time it was as if my body and soul already knew the distinctions.

Glancing at my right temple, he reached across me and buckled my seat belt. "Wait." Closing my door, he returned to the hangar.

I watched in awe and shock as he pulled on the mammoth door and steadily walked it shut, as if it took no effort at all. If it weren't for his huge muscles bulging at the confines of his long-sleeved dress shirt, I would've almost thought I would be strong enough to close the hangar.

Caught up in watching his tall frame move with the grace and ease of both a predator and a warrior, I didn't stop staring at him until he made another visual scan of the property and looked directly at where I was sitting.

My heart leapt, and I dropped my gaze.

I didn't even look up when he got in the driver's seat.

Focusing on my lap, I inhaled his scent as he started the car, but then I smelled the other scent a second before his huge hand was in my line of sight.

Face up, palm open, in the middle of his hand sat a single yellow plumeria.

My breath caught, and my heart raced.

I looked up at him.

Sitting perfectly still, his glacial eyes intent on me, he said nothing.

Fighting tears that I couldn't seem to turn off, I said the only thing I could, even though it seemed like not nearly enough. "Thank you, Sir." Taking the gift from his hand that had both pleasured me and picked a flower for me, I brought it to my face and inhaled.

He put the SUV into gear and swung the vehicle around with skill and familiarity.

Smelling my flower, watching him drive, taking in how his veins and muscles moved, how he focused on the road and the rearview mirrors, how he did it all with the same intense stare as when he focused on me, it struck me.

The man lived in his head the same as I lived in mine.

He didn't speak unless it was necessary.

He didn't try to fill the silence.

And he wasn't asking me questions.

In that moment, he felt like the man who had called me Atala.

I knew I didn't know him. I didn't even know his name. But I felt as if I knew the important parts of him. The man who called me by the name he said was mine, he was different than the man who called me sub and Butterfly. I didn't know how to explain it, but when he called me Butterfly, there was a distinct difference from sub, except it felt like it was the same.

It was almost as if there were two versions of this man.

The version who could fly a plane, call me Atala, tell me he would keep me safe and that I could trust him.

Then there was the version that would call me sub or Butterfly and warn me that I only had seventy-two hours with him right before he made my body come alive with fire, only to turn around and tell me I could walk away from him.

Both sides were controlled and intense.

But the Butterfly and sub side was as fierce as he was handsome.

Lost in my thoughts, I didn't realize we had left darkened roads with no habitation until he was speeding down a multi-lane road with lights and buildings and traffic and people.

Suddenly uncomfortable at the loss of false privacy of our cocoon, I shifted in my seat and stared at the too-bright colors of passing lights of densely packed civilization.

"Speak, sub."

Startled, I clasped the hand that was still holding the flower under my nose and brought both hands to my chest. "I'm sorry, Sir?"

"Something upset you just now," he stated as if he could read my thoughts.

"I'm fine, Sir." Was I? A clock somewhere ticking down from seventy-two hours, a yellow flower in my hand, a pair of my underwear in his pocket, and the intimate place between my legs still feeling the after-effects of his invasion, I didn't know what I was.

All I knew was that I felt as if I should feel shame for begging him to touch me, but I didn't. He had erased that notion when he'd said it was a privilege to touch me. I was still shy, I was still in almost disbelief that it had happened, but more than all of that, I felt him every time I moved, and that eclipsed everything.

"In a few minutes, we're not going to be alone. Do we need to talk about what happened on the plane?"

Heat immediately flushed my face, and I looked out my side window. "No, thank you, Sir."

I felt more than heard his inhale, then his voice came quieter, deeper. "Did you like my hands on you, sub?"

Oh God. "Yes, Sir."

"In you?"

Oh God. "Yes, Sir," I answered, my voice quieter.

"Do you remember what I said to you?"

I closed my eyes and drowned. Then I heard his voice, his words—*Every second I get to touch you is a privilege. Making you come was the second-best moment of my life. Never forget that, Butterfly*—and I was floating. "Yes, Sir," I whispered, reliving it, knowing I would never forget it.

His tone grew with authority. "Open your eyes, sub."

Goose flesh raced across my skin as my womb pulsed with the memory of his touch, and I did exactly what he commanded.

Glancing at me, he turned into an underground parking garage of a high-rise. "How did it make you feel?"

I didn't know if he meant his words or the act, but it didn't matter. The answer was the same. "Like I was floating, Sir."

"Good." He pulled into a parking spot, cut the engine and cupped the back of my neck. Then he frightened me. "Remember that feeling the next time you get upset. Remember my touch." Abruptly releasing me, he opened his door and issued a stern order. "Wait."

I didn't even have time to catch my breath.

My door was open, my seat belt was undone, and he was taking me by the arm.

THIRTY-SEVEN

November

Taking her arm, forcing myself from the dominant I was to the trained military hacker I'd become, I scanned the garage and led her to the elevator.

Except I couldn't fucking flip the switch.

I couldn't compartmentalize.

Every step making me more pissed off, I hit the call button with the side of my fist and tried like hell to tamp down the jealous thoughts running rampant in my head. I didn't want to take her into AES headquarters. I didn't want any of those pricks setting their eyes on her. And I sure as fuck didn't want a single one of them speaking to her.

Rationally, this was the safest place I could bring her.

Zulu would've gotten Alpha back by now. Delta and Echo had been on-site when I'd briefly checked midflight from my laptop. Whiskey was coming in from an assignment. The entire building was wired with a system I'd installed, and no one was getting in or out without me knowing about it.

AES was safer than even my residence.

Because here I wouldn't be alone with her, and that was exactly what I needed while I got behind my screens and tracked that fucking asshole Check Mate.

Flinching when I hit the elevator call button but not saying anything, she dipped her head and stood exactly one step behind and to my left.

Possessive, I amended my instructions. "When I'm not walking, sub, stand at my side."

"Yes, Sir." She quickly took a step forward.

The doors opened, and I had to refrain from putting my hand on the back of her neck and walking her in. Knowing I needed to test her but not wanting to and, sure as fuck, not wanting to trigger her, but selfish enough to want it to happen outside the offices if it was going to happen again, I bit out a series of questions.

"What do you say if someone asks who you are?"

"No one, Sir." Her head lowered, she didn't look up.

"Where are you from?" Her hair hid the scar on her head, but in the fluorescent lights of the elevator, the GSW scars on her arm and her bruised face stood out like a fucking beacon. Add in her disheveled hair and wrinkled dress and it painted a picture I knew every prick at AES would assume was domestic violence.

"Nowhere, Sir."

The fucking irony was that she'd never looked more beautiful to me than how she was now. Scarred, tear-stained cheeks, and the part that only I knew—finger fucked until she'd sobbed—she was more than beautiful. She was mine. "Who am I?"

"Sir... *Sir*."

I wanted to fuck her right here in the elevator and walk her into AES with my seed dripping out of her tight cunt right before I downloaded the footage from the elevator security cam. Then I'd have something to watch over and over after I set her free, because no matter how much I thought she was mine, she wasn't. "Who are you?"

"Sub."

She was never mine to begin with. "Where are we?" No one owned a butterfly.

"I don't know, Sir."

"Good." Giving her one last word of praise as the doors opened, I spared her a glance. "Head down, obey my commands, speak only to me and only if spoken to. Understand?" Telling myself I was doing this to protect her, to keep her from being overwhelmed with questions, to prevent another seizure episode, to keep her identity secure, I fucking lied to myself.

I was doing it because this was who I was.

Controlling, exacting, and possessive.

"Yes, Sir."

I nodded once. "Follow me."

Walking into the command room ahead of her, I tipped my chin toward the corner behind my desk and issued a command. "Wait."

Alpha and Delta immediately looked up from one of the workstations, glancing from her to me.

She tried to hide it, but I saw her take a quick, furtive glance around the room.

"Head. Down. Corner," I ordered in quiet warning, enunciating each word of my command with lethal dominance.

She fluttered to position in the corner, but then she took even me by surprise.

She dropped.

Her bare knees hit the cold floor as her palms slapped against the specialized electrostatic dissipative resinous flooring, only partially breaking the impact of her rushed fall. It was the same reckless drop she'd done four years ago, one I knew would give her bruised knees and red palms. Marks that I didn't put on her body. Fury made my jaw tick.

Alpha's expression turned lethal. "November."

Frightened, underdressed for the air-conditioned command room, she flinched at Alpha's commanding tone.

"Floating," I reminded her with quiet command before glaring at Alpha and waking one of my monitors.

Not taking the fucking hint, Alpha threw me a warning look right back. "November, my office." Striding toward Butterfly, pulling a chair out, he gave her an order. "Sit here. We'll be right back."

Grabbing a new burner cell, I opened my laptop. "She won't listen to you."

Her head already dropped, clasping her hands in her lap the exact way I'd taught her, she sat back, resting her ass on the heels of her boots.

Delta crossed his arms. Alpha's hands went to his hips. They both fucking stared at her.

"Explain," Alpha demanded.

My dick perpetually hard since that kiss, I sat at my desk and logged into the network before waking two more monitors. Then I turned in my chair and spared Alpha a single, dead-locked glance. "Because I trained her."

"What?" Alpha asked, incredulous.

"Sub," Delta stated, turning back to his computer.

Alpha dropped his tone to a lethal calm that would've worked on anyone else. "This is a security breach. No non-personnel in the command room. Get her out of here."

"I have work to do."

Alpha fucking snapped. *"Now."*

Turning in my chair, I faced her. "What do you see, sub?"

She said nothing.

"Permission to speak," I added.

"My lap, Sir," she barely whispered in a voice I'd dreamt of for years.

"What else?" I demanded, wanting my hands on her.

"Whatever you tell me to see, Sir."

Right answer. "Where are you?" I demanded.

"With you, Sir, at your feet."

"Where, physically and geographically?" I specified.

She hesitated. I knew why. Alpha didn't.

"Answer," I ordered.

"Permission to speak freely, Sir."

"Not granted. Simple question. Answer."

NOVEMBER

Her hands pressed tighter together. "In a building, many floors up after an elevator ride, in a cold room, Sir."

Sick pride only reiterated why I needed to set this Butterfly free. "Geographically?"

"Warm, humid air scented of ocean."

"Ocean, what?" I asked lethally.

She flinched and quickly amended. "Warm, humid air scented of ocean, *Sir*."

I fucking inhaled. "Who are you with?"

"You, Sir."

I tested her memory from before the second seizure. "My name?"

"Sir."

I made a mental note to call Talerco back and have him get her set up with a specialist. "Who else are you with in this room?"

"No one, Sir."

"And if I give you permission to look up, observe your surroundings, then answer the question again, who would you see?"

Her voice dropped. "No one, Sir."

"Because?"

She didn't hesitate. "I am no one. I see no one, Sir."

I let her whisper hang in the air. Then I looked at Alpha and held his gaze for two fucking seconds before turning back to my laptop.

"November. My office. *Now*." Alpha walked out of the command room.

I stood. "Wait, sub." I lowered my voice so only she could hear. "Remember."

Delta glanced over his shoulder at her, then me. "Do I need to keep an eye on her?"

I ran backgrounds and tracked every damn employee at AES. I knew who the hell Delta was, and I knew what he was capable of. Meeting his gaze, I gave him the only warning he would get from me. "Look at her again and I will end you."

Not saying a damn word, Delta focused back on his computer.

I typed a command on my main machine, bringing up a tracking program I hadn't even told Conlon about, a program that was the main reason why we were here, and I entered a few keystrokes to start a search. Then I waited until the program kicked in before sparing her a glance. "Eyes on me, sub."

She looked up.

For a split second, I was struck all over again by the color of her teal eyes. "Good?"

She nodded.

"Words," I demanded, needing to hear her voice.

"Floating, Sir," she whispered.

I stared at her for a second. Her tone was off, not pre-seizure off, but definitely not okay. "Something you need to tell me?"

"No, Sir," she whispered even quieter.

Fuck. My comment to Delta. "Do you feel threatened by me?"

She shook her head but frowned and quickly stopped. "No, Sir."

"By anyone else here?"

She dropped her head, and I fucking clued in.

No memory, no resources, no one who knew her, she was fucking frightened of men, and rightfully so. The reality of what the past four years must have been like for her sinking in even further, it fucking destroyed me. I needed to get her out of here, STAT, but I also needed time for the program to work and to double-check Conlon's hacks.

Fuck.

Grabbing another burner from my desk, I quickly programming a number in. Then I squatted in front of her and grasped her chin, bringing her face up so I could see her eyes.

"You are not in any danger here. You are safe. That's a promise I'm making you, one you need to trust. No one is going to touch you, speak to you, or harass you. But if you feel threatened or frightened, you call me. The number's programmed." Taking

NOVEMBER

her wrist, I placed the cell in her hand. "You don't even have to speak. If I see the number come up, I'll be back here in less than thirty seconds. Understand?"

Biting her bottom lip, eyes welling, she nodded.

"Confirm, sub."

"Yes, Sir," she barely whispered. "But do you have to go?"

"Ten minutes, max, and I'll be back. Hold the phone the entire time."

She started to nod, then stopped and gave me her frightened whisper. "Yes, Sir."

I watched her for two more seconds. Then I quietly but firmly reprimanded her. "Don't lie to me again. If I ask if you're good, there is no wrong answer. There's only the truth. Are you good for now?"

"Ye—" Stopping herself, she amended. "I think so. Please hurry, Sir."

"Copy." Standing, I glanced toward Delta.

His back was to her.

I walked out of the room.

THIRTY-EIGHT

Atala

THE FRIGHTENINGLY LARGE, MUSCLED MAN WITH DARK HAIR WAITED to speak until after the door clicked shut with a whooshing sound.

"You need help, woman?"

I had only caught a glimpse of him when I'd entered the room, but it was enough. I would never engage with a man like him. Not here, not anywhere. Not even if I had been on a crew job and he had been the captain.

I would have avoided him at all cost.

Remaining perfectly still, somehow hoping it would make him leave me alone, I said nothing.

He shifted in his seat, and the faintest creak of leather sounded.

Anxiety prickled and goose flesh raced across my arms but not in the way when Sir touched me. This was wholly different.

"Are you cold?"

I was, but that wasn't why my flesh reacted. I had heard the menacing words Sir had said to him before he left the room. I didn't know if Sir had meant the threat as literal or figurative, but it'd terrified me either way. Except I foolishly wasn't afraid of Sir or what he clearly was capable of. It wasn't even that he had threatened to end the other man's life. It was every possible reason why he'd felt compelled to give that man the warning in the first place that was making my breath short and my mind panic.

And now that man was focusing his attention on me, and it was all I could do to stop myself from trying to figure out how to

NOVEMBER

use the cell phone in my hand that Sir had left me. But there was also one other reason I had not tried to use the phone.

A small push feathered against my mind.

It was the sound of the leather creaking from the chair.

No, it was more.

It was that sound combined with the fact that I was on my knees, which I still didn't know why I had dropped to my knees, but it had felt almost familiar, like it was expected or I knew it was expected.

But that sound of the leather chair creaking, being on my knees, the cold floor—something about it....

Before I could try to piece any of it together, the man spoke again.

His commanding voice was deep like Sir's, almost darker, but it was completely different. If voices had a shade, his was void of all color, whereas Sir's voice was midnight navy, like the depth of the Mediterranean on a moonless night. "You have permission to answer my question, sub. Are you cold?"

The language was right. His tone was full of authority, and my throat moved with a swallow as if I were preparing to speak, but this man was not Sir. Despite what my body may have been doing, my mind knew the difference.

I still said nothing.

"Mm-hmm." Ominous power vibrated from his throat. "And what if I put my jacket around those bare shoulders, sub?"

Fear sucked every ounce of cold air from my lungs, and it was all I could do not to react, but my hands, they tensed.

"Message received," the darkly frightening man stated calmly before his tone turned to something more than lethal dominance. "But listen very carefully, sub, because I'm only going to say this once." He paused. "If you need out from under November, you look me in the eye and blink twice." He repeated himself. "Blink twice, and I'll remove you from this situation, no questions asked, and he'll never be your master again."

Shock warred with a traitorous tremor of fear that shot up my spine and shook me from my battered knees to my broken mind.

Too late, I heard the creak of leather.

A creak that happened after my telltale tremor.

When he spoke again, his voice, his presence, they were much closer, even though I never heard his footsteps. "I saw that tremor, sub, and now we have a problem." With the gentlest of touch, two of his fingers slid under my chin and he tipped my head up.

I couldn't stop myself.

My gaze landed on his and the sharp, inhaled breath coming from my lungs was involuntary.

Penetrating green eyes looked down at me as he sat in Sir's chair. "I heard November, loud and clear. I'm not only looking at you, I'm touching you. His threat meant nothing to me, not when he said it, but especially not when I offered you an out and you trembled. So here's the new deal. Unless you give me a sign that this is consensual, I'm going to interpret that tremor as fear and make the decision for you. Nod once if you're here of your own free will." Releasing my chin, he leaned back.

November.

November.

He had called Sir "November." And now I was realizing the other man had called him November also, and suddenly I remembered it. I remembered the unusual name, but I didn't know how. I just knew it fit.

November. Cool like the month.

I wanted to think about that.

But the man in front of me was staring, and I had hesitated. It was only for a couple seconds, but it was enough for me to see the look in his eyes.

Quickly, I nodded once and dropped my head.

But the truth was I didn't know what was or what wasn't my own free will.

NOVEMBER

My body betrayed me around Sir, and my mind betrayed me always. I couldn't even tell if the name Sir had given me was real.

All I knew is that when a cool-eyed, angry-looking man walked into that bar and issued a single command, I had the first sense of belonging since I'd woken up in a decrepit barn with blood-soaked, rotting wounds.

So I'd followed him.

But when I'd gotten outside and he'd come at me, for a fraction of a second, I'd smelled it.

The amber, musk and cedar-scented wintery freshness of cool mountain air, swirled together like a memory, and suddenly, for that single moment, I hadn't been lost.

Then his dominant voice, followed by his unyielding commands, resonated through my very soul and I didn't think. Muscle memory or sheer desperation, or maybe it was simply the punishing fear and loneliness I'd been living with for so long had finally defeated me, so I'd followed him.

My mind didn't know why.

But my body did.

Even now, with Sir's scent lingering despite the large, dark-haired man in front of me who brought his own energy, his own scent, and his own very dominant but very different presence than Sir's, I knew I was supposed to be here with the man they'd called November.

His scent, his name, his eyes when he looked at me, it all somehow fit together. More than anything else in my life had fit together in the past four years, so I knelt.

But the green-eyed man wasn't finished.

His fingers sliding under my chin again, tipping my head up, he stared at me as he had before, but this time it looked more like he was studying me instead of being angry.

Not wanting him to touch me, I averted my gaze.

He dropped his hand. "GSWs, head and arm. Who're they from?"

Startled, I dropped the cell phone as my right hand moved to my upper left arm and my fingers covered the front part of the scar. But the back of my arm, the left side of my head, I couldn't do anything about them except slightly turn away from him. I didn't know what GSW meant, but I only got more upset because I didn't think anyone could see the scar on my head. Not when I wore my hair down.

Lowering my head even further, resting my chin on my left shoulder, I foolishly thought I would be spared from any further scrutiny if I simply didn't look at the green-eyed man. But the door to the room burst open with a heavy hand, and a new male voice was posturing.

"Delta, you dumb motherfucker. I thought you were supposed to be the smart one of us outside of Alpha, but sitting at November's desk is a surefire way to get your ass kicked. Not that I wouldn't like to see the fuck outta that match up, but—" The footfalls coming up behind me abruptly stopped as a distinctive sound of metal sliding echoed. Then the new man's voice dropped to a lethal growl. "You've got two goddamn seconds to start explaining why a beaten woman is at your feet, motherfucker."

Hearing that sound, it was instant.

The slide, the slight click of metal, fear clawed at every single one of my senses, robbing me of all breath. Pain shot through my head and spidered down to my arm before crawling across my skin like a million little needles puncturing me everywhere.

I flinched, then cowered, and I was there.

Dizzy, breathless, I crossed my arms tight around myself.

The man he'd called Delta pushed back in Sir's chair and stood. "Not mine. She's November's, and you're scaring her." Retreating, I saw his heavy boots cross the room.

"What. *The fuck?*" The new man muttered a string of words in a different language as his boots, equally heavy, appeared in my line of vision before he squatted in front of me and shoved a huge gun into a holder on his belt with his heavily tattooed arm and hand. "November do this to you, sweetheart?"

All I could think about was that sound.

That metal sound.

My ears began to ring.

My body started to shake.

"Hey, hey, hey, sweetheart, I'm not gonna hurt you."

My vision flickered.

Tattooed arms reached for me.

"Motherfucker."

I was drowning.

THIRTY-NINE

November

WALKING TOWARD ALPHA'S CORNER OFFICE, I PAUSED IN THE hall and pulled out my new cell to call Conlon.

He answered on the first ring without a trace of his usual mocking banter. "November?"

"Affirmative. Sitrep."

"Jesus fucking Christ, Rhys. That site, the timeline? *Fuck.* Seventeen years? This prick Check Mate even hacked you at Cyber Command. And for the record, *Cyber Command*? No wonder you're a goddamn genius. Not to mention Bosnia. I half thought Zulu was bullshitting me when he mentioned hell rained down on that mission."

Ignoring his comments, already regretting giving him access to the site where I kept every piece of intel I had on Check Mate and the events surrounding it, I asked what I needed to know. "Flight status?"

"Right, right, the plane's down, and I already made the call to your contact. He said he's on it. As far as the FAA is concerned, you and the G60 are at the bottom of the Mediterranean. But fuck, does Alpha know about any of this? Does the Air Force? Hell, does Alpha know yet you sank one of his fleet? Metaphorically speaking, of course, but... Christ."

"Alpha will be read in on what he needs to know. Everything else stays buried. If there's a leak, I'll know where it came from and I'll eliminate the problem. Understand?" It wasn't a threat. It was a promise.

NOVEMBER

"Right." He half-chuckled. "Got it. Don't fuck with you, and perjury over treason is my new mantra."

I glanced at my watch. "Hotel in D.C. swept?"

"Affirmative."

"What'd Blade find?"

"After I combed security footage and found a kid at the exact location and time stamp your software came up with, I ran facial rec and got a hit. Johnston, Mark. Blade ran him down. He's a college kid who took an anonymous job posting from a gamer forum four years ago for a thousand bucks. Instructions were brief. Buy a burner, wait, one day he'd have to send a two-word text to a TBD number, then dump the burner, said number being provided at a future date. And you guessed it, those two words are synonymous with your favorite stalker hacker. The kid also told Blade he'd almost forgotten about the job because it'd been so long. Then he saw a post in the forums earlier today, sent the text, and dumped the burner in a trash can outside his dorm. Blade retrieved the cell in case you want it. I'm tracing the gamer tag of the contact that posted the job and sent the instructions, but it's bouncing all over the fucking place."

"You won't be able to trace it." Not with his software. But I could. "Send me the gamer tag and IP address."

"Copy. You want it sent to your personal setup or work?"

"Command room. I'm at headquarters now."

"Done."

"Did you chase the thousand-dollar payoff Johnston said he received?"

"No, I'll run it down now."

"I'll do it in a few minutes. Send me everything you have on Johnston." I started walking. "I'm heading into Alpha's office now. Then I'll be behind my screens for ten, fifteen minutes. After that, I'm getting her out of here and going dark for a few days. You'll need to cover for me at AES."

"Copy that, but wait." Conlon hesitated. "The kid isn't all that I found."

"Meaning?" I glanced at my watch again. I'd told Butterfly ten minutes. This conversation was eating up too much time.

"Right." Conlon exhaled. "Okay, I'm just going to ask. Your notes indicate a fifth terrorist was picked up from a sailboat in the harbor, but then the trail and your notes on it end there. Did you run down military satellite imagery from around the time the terrorist cell boarded the boat in Havana Bay?"

"No." I couldn't. "I attained that intel right before we were taken hostage, and I left the service immediately after Bosnia. It's irrelevant now anyway and not worth running." He'd know what the risk was for hacking that level of military security to access those satellites. "That fifth man, who I'm assuming is Check Mate, was smart enough not to get caught on any surveillance. Satellite imagery won't make a difference."

Conlon paused. "I have a contact who's a military intelligence officer. I made a call."

I fucking froze. Then rage hit. "You *what?*"

"This isn't going to come back on you or the woman, I promise. My connection was able to pull the sat images—"

"Do you fucking know what you've done?" *Goddamn it.* I knew, *I knew*, I shouldn't have involved anyone. This was why I operated solo. This was exactly why I never should've fucking brought him in.

"It was secure," he argued.

The second he'd made that call, nothing was secure. My anonymity was gone. Her life was now in danger from not only Check Mate but every fucking government agency the U.S. had. Fuck, *fuck*. "No, it goddamn wasn't secure."

"It's a trusted source," Conlon kept justifying. "We needed to see those sat images."

Arrogant, ignorant and fucking blind to the facts, he hadn't stopped for one goddamn second to look at the reality of this. The

NOVEMBER

only person who'd inquire about that op and time frame now, after all these years, was me. And if I was asking, there was a reason. Which meant Cyber Com was already alerted. FUCK.

"There is no goddamn 'we.' You're off this. *Now.*" Putting him on speaker, I pulled up a preprogrammed command I had ready for this exact worst-case scenario, and I hit the fucking key to wipe the entire second dark web site I'd sent him to. Then I bit out orders. "Disengage Blade, get rid of the burner he found, and destroy the machine you used." I took him off speaker. "Never fucking speak of this again. You hear me?"

Pause.

"*Conlon,*" I barked.

"I found a lead."

About to fucking lose it, I gripped the cell. "What lead?"

"You missed something in Cuba."

I didn't miss a goddamn thing. "No, I didn't."

"Right." Conlon inhaled, then tempered his delivery. "You look at data. I look at the story."

"You didn't look at anything except your own goddamn ego."

"Right." Dismissing the insult, he kept fucking talking. "You're a trained hacker with skills we both know I'll never be able to touch. You unearth and collect facts, then put the literal millions of pieces of intel together, and you do it faster than should be humanly possible. I don't have that skill set, so I come at it from another angle. This is me seeing another angle, and I want to check on a hunch. I apologize for not reading you in before I called my contact, but what's done is done. I know the woman's alive, and her facial rec is on every terrorist watch list the U.S. has. While they're not actively looking for her, the fact is she entered the U.S. today with a passport that has her picture, and if I found that with a few keystrokes, so can the authorities. Her clock's ticking, and we both know the risks associated with attempting to hack that terrorist watch list, which would net temporary results at best. And the alphabet soup agencies aren't going to do a damn thing to remove her unless they have substantiated evidence of no wrongdoing. Bottom line, you need proof, and I have a hunch. The way I see it, you've got nothing to lose in letting me run this down. Ten, twelve hours. If I'm wrong, no one's the wiser. If I'm right, you have a chance to end this for her. Which I'm assuming, from everything I read and everything you had me do tonight, is your end game."

I wanted to kill him.

But he was right, and I was already putting those fucking pieces together that he mentioned. Cuba was less than an hour flight from here, which meant he wasn't chasing a lead in Cuba. He was going somewhere near Bosnia. "Where exactly are you going that you need ten hours?"

"Would you tell me if the situation was reversed?"

No. "Yes."

"Right." He chuckled without humor. "Since you already brought in Romeo, I'm using him, and before you ask, everything's off the books. He's secured a plane that won't trace back to us or AES, and I'll be in touch in twelve hours or less."

"You have ten." Fucking livid, I hung up and strode into Alpha's office.

Arms crossed, leaning on his desk, Alpha stared me down as I entered. His unreadable, locked expression no different than the first time I met him when he and his team breached that fucking compound in Bosnia, I had to remind myself it was why I'd come to work for him. Geared up in a full combat loadout or wearing a custom suit, Adam "Alpha" Trefor was always the same. A warrior first, man second. He was a leader, and he was always ten steps ahead.

"Is it her?" he asked.

Giving him plausible deniability, I said nothing.

"Explain," he ordered.

Beyond fucking agitated with this bullshit, needing to get back to her, I didn't remind Alpha I'd never called him out on any of his decisions, operationally or personally. I shouldn't have to explain mine.

I didn't say a damn thing.

"This is a two-way street," he stated. "You know my dealings, all of them. I've trusted you with that intel in case something happens to me. Until now, I've never had reason to question that trust. But when you bring a terrified, battered woman into my command room and make her kneel at your feet, I'm done respecting your boundaries. Start talking or walk. You of all people never bring problems into this office."

My jaw ticked. "She's not a problem."

Alpha dropped the battered woman play and showed his real hand. "I captured an image of her from our security cameras and ran it. She's on the terrorist watch list, and there's a scar from a gunshot wound on her arm. I'm betting there's also a scar on the side of her head." Alpha paused to see if I'd say anything.

I didn't.

He continued. "AES's entire business model is based on high risk. Risks no one else is willing to take. But we don't bring that risk to our doorstep and walk them into the building. We also don't stage a catastrophic crash of one of our Gulfstreams into the fucking Mediterranean with you on board and enlist the Hellenic Coast Guard to cover it up before stashing the plane at Roark's. Not without good reason. So I'm going to ask one more time. Is it her? And if so, who else knows she's alive besides me, Conlon, Roark, Echo and Delta?"

I didn't have time to answer.

Carrying an unconscious Butterfly, Echo kicked open Alpha's office door, strode to the couch and set her down.

Before I could get to her or ask what the fuck he'd done, Echo turned on me.

"This is for fucking her face up, motherfucker." His fist slammed into the ride side my face with the precision and force of a trained Navy SEAL.

Guilt hitting with a force harder than Echo's blow, I didn't block him. I didn't even sidestep as he swung again.

"These are for her goddamn gunshot wounds." His second punch stuck the left side of my head, immediately followed by another aimed at my arm.

Tasting blood, reeling back, I stumbled, but I didn't fall. I took the goddamn hits.

"*Enough,*" Alpha barked.

Ignoring him, Echo landed a fourth punch right below my sternum. "And that, *motherfucker*, is for doing whatever the fuck you did to her to make her so fucking scared she passed the fuck out."

I doubled over. Echo drew his 9mm. The barrel hit my forehead, and I palmed my Glock.

Then I was upright, my aim squarely between his eyes. "You fucking touch her again, unconscious or not, you're a dead man."

"You first, motherfucker. I'm not the one hitting women."

"I didn't goddamn hit her." But I may as well have.

"Echo, November, stand down," Alpha ordered.

Glaring at each other, neither of us moved.

Alpha snapped. "*I said, stand down.*"

"Sir?" a broken butterfly whispered.

Echo dropped his aim. I holstered my Glock. All of us turned to look at her.

Terrified teal-blue eyes met my gaze.

I didn't hesitate.

I picked up my butterfly.

FORTY

Atala

I HEARD YELLING, AND MY EYES OPENED.

Then I was panicking worse than I ever had before.

The tattooed man punched Sir, and as Sir doubled over, faster than I could blink, he pulled a gun and pressing it against Sir's temple.

Bleeding from his nose and lip as if he'd also been punched in the face, Sir pulled his own gun from the small of his back and immediately came upright, his aim directly going to the tattooed man's forehead.

I didn't care that Sir was pointing a gun at the tattooed man or that he looked ready to kill or that he and the tattooed man and the man from the cold room were all arguing and barking orders.

All I saw was the gun pointed at Sir's head, and I couldn't breathe. "Sir?"

At the sound of my voice, the tattooed man lowered his arm, Sir tucked his gun somewhere behind his back, and all three men turned to look at me.

For one heartbeat, I saw pain in Sir's eyes.

Then he masked it and was at my side in two paces, reaching for me.

In the next moment, he picked me up.

One arm under my legs, another behind my back, he brought me to his chest and turned toward the door.

Glaring at Sir, the tattooed man opened the glass office door, but he didn't speak.

None of them spoke.

Holding me tight, Sir walked out of the office and down the hall.

Then his lips were against my forehead and his deeply quiet voice was washing over me. "You're okay, Butterfly. I got you. You're okay."

Tucking my head against his chest, I dared to brush my thumb over the blood trailing down the side of his mouth. "You're hurt, Sir."

"I'm fine." He shouldered his way through a door and walked us into a bathroom. "What did Echo say to you?" He carefully set me on the counter next to the sink.

"Echo?" I watched the muscles in his arms as reached for a bunch of paper towels.

"The man with the tattoos. He's the one who carried you into Alpha's office." Turning on the tap, he soaked the paper towels, then squeezed them out.

"Alpha is the man who left the other room before you did, Sir?"

"Yes." Stepping between my legs, he pressed the cold, wet paper towels to my forehead and gently wiped. Then he pressed them to the right side of my face despite the fact that he was the one who was bleeding. "You didn't call me."

"The phone." *Oh God.* "I…" I had to stop and think about what had happened to it. "I dropped it. I'm sorry, Sir." I grasped his wrist. "I should be helping you, Sir."

"I take care of myself, sub." Gently taking my hand off him, his voice deceptively calm, his gaze searched my face as he wiped across my cheeks, but he didn't look at my eyes. "Were you shaking when Echo picked you up?"

Shame crested the height of my embarrassment. The bad thing had happened again. But it'd felt like it'd only been for a moment, because one second I was in the cold room and the next I was in that office. I could remember everything right before and right after, so it hadn't been anything like previous times, but it'd still happened, and I didn't want Sir angry with me. "Yes, I think so," I whispered. "I'm sorry, Sir."

This time, his eyes did meet mine. "What did I say about apologizing to me?"

"Not to do it, Sir."

"That's correct." He reached over and rewet the paper towels as he clipped out a single word. "Conversation." He shut the water off and glanced in the mirror as he quickly cleaned the blood from below his nose and the side of his mouth. "Tell me what Echo said to upset you."

Everything that had happened in the cold room came back. "It wasn't something he said."

For a single moment, every muscle on Sir's body went stiff. Then he tossed the soiled paper towels in the trash, braced his hands on the counter on either side of my hips and looked at me with barely concealed anger. His voice low and threatening, he spoke each word as if they were their own question. "Did he touch you before he picked you up?"

I was shaking my head before he finished asking. "No. It was a sound."

Sir inhaled. "What sound?"

I hesitated.

"What sound, Butterfly?" he demanded.

"The sound of Echo's gun," I whispered, feeling as if I were saying something very, very bad.

"I didn't hear a weapon discharge. Which sound, specifically?"

My voice came even quieter. "The metal sliding sound. When he pulled it out of its holder and put it back."

Sir's nostrils flared. "Echo drew his weapon on you?"

"Not on me, the other man in the cold room."

"Delta. The command room. Why?"

"He-he thought Delta had hurt me."

Sir studied me for half a second. Then he asked the question I was hoping he wouldn't. "What was Delta doing?"

I couldn't stop it. Tears welled. "Please don't be mad at me."

All at once, his eyes closed and his chest rose with a deep inhale. Then he looked back at me and took the sides of my face in his hands. "I am not now, nor will I ever be angry with you. I'm livid at Delta and Echo, but not at you, Butterfly. Do you understand me?"

Tears slipped down my face. "Then why do you only want to be around me for seventy-two hours?"

His expression shut down. "That's not because of you," he answered vaguely.

"I don't understand."

"You will." He dropped his hands from my face. "What did Delta do?"

My thoughts spun, and I didn't believe him. It was because of me. It had to be. Why else was he closing off his expression and letting go of me? "Delta spoke to me," I admitted.

The sides of his face starting to discolor with bruises, his jaw muscles shifted. "What did he say to you?"

I dropped my gaze. "That he would take me away from you if I needed him to."

Quiet, controlled, Sir spoke. "Look at me, Butterfly."

I met his eyes, but instead of the anger I was expecting, I saw an even more closed-off expression, one that was so locked down it was void of any emotion. Then he said the last thing I was expecting.

"Delta wasn't wrong to say that to you."

Fear flooded my veins. "But you told him not to talk to me."

"That was on me."

My mouth opened then closed. I didn't understand what was happening. I didn't understand where the man from the airplane had gone. It was as if I was staring at a completely different person.

"Speak freely," he demanded.

"I don't understand." I knew there were two sides to him. I'd seen them. But I hadn't seen this version of him yet, and it was frightening me.

Before he could say anything else, the door to the restroom opened and a man wearing a black T-shirt and black cargo pants walked in. With a vacant look in his eyes, he nodded at Sir and set a cell phone on the counter.

Not stepping away from me, not moving at all, Sir glanced at the man. "You were supposed to destroy that."

"You would've regretted it." His voice as hushed as a shadow, it barely moved through the air as he reached in his pocket and placed a very small, thin square on top of the phone. "And I don't take orders from anyone except the source. Lifted fingerprints and ran them. Emailed you the results. You're going to want to look at them."

"Did you read Conlon in on any of this?"

"No." He turned to leave.

"Blade," Sir called after him.

The man named after a knife glanced over his shoulder and met Sir's gaze with a raised eyebrow.

"You on assignment?" Sir asked.

"Not if you need me." Without further comment, he walked out of the bathroom, never having looked at me once.

Sir pocketed the phone and the small square thing. Then he reached for me. "Time to move."

Suddenly uncomfortable with him picking me up, not wanting to see the look in his eyes, I focused on the floor as I leaned away from him. "I can walk, Sir."

For a brief moment, he didn't move. He didn't speak.

Then he stepped back and turned toward the door.

Pushing off the counter, I glanced at the mirror.

Black hair, teal eyes, messy hair, a wrinkled blue dress and a bruise on the right side of my face I didn't remember getting.

I stared at a stranger.

Then I followed another stranger out of the restroom.

FORTY-ONE

November

I FLIPPED THE SWITCH TO MY MILITARY TRAINING.
I fucking had to.
If I saw her suffer one more of those episodes, I'd no longer be a highly trained Cyberspace Operations Officer. I'd be a possessive-as-hell dominant, picking my sub up and walking off the goddamn grid as I condemned her to a life not only on the run but one where my very presence fucking triggered her PTSD.

Focusing up, not touching her, I walked out of the bathroom. I heard her on my six. I smelled her. I fucking felt her.

But I didn't acknowledge her.

Swiping my access card to get into the command room, I held the door for her to enter, but I still didn't look back. Going to my desk, I moved the chair back with my boot and issued an order. "Sit."

Not checking to see if she obeyed, ignoring Delta at the other end of the room and the cell phone that I'd given her that was now next to my keyboard, I leaned over my desk. Pulling up the email Blade sent, I read it. Then I fucking read it again.

The college kid wasn't just any kid.

He wasn't even Mark Johnston. Before seventeen years ago, Mark Johnston didn't exist.

But his fingerprints did.

Russian. Matvey Petrov. The son of Elizaveta Petrov. Both granted asylum seventeen years ago.

Toggling screens, I pulled up Conlon's intel. Then I accessed my software program, started two new searches and began pulling at the threads.

Ten minutes later, I had almost all the pieces and I knew where Conlon was going. Now all I needed was confirmation from him and to follow my own damn hunch.

Scrubbing my searches, I shut down my machines and pulled out my cell to send a text to Talerco. Turning to lean on my desk and get eyes on her, I scanned the length of her as she sat in my chair, head down, hands in her lap.

She didn't look up.

I typed the text.

> Me: *It's November. She had another episode. I didn't see it. She was with Echo, but it seemed to not have lasted as long and she retained memory from directly before the event, but she has no memory of the episode she had on the plane or meeting you. Is it safe to take her home and let her sleep or do I need to get her seen tonight?*

Talerco answered almost immediately.

> Talerco: *What's her current status?*
>
> Me: *She's sitting.*
>
> Talerco: *Calm?*
>
> Me: *Appears to be.*
>
> Talerco: *How many sedatives have you given her?*
>
> Me: *Just one before the flight back to Miami.*
>
> Talerco: *Break one in half, offer it to her when you get back to your place. I'll make some calls tomorrow and get her an appt with a specialist.*

I gave him full disclosure.

> Me: *She doesn't know I gave her one before the flight. I put it in her drink.*

Talerco: *JFC*

Me: *Offering doesn't seem like the right course of action at this point.*

Talerco: *Again, JFC. Did you try talking to her? Calmly like I told you to??*

Me: *About?*

Talerco: *Christ. I'm on my way over. Don't do shit till I get there. And by shit, I mean don't drug her or scare the fuck outta her. Thirty minutes. Try to be fucking normal for half an hour.*

Me: *Copy.*

Talerco: *Jesus. Agreeable Rhys. Now I'll be there in twenty-five minutes.*

Me: *Copy.*

Talerco: *Just fucking stop. OMW*

Pocketing my cell then grabbing hers, I held it out to her as I picked up my work laptop. "We're ready to go, sub."

Her gaze cut from the phone to me, but she didn't take it and she didn't get up.

I fought from touching her. "Permission to speak."

"Do I need the phone, Sir?" she asked so damn quietly.

I read her anxiety and the meaning behind the question. "No." I pocketed her cell. "Come."

Exhaling, she stood and followed me out of the command room and into the elevator. Not speaking, not looking anywhere except at her own damn feet, she kept to my left, once pace behind, hands clasped in front of her.

I knew she was stressed.

I knew she was afraid.

I could fucking taste it, and I wanted to put my hands on her. I wanted to stop whatever thoughts she had that were drowning her innocence in fear, and I wanted to replace them with my dominance.

But butterflies weren't made to be caged, and I'd already broken one of her wings.

The raised flesh of the gunshot wounds on her arm stood out in stark relief under the harsh lights of the elevator, reminding me of who I was and what I'd done.

Reminding me why this teal-eyed, exquisite creature had no memory.

A terrorist cell may have boarded her boat, but I was the one who'd dissected every part of her life, robbed her of all privacy and taken her from everything she'd known.

Distracted, not checking the building's security cams from my cell before the elevator hit the garage level, I was taken off guard when the doors slid open.

Leaning against a support pillar, Blade tipped his chin at me but then scanned the garage like I should've already done.

"You forget something?" Stepping in front of her, blocking her from his sight, I held my hand down and back, giving her a silent signal to wait and stay behind me.

Two small hands wrapped around my wrist and gripped tight.

Blade pushed off the column. "No."

"Alpha send you?" Blade was a chameleon. He was also lethal. Alpha would send him in whenever we needed backup that couldn't be spotted. From behind my screens, I could track Blade, but in the field, no one ever saw him.

Blade scanned the garage again. "Haven't spoken to him." He glanced purposely at the company Range Rover I'd driven from Roark's earlier. "Sometimes overwatch needs a sheepdog outside the wire." His gaze briefly cut to mine. "Not like you to miss me on security cams." He paused. "Twice." His point made, he turned to leave. "Got your six." Moving silently in the opposite direction from the line of AES company vehicles, he disappeared around the elevator bank.

Pulling out my cell phone, I brought up the security feeds for the building, toggled to the cameras covering the garage and scanned to see which vehicle he got in. When I saw it was one of his trucks with tinted-out windows, I pocketed my cell and gave Butterfly my attention. "Good?"

She glanced after Blade, then realized she was still holding on to me and quickly let go. "Yes, Sir."

Shoving down my dominance, I made it as far as the damn Range Rover.

Then I was buckling her in, grasping her chin and staring at the fear in her eyes. About to order her not to be afraid of a goddamn thing when she was in my presence, I caught myself.

Inhaling to temper my shit, I dropped my hand and my voice and told her what she needed to hear. "You're safe."

A wild butterfly looked into my eyes. "I don't know which side of you is telling me that."

I fucking stared at her for five seconds before I recovered. "There's only one of me."

She lowered her gaze.

Then she did what no one else ever had.

"I think there is the side of you that calls me sub and the side that calls me Butterfly, and I think they are not the same." Her teal eyes met mine. "I think the two sides are at odds."

She fucking saw me.

FORTY-TWO

Atala

SAYING NOTHING, HE CLOSED MY DOOR, GOT BEHIND THE WHEEL AND started the SUV.

Daring to glance at him as he pulled the vehicle out of the garage and into the night, I couldn't tell if he was angry or displeased with me, and I wasn't sure I would ever know.

I shouldn't have said what I did.

But I couldn't tell if he was giving me the truth or what he thought I wanted to hear, and I had so many questions stacking up, I wasn't even sure it was worth asking anymore, so I'd told him what I thought instead.

Not that it had mattered.

No matter what side of him I was encountering, this man kept most all of his thoughts to himself. I didn't even know if I could trust that he would tell me what he knew when his three-day clock ran down to nothing.

Suddenly exhausted, I turned toward the window and the passing lights of a city more brightly colored than any other I had ever seen, even under the shadow of night. Leaning my head against the cool glass, I felt the bruise on my face, but before I could wonder again how I'd gotten it, his voice was filling the silent interior of the car.

"Atala."

Sharp and quick and not a question but a statement, I answered anyway, except I didn't use Sir because his tone and how he said my name told me I wasn't speaking to Sir. "Yes?"

I heard the roughness of an almost angry-sounding, inhaled breath before he gave me an order. "Speak."

I didn't know how he always seemed to know when I was lost in my own thoughts, but he did, and since he was giving me the opportunity, I danced around a question. "The other men called you November."

He turned a corner and drove onto a bridge. "It's my call sign at work."

"But not your real name." Watching the moonlight sprinkle across the water and the boats littered about, I carefully didn't phrase my response as a question.

"No."

I waited.

He gave me the opening. "Are you asking my name, Butterfly?"

I turned to look at him. "I am."

His gaze intently focused on the road, the streetlights making a pattern on his face, the vehicle our cocoon, he told me what I had been desperate to know. "Nathan."

Nathan.

I tasted his name, I said it in my mind, and I tried to make it fit. But Nathan wasn't November. It wasn't cool and elusive and dangerous if you turned your back on it. It didn't seem right, and I couldn't remember it. "Did I know that before?"

"No."

Maybe I had called him November or by his surname. "No last name?"

He turned off the street and drove into another underground parking garage. "I have one I use."

One he used? I dared to ask. "What is it?"

He pulled into a parking spot, cut the engine and turned in his seat to look at me.

Then his deep, haunted voice didn't touch my memory, but it cut through my heart. "Rhys. Nathan Rhys."

FORTY-THREE

November

STARING AT MY BIGGEST MISTAKE, THE GHOST OF HER VOICE PLAYING in my head same as it had every day for four years, I told her. "Rhys. Nathan Rhys."

Right here, yes, sir.

"Nathan Rhys," she repeated quietly.

Not telling her she was the first woman I'd ever slept with who knew my real first name, I killed the engine. "Wait." Grabbing her leather jacket and our bags before getting out of the vehicle and pulling out my cell, I checked the security feeds for both the building and my place for any breaches. Then I ran a quick search for any attempted hacks.

All clear.

I opened her door.

Then I saw she'd already released her seat belt, and my jaw ticked at the simple act of dominance she'd unwittingly taken from me.

Her innocent gaze quickly darted to my eyes before she dipped her head. "I'm sorry, did I do something wrong, Sir?"

Jesus, I wanted to break her of that habit. But maybe I was the one who needed fucking breaking. Maybe I needed to give her my damn limits.

Cupping her cheek before I talked myself out of it, I tilted her face up and did precisely that. "We've already discussed this, but you're still apologizing to me, so I'm going to make this perfectly clear. As far as you and I are concerned, there are exactly two things that would warrant an apology. The first is harming yourself or purposely putting yourself in harm's way. The second is fucking another man, which I guarantee will never happen because I would kill him on sight. Do you understand?"

Her eyes wide, she nodded.

"Words, Butterfly."

"Yes, Sir."

The soft submissiveness of her voice and demeanor going straight to my dick, I asked a question I should've asked up front. "Are you going to harm yourself, purposefully or otherwise?"

Her head was shaking before I finished speaking. "No, Sir."

"Good. Then we won't have any problems. Next time I'll undo your seat belt. Come." I held my hand out for her. "A colleague is meeting us upstairs." I helped her out of the SUV.

She waited till I had the door closed before she spoke in a hushed whisper. "Would you really do that… kill someone because of me?"

I already had, and I was going to do it again. "Yes."

She stopped walking and looked up at me.

I scanned the garage, but then I gave her my attention.

Her eyes darted between mine. "Do you always carry a gun? Are you a criminal?"

Not hesitating, telling myself I was aiming to scare her away, I answered, but in truth I was testing her. "Yes, and yes."

She slowly nodded like she knew the first thing about what I was capable of. "You don't seem bad."

I wanted my hands on her. I wanted to show her exactly how fucking bad I was, but every time I thought of sinking inside her, the very next second I was watching her die. Telling myself for the hundredth fucking time not to touch this woman, I did it anyway. "Perception is misleading." I snaked my hand under her hair and palmed the back of her neck because I was tired of fighting it. "Let's get you upstairs."

Leaning into my hold, not saying anything else, we rode the

elevator in silence. Then I led her into what I referred to as my work penthouse. The place I came to sleep when I wasn't at AES or out on assignment.

Two paces inside, she halted. "You... live here?" She looked from the floor-to-ceiling view of the ocean to the designer furniture that'd come with the place before glancing at the kitchen and down a hall that led to three bedrooms and an office.

A new wave of guilt hit me in the chest. "Yes."

I hadn't asked the details of where she'd been for the past for years because part of me selfishly didn't want to know. Crew quarters were better than dozens of other scenarios she could've wound up in, but living in a bunk on a boat wasn't an eight-figure penthouse in Miami Beach with proper security. Compartmentalizing, I dumped our bags on the dining table. "Talon Talerco will be here in a minute. Then I'll make us food. What do you eat?"

"I'm not hungry, thank you. Who is Talon?"

I fought not to show a reaction. "He's a colleague and a former military combat medic. It's been a long day. You need to eat. Food preferences?"

Nervous tension stiffened her entire body, and she clasped her hands. "I, um, just... fish or rice or oatmeal." She looked at me with alarm. "Medic?"

"Yes, medic." *Fish, rice, and oatmeal?* Her expression when she drank the Coke on the plane suddenly coming back, I put pieces together that were painting an alarming picture. "What do you eat besides seafood, rice and oatmeal, Atala?"

"Coffee?"

Fucking coffee. As food. "What else?"

Her hands twisted. "Water." She looked away. "Some fruit if it's plain."

"Eyes on me," I demanded.

Her gaze immediately came back to mine, but she held her hands tight

I fucking asked. "Do you have a problem eating food?"

"My stomach," she blurted.

"Explain."

Like a torrent, she let loose, giving me her fear and anxiety wrapped around intel I never considered. "It's just... I don't know what I like. I can't remember what I eat. And on the yachts, they had so many foods, but everything was either too spicy or had so many ingredients it hurt my stomach or burned my throat, and I just... I couldn't eat it. But I like food. I like grilled fish. I like rice. I like to drink coffee when I watch the sunrise, but I don't like any of those heavy creams or flavors people put in coffee. They taste too sweet or make my stomach hurt. I like it just plain. Mostly, I like the smell. Coffee with a sunrise is... comforting. And I like oatmeal. It's nice. It feels warm when you eat it. I liked when one of the chefs on one of the yachts would put cinnamon and a brown-colored sugar in it. Sometimes bananas or apples. But I can't remember what else I ate... before, and I don't know what foods will make me feel sick. So I just, I eat plain."

Fish, rice, oatmeal, bananas. All things she would've eaten growing up how she did, but dairy, meats, and fresh vegetables would've been expensive and not easily accessible. "Understood. I'll make something plain to eat in a few." Waking up my home machines that took up half my dining table because I'd never bothered setting up a home office here, I tipped my chin at her backpack and leather jacket. "Grab your passports and credit cards. I'll be back in thirty seconds."

Striding down the hall, I grabbed what I needed out of my safe and came back to the main living area as she was zipping up the hidden pocket in her jacket.

Either trusting or tired, she didn't ask questions. She simply handed over what I'd asked for.

Working quickly before Talerco showed up, I secured the burned passports and credit cards in my bag to dispose of later and angled my middle screen. "Step over here, behind the monitor, and face me."

NOVEMBER

She did as I asked.

I took her picture, fed it into my software, turned on my specialized printer and made her a new passport. Then I pulled the trigger on a full ID setup I'd put in place for her years ago and was opening a new bank account and having a credit card overnighted when my cell pinged with an alert for the security system.

I glanced at the screen. "Talerco's here." I was headed toward the door before I realized she hadn't moved. "Atala?"

When she lifted her head and I saw how damn lost she looked, I got fucking hard. That's how my sick head worked. That's what this woman did to me. What she'd always done to me, except now the desire to dominate her, to fuck her so hard she'd feel me for days, was layered with so much damn guilt I didn't know who the hell I was.

But I knew I couldn't keep her in the dark anymore.

She was struggling to understand, and I was being an asshole, but fuck, those seizures, PTSD or not, three in one day was too damn much. Hell, one was too many. I couldn't be responsible for doing that to her, but Jesus I wanted to touch her.

Fate fucking with me, a knock sounded on the front door, and I was staring down the past all over again.

Losing control, running out of time with her, I stood on a precipice again.

Conlon on the move, the window closing on tracking Check Mate, Talerco waiting—I had to do the right damn thing, but fuck. *Fuck.*

The knock came again. "Hacker Boy! Don't make me walk in on you two lovebirds."

My hands fisted, and I hesitated. "Tell me no, Atala."

My teal-eyed butterfly disobeyed me with a pained whisper. "I can't."

Two words sending me over the edge, I moved.

Fisting her hair, tilting her head back, I slammed my mouth over hers and demanded entrance.

Her lips parted, and I sank my tongue in.

But I didn't just kiss her. Gripping her hip, pulling her against my raging hard-on, I consumed her.

For five fucking seconds, I let my dominance out.

Melting into me, submissively kissing me back, my Butterfly fluttered.

Then I broke the kiss and strode toward the front door.

FORTY-FOUR

Atala

HE TOLD ME HE WOULD KILL FOR ME. Then he took my passports and credit cards, kissed me like I was his last breath and strode with anger toward the front door of his extravagant penthouse that didn't have a single personal belonging except for his expensive computers.

A blond-haired man walked in with a mischievous grin and slapped Sir on the shoulder. "Lovebirds." He winked at him. "Knew it."

Low and threatening, Sir said the man's name. "Talerco."

He chuckled. "Nothin' doin', nothin' doin', Hacker Boy." Walking past Sir, the green-eyed man smiled at me. "Fancy meetin' you here, darlin'. How you feelin'?" Setting a big, black bag with a red cross stitched on it onto the table, he stopped a foot away and eyed me.

That's when it happened.

The scent of coconuts and beach struck me, and I sucked in a sharp breath. *Oh my God.* I remembered. "The plane. You were on the plane."

His smile softened. "There she is," he said almost affectionately. "Knew you couldn't forget me, Miss Atala." Casually taking my chin, he turned my head to look at my bruise. "I'm unforgettable, aren't I, darlin'?" He didn't wait for an answer. "Come have a seat on the couch for me." Releasing my chin, grabbing his bag again, he moved toward the sitting area of the penthouse.

I looked at Sir. His hands fisted and shoved in his pockets, he looked at me wearily.

"Come on, darlin'. I don't bite, promise. Just wanna check you out real quick, see how you're doin'. Then Hacker Boy over there can stop breathin' fire at me and go back to bein' his usual not-normal self. Sound good?" He set his bag on the coffee table.

Sir nodded once.

Trying to remember more than Talon's scent or that he was on the plane before I woke up with my head in Sir's lap, I went to the couch and sat.

Talon lowered his tall, muscular frame to the coffee table and sat facing me. "How you feelin'? Any dizziness? Headaches? What do you remember from the first time we met?"

I glanced at Sir.

He was staring at me like I was made of glass.

"It's okay, darlin'. Nothin' you say ain't gonna be anythin' me and Hacker Boy haven't heard already. Ain't that right, Rhys?"

"Yes," Sir answered.

"See?" Talon smiled as he reached for my wrist and held it with two fingers on one side, one on the other. "What do you remember, darlin'?"

"Just that I met you," I admitted.

"That's good," he said absently as his gaze drifted to the left side of my head. "You been feelin' dizzy? And headaches?" He released my wrist.

"Not right now."

"Good, darlin', that's good. You know why I'm here?"

Shame washed over me, and I dropped my head. "The bad thing. The…" I couldn't say it. "The bad thing that sometimes happens."

"Hey, hey, hey." He tipped my chin, but he didn't do it like Sir did. Using just his knuckle, being gentle, he lifted my head. "There ain't nothin' bad about you, and I want you to hear me when I say what I'm gonna say next. You listenin', darlin'?"

NOVEMBER

"Yes."

His accent fell away, and he spoke succinctly. "There's nothing wrong with you. Say it for me."

"There's nothing wrong with me," I whispered, desperately wanting to believe him.

His accent slid back into place as his voice quieted. "That's right, darlin', nothin' wrong. You are how you are, and for right now, all's how it should be." Dropping his hand, he leaned his arms on his legs. "So knowin' that, we're not gonna call it 'the bad thing' anymore. We're gonna give it a new name, and we're gonna call it '*time out*.' Just a little time out when you're feelin' like you need a break. But this new name comes with a new responsibility. Any time you're feelin' like you got a headache comin' on, like you need to take a break or like things might be feelin' a little stressful, you're gonna tell Rhys, and you're gonna tell yourself that you're just takin' a time out. That it's *okay* to take a time out. Then you go get horizontal, get yourself comfortable, and you take that time out without worryin'. You hear what I'm sayin'?"

I looked at Sir.

He didn't nod. He didn't move at all. He just stared.

Talon asked it another way. "You understand you're gonna give yourself permission to have a time out and that you'll be okay?"

"Yes." No.

"That wasn't too convincin', but I'll take it for now. Do you also understand that you don't need to apologize for it? That no one's gonna be mad or upset with you?"

I looked down at my lap. "I guess."

"Good, that's a start, and that's all I'm asking. But I got two more questions for you. You ready?"

I nodded.

"Can you look at me, darlin'?"

I did as he asked.

"Thank you, darlin'. Okay, question number one. You mind if I schedule a doctor appointment for you just so we can get an

X-ray of that wound on your head? Not because anythin's wrong. Just so we can get a picture of that pretty head of yours and see if maybe there's some kinda medicine that can help you with those headaches. I'm not sayin' that you necessarily need anythin', but we won't know unless we take that picture. That sound good to you?"

I remembered Sir's conditions. I also remembered his timeline and his promise. "When?"

"I'm not sure. Could be tomorrow, could be a couple weeks. Depends on how busy the doctor is. How 'bout I make the call in the mornin', set it all up, then let you know, sound good?"

I didn't want to, but if it would help me remember, I would do it. "All right."

"Good, darlin', thank you. Okay, last question, but it's two-part. Try and remember the last few times you had a time out. Were you feelin' a little panicked? Maybe short of breath? Your heart racin'? Feelin' like you needed to get up and get out of wherever you were? Maybe your ears even started ringin' or your vision started tunnelin'? Any of that sound familiar?"

I blinked. How did he know? "Yes," I admitted, embarrassed. "All of that."

He nodded sympathetically. "That's called a panic attack, darlin'. Most everyone has 'em. Never fun, but the good news is I've got somethin' to help all those symptoms. Small little pill called Xanax. Fast actin', makes you a little tired for four hours, but it stops that panicked feelin' and calms it right down. Would you like me to give you some of these pills so you can have them on hand in case you want to try one? Maybe take one the next time you feel a time out comin' on? See how it helps?"

"Will it help with my memory?"

"No, darlin', unfortunately it won't, but it'll relax you, and I think it'll give you some control, which might make you feel a little more secure about havin' time outs."

To be able to have some control over the bad thing, the time outs, when they happened? It sounded impossible, but I wanted that. I wanted it so badly, but I was embarrassed to say that in front of Sir.

As if reading my hesitation, Talon spoke up. "Ain't no shame in this, darlin'. We all take medicine at some point in our lives, and this isn't somethin' you need to feel bad about or worry that you'll need to take it the rest of your life, or any other negative thing you may be thinkin'. This'll just be a few pills to have on hand until I can get you an appointment with a doctor who's a specialist in this and deals with patients who have time outs all the time."

I couldn't stop myself. I glanced at Sir.

To my surprise, he nodded once.

Relief washed over me, and I glanced back at Talon. "Thank you, I would like that, please."

"You got it, darlin'." Talon reached in his bag and handed me a small bottle that had what looked like two dozen little pills in it. "All right, darlin'. Here's how they work. You feel a time out comin' on, feel free to take one pill, then go lie down. If you want to take one pill before bed, you can do that too. You can take up to three pills a day, one every four hours, but I don't want you takin' more than that. If you're feelin' like you need more, or if you feel like they're not doin' their job to calm those nerves down, and we haven't gotten you to your doc appointment yet, you let Rhys know and he'll call me. I'll be back here in a hot minute, and we'll figure out either a different dose or a different prescription and get you sorted out. I don't think you're gonna need that. I think these'll do you just fine, but wanted to let you know you have options. You have any questions?"

Clutching the bottle in my hands, just knowing I had them, even though I was frightened to try one, for the first time I felt a sense of hope. Maybe I wouldn't have to have the bad thing, the time out, happen for the rest of my life.

"No, and thank you very much," I said sincerely.

His smile was reserved. "You're quite welcome, darlin', and it was good seein' you again." Standing, he shouldered his black bag.

"I'll let Rhys know when I get that appointment scheduled. In the meantime, you call if you need anythin', all right?"

"Yes, thank you."

"Nothin' doin', darlin', nothin' doin'. Keep Hacker Boy in line for me." Smiling, he walked toward the door but paused to slap Sir on the shoulder again. "That's how it's done." He let himself out.

Sir waited until the door closed behind Talon. "Good?"

I wanted to weep with relief at the same time as I wanted to drown in shame. "Yes."

"You hesitated." His hands still in his pockets, he didn't come toward me or move at all.

"I'm fine, but I wouldn't mind a shower, Sir." Realizing how I slipped in and out of calling him Sir depending on his cues, or my need to feel as if I pleased him, I hadn't minded, but right now, I just needed a moment to think. I didn't know what was right or wrong. Talon made the pills seem normal. Sir had nodded. The bottle in my hands felt like hope, but I still needed a minute.

Sir tipped his chin toward the hall. "Bedroom at the end. Towels are in the linen closet. I'll let you know when food's ready." He turned toward the kitchen.

Picking up my backpack, I walked down the hall past three bedrooms before I entered the one on the end, and I immediately knew it was his.

It smelled like him.

It also had a different décor from the rest of the penthouse. Instead of whites and light gray and pale turquoise, this room was all dark grays, from the thick carpet to the bedding to the color on the walls. The bedroom was like the month of November, and even though I always preferred warm sun, I immediately loved it.

What I liked even more was the balcony with large, comfortable-looking lounge chairs, and I foolishly imagined myself sitting there, watching a sunrise with Sir while we drank coffee. Then I was desperately wondering if we had ever had a moment like that.

Lost in the fantasy of what could be, trying to remember what had been, clutching the bottle of pills, I was still standing at the large slider doors when I barely heard footfalls. A second later, his cool, masculine scent washed over my very being like both familiarity and a memory I couldn't reach.

Then his voice came, low and hushed, but deep and full of his dominance that was laced with authority. "What are you doing, Butterfly?"

Butterfly.

His tone as seductive as if he were calling me sub, my body instantly reacted. The sudden ache between my legs was so painful and needy, I was back on that plane, and I wanted to drop to my knees as badly as I wanted him to touch me again.

But my mind?

My mind was sending alarm bells so loud, I could almost taste copper because this wasn't the plane. This moment was in his bedroom, with his bed right behind us, and there wasn't a life raft in the world that could stop me from drowning in this man.

I already had.

Because in the next moment, the whisper left my mouth before I could stop myself from giving him my vulnerability. "Trying to remember, Sir."

The man named after a month as dark as this room did not respond.

He stepped up behind me, wrapped one arm around my waist and brought me back against the solid heat of his strength as if to protect me. Then his lips touched the bare skin of my shoulder right before they landed on the left side of my head. "Maybe you shouldn't."

Hurt crushed the very vulnerability I had given him. "Because that would be better?" For him?

He stared over my shoulder at the dark surf for a long moment. "If memory could be selective, I would choose that for you, Atala." Then he inhaled deep and stepped back, leaving me as cold as his name suggested. "Come. Food's ready."

FORTY-FIVE

November

WATCHING HER PICK AT HER FOOD LAST NIGHT AS IF FRIGHTENED to eat had been a new version of hell. But then she'd showered by herself and skittishly crawled into bed in nothing except a worn, thin tank top and those fucking plain underwear I wanted to rip off her. I'd lasted two seconds watching her huddle on the farthest edge of the mattress before I'd pulled her back to my chest and wrapped an arm around her.

Then she'd told me she needed a time out.

Fucking gutted, I'd grabbed her pills and gave her one.

She'd curled into a fetal position, whispered she was afraid of doctors, then fell asleep.

I spent the next four and a half hours blaming myself for every damn thing. Then my cell rang before dawn with a call from Talerco.

Now I was sitting in a fucking waiting room at a hospital where I'd been the last three hours while Talerco was with her who the fuck knew where and I'd been banished to the goddamn sideline.

I fucking got it.

Talerco didn't trigger her seizures.

But I'd made her a promise that I'd be with her, and every damn minute that ticked by was making me more on edge.

Pulling out my cell, I dialed Conlon again, but it went straight to voice mail, same as it'd been doing since last night.

NOVEMBER

Glancing at the time, knowing what I had to do but putting it off, I sucked it up and made another call.

Neil Christensen answered on the first ring in Danish. "Ja." Construction noise sounded in the background.

"It's November. I need a favor."

"Hold."

The call was muted for a few seconds then he came back on the line without the background noise. "Go."

"I need a secure waterfront property with a deep water dock, preferably furnished and with a security system already in place. Nothing anywhere densely populated. I also need a boat, cruiser, something between thirty and fifty feet, newer, fully operational, and I need both STAT."

"Purchase or lease?"

"Purchase. Cash."

"Budget?"

"Don't care."

Christensen paused, then, "Three property possibilities. Key Largo, Atlantic side, seventy-foot deep water dock, secure, new construction, end of canal, direct ocean access. Tavernier, Gulf side, refurb, long dock, beach, smaller property, stilts, gated entry. Islamorada, large property, deep water dock, end of canal."

"And a boat?"

"I have a client selling both his Azimut 50 Fly and Azimut Atlantis 45."

"Can either be captained by one person?"

"Experienced captain, yes."

Scrubbing a hand over my face, I did what I never fucking do. I deferred. "Which property and which boat would you choose?"

"Who is it for?"

"Female. She previously ran fishing charters by herself on an old, forty-six-foot Bertram in the Greater Antilles."

Christensen didn't hesitate. "Largo property and the fifty-foot flybridge."

"Is the property furnished?"

"Staged with option to purchase."

"I'll take both. How soon can you make all of this happen?"

"Level of urgency?" Christensen asked.

"Urgent."

"I will draw up the paperwork today and bring it to you later tonight."

"Copy. Amount of funds to transfer?"

"One-point-two for the Azimut, six-point-nine for the property." He gave me an account number. "The Azimut is in Miami. I will have it delivered to the Largo property by end of business today."

"Thanks. Transferring eight-point-one million now."

"Text the purchaser name for the paperwork. I will be at your penthouse at twenty-one hundred hours."

"Roger. One last favor?"

"Ja?"

I asked.

"Done." Christensen hung up.

I made the transfer and sent him a text with the name of one of my shell corporations. Then I glanced for the hundredth time down the wing of the hospital where Talerco had taken Butterfly.

Five minutes later, my elbows on my knees, my head in my hands, someone approached my position.

I knew it was Alpha without looking up. SEALs moved differently. Silent, stealth, but everyone had a footprint.

Not saying a word, Alpha took the seat next to me.

"Talerco's getting her an MRI, and they're running some other tests."

"I know," Alpha answered.

I didn't bother asking how. Alpha held his own hacking, and I hadn't gotten into the hospital's records yet to expunge her history. I was waiting until I had answers. "Then you know this is all my fault."

NOVEMBER

"Considering I saw you draw on Echo and threaten to kill him if he touched her again, I'm going to say whatever happened to her is those Russian terrorists' fault and you're shouldering the blame because you have feelings for her."

"It doesn't matter what I feel."

"Since I haven't seen you show emotion once in four years, I'd argue that point, but we can come back to that. You want to tell me what's going on?"

"The less you know, the better. You already figured out she's on the terrorist watch list. You don't want any of this coming down on AES. It'd jeopardize your security clearance and our government contracts."

"Is that why you kept me in the dark?"

"Yes." That and I'd never wanted to share Butterfly with anyone.

"I'll worry about AES and my security clearances. Read me in."

We'd been in a hospital for hours, her image had been caught on dozens of security cameras by now, and I was sitting on my ass, letting it happen because I couldn't fix her.

Past the point of keeping this contained, I fucking inhaled. Then I started talking. "I was supposed to zero in on that Russian terrorist cell's location four year ago and send in a drone strike. But when I saw her with them, I couldn't do it. I knew she wasn't part of their cell. She didn't deserve to die. I'd watched every second of footage I had on her countless times, and I didn't see the slip, but I had my orders."

"The slip?"

"Every terrorist I ever brought down had it, that *slip*. More than a tell, if you looked hard enough, watched long enough, you saw it. They'd fuck up, and I'd catch it. Then I knew. Sending in a drone strike or a team, whatever the mission called for, if I saw that slip, I didn't question it. I made the call and eliminated the threat. I did my job."

"She didn't slip."

I glanced at Alpha. "Not once." I looked down the hall. "I couldn't kill her. Not how I found her."

"How you found her?"

"Young and alone, hosing off the decks of an almost fifty-year-old crawler in Cuba." That moment she'd looked up as Alekhin and his men came down the docks. I'd never forget the innocence on her face, her expression. But then I saw her eyes, and there was no mistaking the same damn thing I saw every time I looked in a mirror. Solitude. Except she hadn't looked like she was wearing her isolation as a badge of honor. She'd looked lost. The kind of lost that made me want to rescue her, but I didn't fucking rescue people. I hunted, hacked and tracked. Then I eliminated them. But this woman had been different from the moment I saw her.

"What happened?" Alpha asked.

"They got to her." I checked the hallway again before glancing at my watch. "Four of the Russian terrorists from Bosnia boarded her boat. She chartered out of the marina, and I didn't see them on my screens again until three months later when they berthed at a private dock in Key Largo." By then I'd had my plan.

"Bosnia's a long way from Key Largo," Alpha stated.

"It is." I condensed the rest. "I'd decided I was going in. My plan was to pull her and get her off the grid, but I needed a window of opportunity. So instead of reporting when the cell landed on U.S. soil, I erased my tracks, planted a detour and bought myself a couple hours. A few security feed hacks later, I grabbed her when they went into a bar in D.C. All I had to do then was get her to the next step. But I hesitated, they grabbed us, and I woke up restrained in that compound in Bosnia while she was at my feet, taking a beating." Fucking enraged all over again, the memory played on repeat. "Using her as leverage, the head of the cell demanded I tell him what I knew." Glancing at Alpha, I admitted my worst goddamn mistake. "I told him to fuck off, and he shot her in the head."

NOVEMBER

"Yo, Rhys."

My gaze cutting past Alpha, I was already on my feet and moving.

Walking a terrified-looking butterfly through a set of double doors, Talerco came down the hall.

Pissed that he had his hand on her back, fucking livid that she looked so damn scared, I didn't hesitate. Cupping her face, I pulled her to me. "Butterfly?"

Teal-blue eyes welled as she looked up at me and whispered, "Time out, please."

"On it." Tucking her to my side and wrapping my arm around her for support, I paused only long enough to glance at Talerco and mouth *seizures*.

He shook his head once. "She's all good. Little claustrophobic. Papa tango sierra delta." He handed me paperwork. "Test results, prescription and resources." Moving into her line of sight as I shoved the papers in my pocket, Talerco glanced down at her. "You did good, darlin'. You got my number if you need anythin'."

"Thank you," she whispered, sounding like she was about to fall apart.

"Nothin' doin', darlin'." Talerco looked back at me. "You know where to find me."

"Copy. We're moving." Turning her toward the exit, I glanced at Alpha and asked for a favor so I could get her out of here. "Total scrub?" He'd know what I meant.

"Consider it done."

"Thanks." Pulling her in closer, I got us out of earshot and asked, "Can you walk to the car, Butterfly, or do you need me to carry you?"

A tremor shook her small body. "I-I can walk."

I let her have her dignity until we cleared the hospital entrance. Then I was done. I picked her up.

She let out a small gasp, but her arms wrapped around my neck and she tucked her head against my chest.

I fucking breathed for the first time since we'd walked into the damn hospital.

Then I carried my broken butterfly to the car as Talerco's statement replayed in my head.

Papa tango sierra delta.

PTSD.

FORTY-SIX

Atala

His scent filled my very being and descriptive words I didn't know how I knew the meaning of drifted into my thoughts. Amber, musk, cedar—cool like wet concrete in winter, like how that city with the bar smelled—all of it mixed with the scent of fresh laundry and the soap from his shower and swirled together as if it were more than this moment.

It felt like a memory.

From today, yesterday, four years ago, I didn't know.

It was one of the hundreds of questions I wanted to know the answer to at the same time I just didn't want to know anything anymore.

Thankful I was out of that loud tube and the hospital, I only wanted this moment, lying beside him in his bed after he'd picked me up, driven us here, carried me into the penthouse and laid me down before closing the curtains. Then he'd asked without judgment if I needed a pill.

I'd said no, and he'd merely nodded, kicked off his boots and lay down next to me.

Now here we were, and I was floating in his closeness, in the comfort of his quiet but consuming presence. If I allowed myself to think past this, I knew I would've wanted more. I'd want his arms around me.

I'd want more than that.

But he'd carefully lain so he didn't touch me, and he hadn't spoken.

I didn't know if I was supposed to be concerned by it or fill the void or if he expected anything more of me, but for the first time since I'd woken up in that barn, my mind, my thoughts, they settled in a way that felt… right.

Inhaling deep, taking my fill of his scent as much as I could, I breathed in the moment.

I breathed in his stillness.

I wanted to crawl inside it and live there for as long as I could, but stress and not much sleep must have taken hold, because I didn't realize I'd finally closed my eyes and drifted until his deeply reserved, quiet voice tingled across my bare skin.

"I rob people of their privacy."

I said nothing, but I shifted one leg, subconsciously positioning it closer to him.

"I hack what others take for granted," he continued, not moving, his stillness absolute.

"A hacker." Yes, he had said. Using his computers, his strong hands that flew across his keyboards, I had seen him work. I didn't know or understand the how of it, but I knew Sir was intelligent. Much more intelligent than he let on to me, to the men he worked with, to the world. Choosing instead to remain silent most of the time, I didn't know what had made Sir this way, but I understood it. I choose the same silence, but for very different reasons.

"A hacker," he repeated as if the word was meant to convey something other than what it was. "But I've only ever stolen two things in my life."

Momentarily forgetting the instinctual notion that I was mindful of this man, that I felt compelled to defer to him, to acquiesce to his voice and commands, that when I did, I felt safe in those brief moments and the world made sense. Forgetting all of that, forgetting to ask permission because it made me feel as if I belonged to him, I turned toward him and I asked a question. "What did you steal?"

NOVEMBER

Staring at the ceiling, one hand under his head, his bicep straining the crisp, fine material of his shirt, his other hand rested against the hard muscles of his abdomen as his fingers lay precisely side by side with only this thumb spread out. "The first thing was a computer." His chest rose and fell twice with even breaths. "I was eleven. We were in the schoolyard. It was recess. All the kids were playing except this group of a few boys. One of them was rich. He had a laptop, brought it to school and flaunted it whenever the teacher wasn't looking. That day he'd snuck it out to the playground. He and the other kids were huddled around it as he bragged about some video game I'd never heard of. The teacher caught on and reprimanded him, told him to take the computer back to the classroom. He did, and I waited a minute. Then I snuck off the playground, grabbed his laptop and the power cord and left school."

"Did you get in trouble?" I had no memories of school.

"No."

I didn't understand. "How did you explain your absence when you left school? They must have suspected you'd taken it."

"I never went back."

I didn't know much about the cost of things, and I wasn't sure of all the laws or rules of society, but stealing a laptop and never going back to school didn't seem like something that would go unnoticed. "The police didn't come looking for you?"

"The cops didn't know where to find me. That year, we'd moved three times since school had started. No one knew where I lived."

How was that possible? "Don't schools keep track of the children?" I had passed some schools in my travels since I'd left the old woman's farm. I saw how the adults kept the children herded like a mother duck led her ducklings. Whether they were on playgrounds, in lines for busses, crossing streets, it all seemed very... controlled.

"Not kids like me."

I frowned. "I don't understand what that means."

"I was poor." His voice lowered. Then he spoke his next words as if they were an angry admission. "My mother was negligent."

The words struck me in the chest, hurting my heart, and all at once my body felt too tight and I badly wanted to reach for him. "I'm sorry."

"Why?" he asked without emotion. "Do you think you knew any different?"

The need to reach for him fled as fast as it'd come. Not knowing if I was being reprimanded or insulted, I pulled my arms in close and whispered the only two words I'd become adept at, the two he'd told me repeatedly not to use but I couldn't seem to stop. "I'm sorry."

The rise of his chest was steep as he took a deep inhale before letting it out slow and speaking in a tone so low and laced with so much anger that it filled every inch of the room. "Your father was an abusive alcoholic."

Shock hit me as sure as if I'd been slapped across the face. Then he spit out a parallel even more shocking.

"My mother was an abusive drug addict. We're no different."

We were so different that I didn't have words for how different we were.

I was no one with nothing, and he was a highly intelligent, highly trained computer hacker working at a security company with private jets and other military-trained coworkers, living in a house so full of expensive furniture and electronics and fancy things that I didn't even have names for all of it, except rich. He was very, very rich.

My only belonging that I was even remotely sure was mine was a bloodied matchbook.

Ashamed, embarrassed, hearing his exact words when he'd used past tense when he spoke of our parents, I wanted to sink away from this moment and never surface in it again.

NOVEMBER

I didn't care what he'd said.

The military-trained, alpha, dominant man next to me was wrong.

We were nothing alike.

More distraught than when he walked away from me in that bar, I rolled over.

FORTY-SEVEN

November

ROLLING TO HER SIDE, SHE GAVE ME HER BACK. Her pain filling the whole damn room, I could taste the memory of her mouth after I'd taken her virginity. My cock hard, the dominance I was holding back becoming an incessant pounding the more fucking helpless I felt to help her, I lay there.

Not touching her.

Not comforting her.

Not sinking inside her.

I was beyond relieved she didn't have a seizure disorder, but that didn't mean she would suffer any less. How the fuck was I supposed to fix PTSD?

I couldn't, and it was killing me, which was why I'd stupidly told her about my shit past and her father. I thought if she knew some of the facts about me, about herself, she'd realize she wasn't leaving any great memories on the table, and it'd be one less thing for her to stress over.

But she'd turned her back, proving there wasn't a damn thing my presence was doing that was helping her.

I needed to get behind my screens, get a hold of Conlon, and fucking take down Check Mate. That was how I could help her.

Except I didn't move.

Selfishly lying there, I took the moment because even with her back turned, this woman gave me more peace than I'd ever felt.

Soft, hesitant, her voice dipped, then landed on my conscience. "You're not saying anything."

NOVEMBER

Neither was she.

She wasn't even asking about her father. Not that I blamed her. I didn't talk about my past. What I'd told her was more than I'd ever said to anyone about the woman who'd brought me into this world. The same woman I'd watched die as she overdosed on the floor of our second subsidized housing apartment because she'd burned the first one down. I'd sat there helpless, holding her head in my lap as she convulsed, not knowing what the fuck to do because we didn't have a phone, and I was twelve years old. Part of me didn't think she'd die. She'd OD'd before and woken up, but that last time, she didn't.

She'd stopped breathing, turned blue, then foamed at the mouth.

I sat there for a fucking day, staring at her body before her dealer showed up, pounding on the door, yelling about money. I grabbed the laptop I'd stolen, shoved it in my backpack and climbed out a window.

I fucking hated her.

Same as I hated the man who'd thrown away Butterfly while he'd buried himself in a bottle.

Shutting the door on both our pasts, I gave Butterfly another truth she didn't need to hear. "There's not much I can say." I was out of safe topics with her.

"You didn't tell me the second thing you stole."

If she was aiming for avoidance, she'd picked the wrong damn question. Turning my head to watch her body when I told her, I gave her the answer. "Your virginity."

Her shoulders stilled on an inhale. Then her voice not only went quiet as hell, she slipped to her innocent, hesitant, submissive voice. "To steal means to take what is not yours."

"Turn over and look at me, Atala."

Flinching at my command, she hesitated, but then she turned and gave me those teal eyes I'd never get enough of. The same eyes that'd haunted me for the past four years.

I gave her an order because I knew that tone of voice, and I knew she'd need the dominance. "Speak freely."

"Did you take me by force?"

"No." Not nearly as much as I could have.

"Then how was it stealing?"

"I took you forcefully, not forcibly, but I still took." I took advantage. I took what I wanted. I took what she'd never get back. She'd deserved better.

"Were we… a couple?"

My jaw ticked. "No."

Her gaze cut to my tell, then she looked away. "Did you even like me?"

Too damn much. I grasped her chin and brought her eyes back to me. "Yes."

"Then why weren't—"

"It was one time, and it was rushed. Minutes later, we were taken hostage by terrorists."

"Is that when you saw me get shot?"

I had to take two fucking breaths before I answered. "Yes."

Watching me like I was watching her, her expression so damn lost, I wanted to put her under me and dominate the fuck out of her until I wiped every ounce of doubt off her face. Then I wanted to fuck her memory back so she'd remember me. So she'd remember exactly how it felt when I took her virginity.

I was so goddamn selfish, I didn't know who the hell I was anymore.

The second her memory came back, so would Bosnia.

She didn't deserve that. My Butterfly did *not* deserve that.

Except she wasn't mine.

She never had been.

Pulling out of my grasp, she looked past me. "Did you… like being with me?"

Every question cutting deeper, I should've gotten up and walked away. Ending this conversation, severing any connection to her, setting her up somewhere safe, getting her help, letting her get on with her life—all of it would've been better for her than lying next to me. But I was too greedy to let her go yet.

"Yes," I answered truthfully.

"Did I like being with you?"

I broke her, then I got her kidnapped and shot. "You cried afterward." Like wasn't part of the equation.

Her gaze immediately cut back to mine. "Because I was hurt?"

Fucked, sodomized, and bloodied, she'd been a sobbing wreck, and I'd gotten off on it. "You were emotional."

"Why?"

I wasn't doing this.

Sitting up, I pulled on my boots, then stood. Riffling through her backpack, finding what I needed, I tossed a pair of worn jeans on the bed. "Get dressed."

Striding into my closet, I threw on my leather, holstered my Glock G17, then grabbed two helmets from the top shelf in the back. Helmets that were identical to the ones we'd had four years ago.

When I walked out, she was standing at the foot of the bed, jeans on, tank top, no bra.

I stared at a night four years ago.

She stared at a stranger.

My voice rough, my tone rougher, I tipped my chin at her boots. "Put those on." Short, lace-up, not like the ones she'd had, these were more practical. I hated them.

Sitting on the edge of the bed, she made quick work of it. By the time she stood back up, I was ready.

I held her leather out for her.

Silently stepping up to me and twisting to slip her arms through the sleeves, she then turned back to face me and waited.

She fucking waited.

Muscle memory, her naturally submissive personality, or a true memory locked somewhere in the depths of her scarred head—I didn't know. Maybe it didn't matter.

Same as that fateful night, I zipped her jacket. A jacket that now had a stitched bullet hole on the left arm.

My hand went to the back of her neck. "Let's go."

FORTY-EIGHT

Atala

Holding two helmets, keeping one hand on me, wearing a leather jacket that almost matched mine, my nerves sang from his touch as he took me down the elevator to the garage.

Bypassing a rugged-looking Jeep and the Range Rover with heavily tinted windows we'd ridden in, he kept going. Passing two shining, polished, sleek-looking motorcycles—one red, black and chrome, the other all black—he strode to the rear of the garage, toward a dust-covered tarp. Then he released me to grab it single-handedly and he yanked it off with one swift tug.

A flurry of particulates filled the air as the tarp dropped to the ground, revealing a scratched, beaten-up motorcycle. It looked like it had been expensive at one point, but now it just looked broken and bruised, like it'd been in an accident or maybe slid across rocks, then someone put it back together without concerning themselves about cosmetics.

When he put the key in, before he turned it, I had a moment of doubt.

Then the garage filled with the loud rumbling of a motorcycle as he stood next to the beast and revved the engine a few times before pulling out his cell phone.

The smell of gas surrounded us as he swiped on his phone a few times. The garage door opened, then he was turning me to face him and fitting a helmet over my head.

His fingers brushed the sensitive skin on the underside of my chin, and I shivered as he secured the strap.

If he noticed, he didn't comment.

He didn't say anything at all.

Putting his own helmet on, he straddled the scratched-up bike and revved it again as he toed the kickstand and backed up. The visor on his helmet up, I could see his eyes and half his face as he tipped his chin. Then his voice came through my helmet as if it had a built-in speaker. "Get on."

I hesitated.

Both at hearing his voice so intimately over the roar of the engine and because I couldn't remember ever riding on a motorcycle.

As if sensing my wariness, his voice came again. "You've ridden before. Brace a hand on my shoulder, swing your leg over and use the foot pegs."

My gaze cut to the foot pegs as if I knew what they were. Taking it as a sign, but more, wanting to know what it felt like to ride on a motorcycle, wanting to have my arms around him, I did exactly as he instructed.

I got on.

The motorcycle looking like it was built for racing, not riding, the back seat was higher than his and much more narrow, but I shockingly fit. And once I wrapped my arms around his waist, careful of the gun I saw him holster before he'd put his jacket on, I naturally curved against the hard strength of his back and turned my head.

My heart suddenly racing, I laced my hands.

His voice came through the helmet again and touched my soul. "Good?"

I didn't know what I was. "Good."

He carefully pulled out of the garage, and it magically shut behind us.

I had a fleeting thought that it still felt wrong to not call him

Sir, but then he revved the engine again and we were off like a shot, and I wasn't thinking at all.

The wind whipped past us, carrying away all of my fears and anxiety, and we flew down the road, freer than a bird.

I didn't know I was smiling until my cheeks shifted inside the helmet.

"I like this." My voice excited, adrenaline surging through my veins, I couldn't remember the last time I'd smiled. "I *really* like it." Aside from when Sir touched me, I couldn't remember anything I'd liked more. Except there was something that came close, and I started to say it, but then I stopped myself. "This is..." Trailing off, I felt foolish.

I knew my thoughts and words, the way I spoke, it was different than him. I wasn't nearly as smart, not with anything that I could remember. I wasn't experienced or sophisticated. I didn't know how to do anything except knot ropes, crew and make oatmeal. But none of that compared to him.

He could fly private jets and drive a motorcycle and make his hands fly across a computer keyboard like he was conquering the world.

His tone shifted to that unyielding tenor that was without emotion. "This is what?"

I wanted to say never mind.

I wanted to tell him I was being foolish or childlike, but I also wanted to actually tell him what I was thinking. When he spoke like that, when his voice took on that tone of authority, I wanted to lose myself in him and just... follow his lead, not have to think.

"Atala," he stated in that same tone as his voice filled my head from the secure-fitting helmet surrounding me.

I was speaking before I realized I no longer felt too foolish to speak my thoughts. "I was going to say this is almost like diving into the ocean from the upper deck of a yacht, but better. The rush of the wind, the feeling of flying, it's different. It isn't interrupted by that first moment your body breaks the surface of the water, or later when you need to come up for air. It's like the moment when you first jump, but it keeps coming. Like we're flying."

"Did you jump off the upper decks when you were crewing?"

"No crew members were supposed to on any of the yachts I worked on, but sometimes I would anyway when I knew no one was around." When I knew I wouldn't get caught.

His shoulders stiffened. "You did it by yourself?"

"Yes. I liked being in the water more than I liked being on the boat," I admitted.

"You like swimming."

The way he said it, the sudden shift in his tone, deeper but quieter, I didn't know if it was a question, but I answered it anyway. "Yes."

"Hang on." His hand briefly landed on my thigh and squeezed.

My heart rate exploded.

He hit the gas, and shifted through the gears. Then we were truly flying.

My smile spread as my arms tightened around him.

Was this happy?

Did I care about memories?

Could it be this easy to feel free?

His deep voice came through the helmet again. "Good?"

I said it again because I wanted to say it a hundred times. "I *really* like this." I wanted to make a forever out of this moment.

"Good." He pulled the throttle, and we went even faster.

A small, surprised but happy, almost-laugh escaped, and the sound was as unfamiliar to me as my life before a few years ago.

Quiet, so quiet I didn't know if I was actually hearing it or imagining it, a single word floated into my helmet and into my heart. "*Butterfly.*"

FORTY-NINE

November

SHE LAUGHED.

I was doing ninety-eight on US 1 at nineteen hundred hours, unnecessarily risking her life, taking her to the one place that could destroy her protection of amnesia, and she was laughing.

"Butterfly."

My Butterfly.

Finally free.

On a motorcycle that'd almost killed her once before.

I needed a new word for fucked-up.

She needed a Talerco, Echo or Delta, or just about any other asshole more honest than me right now, but just the thought of anyone speaking to her, let alone touching her, made me want to kill.

Her arms tight around me, pushing the Streetfighter past what I should in its current condition, I didn't tell her I was going fast to reduce the amount of time we were out in the open, exposed. I didn't tell her I had my Glock because a fucking hacker thought our lives were nothing more than a game of chess. And I sure as hell didn't tell her the sound she'd just made was better than her cry of pain when I took her virginity.

I just fucking drove.

Telling myself I was giving my Butterfly her wings back.

I drove her all the way to the secluded marina I'd bought through one of my shell corporations four years ago.

Pulling up to the old, defunct marina, I brought us to a stop in front of the dry storage warehouse that looked worse than dilapidated on the outside. Using my cell, I scanned the security feeds I had for the place as I used one of my software programs to open the bay door.

Her sweet voice came through my helmet. "Where are we?"

"You'll see."

I pulled us in, remotely shut the door, then drove with only the Streetfighter's headlight as a guide to the back of the cavernous building before turning the bike around to face outward in case we had to make a quick exit.

Cutting the engine, I used my cell to turn on the warehouse's lights, then I toed the kickstand down.

Getting off the bike, she glanced around with her helmet still on.

I swung my leg over the bike. "Come here, Butterfly."

She stepped up to me. "There are boat lifts, but no boats."

"I know." I took her helmet off, then mine, and grabbed her hand. "Come." Praying like hell I wasn't about to send her into an episode, I didn't warn her where I was taking her.

I led her out the back door of the dry storage and took her down the dock to the only boat berthed.

Then I walked her onto her 1975 forty-six-foot Bertram Sport fishing boat and dropped her hand.

Standing mid-deck, the nighttime spotlights from the docks falling across her face, she looked around, then looked at me with confusion. "Sir?"

Treading lightly, I gave her half a truth. "This is part of your past."

"This boat?"

I nodded. Then I told her. "It was yours." I watched her for an adverse reaction, but she didn't say anything. "You grew up on this boat."

Inhaling sharply, she turned her back on me. "Thank you for, um, showing me." Her finger trailed the pitted gunwale, then her voice got dangerously quiet. "That's nice of you."

I scanned the waters and mangroves around us. "Whatever you think I am, nice isn't on the list."

She inhaled again, this time deeper. "Maybe it is now."

"No, it's not, Atala." I hated not calling her Butterfly. She didn't move through her surroundings, she wasn't grounded, she wasn't even fucking real. She fluttered, and I was staring at a ghost.

Either ignoring what I said or lost in thought, she ran her hand over the cabin slider. "Is it unlocked?"

"Yes." The boat was exactly as I'd found it before I'd had a marine tow service bring it here.

Opening the slider, her steps barely making a sound, she ducked her head from muscle memory, whether she realized it or not, and slipped below deck into the main cabin.

Staying topside, keeping an eye on her and our surroundings, I watched in fascination as she turned in a circle, then briefly closed her eyes and did it again while inhaling deep. Looking back around at everything that I'd left largely untouched after searching for clues, she ran a hand over some of her clothes that were in a neat pile.

"What do you think is not nice about this?" Using two fingers, she picked up the top of a string bikini that was old four years ago. "You're showing me where I came from." Gently releasing the nothing piece of material, she neatly put it back how it was. "That's more than anyone else has done for me." She frowned. "I think. Except for the old lady."

"Old lady," I stated, suddenly focusing all my attention on her.

"Yes." She picked up another small bikini. The yellow one. "I wore this?"

"Yes. What old lady?"

"The one from the small farm and broken barn in the woods. Where did I live that I wore these clothes?"

Farm in the woods. *Fuck*, that was it. "Nowhere." I needed to get behind my screens.

She glanced up. With confusion etched across her face, she looked almost as young as she did when I first saw her on my screens. "What do you mean, nowhere?"

"You did fishing charters, mostly in and around the Bahamas. You didn't have a home, you lived on this boat, but you indicated you frequently anchored in an atoll at the southern end of the islands. What old lady are you talking about, Atala?" I needed to get a hold of Conlon, STAT.

Staring at me wide-eyed, she blinked. Twice. Then she came up the stairs. "That's how I knew how to crew. That's how I knew the proper terms for yachting." She looked around the deck.

"Yes." Losing patience, wanting to put my hands on her to get her to answer my question, I instead used my dominant tone. "Tell me about the old lady and her land."

She crossed her arms. "I, um…" She looked around the boat. "I don't know more than that. It was barely a farm, not much land was cleared. There were chickens, a goat, and an old barn I stayed in. It was cold. I tried to patch the holes in the old, rotting wood with whatever materials I could find. I knew how to use a hammer. But she didn't stay in the barn with me. The old lady had a small, one-room house. She lived there and she, she, um…" Butterfly circled a finger around the left side of her head without touching herself. "She tended to that."

I said it for her. "The gunshot wound."

The color drained from her face, and her arm went back around her middle, joining the other one that hadn't left as her voice dropped to a whisper. "Yes, that."

Two things struck me at once. She wasn't facing the truths I'd given her, and she wasn't understanding physiologically what was happening to her. The first I addressed immediately, without any filter. "You were shot in the head by a terrorist, Atala."

NOVEMBER

Turning away from me, her voice got even quieter. "If you say so."

"Look at me," I ordered.

She turned back, but her gaze was solidly locked on her feet. "Why do you do that?"

"Do what?"

"Demand that I look at you."

Fighting every instinct I had, I didn't touch her. I didn't grip her hair. I didn't make her feel the sheer force of my strength while giving her every ounce of attention.

I didn't show her how she was the center of my goddamn universe.

I reined it all in and kept my tone level, but I was done being *nice*. "Do you want my attention when you speak to me? Do you want me looking at you? Giving you my eyes? Listening to your words, hearing what you say, watching how you say them?" Ruthless, not waiting for an answer, I played dirty. "Or do you want me staring past you or looking at another woman?" I didn't need an answer because I knew this woman. Memory or not, the core of her, the scared, attention-starved little girl she was down deep, I saw that part of her. I also saw the strong woman who'd survived against all odds. I saw her, period.

Now she needed to see me.

"Eyes on me, Atala. Right now."

She looked up.

"You were shot in the head," I repeated.

Tears welled.

I said it again. With detail. "You were shot in the head at close range with a 9mm Beretta."

She started to shake. "Why are you doing this?"

"Because you don't need to shake, you don't need to lose consciousness, and you *do not* have seizures." She needed to hear the truth. She needed to feel it, cry, scream, be fucking angry, and she needed someone to be with her when she did, and I was that someone. Goddamn it, I was *her* someone. But our time was running out, and I needed to do this now. "You have PTSD, Atala."

She sucked in a sharp breath and started to turn again.

"Don't look away from me right now." Taking her arm, I made her face me. "You have Post Traumatic Stress Disorder. You do *not* have a seizure condition. You're traumatized from what happened four years ago, from your childhood, from your father. You're not remembering because your brain is trying to protect you. But if you want to live, if you want to breathe through that fear, you have to learn how to walk with the trauma. You can't sidestep PTSD, Atala. You have to live with it." Tears streamed down her face, but I wasn't finished. "You have to walk through it." Allowing myself the one gesture, I gripped the back of her neck. "You can face this."

Same as the way she'd cried on my lap all those years ago, quiet, reserved, desperately trying to hold it all in, she let a small sob escape. "I can't do that."

"Why not?" This woman didn't have the military at her back. She didn't get sent to college on the government's dime. She didn't have a Deputy Commander who took her under his wing. She'd had an alcoholic father who'd treated her like hired help and a hacker who'd gotten her shot in the goddamn head, but she was still fucking standing. Not just standing, she'd walked across Eastern Europe, stretched ten grand out over four years, gotten jobs and made her way to the U.S. all because of a fucking matchbook. There wasn't anything this butterfly couldn't do. Which was exactly what I was about to tell her when she whispered two words that gutted me.

"I'm alone."

Hating myself more than I ever had before, I made her an empty fucking promise. "I'm right here."

Unlike four years ago, she didn't just quietly suffer, she fucking broke.

Standing in the middle of her piece-of-shit boat, covering her face with her hands, looking so goddamn small and broken, she burst into tears and sobbed.

For two seconds, I stood there and stared.

I stared at her brokenness.

I stared at her utter beauty, I stared at a woman who was stronger than I ever was, and I stared at a woman who was finally facing her past.

Then I did what I'd done four years ago.

I picked her up and sat down with her on my lap.

Except this time, I didn't punish her for the demons in my own head.

Doing what I should've the first time, knowing damn well that life didn't offer second chances, but by some miracle here it was, I wrapped my arms around her tight and I gave her the only brand of comfort I knew how to give. I gave her my dominance.

"Cry it out, Butterfly. Give me the tears." I stroked the length of her hair. "Give me every last one." I was going to shoulder them all for her.

Then I was going to do what I did best.

I was going to hunt.

FIFTY

November

I DROVE US BACK TO THE PENTHOUSE JUST AS FAST, BUT THIS TIME, SHE didn't laugh.

She didn't say a damn word.

She also didn't tell me she needed a time out or call me Sir.

Both were progress, but the latter I hated.

I got us upstairs, quickly made her food and had to refrain from calling her sub and ordering her to eat it when she said she wasn't hungry, but I did give her a look.

She began to eat, and I got behind my screens.

I was still behind them when I heard her get off the stool at the kitchen counter and come up behind me.

"Do you like when I call you Sir?"

Typing, I paused for only half a second. "Yes."

"Do you like to be called Nathan?"

"Only by you." Only when necessary. I picked Nathan back up after Bosnia for the same reason I choose Rhys. A punishment and a reminder of who I was.

She was quiet for a few seconds. "I have a hard time thinking of you as Nathan."

"I haven't gone by my given name for a very long time." I was pissed I still hadn't heard from Conlon, but I'd found their ghost plane, and they'd been back up in the air for hours already, en route to Miami.

"Why not?"

I gave her the easier answer. "I don't prefer it."

NOVEMBER

"Do you like November better?"

I liked Sir. Again, I gave her the easier answer. "Yes."

"I think it suits you." Her voice dropped to an innocent murmur. "Butterflies in November."

Sir suited me. I didn't acknowledge either of her comments.

Her feet shifted, and uncertainty filtered into her tone. "What was it like?"

"What was what like?" Distracted, I entered one more search into my software.

"Between us." Her voice pitched quieter. "Sex."

My hands froze on my keyboard. Then I turned in my chair. Nervous, biting her lip, she looked at her feet.

I waited.

Without lifting her head, she brought her gaze up to mine. "For me or for you?"

The question catching her off guard, she hesitated. "For you."

"I manipulated your body, controlled your movements and held you down." I watched every inch of her face for a reaction. "I dominated you." Nothing in her expression changing, she didn't so much as blink, but her breathing, her pulse, they sped up.

Her voice dropped to a whisper. "Is that what you like?"

"It's who I am." Who I was.

She nodded with the same damn innocence, the same acceptance she'd had four years ago. "You like to control... that."

She was still so fucking untouched, unaffected by the shit in this world, even after everything she'd been through. Not for the first time, I wondered just how selfish my motives were for trying to get her to remember a past that wasn't worthy of a single ounce of her purity.

I gave her complete honesty. "I liked controlling you."

Lifting her head, she met my comment not with shyness, but with curiosity. "Why?"

In a constant state of arousal around her, no matter how many times I told myself to stand the fuck down, my cock pulsed at the memory of being inside her. "Because no one else had. Not in the way I touched you," I added, knowing she deserved a better answer.

"Because I was…" Dropping her gaze, her throat moving with a swallow, her voice came even softer. "Because I was a virgin."

I wanted my mouth on hers, my hands in her hair. I wanted to drive so deep into her that memories no longer mattered for either of us. "That was part of it."

She nodded again, this time quicker. "So you don't only like, you know…." Trailing off, her eyes darted to mine before looking away.

Jesus, I wanted to dominate her. "It wasn't only about your virginity, Atala."

"What was it about, then?"

Staring at an innocent Butterfly, my selfishness hit a new level. "You can be free of anything but yourself."

Her teal-eyed gaze drifted. "What I am—this isn't freedom."

I said what I should, not what I wanted. "Soon enough, you'll be free to live your life." I wouldn't clip her wings.

She looked back at me. Just like four years ago, she didn't hide the fear or anxiety in her expression. "Is that what you want?"

"I want you safe." From me, from Check Mate, from a terrorist watch list.

"Thank you."

I didn't reply.

"May I ask one more question?"

I tipped my chin.

Color flushed across her cheeks. "What was it like for me?"

"What was what like?" I knew what. I wanted to hear her say it.

Her head dipped, and her voice dropped. "Sex… with you."

Jealous rage hit. "With me," I stated.

"Yes," she answered like it was a fucking question.

My jaw ground. "How many men have you had sex with, Atala?"

"None that I remember."

I fucking exhaled. Then I went back to my screens because I didn't want to answer her question.

Not letting it go, she asked again. "What was it like for me?"

Turning back to her, I took in every inch of her innocence before I ruined it. "Pain."

Her gaze immediately shifted away from me. "Because it was my first time?"

I wanted to break her of that habit. I wanted to spend a fucking eternity breaking her of every insecurity and fear that took her attention away from me. "Because I wanted you to feel pain."

"Why?" she whispered.

Because I was fucked-up. "That's who I was. I wanted to hurt you." Then I'd wanted to make her feel good, but she'd denied me that, and I'd been fucked ever since. So fucked, I hadn't touched another woman.

Her eyebrows drew together. Then she threw me. "But you didn't want to hurt me like… this." Using two fingers, she barely touched the left side of her head.

"No."

She nodded slowly, like she was mentally piecing shit together before saying the last thing I expected. "You wanted me to feel pain, but you didn't want to hurt me."

I stared at the beautiful creature in front of me and wondered for the first time what truly made someone intelligent—being left to your own resources or having every advantage at your fingertips. "You can feel pain without emotion." Physical pain. "But you can't experience hurt without pain." I'd wanted both from her.

Long, wild hair, ethereal, teal-eyed, my innocent butterfly spoke with an intuitive awareness that could only come from having survived a shot to the head. A shot I may as well have pulled the trigger on. "Feelings hurt like physical pain."

I gave her every reason why she should stay away from me. "When I took your virginity, I wanted to hurt you, and I wanted to make you feel pain. Deep pain. Then I wanted to give you pleasure more intense than any pain I'd inflicted or any hurt you'd experienced before me." Then she would've remembered me.

Her throat moving with a swallow, she picked out the one word she should have. "Wanted?"

"Yes, wanted."

"And now?" she barely whispered.

I held her gaze. Then I made her a promise. "I'll eat a bullet before I ever hurt you again."

Her lips parted with a sharp inhale, but it was her expression that gave her away. "Don't say—"

"Don't lie to yourself about who I am," I warned.

"I don't think I am the one who is lying."

"Facts are facts. I am who I am. You're who you are." The two didn't fucking meet.

The tone of her voice dropped to one I'd never heard before. "You're not going to touch me like that again, are you?"

My jaw rigid, my chest fucking tight, I forced myself to say it. "No."

"Because you think you'll hurt me."

"There's no pretense. It's who I am, Atala." No matter how hard I'd try, sooner or later, I'd slip. I'd be the one losing the façade, and I'd fucking hurt her.

Her expression fell, and a knock sounded at the door

Expecting Christensen, I stood and made it one pace before her quiet voice hit my back.

"I think you're wrong."

Pivoting, I stepped into her. Gripping her chin, dominating her with a ruthless, lethal tone, I bit out a question that wasn't a question at all. It was an insult. "What fucking part of the conversation about me wanting to hurt you do you not understand, Atala?"

She flinched in fear, but she didn't back down. "There's more than one way to lie."

Fucking enraged, at myself, at that fucking piece-of-shit Check

NOVEMBER

Mate, at her father, at my mother, at every goddamn part of my fucked-up past that made me who I was, I didn't look down at a butterfly. I glared.

Her voice dropped to a whisper more crushing than an IED. "I think you're lying to yourself."

The knock came again, and my cell vibrated with a distinctive pattern I'd set for an incoming video call.

Releasing her, I walked to the front door and opened it. Tipping my chin at Christensen to enter, I answered my cell.

His usual affable expression absent, Conlon's face filled the screen. "Took a little longer than I expected, but I think I've got something. Put your woman on."

Ignoring Butterfly as she stood back with her arms crossed, Christensen walked in and laid out paperwork on my dining table.

"Show me first," I told Conlon.

"Won't mean anything to you," he argued.

"Conlon," I warned as Christensen handed me a pen.

"Right." He flipped the screen and used his cell to show me a video on his laptop. Mountainous forest as far as you could see, small clearing with an even smaller pasture, two dilapidated buildings in the distance.

"Location?" I demanded, signing paperwork.

"Realistically? The middle of nowhere. Geographically, northeastern Romania. Put her on, she needs to see this. I think you know why."

Christensen shuffled papers, laying out more for me to sign.

I held up a finger to him as I walked over to Atala. "I'd like you to look at something."

Not meeting my eyes, she nodded.

Stepping in on her six, I brought my arm around and held the phone in front of her. "This is Victor. He's going to show you a video."

Conlon smiled his playboy smile. "Right. Hello, love. You can call me Vance." The fucker winked. "Just wanted you to see something. Tell me if you recognize anything, all right?"

"All right," she quietly replied.

Conlon stared at her for a second. "Right. Here we go." He flipped the camera angle and showed her what he'd already shown me.

She sucked in a sharp breath.

Both Conlon and I heard it, and he flipped the camera angle again, his face filling the screen. "I take it you recognize this place?"

"The old woman's barn."

"Right. Barn might be a stretch, darling." He pasted on a disingenuous smile. "Nice to meet you, love. Let me talk to November for a minute?"

Stepping back, I took the call off video. "Victor, hold." Muting him, I glanced at her, but she still wouldn't look at me. "Atala."

No eye contact. "Yes?"

"Look at me," I demanded.

"No, thank you, Sir."

God-fucking-damn it. I grasped her chin, hard. Then I lowered my voice. "No matter what you may think of me or my actions, your safety and well-being are my only priority. That said, I don't care how angry you get with me, if I tell you to look at me, you look. If I ask you a question, you answer. This isn't a test of wills. This is nonnegotiable. Understood?"

No response.

"Do you need me to force a reply out of you right now?" I wasn't playing games with her.

She gave me her voice and her eyes. Then she gave me attitude. "You said you would take a bullet before you harmed me."

Inhaling fucking twice to control my anger, ignoring her lashing out at me, I asked what I needed to know. "Will you be all right if I walk into the other room for five minutes and take this call?"

Embarrassment instantly colored her cheeks, and her voice dropped to a whisper. "Yes, Sir."

NOVEMBER

"I want you to come get me if that changes or if you need me. Understood?"

"Yes, Sir," she answered even quieter.

"Good." Releasing her, I glanced at Christensen and switched to Danish. "Will you keep an eye on her?"

"Ja."

I strode to my bedroom for privacy and took the call off mute. "Conlon."

"Right. So guess who owns that farm?"

"Varvara Petrov."

"Right," Conlon drew out. "Sister of Elizaveta Petrov."

"And aunt of Matvey Petrov, aka Mark Johnston."

"Our lying college student with a burner," Conlon added. "How the hell did you beat me to this?"

"Fingerprints off the burner. Reverse trace. How did you track this down?"

"Sat images from Cuba four years ago. I combed the marina, but then I started searching nearby beaches because I was wondering how the hell someone gets on a boat without ever being seen at a marina. Turns out, you swim from a nearby beach, and guess who went for a swim and never returned to shore?"

"Zakhar Petrov." I'd found the birth certificate, but I hadn't been able to find an image of him yet.

"Zakhar Petrov," Conlon confirmed. "The son Varvara Petrov thinks is dead. The same son her sister turned over to Russian authorities for hacking and making terrorist threats right before Elizaveta asked for asylum for her and her young son."

Right now, I didn't care about the asylum angle. I needed a picture of Check Mate. "Do you have a screenshot of Zakhar from those sat images?"

"I have one better. I already ran the screenshots through your facial rec software, and I got a hit right before I called you. Guess whose image came up on a Cuban passport?"

Cuba.

He was under my nose this whole goddamn time. "Send me those images, and I need you to ask Roark something for me."

"Done and copy. What do you need?"

I asked.

"On it."

"Thanks."

I hung up, grabbed my go bag, and strode back to the living room.

FIFTY-ONE

Atala

ASHAMED BY WHAT I HAD SAID TO SIR, BUT ALSO FEELING AS IF I had needed to say it, I stood as silent as the giant, frightening man by the dining room table who didn't say a word.

I didn't think I could be more anxious until Sir came back carrying an envelope and a large duffle that he set down on the table next to his fancy black bag that held his laptop. Glancing at the other man, Sir spoke to him in a different language.

The other man barely moved his head in a single tip of his chin.

"Tak," Sir replied to the man before turning his attention on me. His expression lethally controlled, he pulled out a chair and switched back to English, giving me a sharp order. "Sit."

Startled by his tone and by the look in his eyes, I flinched.

His nostrils flared with an inhale. Then he pulled out another chair, angled it to face the first one, and he sat. Leaning his elbows on his knees, he clasped his hands and quieted his tone. "Sit, Atala."

Atala.

My stomach dropped, dread choked my throat, and I fought tears.

Then he made it worse. "Please."

Biting the inside of my cheek, and feeling the sudden throb of a headache, I took the seat facing him. Then I clasped my hands tight, lowered my head, and silently pleaded.

Please, please don't let this be what I think it is.

Warm hands covered mine. "Look at me, Atala."

His voice came out in a slightly more subdued version of his previous tone, but there was no mistake in how he said his words. It was not a request.

I met his cool-eyed gaze.

Then he began to speak.

"You grew up on a fishing charter operated by your father in the Greater Antilles. Your mother died in childbirth, and your father raised you to call him sir or Captain. He taught you to crew, read and follow his orders. He did not nurture you. He did not call you by your name, and he kept you just isolated enough to control you with fear and mistrust of the outside world. He drank and used you for manual labor. A few years before I met you, you said he died in his sleep. You buried him at sea in the northern Bahamas where you believed your mother to have been buried. Then you took over operating the boat and ran your own charters."

Sir's chest rose with an inhale as his hands tightened around mine.

"You more than know how to crew, Atala. You know how to captain a vessel. Remember that."

Captain.

I didn't have time to process that before he kept speaking. "As I told you, your name is Atala Rose. That's your first and middle name, but you were unaware if you had a last name, and I wasn't able to find any record of your birth or any legal documents on you. I do not know your last name, and I never asked if you knew your father's legal name, but I'm going to assume you did not. The boat you operated had no registration, no insurance and no history of ownership. I can only assume your father destroyed the documentation and covered his tracks, but I don't have any answers as to why. All I know is that your accent is American, so I assumed your father was American, but again, I have no proof. All of this is to tell you that part of the reason you may not be remembering your past is that there wasn't much to remember. Besides your name and your life on the Nalleli Rose, which you did not speak of with any sort of fondness when you referenced your upbringing, you didn't give me any more details."

My chest started to hurt as much as my head. "Was there anything good in my life?"

"When I first saw you, you were cleaning off the decks, and you looked both at peace and comfortable with your task." He paused.

I had to ask. "Then what happened?"

"Four Russian terrorists boarded your boat at a marina in Havana Bay, Cuba, and held you at gunpoint. You chartered out of the marina, and for the next three months, you were their hostage while they plotted an attack against the United States."

Oh, dear God. "What kind of attack?" Had I helped them?

"I don't have the exact details, but even if I did, I would not and could not tell you. All I can say is that I'm former military, U.S. Air Force. I was a Cyberspace Operations Officer named James Hunter, and the Russian terrorists were stopped." He paused. "But not before they took us both hostage, relocated us to Bosnia for interrogation, and shot you while I was restrained." His chest rose and fell twice. "I'm the reason you were shot in the head and the arm. I'm the reason why you've lost your memory."

No. It couldn't be him. Tears welled and spilled down my cheek. "I don't understand. You said I was taken in Cuba. You were in the United States military. How did you get taken hostage when they already had me?"

He stared at me. Then he crushed my heart. "I was ordered to eliminate the terrorists with a drone strike, and in the process, end your life as well."

Yanking my hands free, I stood. "I don't want to hear this."

He slowly rose to his feet, but his voice, his words, they kept coming. "The terrorist cell landed on U.S. soil. They had you with them, and the U.S. considered you a threat as well, so the drone strike was imminent. But I'd been watching the security footage I had of you for months. I knew you were innocent, and I couldn't let you die. Devising a plan to extract you, I lied to my superiors, evaded my security detail and covertly approached you after the terrorists entered the bar where the matchbook you have is from. I offered you a choice. I said you could come with me or take your chances with the men who'd abducted you. You didn't know they were terrorists or what they were planning, but you knew it was bad, and you made a choice. You came with me. I got us out of that bar and back to my place. I made you those passports, gave you cash and access to an offshore bank account and told you how you were going to escape."

"Stop," I cried. I couldn't hear any more.

He didn't listen. "But then I made a catastrophic mistake." He gripped the back of my neck. "Same as I'm doing right now. I couldn't keep my hands off you." He stepped into me. "I had to have you. I had to taste you. I wanted to drown in your natural submissiveness because that's who I am. That's what I do." He angled my face up to his.

"*Stop it.*"

"I took you. I took your virginity. Then I got you killed because I didn't get you out soon enough, and the terrorists found us at my place."

"*No,*" I sobbed, pulling away from the one man, the only person I could ever remember trusting. "Stop it. *Stop it!*"

"I broke your wings, Butterfly. I fucking broke them, and I'd do it all over again just to steal that moment with you." His voice cracked. "I'm sorry. I'm so fucking sorry."

Sobbing, my knees started to shake.

But my Sir, my cold month, my savior, he didn't reach for me. Holding my neck, he stepped back.

"Wait, no, stop, Sir!" No, this wasn't happening. *This wasn't happening.*

No longer looking at me, he spoke over my head. "Grab her."

Muscled arms wrapped around my waist, and Sir let go of me.

NOVEMBER

My Sir let go of me.

"No! No, no, NO." My legs gave out, my body doubled over the wrong arms, and I choked on my crushing despair. "Please, *please*, don't! *Don't leave me, Sir!*"

Sir ignored me. "You know what to do, Christensen."

"Ja."

"SIR!"

Grabbing his two bags, leaving the envelope, Sir didn't even look back.

My vision twisted, my ears rang, my heart shattered, then I was there.

Drowning.

FIFTY-TWO

November

I STEPPED OUT OF THE SHADOWS. "YOU SHOULD BE MORE AWARE OF your surroundings."

Not so much as a flinch, Deputy Commander Bradley turned away from the cabinet where he was about to pour himself a drink and chuckled without humor. "Thought I saw the last of you." He held a glass up. "Drink?"

"No."

"Right. Not your vice of choice."

Slip one. "Correct." Something he wouldn't know unless he'd studied me.

Slowly going through the motions of pouring himself a drink and buying time, he filled his glass half full with his preferred vice. Taking his scotch, he walked past me to his desk chair. Still stalling, he took a swallow. "It's been a while."

"I've been around." After landing at Tipton two hours ago on the Gulfstream I'd flown from Roark's that I'd set up with a new tail number and fake ownership papers that traced back to a shell corp, I'd made a pit stop at the Pentagon. Intercepting a shocked Perkins before he'd walked in for his shift, I'd blackmailed him into grabbing me something from the command center. Specifically, something from Bradley's office within the command center. Twenty minutes later, he'd come back out, and I'd had my proof.

Bradley's chuckle returned right before he outed himself, purposely or accidentally. "I heard."

Slip two. He hadn't heard shit. I'd been more than careful. If he knew something, there were only two possibilities. "I'm sure you hear a lot."

"Unavoidable in my line of work." He took another swallow.

I took note of how he said *work,* not duty. "The internet never sleeps."

"Neither do terrorists." He drank again, this time finishing what was left in his glass. "I'm assuming there's a reason you're here?"

I hated him. "You're going to do me a favor."

He smirked. "I'm sure anything you could possibly think to ask of me, you could do yourself."

He was right. He also downplayed the fact that I didn't ask him for a favor, I told him he was going to do it. "Correct again." He knew what was coming.

He leaned back in his chair. "Then why ask?"

I ignored his question. "It's going to come from official channels." It had to be irreproachable. I laid out what I wanted. "Four years ago. Cuba. Female hostage taken by the Russian terrorist cell. Remove her from the watch list and delete all intel on her."

"I'm not going to—"

I set my cell on his desk with the expedited DNA test results showing.

"What is this?"

He knew exactly what it was. "Incentive."

He smirked. "If this is what you've been up to the last four years, son, I suggest you get your head on straight, pronto."

I swiped to a new screen, then another, then another. Separate, the DNA test, the images of Zakhar Petrov's fake Cuban passport, the picture of the farm with the old woman, the image of Mark Johnston, aka Matvey Petrov, it didn't mean much. Together, they painted a picture.

"Over twenty years ago, you were stationed in Germany, trying to climb the ranks as you weeded out cyber threats you weren't very adept at finding. So you started to enlist the help of any foreign hacker you could find, either using them to get results or using them to trap and net American hackers you could then force into service. Except you fucked up." I pocketed my cell. "Zakhar Petrov."

Decades of practice, he didn't blink. "I'm supposed to know who that is?"

"He knows you." And I should've seen this bullshit seventeen years ago. "He's the cousin of your bastard son, Mark Johnston, aka Matvey Petrov. The same son you helped get asylum for, along with his mother seventeen years ago when you lost control of Zakhar Petrov after he baited me into hacking the NSA. My guess, he wanted a bigger payday."

"I'm the face of Cyber Command, son. You think anything you say or show me on a damn cell phone is going to condemn me? Those pictures prove nothing."

"They don't have to. Facts are facts." His career would be over. So would his freedom. There wouldn't be a court of law or defense of reasonable doubt. Not for treason. The military would do what they did best. They'd take care of their own problems. I repeated my request for the second and last time. "Remove the woman from the watch list. Delete all intel on her, then hand in your retirement papers."

Bradley held on to the charade. "I can't make names disappear off the terrorist watch list just because you sneak in here with a personal agenda, son. Do I look that stupid or like I have that kind of authority?"

He had exactly that kind of authority. "You have one hour. Delete all trace of her, submit your retirement paperwork, and I'll delete the evidence of your multiple counts of treason." I turned to leave. This time out the front door because I'd already disabled his security system, something he should've noticed.

"Hunter."

I glanced back.

Standing over his desk, he looked exactly like what he was.

NOVEMBER

A fucking failure in a uniform he didn't deserve to wear. "For the record, I did you a favor pulling you out of that shit existence you were living. A studio apartment, minimum wage fixing computers for a box-chain store, hacking at night?" He scoffed. "The Air Force made a man out of you."

"You did yourself a favor." He had no idea how fucking lucky he was. "Make no mistake, you're only still breathing right now because you serve a purpose. Stop serving it, come after her or me, and your corpse will make Bosnia look like child's play." I walked out the front door and got in my car.

Then I pulled up both the audio and video feeds I'd installed in his study.

At two minutes past twenty-three hundred hours, he made the call. Then he emailed his request for retirement.

Six minutes later, I hacked Cyber Command.

Her name was wiped.

The lights in the study turned off, a light went on upstairs, then nineteen minutes later, it went off.

I waited an hour, then snuck back into the Deputy Commander's study, removed my equipment and got back in the car. Using a new burner, I dialed a number.

The call connected after the first ring. "Go."

"I'm on my way."

"ETA?"

"One hour, forty-five minutes."

"Copy."

I hung up and drove back to Tipton.

FIFTY-THREE

Atala

WARMTH ON MY FACE, MY ARMS, I SWAYED.
I was floating.
No, my head was hurting.
I couldn't float with my head hurting.
And my chest hurt.
Everything hurt.
Like a crushing wave landing before you swim under it.
"You are awake," a deep, accented, male voice said. "We are here."
Here?
"You may wake up."
My eyes opened. Then I was blinking against the bright, hot sunlight.
Car.
I was in a car.
No, a truck.
I inhaled, and a seat belt pushed at my chest, and then it struck me all at once, worse than a thousand crashing waves.
Sir. *Sir.*
He was gone. He'd left me. My seventy-two hours had expired, and he'd tossed me away.
Tears welled.
"There is help for everything except death," the accented voice said.
I turned my head.

He was huge—even bigger than Sir—and frightening, and he was looking at me with cold, gray-blue eyes that were almost like ice. "That was you, at Sir's. But that was last night. Now it's morning."

"Yes," he stated, sitting perfectly still.

"I had a time out?" I foolishly asked.

"Ja."

I didn't know what that meant, but I assumed it was a yes. "You have an accent."

"You have PTSD."

I said nothing.

He glanced out the front windshield. "We are here. Stay. I will open your door."

He got out of the truck and scanned the long, pebbled driveway and the house beyond that had the ocean lapping at its back steps as if trying to claim them. Then he opened my door and stepped back just enough for me to get out. "Can you walk?"

I didn't know. I didn't know where I was. I didn't know him. I didn't know why I was here. I only knew one thing. "You said there is help for everything except death, but I already died." There was no help for that. He'd said so.

"You are still breathing."

In that moment, it didn't seem like much of a consolation. "Who are you?" I couldn't remember his name.

"Neil Christensen."

"How do you know Si—Nathan?"

"We are acquaintances."

Beyond tired, beyond knowing who to trust or what I could or should say or not say, I simply spoke my mind. "That's not very reassuring."

"It was not intended to be. It was fact. I know Talerco and Trefor."

"Trefor?"

"The owner of Alpha Elite Security. You may know him as Alpha."

"Is that the name of the company Nathan works for?"

"Yes. Do you need help stepping down?"

Embarrassment struck. "No, thank you. Where are we?"

"Key Largo."

I tried to piece together the timeline between the very early morning sun and Sir walking out late last night. "How far is this from Sir's penthouse?"

"Two hours."

"Did you put me in the truck?"

"Talerco did."

"Talon was here?" I didn't remember seeing him at all.

"He was in Miami. He stayed with you last night. I went home, then came back this morning. He put you in my truck. I drove you here."

"Thank you." It wasn't the right response. I wasn't sure I was thankful for anything right now, but I didn't know what else to say.

"Come," he ordered, not unlike how Sir gave orders.

More than embarrassed, and feeling like I had sea legs, vowing not to take any more of those pills, I helped myself get out of the huge truck. "Were you in the military too?"

"Ja. Jægerkorpset."

"Jæger—what?"

"Danish special operations forces." He led me toward a huge house.

"Danish?" I tried to focus on anything other than what was happening. "Then how do you know Talon and Alpha? They speak with American accents." I barely glanced around at the lush, tropical grounds because my gaze was drawn to the clear turquoise water beyond the property.

"We served together in Afghanistan." Pulling out his cell phone, Neil paused. "Wait." He did something on his phone, and the gate at the front of the property opened.

NOVEMBER

An expensive Jaguar driving too fast pulled in and stopped right next to us as a tiny, dark-haired, beautiful woman got out and smiled wide. "Oh, my God. You didn't tell me she was so pretty, Viking. Look at her eyes!"

"Viking?" I asked, but Neil didn't answer me. He let out a low sound of warning that was almost like a growl.

The woman didn't miss a beat. Waving a dismissive hand right before she rushed me and hugged me quick and hard, she laughed. "Ignore my husband, he thinks he isn't a Viking, but he is." She went up on tiptoe, grabbed the front of his perfectly pressed shirt and kissed him.

He gripped her by the back of the neck and pulled her away from his mouth as he spoke low and threatening to her. "Do not spread falsehoods."

She let out a seductive laugh and smiled flirtatiously at him. "Wouldn't dream of it." Looking back at me, happiness sparkled in her eyes. "See? *Viking*," she loud-whispered, conspiratorially.

"Ariella," his deep voice reprimanded.

She patted his chest and stepped away from him. "Got it. No falsehoods." She smirked, complete with an eye roll. "Let's get to the fun part." She clapped her hands once. "I got clothes and shoes, and ohh, you're going to love them!"

Shocked, I blinked. "You went shopping… for me?" *For clothes?*

"Yep. Didn't even have a budget." She laughed. "Viking said November said to get you whatever you needed, and, girl…" She paused to look at me with a quick flash of sympathy. "I think you were about due." She smiled again. "But don't worry, I kept it simple like November requested." She opened the passenger side of the car, and it was filled with shopping bags.

Anxiety hit me fast and hard. "I, um…" I panicked. "I can't afford any of that." I had no money, and Sir had taken the credit cards, and *oh, God.* How was I going to live?

"You don't have to." The lady's voice turned soft, like she knew what I was thinking. "November paid for it. And while I don't personally know him, he works at AES, and, honey, those men can afford a lot more than one shopping trip."

"Ariella," Neil stated.

She glanced at him, but she didn't give him attitude this time. "I hear you, but I'm not saying anything that she probably doesn't already know."

"I am taking her inside," Neil replied to her. "I will come back for the bags."

"It's okay, I got it. Show her around, and I'll put all these away." Quickly reaching for me, the woman who smelled expensive and looked so beautifully put together hugged me again, fast and hard, but this time, she whispered in my ear. "I know these men can be scary, but they look after their own. Once you're in, you're family. You're going to be okay."

I couldn't stop myself. Tears welled, and I whispered back. "Sir left."

The dark-haired woman pulled away but held my arm as she looked at me with compassion. "Give it some time."

"He isn't coming back." I didn't know if I was telling her or myself.

She squeezed my arm. "I'm so sorry."

"It is time," Neil said, before barely glancing at me. "Come."

"Go with Viking," the woman who couldn't have been much older than me urged. "He'll show you around."

Moving with nothing more than momentum, I followed a man who had the size and disposition of a Viking into a custom-built designer home that was the most expensive house I ever remembered being in. Then he gave me an envelope with a new passport, new credit card, a driver's license I didn't even look at, and login information for a bank account before he acknowledged the brand-new-looking, fifty-foot yacht berthed at the house's private dock.

He said everything was mine.

All of it.

The furnished house, complete with plain food stocked in the refrigerator and cupboards, the flybridge yacht, the clothes his wife had put away in the main bedroom—even a Jeep that was parked in the garage that I didn't know how to drive.

I needed a time out.

I needed it so bad, I barely remembered telling them thank you and declining the woman's offer to stay and make us all dinner.

I closed the door behind them, and barely managed to use the cell phone security app that Neil had installed and shown me, to lock it.

Then I grabbed my backpack and the envelope and went upstairs to the big bedroom as my head started to pound so hard, my vision tunneled.

My resolve gone, I reached for the bottle of little pills and took one.

Then I curled into a ball on a bed as big as the one Sir had, and with shaking hands, I pulled the passport out of the envelope.

My heart racing, my breath short, I opened it and read the name.

Atala Rose Rhys.

I burst into tears.

FIFTY-FOUR

November

WAITING FOR ME AT EXECUTIVE IN HIS SEAPLANE, ROARK DIDN'T comment as I got on board and tossed my gear in before closing the door of the older Cessna.

But Missy did.

She barked when I took second chair and strapped in. "She still pissed at me?"

Taxiing across the dark apron, Roark checked in with Executive Tower before answering me. "She has a long memory."

Fucking great. "You got the coordinates I texted?"

"Yes." Lining us up for takeoff, he throttled the single-engine turboprop.

"I need you to make a pit stop first." I gave him a different set of coordinates.

Roark glanced at me. "That's in Largo."

"I know. I just need a touchdown." I had to fucking see that she was okay.

Roark didn't comment, and thirty minutes later, he was bringing the Cessna down on the water.

I pointed to a neighboring house and dock that I'd already hacked security feeds on to make sure no one was currently in residence. "Pull up over there."

"Copy." He angled the seaplane in expertly.

I opened my door. "Five minutes."

I didn't wait for a response. Already off the plane, I cut across the property and pulled out my cell. Logging into the security system that Christensen had given me access to, I saw she'd locked the doors and turned off all the lights in the house, but she hadn't set the alarm.

Shoving down my anger over the alarm not being set, I let myself in the back door. Then I went looking for her.

Thirty seconds later, I found her.

Curled up in fetal position in the middle of the king bed in the main bedroom, the passport was open next to her.

Her hair splayed, her chest rising and falling, even in sleep, I could tell she'd had a rough night. The bottle of pills on the nightstand only confirming that fact, I was both fucking gutted and so damn relieved to see her, I didn't want to leave.

But I had to.

Quietly walking over to her, I leaned in and barely pressed my lips to the left side of her head. "Sleep, Butterfly," I whispered.

Forcing myself to take a step back, I stared at her for another ten seconds.

Then I left the way I came, locking the door behind me.

Four minutes and thirty seconds later, I was back on Roark's seaplane, and he was pulling away from the dock.

He didn't speak until we were back up in the air. "She good?"

"No." But she was breathing. "Flight time?"

"Forty-seven more minutes."

"Copy. Gearing up."

Roark nodded, and I climbed in back as Missy side-eyed me.

With the precision of a highly trained pilot, exactly forty-seven minutes later, Roark was landing the Cessna in Havana Harbor.

Shouldering my tanks, pulling on my fins, I secured my mask. "I'll be in and out."

Roark glanced back at me. "You got thirty minutes, at most, before we start taking heat either from the Cuban coast guard or pirates."

"I won't need thirty." Opening the back door, I stepped out

onto the float, positioned my regulator, then dropped into the dark water.

Checking my underwater navigation board's compass, I set off.

Seven minutes later, I surfaced just enough to check the name on the old sailboat.

Then I sank back below, pulled off my fins, secured them to my dive belt and unstrapped my rifle. Resurfacing, taking out my regulator, I quietly climbed aboard.

Lights on below, cabin door open, the fuck didn't even hear me coming.

His back to the deck, headphones on, open fifth of vodka next to him, he was typing away on a laptop when I descended the three steps and pressed the end of my silencer against the back of his skull.

Fucking freezing, he slowly raised his hands.

Then Zakhar Petrov turned to look at me.

"Do you know who I am?"

The smug fuck pushed one side of his headphones off. "James Hunter. Took you long enough, *comrade*. I found you again three days ago," he bragged. "Well, I found the prude bitch. I knew if I kept her alive after Alekhin was too stupid to make sure his aim wasn't shit, you'd eventually show up. All I had to do was wait. And watch," he added, baiting me.

"You took her to your mother's."

He snorted. "More like dumped her. I wasn't going to nurse her. She didn't even put out."

I refrained from pulling the trigger. Barely. Then I called him on his lie. "You didn't track me three days ago." I knew my skills. "Who gave you my cell number?" It was the one piece of intel I was missing.

"Is the Deputy Commander's favorite hacker really that stupid?" He outright laughed. "I didn't need your exact cell number. I knew you'd chase her. All I had to do was hack every service provider, triangulate the position around that bar, then send an anonymous text to every cell in the area." He gave me a smug look. "You seriously didn't notice everyone around you checking their cell phones at the same time?" Shaking his head, he smirked as he made air quotes. "*Check mate.* What a joke. You were stupid enough to fall for it when Bradley paid me to plant it the first time. Then four years ago, I didn't even need a payout. I saw you looking at those idiot terrorists who hired me. You made it too easy. That time was just a bonus. But when the prude bitch showed back up a few days ago?" He laughed. "That was just for fun. Who's the better hacker now, *comrade*?"

I pulled the trigger.

The back of his head exploded, coating his laptop and half the cabin in brain matter and blood.

Using the end of my rifle, I tipped over the bottle of vodka, spilling it all over his setup. Then I turned on his hot plate, dragged it close and threw a shirt over it. Finding three more bottles of vodka in the small galley, I strategically emptied them around the sailboat's interior before I stepped out of the cabin and secured the door.

Dropping back into the water and positioning my regulator, I pulled on my fins and glanced at the navigation board's compass again.

Then I swam.

By the time I was back on Roark's Cessna, the twenty-seven-foot Albin trawler was engulfed in flames.

Lifting the seaplane into the air, Roark glanced at me. "Mission accomplished?"

"Almost." I had one last thing I needed to do.

"Back to Executive?" he asked.

"Back to Executive," I confirmed.

FIFTY-FIVE

Atala

I DREAMT OF HIM.

It was so real, I could smell him.

New house scent was all around me—paint, drywall, new carpet—but I swore I smelled him too.

Amber, musk, cedar, winter, fresh laundry and soap.

Inhaling for the countless time since my eyes had opened to the early morning sunrise coming in through huge picture windows overlooking the ocean, I grasped at the hint of his scent.

I hadn't even moved.

I was afraid if I did, I would lose his scent and he would be gone forever, and I would be alone.

All alone.

In a mansion on the ocean with a car, a yacht, and a bank account.

This wasn't real.

None of it was.

I tried to tell myself I was in the bad thing and I was stuck there.

Except I knew I wasn't.

My face was warm, my body wasn't shaking, and I was looking at the most beautiful ocean I could ever remember seeing.

Inhaling one more time, I thought of the stern Danish man's words.

There is help for everything except death.

You are still breathing.

NOVEMBER

Every single thing about my life was different than before I met a cool-eyed man who called me Butterfly, but the Danish man was right.

I was still breathing.

And I couldn't lie here forever.

Reminding myself that I'd been alone for years, telling myself I could do it again and that I should be beyond grateful for everything Sir had done for me, I forced myself to get up.

Then I glanced at the view again and walked into the closet.

I sucked in a shocked breath.

Dresses, pants, shirts, shorts, tank tops, swimsuits, shoes—so many shoes.

Tears welled.

Maybe everything had seemed simple to the Danish man's wife, but I'd never had so many clothes, and I'd never had anything even close to as nice as everything she'd picked out for me.

Everything that Sir had paid for.

Trying not to cry, looking at all the clothes, I didn't know what compelled me to choose what I did, but I grabbed a teal blue bikini that was almost the same color as my eyes and a short, bright-yellow sundress.

Rushing into the bathroom that was bigger than any I had ever seen on even the yachts, I quickly pulled off my worn clothes and put on the new ones.

The bikini fit perfectly, and the dress made me look almost as sophisticated as the woman who'd bought it. But my long, un-styled hair and makeup-less face? I would never be what that woman was.

I would never be what Sir wanted.

Tears fell, and my swollen eyes turned red.

I repeated the Danish man's saying.

You are still breathing.

I said it over and over as I walked out of the bathroom, down the wide stairs, and found the huge kitchen. I was still saying it when I made coffee using a machine like they'd had on the yachts that made single cups from little pods.

Then I was about to take the mug with the familiar scent of coffee out to the dock when a doorbell sounded right before a sharp knock.

"Open up, darlin'! I know you're in there!"

Talon.

Rushing to the front door, I opened it.

Smiling wide, the green-eyed, blond man took me in with one quick glance, then walked past me with both his black bag with the red cross and another smaller bag over his shoulder. "Thought I was gonna have to bust down your door, Miss Atala Rose. Which, for the record, a name like that's so fittin', it just ain't fair. I can't even nickname you. Although…" Pausing, he looked at me and grinned with mischief. "I could call ya Butterfly right in front of Hacker Boy and watch him lose his shit. That might be worth gettin' my ass kicked." He winked.

"What are you doing here?" I'd never had company, let alone a place to have company. Not knowing what to do or how to act, I reverted to my crewing experience. "Would you like a coffee?"

"I'm all good, darlin'." He drew the word *all* out. "My women took care of me this mornin' before I came down here."

Women? Suddenly uncomfortable, I stepped back.

Talon chuckled at my reaction before holding up his second bag. "Brought ya a present." He walked toward the kitchen island and took a stool. "Nice digs, by the way. Didn't think Hacker Boy had it in him. Kinda figured him for somethin' darker, more of a cave-dweller kinda vibe, but hey, who's judgin'? Come have a seat. Let me show you whatcha got."

I walked over with my coffee, not sure if he was joking or insulting Sir, but feeling the need to defend him, nonetheless. "Nathan doesn't live in a cave. He has a penthouse." And a marina, but I didn't think I should mention that.

"Nothin' doin', darlin', nothin' doin'." Pulling a laptop and a power cord out of the bag, he reached across the island to plug it in before opening it and turning it on. "Brand spankin' new, set up for ya by yours truly, your very own laptop." He turned it to face me. "You know how to use one of these?"

"No," I admitted, holding my coffee close.

"Real simple, just two things you gotta know, all right?"

I wasn't sure I liked where this was going, so I didn't answer. Turned out, I didn't need to.

Talon moved his finger across the small pad in front and hovered over a little icon. "You hit this." A screen came up that looked like a picture frame. "Then you hit this little video camera icon." He pressed it. "And wait a sec."

A little circle turned like a timer, then the screen filled with the image of an older woman sitting at a desk.

She smiled kindly.

"Hey, doc," Talon said affectionately as he leaned closer to me, and our image appeared in a small box at the top right of the screen. "This is my friend, Atala, I told you about." Talon nodded at me. "Atala, this is Miss Genny Grace, and she's an expert in all things PTSD."

I flinched at both the word and being blindsided by Talon, but his arm wrapped around my shoulder and kept me from bolting.

"Hello, Atala," the woman replied with kindness in her voice. "I'm getting the impression that Talon didn't warn you about this quick meet and greet this morning."

I somehow found my voice. "No, ma'am."

"Guilty," Talon admitted cheerfully.

She frowned at Talon before looking back at me. "Well, regardless, I very pleased to meet you, and if you're interested, I thought we could virtually get together once a week for an hour and chat. Maybe I can provide some insight for you, or we could just talk about how you're doing, or talk about anything at all. Would you like that?"

My heart started to race. "Are you a doctor?"

"I'm a trauma counselor, dear."

Trauma. Counselor. Not a doctor. "And you just want to talk… to me?"

She smiled. "Very much so."

"Why?" I asked.

"I like to hear people's stories. And if I'm being completely upfront, I like to help them."

Help me. With trauma. But I didn't know my story. "May I please speak to Talon for a moment?"

"Of course, dear. Just mute me."

"This is how." Talon dropped his arm from my shoulder, then showed me how to hit mute before he looked at me. "You got a question, darlin'?"

"Is this about the bad—the time outs?"

His tone, his demeanor, they turned serious. "Yes, it is."

"I don't have a story. I can't remember anything."

"That's okay," he reassured. "You can still talk to her."

"I took a pill yesterday," I blurted.

Talon didn't so much as blink. "That's fine. That's what they're for. And just so you know, Genny's helped a lot of military veterans with PTSD, and I thought she could help you, or at least give you an opportunity to talk to someone who is well versed in the subject matter."

The overwhelming instinct to look for Sir, to look to him for approval crushing me, I asked the only person I could ask. "Would you talk to her?"

"Yes."

"Okay." I nodded as I inhaled. "Okay. I can do this."

"You already are, darlin'." Winking at me, Talon hit the mute button again. "We're back, and we're good to go, Doc. How 'bout weekly appointments to start?"

"That's fine with me. Is that all right with you, Atala?"

"Yes, ma'am."

NOVEMBER

The woman smiled again, and I liked it. "Call me Genny, Atala. How about we meet on Fridays at one p.m.?"

"Okay."

"Great. See you this Friday, Atala." She glanced toward Talon and gave him an almost stern expression. "No more shenanigans, Mr. Talerco."

Talon smiled wide. "I make no promises." He laughed, Miss Genny shook her head, and Talon ended the video call before glancing at me. "Proud of you, darlin'. You good for now?"

I didn't know what I was.

I just wanted to be on the water.

So, I told him that. "I'm going to go for a swim now."

"Sounds good, darlin'. Nice day. Fresh air will do ya right." He stood and grabbed his black bag with the red cross, but he left the bag he'd brought the laptop in. "You need anythin' else from me right now?"

"No, thank you." I suddenly really, really needed to be in the water, and I needed to be there now before I broke down and asked him where Sir was.

"You have my number. Don't hesitate to use it, but I'll be in touch." Talon turned toward the front door. "I'll let myself out, darlin'. Enjoy your swim."

I was already grabbing the keys to the fifty-foot yacht the Danish man had left on the counter.

Talon walked out the front door. I walked out the back.

Twenty minutes later, I was on the flybridge in the middle of a sea of turquoise with tears running down my face as hot sun cradled me in familiarity.

Sir was right.

I knew how to captain.

I would have to learn a million things on this fancy boat, but that could wait.

I'd found a deep enough spot, the anchor was dropped, I'd

stripped off my dress, and I was already climbing to the top of the flybridge.

Then I jumped.

For two seconds, I was flying.

Flying and crying.

Then I plunged into the warmest water I ever remembered and stretched my arms, my legs and my lungs, and I just swam.

I swam until I couldn't hold my breath anymore.

Then I surfaced, rolled to my back and was floating on the soft swells when it happened.

I heard Sir's voice, clear as day.

They call me Hunter.

Gasping because it was so clear, so real, I picked my head up and treaded water as I looked all around me.

Then I looked again.

They call me Hunter.

Inhaling deep, my eyes closed, and I knew what it was.

A memory.

A memory.

Both bitter and sweet, I didn't care. I wanted every memory of Sir I could remember.

With a sense of new purpose, I swam back to the Azimut and jumped off her flybridge two more times.

I didn't remember anything else, but I was okay.

Content, my skin warm, my muscles tired, I captained the yacht back to the dock using only my sense of direction and landmarks I'd paid attention to when I'd chartered out.

Concentrating on pulling her into her berth, making sure the bumpers kept her pretty hull unscratched, I didn't look up until I cut the powerful engines.

Then my heart stopped.

Standing on the dock with his hands in his pockets, Sir met my gaze.

FIFTY-SIX

November

I pulled my Ducati Diavel 1260 S up to the gate at the front of the property.

New, modern, elevated for storm surges, thick tropical vegetation everywhere, tall privacy fencing blocking the view of the place from any neighbors, unobstructed water views, the house was a good fit for her.

Using my cell, I opened the gate.

Driving down the long pebble driveway, I pulled around to the garage, but not before I saw the dock and what was noticeably absent.

Parking the bike under the single carport next to the three closed garage doors, I swung my leg over, removed my helmet and grabbed the bag I had strapped to the rear seat. A fresh go bag I shouldn't have even brought. A bag I'd thrown her helmet in because I couldn't let go of the sound of her small laugh when she'd been on the back of my bike with her arms wrapped around me.

But fuck, I wasn't supposed to be doing this.

I wasn't supposed to stay or take her for a ride.

I was here to tell her one thing, and one thing only. Then I needed to leave.

Leave before I fucked her up even worse.

Don't stay. Don't give her hope. Don't fucking hurt her.

I repeated it in my head, same as I'd been telling myself the whole ride down here. But my head and my actions were at odds, and I packed the damn bag, justifying a change of clothes in case it rained. Then I'd gotten on the bike because I didn't just want to see her, I needed to see her.

And she needed to know she was free.

Holding on to that thought, I let myself in the house.

The first thing I saw was a laptop on the counter I hadn't given her, and the second was a full cup of coffee.

Dumping my stuff on a chair, I touched the mug.

Cold.

I woke the laptop. Then I checked the history.

Video chat app.

My nostrils flared, and I pulled out my cell. Using my own software, I traced the number.

Genny Grace. Trauma Counselor. Specializing in PTSD.

This was Talerco's doing. Had to be.

I hacked her cell, checking for calls, but there weren't any. There also wasn't any activity on the security app with her login since last night. Checking the camera feeds, I scanned the front door's camera activity from earlier this morning because the laptop hadn't been here last night. I would've noticed it.

Three minutes past oh-eight-hundred, Talerco had knocked on the door, but there was no history of her opening the gate.

I checked the front gate camera.

That fucking prick.

I dialed his number.

Talerco picked up on the first ring. "You come to your senses yet, Hacker Boy?"

"If you use the gate code to gain access her property again, I will break both your arms, which is a fucking courtesy."

The asshole chuckled. "Courtesy, huh? What makes me so special? 'Cuz rumor has it you threatened to end Delta and kill Echo, and now all I'm gettin' is my arms broke. You goin' soft, Hacker Boy?"

"The trauma counselor," I ground out. "Genny Grace."

"Christ, you *are* Hacker Boy. Well, you're welcome. And just so we're clear, you fuck with her head anymore, and I'll break more 'an your arms. Now quit callin' me and go be fuckin' normal to your woman. She misses you."

I froze. "She said something?"

"No, but she didn't have to. Pull your head outta your ass, and you'll realize that butterfly of yours ain't got eyes for no one and nothin' 'cept you. Not sure how the fuck that happened, but there you have it. You're welcome. Next time you call, I'm chargin' you." He hung up.

I closed the app, shut the computer, pocketed my cell and walked out to the dock.

Scanning in every direction, I saw a few boats, but none that were fifty feet with a flybridge. Deciding to wait in the air-conditioned house instead of the heat, I'd made it halfway up the dock when I heard a boat come around the end of the peninsula the house sat on.

Pivoting, I looked back out at the water.

My heart fucking stopped.

Standing at the helm on the flybridge, hair blowing behind her, wearing nothing except a turquoise bikini, my Butterfly brought fifty feet of boat in and swung it around, parking the yacht fucking perfectly.

Butterfly wasn't a sub.

She was a goddamn queen.

Captivated, I stared.

Freer than I'd ever seen her, she cut the engines then glanced up, and her gaze met mine.

I was struck.

My hands in my pockets, my feet rooted, I couldn't have moved in that second if my life depended on it.

All I could do was drink her in.

My Butterfly.

My goddess.

I didn't need to come here and tell her she was free.

She was already flying.

Fuck, she was flying.

Turning, she rushed down the steep steps from the helm, crossed the aft deck, and expertly threw a rope onto the dock from first the stern, then the bow before hopping off the boat barefoot. She was already tying her mooring lines before I had the sense to move.

Grabbing the rope for the bow, I tied down the front of the yacht, and then she was there, standing in front of me, small as hell, in a sexy bikini that matched her eyes, and I knew.

I loved her.

I'd loved her since I first laid eyes on her.

Wanting to kiss her, I brushed an errant strand of hair from her face. "You handle that boat like a captain, Butterfly."

Sucking in a sharp breath at the sound of my voice, her sun-kissed cheeks flushed. Then she gave me her honesty. "I don't know how to use half the navigation equipment yet."

"You'll learn."

"I'll learn," she repeated, as if needing to hear herself say it.

I couldn't stop myself. I ran the back of my fingers down the side of her face. "You're beautiful out there on the water, Butterfly." So goddamn beautiful.

Her voice dropped to a hope-filled whisper. "You're here, Sir."

Sir.

Sliding my hand under her hair, grasping the back of her neck, I took the moment. Bringing my forehead to hers, closing my eyes, I breathed her in. Then I kissed her forehead once and released her. "You don't have to call me Sir anymore." I could never dominate this woman again, but fuck I wanted to. I wanted to watch her fly free on her boat and swim in the ocean, then I wanted to take her inside and make her fall apart under my touch, but she'd done enough falling apart in her life.

"You will always be Sir to me." Guileless, she looked up at me with eyes the color of the water. "Am I no longer Butterfly to you?"

"Atala," I warned.

She dipped her head and her voice turned shy. "You gave me your last name. In my passport."

Sun-kissed shoulders, ocean-air-dried wild hair, she was stunning, and she would always be mine, where it counted. But she deserved the truth. "It's not mine."

She looked back up. "I don't understand."

Taking a breath, I let it out slow. Then I told her. "When we were held hostage, before you were shot, you weren't speaking. I needed to hear your voice. I asked you if you were with me. You answered. 'Right here, yes, sir.'" I choked down the memory. "Those were the last words you said to me."

For five seconds, she stared at me.

Then she whispered, "R-H-Y-S."

"Yes." I gave her an out. "You're free to change it."

"Are you changing yours?"

"No." Never.

"I want to keep it."

"As you wish." I finally told her what I came here to tell her. "You're free, Butterfly."

"Free," she repeated as if the word were foreign.

"Yes. I wanted you to know. You have nothing to fear anymore." Including me.

My beautiful Butterfly didn't say anything, she simply stared at me.

Remembering every inch of her like this, committing it to memory, I turned to go.

"You're leaving?"

Pausing, I forced myself to say what I had to. "Yes."

"Why?"

"You know why."

"Because you think you'll hurt me?"

I turned. "It's not a matter of thinking I will. It's fact, Butterfly. I'm not...good."

"You've been good to me." She glanced at the house, the boat. "How is all of this bad?"

"You know what I mean." I wasn't going to explain to her how the twisted part of me would always want to grip her hair, put her on her knees, make her submit. "There're two sides to me, Butterfly, and one of those sides isn't good for you. I can't hurt you again." I prayed she'd fucking understand and listen to my next words. "Be safe for me. I need that." Fuck, I needed it. Unable to stop myself, I leaned down one last time and brought my mouth to hers. "Fly free, Butterfly." I kissed her once, then I forced myself to step back.

"I can't see my own wings," she blurted.

I said nothing.

"But I took the boat out, I swam in the warm water, and for a moment, I felt it."

I knew what she meant. "Floating."

"Floating," she agreed, her voice dipping in shyness.

Relieved, elated, fucking jealous that she'd gotten there without my touch, there was only one thing I could say. "Good."

"Do you dislike the part of me that can't remember you?"

"No." *Jesus.* "I don't now, nor will I ever hold your memory loss against you."

She nodded hesitantly. Then, "Do you like the person I am now?"

This was killing me. "You know this has nothing to do with like, Butterfly. You're perfect, exactly how you are. Never let anyone tell you any different."

"There are two sides to me as well."

I fucking stilled.

But my innocent, perceptive Butterfly didn't. She kept talking. "The person I was, who I am now, they're different. I have scars and no memories and that stress disorder, but you just said I was perfect how I am. So how come you can't be perfect how you are too? Why do you get to say you're bad and walk away? I like all the parts that make you who you are." Her voice quieted. "Maybe I want to feel pain and hurt and pleasure. Maybe I want to feel alive."

"You don't know what you're saying."

"Maybe I don't. But I know how I feel when I'm with you, and it feels more free than any boat."

My fucking chest tight, I warned her. "Stop, Butterfly."

"Why? You can't hurt me, Nathan Rhys."

My hands fisted. "Yes, I can."

"You can't break my wings."

My jaw clenched. "Walk. Away."

"You can't kill me." Defiant, innocent, brave, stupidly playing with fire, she closed the distance between us. "I already died."

"*Butterfly*," I ground out.

"I heard you out on the water today." Her voice dropped to a whisper. "*They call me Hunter.*"

I fucking froze.

Looking up at me with the wild, teal-blue eyes of a winged creature too fragile to touch, she saw right through me. "Where's the hunter now?"

With a roar, my hands were in her hair and my mouth was on hers.

Sinking my tongue in deep, too fucking gone to think straight, I kissed her hard enough to bruise her lips.

But my fragile Butterfly didn't pull back, and she didn't cry out.

She wrapped her arms around my neck and kissed me back.

Fuck, she kissed me back.

Gripping a handful of her hair, I pulled her off my mouth. Chest heaving, staring into impossible eyes, I gave her one fucking chance. "This is your only warning. Walk away from me right now, Atala." I gripped her harder. "Walk. Away."

Her lips swollen, she didn't hesitate. "No."

My nostrils flared. Then I showed her how truly weak I was.

"If I kiss you again, I'm not going to stop," I warned her. "I'll fuck you. I'll hurt you. I'll control you, and I'll never let you go."

Her face softened with pure submission. "Yes, please, Sir."

I broke.

My mouth slammed over hers. Then I picked her up and I carried her onto her boat.

I made it as far as the closest fucking divan in the cabin.

Ripping her bikini off, unzipping my pants, fisting my cock, I shoved her legs wide with my knee. Then I hovered over her and soaked in every vulnerable inch of her.

Her bare, wet cunt, her perfect breasts, her hard nipples, her swollen lips, her eyes.

Those butterfly eyes.

Leaning over her, bringing my mouth to hers, I fisted myself at her entrance. "*My* Butterfly."

"*My* Sir," she whispered, inhaling my dominance.

I sank inside her.

One torturous inch at a time.

Shaking with restraint, burying myself in her tight, perfect heat, I stroked the very depth of her womb, slow and deliberate.

Shaking right along with me, constricting around my invasion, she cried out.

But then her fingers dug into my shoulders, and she unfurled her wings.

Opening her legs, arching her back, my Butterfly let me in.

Gathering her in my arms, rasping against her lips, I pushed deeper and made her a promise. "Forever my Butterfly."

"Forever," she promised back.

Then we both were flying.

EPILOGUE

November

PULLING THROUGH THE GATE, I ALREADY KNEW THE YACHT WAS OUT. I'd checked security cams before I drove home.

Home.

I didn't give a shit where I laid my head as long as she was there.

Butterfly was my home.

She was my reason.

But she was about to get her ass spanked.

Striding through the garage, bypassing the house, I went straight for the dock because I knew what she was doing.

The early morning sun barely above the horizon, the Azimut fifty yards out, I watched her climb aboard the aft deck, using the swim platform. Wearing a turquoise string bikini, speargun in hand, she dumped her catch in one of the coolers before making her way up to the flybridge.

Barefoot, no dive mask, she deftly climbed onto the gunwale one-handed.

Then she dove into the ocean with the fucking speargun from the highest point on the yacht.

I didn't give a damn that she was a butterfly or that her solitary performance was a vision.

She'd crossed my hard limit. Again.

Surfacing forty-seven seconds later with her fresh kill, she climbed back on board, stowed her speargun, and deftly brought the yacht back home before tying it down.

Minutes later, smiling, she was walking down the dock toward me in nothing but her bikini, carrying two spiny lobsters.

She held them up. "I caught dinner."

My hands in my pockets, I didn't say shit.

Her smile dropped, right along with her voice and the arm holding the lobsters. "I saw them when I had my coffee on the dock." Shifting her feet, she dipped her head to glance at her fresh catch. Then she let out the truth because she hadn't figured out how to lie yet. Not to me. "I thought I would be back in before you got home." She looked back up at me. "You said you had to work late last night, and when you still weren't home this morning, I just…." She trailed off.

"Are my work hours now a direct reflection of your lack of safety?" My voice was even, but my tone said it all.

Color flushed her sun-kissed face as ocean water dripped down her shoulders from her slicked-back hair. "No, Sir."

"Do you dive from the top of the Azimut by yourself, *ever?*"

Her voice got even quieter. "No, Sir."

"And do you ever fucking dive into shallow waters?" I asked, enunciating each word with dominant intent.

The breeze cooler than the water, my tone clear, she shivered. "It's high tide, Sir. It wasn't—"

My eyes narrowed, and her head dropped.

"No, Sir," she whispered shyly, but then she looked back up at me, except she didn't give me the innocent gaze of my Butterfly. She gave me Sub. "Are you going to punish me, Sir?"

Oh, I was going to punish the fuck out of her.

But I wasn't going to spank the shit out of her right here on the dock before bending her over the goddamn live well and fucking her hard until the whole damn island heard her screams and knew she was mine.

I knew my little sub.

I knew exactly what made her tick.

That wouldn't be punishment for her. She'd come hard, over

and over, and take what I gave her, but she wouldn't give a damn if anyone heard or what they'd think.

She only worried about what I thought.

Exactly how I wanted it.

Needed it.

I was control.

She craved being controlled.

Total power exchange—with a few exceptions. The yacht was one, but fucking diving off the goddamn top alone wasn't.

Taking the lobsters from her and dumping them in the live well on the dock, I grabbed her.

But I didn't just pick her up.

I threw her over my shoulder, and my palm landed on her ass with a crack that echoed across the water right before her gasp chased it.

My cock hard, I checked in. "Did that hurt, sub?"

"Yes, Sir."

"Good." I slapped the other ass cheek harder than the first as I walked her into the house.

She cried out.

I kicked the door shut behind me, but then I fucking checked myself, and I checked in. "How bad did that hurt, sub?"

Her voice came softer. "Not bad, Sir."

Taking the stairs two at a time, I slapped her ass again, this time harder and without pause before bringing my palm down on each side.

She yelped as she flinched on my shoulder and dug her hands into the back of my shirt.

"How about that, sub? Did you fucking feel that?"

"Yes, Sir, yes, Sir," her voice broke with a true cry.

"Are you telling me to stop?"

"No, Sir."

"No, or no, Sir? Which is it?" There was a difference. A big fucking difference. And she had all the power right now.

"No, Sir," she said clearly, without hesitation.

My cock fucking pulsing, painfully pushing at the confines of my pants, I threw her on the bed and barked out an order. "On your knees, ass up, head down."

She didn't hesitate.

Positioning herself on the end of the bed, giving me her sweet ass in her thong bikini, her cheeks already red from my touch, I fucking salivated to taste her as I yanked my shirt off and undid my zipper.

Stepping out of my pants and boots, I checked in again. "What's your safe word, sub?" I asked, but I was going to fuck her no matter what. The only question was if I was going to punish her while I did it.

"No, Sir."

"What did I just fucking ask you?" I demanded, stroking my cock as I pulled at the strings on her hips.

The scrap of material fell away, showing me her already glistening cunt. "I'm sorry, Sir. I meant my safe word is no."

"When can you say it?" Dragging two fingers through her wet need as she jerked from my touch, I wiped her desire on the head of my cock because that was all the prep she was going to get if she didn't red-light me.

"Anytime, Sir."

I lowered my voice. "Did you dive from the top of the Azimut alone this morning, multiple times?"

"Yes, Sir," she quietly, submissively replied.

My palm ruthlessly rained down on her ass as I spanked the shit out of her until she was crying and I was panting. My hand burning, her ass a brilliant red, I fucking inhaled. Raw hunger, deep satisfaction, I asked the goddamn question. "Are you ever going to jump off the goddamn yacht alone again?"

"No, Sir," she sobbed. "No, Sir. *Please—*"

I shoved my cock into her tight, dripping cunt to the hilt with one hard thrust.

NOVEMBER

Her back arched, and her scream echoed through our bedroom. Then she was pulsing around me as she came.

My nostrils flaring, my fingers digging into her hips hard enough to leave bruises, I sank into my dominance. Then I started fucking her. Hard.

Driving into her without mercy, bottoming out on every thrust, grinding my hips to hit her G-spot with every stroke, I fucked her through her orgasm and to the brink of another.

"Please, wait. *Oh, God.* I can't, Sir," she cried. Her hands fisting the bedding, her entire body shaking, she begged. "Please, stop. Sir, I can't take… I can't—"

I switched my angle.

Her animalistic moan erupted from her chest as her entire body arched.

Her cunt constricted hard, and I let go.

With a fucking roar, I gripped the assaulted flesh of her red ass and came so fucking hard and deep inside her, I levitated.

Pulse after pulse of my dominance filled her still-throbbing cunt, and everything went right in the world.

Holding on to her until the very last aftershock pulsed through her sweet heat and she sank back to the bed, I leaned over and wrapped my arms around her.

Then, still inside her, I crawled us up the mattress, lay down with her in my arms and kissed her shoulder as I gently eased out.

She flinched, but she didn't complain as my body left hers.

My voice hoarse, I checked in. Except this time, it was more than a check in. "You still with me, sub?" I pressed my lips to the left side of her head.

Reaching back with a shaking hand and fluttering a finger over the scar of my stab wound, she whispered. "Right here, yes, Sir."

I fucking closed my eyes and inhaled. *"Butterfly."*

She knew what those four words meant.

She didn't remember saying them the first time, and I hoped like hell she never did, but she knew their meaning was deeper than any three words we could've said.

Grabbing her hand and bringing her fingers to my lips, I kissed my Butterfly's ocean-scented skin.

"*Sir*," she breathed with a shiver.

Knowing that voice, knowing what she needed, I fisted her wet hair, angled her head, and reverently kissed her.

My little sub unfurled her wings and moaned into my mouth as she wrapped her arm around my neck.

Rolling her to her back, I sank inside her still-wet, tight cunt that was full of my seed. Then I asked again, this time, softer. "How about now? You still with me, sub?"

My teal-eyed miracle looked up at me. "Right here, yes, sir."

I slowly made love to my Butterfly.

Descending to the bilge deck, bypassing the engine room, I opened a full-height storage compartment and pushed life jackets aside. Entering a code into a small, hidden security panel, I pressed my thumb against the fingerprint scanner.

The lock clicked.

Pushing the fireproof, waterproof, steel door open, I stepped inside the vault and secured the door behind me.

Using another fingerprint scanner, I opened the weapons cages and grabbed what I needed before briefly taking a seat at the main terminal of the onboard command center. Accessing an encrypted program, I double-checked the intel. Then I wiped my search history, pulled out a clean burner and dialed.

The call was answered on the fifth ring. "I said I was out."

"New assignment." I rattled off my GPS coordinates. "Twenty-four degrees, fifteen minutes, zero-two-point-two seconds north. Seventy-eight degrees,

NOVEMBER

zero-zero-point-zero-five-point-zero seconds west. Use the Sikorsky S-76D. It's fueled up and ready to go at the hangar in Indiantown. Fly nap of the earth." I glanced at my watch. "You have ninety minutes before first light."

"A matte-black, stolen, unregistered helo flying low altitude over a major metropolitan area, oh-dark-thirty or not, won't go unnoticed. I don't need this kind of heat."

"Then don't get noticed." I hung up.

THANK YOU!

Thank you so much for reading NOVEMBER! If you are interested in leaving a review on any retail site, I would be so appreciative. Reviews mean the world to authors, and they are helpful beyond compare.

Turn the page for a preview of ECHO, the next exciting book in the Alpha Elite Series!

ECHO

Navy SEAL.

Mercenary.

Ghost.

Joining the military wasn't a choice, it was survival. It was also the last place they would think to look for me. Hiding in plain sight, I lived in the shadow of deployments… until an off-the-books mission put me in the crosshairs of my past.

My cover blown, I walked away from the SEALs and sought refuge at the one place where I'd be more invisible than on the Teams—Alpha Elite Security. As a Black Ops government contractor, AES was the world's leading provider of security solutions. High stakes, higher price tag, and complete anonymity. Trained to kill long before the Navy put a gun in my hand, I fit right in.

Legally aiming my rifle, taking any AES assignment that guaranteed action, I lived to fight. But then I made a mistake. One single misstep and I was face-to-face with the only woman who could kill me faster than a bullet.

Code name: Echo.
Mission: Evade.

ECHO is a standalone book in the exciting Alpha Elite Series by USA Today Bestselling author, Sybil Bartel. Come meet Echo and the dominant, alpha heroes who work for AES!

WHISKEY

Mercenary.

Navy SEAL.

Unconventional Operative.

I didn't join the Teams. I was recruited. They called me the Specialist. They said I had a unique skill set. I knew who I was.

For eight years, the Navy tried to rein me in with their tactics, techniques and procedures. They told me to adapt and overcome. I didn't adapt. I did my job.

Now I worked for Alpha Elite Security. If you called me Specialist, I'd eliminate you before you took your next breath. If you recognized me, it was already too late. I lived by my instincts and used the resources around me. No target was out of my scope…until my boss unknowingly handed me the only assignment that was.

The one woman I couldn't kill.

Code name: Whiskey.
Mission: Eliminate.

WHISKEY is a standalone book in the exciting Alpha Elite Series by *USA Today* Bestselling author, Sybil Bartel. Come meet Whiskey and the dominant, alpha heroes who work for AES!

DELTA

Dominant.

Mercenary.

Navy SEAL.

I had one job on the Teams. Predict the unpredictable. See what no one else saw. Analyze, assess, anticipate. Then execute with deadly force.

Calculating the enemy's moves, including the ones they hadn't thought of yet, was my specialty. I did it for the Navy and now I was private sector, utilizing my skills at Alpha Elite Security. I had a hundred percent mission success rate…until her.

Make no mistake, I saw the blonde coming. I predicted her every move. But this time, I wasn't going to stop it. I was going to do something much worse.

Code name: Delta.
Mission: Dominate.

DELTA is a standalone book in the exciting Alpha Elite Series by *USA Today* Bestselling author, Sybil Bartel. Come meet Delta and the dominant, alpha heroes who work for AES!

ACKNOWLEDGMENTS

As I write the last page of NOVEMBER, I cannot help but feel a bittersweet sense of accomplishment. I think every book an author writes is a testament of perseverance, and every story a culmination of the emotional trials and personal journeys we experience in life. I just never imagined, not even in my worst nightmares, that I would be experiencing this journey called life without my only child, my son, Oliver Shane.

Twenty-three months ago, (as I write this), my Sweet Boy, at the tender age of fifteen, passed away tragically and unexpectedly in his sleep from an undiagnosed birth defect in his heart that is so rare, less than 1% of the population has it.

I cannot help but think about the correlation between that rarity and my beloved son.

Oliver was a rare and extraordinarily intelligent, compassionate, and gentle soul. Born with an autoimmune disease, he not only overcame the obstacles life threw at him, he thrived. Oliver was a straight-A student with a 4.45 GPA. He was an incredibly talented cello and piano player, a black belt in Karate and Jiu Jitsu, and a compassionate friend to everyone he met. Oliver had so much perseverance and determination that I was, and still am, in awe of him.

There are no adequate words for the grief of this ruthless separation. I am, however, consoled by two humbling and incredible events that have taken place.

By the hand of God, and facilitated by Oliver's orchestra director, along with the generous donations given in his name, the music Oliver was writing before he passed was turned into a full orchestral piece called *Oliverian Fantasy,* by the amazing composer, Brian Balmages. I hope everyone hears Oliver's melody, and I hope orchestras and symphonies around the world play this incredible, haunting, and absolutely beautiful piece.

You can listen to *Oliverian Fantasy* sybilbartel.com/Oliverian-Fantasy.html.

Another outcome from Oliver's passing is that there is now the Oliver S. Bartel Memorial Scholarship Trust. Each year, this trust will award a Vero Beach High School Orchestra graduating senior a scholarship to help continue their musical pursuit in college. This is the only scholarship of its kind for orchestra students at Vero Beach High School. You can read about the scholarship at sybilbartel.com/Oliver-Bartel-Memorial-Scholarship-Trust.html.

Lastly, as I write these final thoughts, while I cannot begin to describe the level of grief or put into words the all-encompassing pain of this kind of loss, I want to say this: I love you, Oliver Shane Bartel. There is not a waking moment that I do not miss everything about you. Thank you for being the greatest gift of my life. I am beyond proud of you. I will endeavor to live my moments here on earth with the same compassion, love, fortitude and perseverance you so humbly possessed. I hope this book does your memory justice.

I love you, my Sweet Boy, here, now, always, forever. I love you more than anything.
XOXO
Mom

ABOUT THE AUTHOR

Sybil Bartel is a *USA Today* Bestselling author of unapologetic alpha heroes. Whether you're reading her deliciously dominant Alpha Elite mercenaries or her protector hero Alpha Bodyguards, her page-turning romantic suspense, and heart-stopping military romance all have unwavering alpha heroes.

Sybil resides in South Florida, and she is forever Oliver's mom.

To find out more about Sybil Bartel or her books, please visit her at:

Website: sybilbartel.com

Facebook page: www.facebook.com/sybilbartelauthor

Facebook group: www.facebook.com/groups/1065006266850790

Instagram: www.instagram.com/sybil.bartel

TikTok: www.tiktok.com/@sybilbartelauthor

Twitter: twitter.com/SybilBartel

BookBub: www.bookbub.com/authors/sybil-bartel

Newsletter: http://eepurl.com/bRSE2T

The Oliver Bartel Memorial Scholarship Trust: sybilbartel.com/Oliver-Bartel-Memorial-Scholarship-Trust.html

Printed in Great Britain
by Amazon